Parker was paid to talk to fakers on the phone, and decide which of the day's many events qualified as news. The phone rang. Parker answered.

"This is Allan," said a voice made groggy by too little sleep and too much coffee.

"What's up, Shanahan?"

"We've got tape of the kid that got killed last night."

Parker checked the log that the night editor kept of major incidents. "Oh yeah? Which dead kid is that?"

"Over in Lincoln Square."

"No kidding. There's always a dead kid in Lincoln Square. Call me back later when you've got something that hasn't already happened fifty thousand times."

"I've got a sound bite with a Street Crusader who said it's Mayor Cleveland's fault and Doogie Smith will save the day."

"And?"

"And tears, Parker. We've got tears."

"Hey, if I want tears, I can cry my own."

"These are male tears I'm talking about. Male Hispanic tears: salty, salsa, blubbering machismo. I'll take it to Channel Eight. They love a good cry over there."

"Male Hispanic tears? That's another story. . . ."

Books by Sean Hanlon

Prestor John Riordan Mysteries:
The Cold Front
The Big Dark
The Frozen Franklin
Deep Freeze

Jump Cuts

Published by POCKET BOOKS

For orders other than by individual consumers, Pocket Books grants a discount on the purchase of **10 or more** copies of single titles for special markets or premium use. For further details, please write to the Vice-President of Special Markets, Pocket Books, 1230 Avenue of the Americas, New York, NY 10020.

For information on how individual consumers can place orders, please write to Mail Order Department, Paramount Publishing, 200 Old Tappan Road, Old Tappan, NJ 07675.

JUMP CUTS

SEAN HANLON

POCKET BOOKS

New York   London   Toronto   Sydney   Tokyo   Singapore

This book is a work of fiction. Names, characters, places and
incidents are products of the author's imagination or are used
fictitiously. Any resemblance to actual events or locales or persons,
living or dead, is entirely coincidental.

An *Original* Publication of POCKET BOOKS

POCKET BOOKS, a division of Simon & Schuster Inc.
1230 Avenue of the Americas, New York, NY 10020

ISBN: 0-671-70456-7

First Pocket Books printing August 1994

10 9 8 7 6 5 4 3 2 1

POCKET BOOKS and colophon are registered
trademarks of Simon & Schuster Inc.

Cover art by Dan Cosgrove

Printed in the U.S.A.

For the Eye, the Tooth, and the gang at Channel 2

JUMP CUTS

CHANNEL TWELVE

JULY 16, 6:46 P.M. LEDE INTO FIRST WEATHER BREAK
CAMERA ONE: MEDIUM CLOSE-UP/JANETTE

JANETTE: The Second City with the big shoulders has another nickname tonight: Murdertown, U.S.A. The FBI's latest Uniform Crime Report reveals that Chicago had 857 homicides last year. Alderman Douglas Smith, founder of the Crusade for Safer Streets, says we've earned this dubious honor because the drug gangs are out of control. ROLL SMITH SOUND BITE/OUTCUE: ". . . wouldn't happen if we had more muscle on the street and more guts in City Hall."

JANETTE: Smith wants local community groups to form their own police clubs to protect their neighborhoods from the roving gangs of street toughs that he calls narco-killers. We'll hear more about this on Thursday when the alderman is expected to make the long-awaited announcement that he will run for mayor against Willis Cleveland in September's primary election.

CAMERA THREE: TWO-SHOT/CARL, JANETTE

CARL: Thank you, Janette. I understand you'll be taking a closer look at drugs and the gangs in your series of special reports starting Monday.

JANETTE: That's right, Carl. We're calling our week-long series "The Brotherhood of Death." Brother is killing brother and their mothers have had enough. I think you'll be shocked and surprised.

CAMERA TWO: THREE-SHOT, JANETTE SMILES; TWO-SHOT/CARL, ERNIE

CARL: I'm sure we will, Janette. But right now I'm hot and bothered because my air-conditioner is on the fritz. Where'd you get the heat, Ernie?

ERNIE: We got it from a high-pressure system camped out in the plains. (ROLL U.S. WEATHER MAP) It's blocking out the cool winds and letting warm air come up from the Gulf of Mexico. (ROLL STATE WEATHER MAP) That's pushing temperatures up over 100 degrees for the first time this year. The high pressure is also causing some drought conditions for our friends downstate in Little Egypt. (ROLL DETAIL MAP OF DELTA WITH TEMPS FROM CAIRO, THEBES, KARNAK) The outlook is for more of the same. After the break we'll be back with the five-day forecast.

NEWS MUSIC/PRINT OUT: *MISSISSIPPI BURNING* THEN FADE TO TOYOTA CAMRY SPOT

1

Talking Bulljive Day

THE WEATHER REMINDED MRS. SHANAHAN OF A SIMPLER, MUGGI-
er time before central air conditioning. She dozed to the
lullaby of the police and fire radios, dreaming of her lost
youth. She dreamt of the time when her mother wasn't so
sad, her father wasn't so angry and Mrs. Shanahan wasn't so
afraid of tomorrow. She wasn't even Mrs. Shanahan yet, but
little Helen Gates who won the third-grade spelling bee and
grew up in the house where Diamond-Tooth Eddie was
killed—in a house with teddy bears and lollypops, a rocking
horse and Santa Claus.

She was dreaming about her first day of school when the
radio—tuned to police dispatch—started beeping and
screeching with familiar urgency. Waking up, she was old
again and she wasn't little Helen Gates anymore. Her father
had died many years before and her husband many years
after that. Her son Allan had their anger now and she feared
that his life would be unhappy too. Sometimes her joints
hurt so much that death seemed like an unreliable friend
that had left her stranded at the carnival. She turned down

3

the volume on the other dispatch radios so she could better hear the one that was making all the news.

"Unit Niner, respond code red to 2314 West Altgeld Street, map page 9. Report of eleven-one in progress. Over."

Mrs. Shanahan listened to the radio for a while longer and jotted down specifics on a yellow legal pad: the body, the blood, the woman in hysterics, the paramedics en route. Maybe it was only a domestic, but maybe it was a tourist who had wandered into the wrong part of town and been beaten to death for the fifty dollars in his wallet. Mistakes like that were worth a lot of money to Electronic News Tonight.

When the dispatcher had said everything she was going to say, Mrs. Shanahan flicked open the mike on a two-way radio that connected her to the vintage station wagon in which her son and his partner cruised the streets in search of things that go thump in the night.

"Hear that?"

"Hear what?"

"Some sound is biting me."

Allan Shanahan chuckled. "Oh, come on."

Nat pulled over to the curb, turned off the engine, and held his breath while they listened for the sound of news about to break. The distant wailing of police sirens indicated a gathering of Plymouth Furys in the night.

"There. You hear it now?"

Allan nodded sharply and looked at the dispatch radio, wondering if the sirens were anything worth chasing. The radio's silence suggested that the fuss was nothing special, maybe a hit-and-run driver or a guy gone crazy with a carving knife.

"I guess that's why they call you Nat."

"It's 'Natural Sound' to you."

"Paco 'Natural Sound' Puchinski. Mr. Microphone. He's half-Rican, half-Pollack, and all newshound. But can he drive? Hell, no."

As if to prove this was not true, Nat started the engine and

4

pulled out onto the street. They were driving in the general direction of the Furys, but the sirens soon silenced, one by one, until all they could hear was the labored chugging of their own vehicle. The car choked on its own fuel when Nat eased up on the gas.

Allan adjusted the rearview mirror until he could see the stout and untidy rows of his own teeth. He removed a chunk of something trapped between two choppers and dropped it on his tongue. After swallowing he said, "This car worries me."

Nat patted the dashboard as if the car were a pet about to be destroyed. In fact, it was a decommissioned K-9 cruiser that had been uglied up with a sledgehammer and an acetylene torch. After six months of chasing cops and fire fighters, the vehicle no longer smelled of dogs and cigarettes. Now it smelled of Nat's cologne and Allan's sweat. Outside, the passenger door featured a death's head screaming, and the driver's door a stylized TV camera in brightest red with the words Electronic News Tonight emblazoned in brightest yellow. The hood ornament was a 1940s-vintage radio microphone that Mrs. Shanahan had purchased at a garage sale in Melrose Park along with the dispatch radio that now crackled to life.

"This is ENT dispatch to ENT remote. It's time to go get paid. Over."

Allan picked up the receiver. "What's up, Ma? Over."

"There's a dead one over on the 2300 block of West Altgeld Street. That's map page 9, right next door to the old Piggly Wiggly. Over."

They started to pick up speed and Allan started to worry. He said. "What else, Ma? We need more than that. There's people dying all the time that never make the news. Over."

"Well there's a crowd and some blood and a woman in hysterics—over."

"Got it, Ma. Over and out."

Allan Shanahan braced himself against the dashboard as Nat punched the accelerator. Tires squealed and metal complained as they made for the nearest exit and headed west on Fullerton Avenue into an uneasy night. This was the part of the job that Allan hated: the blurring of his vision, the humming of the engine, the feeling that his partner was a crazy man who wanted to die in flames but didn't want to do it alone. Allan tried to express this with a few urgent grunts.

"Damn!"

"What's wrong?"

"Shit!"

"You okay?"

"Fuck!"

"Not now. I'm driving."

Allan closed his eyes and whispered a little prayer as Nat hunched over the steering wheel and felt the power coursing through his veins. At 85 mph, it wasn't just a Plymouth wagon anymore but a souped-up, reinforced chariot from hell with a microphone on the hood. Pedestrians ran for cover and cars pulled over to the curb as it hurtled up one street and down another, through the night, across the river, and into the heart of the city like a bullet on wheels.

Somebody had just killed somebody else on West Altgeld Street and if they got there in time for some pictures and sound they'd get at least $500 from the affiliates and another $1,000 from "Crime Time Prime" or some other syndicated TV show. Nat thought about all of the things that $1,500 could buy as he put the Plymouth through its paces. He thought about dinner at the Tower Inn as they raced out of the fashionable lakeside precincts of the Near North Side; box-seat tickets to the next Sox game as they hurried through Lincoln Square; about a night of carnal madness with a woman at the airport bar as they plunged down the star-spangled boulevard to the strip where the automobile dealerships displayed their expensive wares. Hondas, Fords, and Toyotas offered mute praise as the station wagon rushed to the scene of the crime. If vehicles could speak, the neat rows of brand-new cars with unblemished tires and five-figure prices would have cheered—and then they would have screamed. Instead it was Allan who screamed, "Watch out!"

It happened fast, but they remembered it slow. Nat hit the brakes, which burned for a moment and then failed. A lot full of Chevys on the right and one full of Subarus on the left competed with each other to see who could fly the most American flags. On the street between them, a city bus had come to rest and been surrounded by a gathering of flashing lights—police blue, paramedic white, fire-engine red. The street was blocked from sidewalk to sidewalk, but the Plymouth didn't care. Nat put the car in neutral and applied the emergency brake with little or no effect. They had no place to go, no way to stop. Allan remembered the biggest mistakes in his life and Nat his biggest accomplishments as the Plymouth hit a dip in the road and picked up even more speed. The flags and the cars and the showroom windows dissolved into a dizzy blur. The blur came into focus for a micro-moment when Nat announced what he feared might be the last decision he would ever make.

"Hang on, bud. We're going for the Subarus."

The Plymouth was like a solid-steel bowling ball careening into cardboard bowling pins. The reinforced bumper and the radio mike, the two-way radio and the TV gear, the photographer and the producer all hit the lot with a thunderous clang followed by a multitude of lesser sounds: the crunching of metal, the flying of glass, the bouncing about of brand-new tires. Some of the Subarus were rammed to the side, crumpling into other Subarus. Others were crushed beneath the wheels of the Plymouth. Three four-door mini-wagons took the full force of the collision and were smashed flat against the brick wall of Al Montoya's Mid-Town Subaru Center.

The imports had acted like aluminum air bags. Although the Plymouth was totaled, its occupants emerged with no broken bones or internal injuries, only countless cuts and bruises. After the hubcaps stopped rolling and the radiator of the Plymouth stopped hissing more heat into the summer night, after the officer who was attending to the city bus rushed over to the scene of this new calamity, after everyone in the bus and on the street stood there torn between mute

7

admiration and speechless horror, then came the sound of the scratchy voice of Mrs. Shanahan, talking to her son on the two-way radio.

"Allan? Are you listening to me? I said it's a bogie after all. Repeat. It is a bogus event. There's a dead body all right, but it's only a domestic. Just another woman with another gun killing another man. The guy probably had it coming, but that's not news. Do you read me? Over."

Hammerhead was working on his first mustache as he walked around the block, brushing back the shorter hairs and tugging on the longer ones. The mustache wasn't part of the dress code, like baggy pants, a tight T-shirt, and hundred-dollar basketball shoes, but most of the Alone Unknown had some kind of hair on their faces. The Eye's face was mostly hair and his body was mostly muscle. Maybe that's why he was making a delivery in Billy the Bopper's car while Hammerhead had to cool his heels walking around the block.

That was the bad thing about living in the back of a Cutlass Supreme, especially with a friend. The good thing was you could always go someplace other than where you were because you'll die in the city if you ever stop moving. Your car will make you free, or at least that's what Popeye said. Popeye, a.k.a. the Eye, always figured that as long as he had a car and a gun nobody would come after him unless they wanted him really bad. The other guys figured that Popeye was worried about gangsters, but he was mostly worried about cops. The Eye had said he'd never go back to Joliet State, that if it came down to going back he'd kill as many cops as he could first so some other cop would kill him back. That way he'd maybe be a story on the news instead of returning to that hellhole.

Billy the Bopper would understand. He was doing some hang time at the Place, thanks to the time they gave him for driving around Lincoln Square on somebody else's tires. After the cops checked the tires, they checked the stereo and the watch and the gun and the trunk full of Reebok "the

Pump" basketball shoes ($99.99 each, not including tax). The only thing the Bopper hadn't stolen was the car itself, so they sent him to Joliet.

Meanwhile the Bopper was letting the Eye use his car to make up for the fight they'd had over Gloria Marti. Popeye had moved from the back seat to the front and Hammerhead had moved into the back so he wouldn't have to live at home and listen to his mother all the time. "Shut up go to school don't hang around with those rotten kids no more clean up after yourself and don't watch so much TV I'm talking to you."

Popeye had let Hammerhead move in to sleep in the back because hang time with Hammerhead was better than hang time with the Truth, who had these crazy dreams from getting dusted and a tendency to grind his teeth while asleep. Nothing was better than hang time with Gloria Marti but she had left the neighborhood to make it as a waitress in a downtown stripper bar.

"I seen a Caddy up by Western," Popeye said when he returned from the delivery. "It's giving me the gimmies and it won't let go."

"Save it for tomorrow," Hammerhead said. "It's getting light outside."

Popeye had that crazy look you get from smoking rot, his eyes shooting BBs all over the place and his hands playing bongo on the steering wheel. "You take the car and I take the walk. Be back like I got a rocket in my pocket."

The two traded places and then Billy the Bopper's car chopped the night into smoke and noise. The heat of the night and the heat of the engine mingled with the hot flush of anger rising to Hammerhead's cheeks. Sweat beaded up on his lips and his scalp started to itch.

He said, "What's the caper?"

For a moment Popeye's fingers crumpled into a fist, but the rot was still kicking in so he bongoed another tune on the dash. This tune was faster than the one before to make up for the beats he'd skipped.

"This is not a caper. This is public service."

"What're you talking about?"

"I'm talking about the way I learned it in the place. Dealing's just another caper and so is robbing folks, but stealing cars is a public service."

"You been smoking too much rot."

"That's true, but so's what I'm telling you. When you steal from a car all you get is some hubcaps and a tape deck and one of them wide-bottom coffee cups that don't tip over, but the cop gets a job chasing you and the owner gets a new tape deck. Some Korean makes his fat selling him the tape deck and the insurance people raise up the rates so they make money too. There's people with children counting on the Eye to go tear down that car."

Hammerhead fought off sleep while Popeye went to work. It was too late for Popeye to be so ripped, too late for Hammerhead to be driving getaway, but that was one of the bad things about living in the back of Billy the Bopper's car. The other bad things were winter storms, dirty laundry, and a pet gerbil named Bilbo that Popeye kept in the cage he had made of the glove compartment. Bilbo had teeth like ten penny nails which he used to grind gerbil food into gerbil turds that smelled like yesterday's puke.

"Fuck you, Bilbo," Hammerhead said to the glove compartment. "You're going to die someday."

Hammerhead couldn't get rid of Bilbo or Popeye might get rid of him, but at least he could dream about doing it—down a toilet, in a blender, or into the path of an oncoming truck. Hammerhead was thinking about baking Bilbo to a fuzzy brown crisp in the microwave at the 7-Eleven when the night was pierced by the sound of a car alarm, the Chicago Whooping Crane. He turned on the engine and waited until Popeye came out of the night with the contents of a Cadillac. These included a half-carton of cigarettes, a pair of wraparound sunglasses, the usual stereo system, and a book entitled *The Self-Help Catalogue* by Sol Kindler.

Once it was safe enough to switch seats, Popeye took the wheel. Hammerhead read a few choice passages from the self-help book while the Cutlass chugged down Elston Avenue. A few bright rays of the breaking dawn were already shining through the wall of high-rise buildings that insulated Lincoln Square from the cooling breezes that blew off the lake.

"It says, 'The first objective of the negotiator must be to separate real from imagined impediments.' "

"No shit," Popeye said. "What's an impediment?"

Hammerhead didn't know but kept on reading anyway. Popeye headed toward the lake, looking for a shady place to park so they could get a little sleep before the hot morning sun turned Billy the Bopper's car into a pressure cooker. He settled on an underpass that cut beneath the steady hum of the outbound lanes of the Kennedy.

Popeye started to snore, Hammerhead started to think, and Bilbo started to chew at the cage that held him in custody. Hammerhead thought about how Popeye had become the unquestioned leader of the Alone Unknown. He was kind of ugly and not very smart. He didn't have any money, and he didn't even have two real eyes. He'd already been in jail twice, and he'd never had a real job, unless you call bussing tables a job, which no righteous gangster did.

Hammerhead dropped a gerbil pellet into the cage and listened as Bilbo began the process of turning it into a turd. Then he dozed off to the one-note melody of cars and trucks escaping to the 'burbs.

He woke up a few hours later. Popeye was shaking his shoulder and looking at him with his glass left eye. He said, "Out of the car, Brother Blood. You're going for a walk."

Hammerhead replied, "How come?"

"I need to go get some taxes."

This got Hammerhead's attention. He propped himself up on his elbow and said, "You got a caper? What's the plan?"

Popeye didn't nod, and he didn't shake his head. He just said, "The plan is get out of the car or you and me will be having words."

* * *

11

Sister Delilah Blue munched on a doughnut from a silver serving tray and marveled at the world in which she lived, at how it got smaller the older she became. When she was a girl, she had dreamed of conquering outer space, of bringing the Word of Jesus Christ to little green folk with big bald heads. When she was a divinity student at the Negro Bible Institute, she forsook such grand ambitions and wanted only to praise the Lord from the pulpit of St. Harold's African Methodist Episcopal Church, thereby saving the planet from the depredations of wicked men. When Willis started running for mayor, she decided that Chicago was the only place she really needed to save. Seven years and two elections later, chaos still ruled the universe. Wicked men still ruled the world, and Chicago still resisted the best intentions of a very good mayor. Delilah's ministry had receded to the parameters of her cozy condo on the thirty-second floor of the Hancock Center. She now would consider her life blessed by God if she managed to save even that.

If her ministry had receded, her waistline had not. As her weight approached the neighborhood of 200 pounds, her shape and texture were becoming like that of the doughnut she was eating. Turning on the intercom, she said, "Myron, please bring me the file on Alderman Smith and then say I'm gone unless it's the boss."

The crisp, clean harpsichord notes of something by Bach tinkled out of stereo speakers embedded in her office walls. The music was cold, hard, and white, like a hailstorm on the brain. Sister Delilah didn't like it much. Her taste ran to gospel, saxophones, and poor folks with the blues, but people expected that of her, so she listened to Bach instead. She didn't like her office either, not the red mahogany furniture or the elaborate Persian rug or the antique display case full of authentic African thingamabobs. Her taste ran to bare floors, modern art, and molded plastic chairs, but she saved all that for her condo in the Hancock. The things she did for a little privacy.

Myron brought in the file and removed the tray of doughnuts. She could see him flexing his scrawny butt as he walked out the door, secure in the false belief that someday Delilah would succumb to his charms, even if she was a sister of the Lord. Delilah would not succumb because Myron looked a lot like Bach sounded, tight, white, and brittle, while her taste ran to men with a lot of meat and a little sweet. And if they had strayed from the path of Jesus, that was all right with Delilah Blue. She would save them with a little glimpse of heaven here on earth.

"Douglas MacArthur Smith," Sister Delilah said to herself as she cracked the folder open. "Why you trying to mess with me?"

The folder was full of newspaper clippings in chronological order. The first was three paragraphs long, ten years old, and announced the formation of the Crusade for Safer Streets, an organization of young men and women dedicated to fighting crime wherever they could find it. Finding crime was not a problem, as 1,587 subsequent press clippings showed. The last story was only three days old and featured intense speculation about the alderman's political future. Would he run for mayor? Would the Street Crusaders start wearing suits? What about those funny hats? Might the public be fooled by a firm chin and shameless promises of a safer tomorrow that would never come?

Delilah had read it all story by story as it happened. Now she read it again, looking for something that would explain the ascendancy of Douglas Smith. Between the first clipping and the last was an American success story that reminded Delilah of her own transformation from storefront savior to mayoral mouthpiece. With more color, different names, and a run-down neighborhood, the headlines could have been about Delilah Blue, Willis Cleveland, and the Community Action Resource Enterprise:

LOCAL GROUP KEEPS WATCHFUL EYE ON ELDERLY
ACTIVIST CALLS FOR MORE COP MONEY
VIGILANTES CREDITED WITH MUGGER'S ARREST
SMITH WINS CLOSE RACE FOR ALDERMAN
CRIME STATS DOWN IN CRUSADERS' NEIGHBORHOOD

13

ALDERMAN HONORED FOR VOLUNTEER WORK
CRUSADER: 'GIVE NARCO-KILLERS THE CHAIR'

Delilah closed the manila folder and set it down on her desk. She thought about the numbers as she watched condensation from the air-conditioner bead up on the windows, looking like an ice cube's view of a city melting down. According to the overnight poll, 20 percent of likely voters were solidly in Doogie's camp. That was less than half of the mayor's positives but very close to the 23 percent that Willis had had nearly eight years before, when the pundits said he never had a chance.

Those were the glory days. Before they discovered what winning really meant, the world they were trying to save was a lot bigger than her condo and Delilah despised the sort of person that she had since become. She remembered the day they knew they had it made, when she woke up and saw that a headline writer at the *Trib* had shortened their Community Action Resource Enterprise to a pithy and positive CARE. The *Sun-Times* followed suit, and she and Willis were on their way. The shorter the words, the bigger the type. That's why the mayor always told reporters that his name was Willis, but they could call him Will, and that his press officer was Sister Delilah Blue, but they could call her Sis.

Myron interrupted Delilah's meditations with a phone call from Will. "What it is, Sis? What it is? What you got for me?" Sister Blue looked at the receiver as if it were emitting a noxious odor. Willis liked to pretend that he was exactly what people expected him to be. He acted the streetwise player, turning on the shuck and jive. He called white guys "dude," black guys "brother," and Delilah "Sis" for short.

"What it is, Mr. Mayor, is not too much. The file. If there's anything there, I don't see it."

"Now which file is it you mean?"

"A folder full of old newspaper clips, everything the paper's ever wrote about the man."

"Well that's your problem then. You're looking in the

wrong place. Doogie don't live on the printed page. He lives in TV land, in that box on the table in your living room."

Many faces gathered around the mayor's TV set. Some of the faces were worried and some were merely bored. Most of them were black or brown. One of them was white. All faces had the glimmer that a little power puts in the beholder's eyes. Distorted by TV, the smaller, flatter face of Alderman Smith spewed forth from the mayor's set with the same kind of look, but his glimmer was more like a spark.

When Smith's sound bite was over, the mayor pressed PAUSE and the image froze in place. "We need to talk about Bulljive Day."

Delilah asked the question on everybody's mind. "What day?"

"Bulljive Day, Sister. Forty-nine days from now. Doogie and me'll be flapping jaw at the Biograph in this debate for the ladies in the League. Live TV and all the rest just before the vote. When the bulljive comes to a bubble, the voters get their due. If we don't win it by Bulljive Day, we're going to lose this thing. It's time to get to work."

They all stayed still for a moment, as if they were stuck on PAUSE like Doogie. Delilah broke the spell. She said, "Sometimes I wonder about the Lord, making a man like that. So evil and so sly, serving up all that Chinese food."

Everyone laughed, especially the mayor. The white guy, a pollster by the name of Donald Boyle, didn't know what he was laughing at. He said, "What do you mean, Chinese food?"

"That's what you get on the TV news," Delilah Blue replied. "Chinese food for thought. It fills you up until your brain is stuffed and then a half hour later you're stupid again."

The mayor chuckled. "Well said, Sis."

"That's because you said it first."

Everyone else chuckled too, and this time the pollster meant it. When the laughter subsided, he approached a chart that described the voting patterns of the city's ethnic groups. "I don't know about Chinese food but I do know Chinese voting patterns. Alderman Smith'll get 90 percent of the yellow vote. The browns're what I'm worried about. We've got a problem if they stay on the fence. The question is, what to do?"

The mayor spoke very softly, which is how he spoke when he wanted to be sure that everyone listened real hard. The pollster held his breath. Delilah cocked her ear. The others made similar efforts to detect his every word.

"I will eat a lot of ethnic food and you will all get muddy. I will take care of the allegations and you will take care of the allegator. I don't know how you're going to do it. I don't want to know so as to protect my precious deniability in the event of lies and crimes and what-have-you. Now if I was a sister of the Lord and my snappy little condo was on the line, I'd work the TV thing real hard. Pull the plug on Doogie's pub and he'll be yesterday's news."

The pollster looked at Delilah and mouthed the word "Pub?" without really saying it.

"Pub is publicity," she said. "Ink. Exposure. Free air time."

The mayor stood up, a signal for the others to leave. "We need to put a real quick stop to all the free pub he gets."

Delilah shook her head. "Or turn it sour would be even better. Bad pub's better than none as far as Doogie's concerned. No problem. I heard about these TV guys'll do anything if the money is right."

2

Shoe Goo Summer

ALLAN KEPT UP A CONSTANT CHATTER AS NAT GUIDED MRS.
Shanahan's Ford down the rolling river of rubber and steel
known as Halsted Street. He talked about the Chicago
Sanitary & Ship Canal and the Italian workers who had built
it and he talked about the elevated train and the way it kept
rolling around the Loop. He said the city was like a crazy
man who seemed to be at peace but was ready to explode at
any moment into fire and blood with somebody's vital
organs leaking out onto the street. Nat listened but he didn't
hear until Allan said, "I think I'm going to die."

"How come?"

"Because it's hot and humid and I'm sitting here breathing air that you just finished breathing."

"Shoe Goo Summer."

"All I know is it feels like I'm wearing a grease monkey's
rag. You know I've got this theory about—what was that
you said?"

"Shoe Goo Summer."

"What's that?"

Nat didn't answer until Mrs. Shanahan's car had eased to

17

a stop behind a CTA bus that belched more smoke, more heat, more sticky summer goo into the midday air. He put the vehicle in neutral and checked the bottom of his shoes to see what had collected there: a few small stones, two cigarette butts, and a flattened bottle cap. He peeled off the bottle cap and handed it to Allan.

"On a day like this, it gets so hot the tar in the asphalt melts and sticks to the bottom of your shoes. My mother would always call it Shoe Goo Summer and she'd make me scrape off all the crud before she'd let me in the house. She pronounced it Chew Goo Summer. Mama was Puerto Rican. This one time, I swear to God, a goddamn rubber is stuck to the bottom of my shoes and my mother's right there looking at me like I'm out getting girls instead of just thinking about them all the time."

Nat held his tongue too late, afraid the word girls might get Allan started. It didn't take much.

Allan said, "I've got a theory. You want to hear it? It's about women, I mean."

"No."

"Okay. Here it is. You know all this stuff about sensitive guys? That's just a female scam. Women only want guys to be soft so they can push us around. Right?"

"Wrong."

"I never met any woman that wasn't tougher than any man when you got right down to cases. My theory is that what the world really needs is more sensitive women, so we can start pushing them around. The whole thing started with advertising, because women buy all the groceries. That's why TV guys're so stupid, like Archie Bunker and Dick Van Dyke. And you know this other theory I've got?"

Nat didn't answer, so Allan talked on. "You notice how a lot of these TV women look kind of goofy when they're not on the tube? This one's got a big nose, and that one's got a monkey mouth, and this one's too short, and that one's too tall, only they all look perfect on the news. The trick with TV is you got to look good in two dimensions, with your features all flattened out. You can have a nose like a loaf of french bread and still look good on television, but if you've got big ears, forget it; 2-D only makes big ears bigger so they look like garbage-can lids."

Nat tried to imagine his partner's teeth in two dimensions. They protruded from his mouth in a wild display of dental exuberance, with each tooth going its own way in a manner that forced his lips back into a permanent grin, mocking the man's naturally gloomy disposition. Allan wouldn't stop talking, so Nat said the two words that were guaranteed to shut him up.

"Janette Baylor."

Allan contemplated the bottle cap that Nat had peeled from the bottom of his shoe. "What about her?"

"Nothing. I was just thinking about how she looks in 3-D."

Thoughts of Janette in 3-D and 2-D kept Allan quiet for a little while. The latest source of the producer's gloom was the fact that Janette didn't care if he died tomorrow, unless it was a story to be read on the late-night edition of Channel Twelve news.

Wanting Janette and not being able to have her combined with the fumes of the CTA bus to put Allan into a comatose state. Nat enjoyed the silence and tried to imagine a more perfect world in which guys who knew how to make money fast also made good traveling companions. He put Mrs. Shanahan's Ford in gear, following the bus to the South Side where they intended to purchase another retired police cruiser to replace the one they had totaled at Al Montoya's Mid-Town Subaru Center.

More heat. More fumes. More daydreams. Shoe Goo Summer reminded Nat of long-lost vacations from school with nothing very much to do, when the punks in his neighborhood used knives instead of guns and smoked pot instead of crack. In those days, the Near North Side was a kingdom to be defended and a canvas to be painted with Day-Glo colors from an aerosol can. Chores were assigned according to skill, which meant that Crazy Horse did most of the stealing and Nat did most of the painting because he had always had this thing about art.

Nat wanted to tell Allan about the good old days, when he was a graffiti artist with a gang of his own and the only bad thing about summer was it would have to end someday. But Allan was too busy thinking about what he could never be or have.

"Janette's different. Special, I mean. Just last night I saw how she's doing this series called 'The Brotherhood of Death.' Good name. I like it. Maybe we'll see her on the street tonight. Maybe we should give her a call, sell her some tape. If we get something really good, I mean."

Allan was too wrapped up in his own yearning to detect the hollow sound of his unheard speech. His gabbing blended into the other background noise as Nat leaned right on the steering wheel and turned onto Roosevelt Road. When the Ford settled into the right lane with the right speed, Nat turned to Allan and said, "This summer is never going to end. It's the greenhouse effect from all those fossil fuels. I read something once where the lake is doing a slow boil, and it'll be gone in another hundred years or so. That's how come the air's so clammy, because the lake is boiling away and that's how come there's all those dead fish. Alewives, they're called."

Allan thought about the heat as they rolled past the shifting bulbs of a bank sign that announced the time, the temp and the current interest on tax-free municipal bonds. He imaged the perspiration beading in the hollows of Janette's body and said, "Here's what I don't understand. The body's 98.6 degrees. So how come I'm here sweating like a pig when the temperature's only ninety-five? If I'm ninety-eight and the temp's ninety-five, then the air should feel cool, right? Don't you think?"

Nat leaned left on the steering wheel, turning onto Laramie. "Let's go down to the lake. We'll buy some beers and jump in the water. We can take the night off and buy a new rig tomorrow."

"That's a negatory. We start playing hooky, and sure as shit somebody big gets killed. There's lots of guys out there with TV cameras looking to steal our business away."

"Hey, I don't want to spoil your fun, but *somebody* is getting killed all the time," Nat said. "News is what we do for a living, remember? And anyway, it's Shoe Goo Summer. One of the things about this time of year is people get mad and they build up steam and they go out and kill somebody. We don't need to roll tape on each and every one."

They stopped at Thirty-Fifth Street, which was all jammed up. The light turned green, then red, then green again, but still they didn't move. An old man with black gums climbed up on the bumper and started wiping the windshield with the sleeve of his shirt. Nat watched him smear a compound of dust, oil, and bum sweat into a whirlpool smudge. He'd ask for a quarter when he was done.

Phil's High-Performance Vehicle Resale smelled like the heart of Shoe Goo Summer—rubber and oil and too much heat with no place else to go. Phil had seventeen old police cruisers lined up for sale. Each one had a spotlight on the driver's side and a rusty ring on top where the party light used to be. He had covered the city seal on each car with a thin coat of off-white paint, but if you looked long and close enough you could still see the fading image of a noble savage looking at an approaching ship with a worried look on his face. Beneath them were the Latin words *Urbs in Horto.*

"What's that mean?" Nat said.

"City in a garden," Allan replied.

"This town needs a better seal. City in a Ditty. *Urbs in Blurbs.* Frank Sinatra. My kind of town. What do you say to that?"

Allan didn't say anything, because before he could, Phil snuck up from behind and announced his presence with a smoker's cough. "Well if it ain't the Electronic Dudes Tonight. You must be working overtime, being back again so soon. How long's it been?"

"November."

Phil made a quick calculation of the ratio of time to money as it applied to Electronic News Tonight. These were important customers who must be milked with great care and good cheer. He walked over to one of his cars and threw his hands into the air. "You are hard-driving fellas and you drive a hard bargain too. I got to give you that."

Phil petted his nearest wreck, as if he expected it to purr. He liked cars more than people and hated to see them mistreated. Cops were bad and journalists worse when it came to driving cars. He said, "This one here's got a hundred fifteen thousand miles and a brand-new transmission. I just installed it myself. Forty-five hundred and you get the tires free."

Allan grimaced at the price. Nat hated the inevitable dickering, so he walked over to the office and poured himself a cup of Phil's forty-weight. He was tired of driving junked-up cruisers, tired of sweating all summer long, tired of Allan and of TV news, and tired of being tired. Phil's coffee didn't help although it did make him more alert to the weariness in his bones.

"Explain one thing to me," Phil was saying to Allan as Nat walked back into the lot. "How come I never see you on TV if you guys are Electronic News Tonight?"

Allan stuck his finger in the exhaust of the car Phil was trying to unload. "This puppy's burning oil."

Phil ignored the comment. Allan said, "We only work at nights, selling tape to the highest bidder. We don't want the glory, and we don't want the mail. We just want the money. That's why you never see us on the tube. That's why we'll be rich at forty."

Phil nodded as if he understood. He didn't. "Well, you wear out cars pretty fast. If you don't want this one, then tell me what you want."

Allan wiped the oil from his fingertip and said, "What do you have that's fast and ugly? Give us four new tires, and we'll pay you by the dent."

Phil chewed on his cigar some more. "How come you always buy ugly cars?"

Nat could hear the quarters clanking in Allan's head as his partner thought about it. Information was money, and he never gave either away, so he lied. "Ugly cars hardly ever get robbed. You want to get robbed, you drive a brand new car. You want to travel around in peace, you buy a piece of shit from Phil's. So what's the special of the day?"

They walked along the row of seventeen stripped-down Plymouths until they reached one that seemed to have rolled away from a shower of cannonballs. Phil said, "What can I say? We sell police cars, so I got Furys." He nodded at a dented heap at the far end of the row. "That one might do the trick. It's a 1990 from Precinct Five, over by Broadway and Foster Avenue. I heard it's got low mileage because the officers in it were always hanging out behind the Uptown Theater, keeping out of trouble. That's what you do if you're smart and you work in Precinct Five."

3

The Truth About the Tooth

THE SQUIRRELS IN MRS. SHANAHAN'S ATTIC WATCHED NAT'S ARrival with more than the usual interest. Nat figured the noise and the smell the Plymouth made as it crunched up the gravel road was what caught their attention. To a squirrel's brain, the car must have seemed like the 'dozer that had leveled their woods late last spring.

Nat had a hard time believing that condos would be built next to the house where Diamond-Tooth Eddie was killed. He also believed it not right that Allan should grow up in the presence of such gangster lore. Allan didn't care about gangsters, and he never paid proper respect to the place in which he lived.

Diamond-Tooth Eddie had been the mayor of Willow Woods during the Roaring Twenties. The town was fifty miles from the city, but one could get there by road, rail, or canal. This made Willow Woods the perfect staging area for the transportation of bootleg liquor. Eddie's uncles and brothers and cousins—half the town, in other words—got handsome handling fees for moving cheap Canadian whiskey from rail to road to canal. Barges were thought to be the

24

best way to move large amounts of liquor into the city quietly in the night.

Eddie's cut for making all this happen was his main source of revenue, gambling his main expenditure. For years the mayor maintained a rough equilibrium between his crime and his vice, but after the repeal of Prohibition his income could no longer keep pace with his outgo. The Capones bought up all his old gambling debts and sent three guys from Milwaukee to collect. Eddie had no money, so they beat him to death with his own sap and left him to die in his own bathtub.

The Shanahans bought the place, bathtub and all, at one of the annual county auctions of delinquent property after unconfirmed rumors about booby traps and a mysterious stench had the effect of lowering the price. A major remodeling eventually uncovered some evidence that pointed to Eddie: a gun, sixteen jars of bootleg whiskey, and a two-foot length of oak branch that had been hollowed out, filled with lead, and varnished to a dark brown gloss. Allan used this device to prop open his bedroom window.

"What a jerk," Nat told the squirrels. "You'd think with living in a place like this he'd help me make my gangster doc."

The squirrels did not reply. They'd been pretty sullen as squirrels go ever since 'dozer day. Nat remembered it because he'd been up all night chopping tape when the machines rolled in at 6:00 A.M. The woods were mostly gone by the time the workers stopped for lunch. Nat and the workers watched the wildlife scramble around for new accommodations. The evicted birds crowded other birds out of Mrs. Shanahan's trees, and a tribe of chipmunks were slaughtered during an ill-advised trek across Archer Avenue. The bugs survived, as bugs will do, and the groundhogs started making abodes in Mrs. Shanahan's garden.

Only the squirrels were able to improve their lives following the demolition of their original habitat. The day after the woods were destroyed, they set up shop in Mrs.

Shanahan's attic and quickly went about the important
business of remodeling her house to suit their needs.

The squirrels disappeared into their newly acquired accommodations when they heard the familiar sound of Allan
crunching gravel in his mother's Ford.

When Allan had parked the car, Nat said, "This new
cruiser's hooked on speed."

"I noticed. When did you get here?"

"Ten ago. Let's call her Genghis Kar."

Allan didn't answer for a while. He was looking at a mind
picture of a fiery crash in which his guts exploded into a
gusher of bloody steam as his bodily fluids were turned into
a gasified protein mist. Firemen, cops, paramedics, and
reporters would rush to the scene. When the fire was extinguished and the protein had congealed into a puddle of
pink, the only parts of the wreck that could be identified
were a vintage radio microphone and a passenger door on
which were inscribed the words Genghis Kar.

Allan said, "If a car's a 'her' you can't call it Genghis.
How about the Madonnamobile?"

"Napoleon Fallapart."

"Meryl Street."

"Alexander the Crate."

"You're obsessed with power."

"And you're obsessed with worse."

"Let's go get the sledge."

The sledge was in the house.

"We're back," Allan announced to his mother, as if she
couldn't tell that by the fact that they were flapping their
shirttails at the vent and dripping sweat all over her rug.

Nat said, "Hello, Mrs. Shanahan. What's the big news
today?"

The old woman consulted a clipboard she'd hung on a nail
near her wide assortment of emergency dispatch radios.
"Not much, dear. A five-car crash on the Outer Drive and
another shooting on the North Side. The shooting was just a
mugger and the affiliates were all in on the crash. I guess

some kids were showing off and spun out into oncoming traffic."

She turned to her son. "You're supposed to call Norm at Channel Eight. He's got a job for you."

Allan nodded. Nat smiled, wondering what was in the old girl's refrigerator. Mrs. Shanahan could read Nat's mind. He was like a big squirrel she'd let downstairs to eat her out of house and home.

Allan said, "The sledgehammer, Ma."

Mrs. Shanahan headed for the refrigerator as if the sledgehammer were tucked between the sliced Velveeta and the tuna casserole. She retrieved the latter and popped it into the microwave. "Eat first. You must be starved."

Allan made another pitch for the sledge, but his mother would have none of that. She regarded the last womanly joy of her life to be the talk of these hardworking men around her kitchen table. She filled them up with workingman's food to the noise of politics, women, and work, work, work.

Allan said, "We need to trim that bite from the chief."

"Let's do a jump cut, then. A jump cut is up-front, lets people know that we're chopping something out."

Empowered by his mother's tuna casserole, Allan banged away at their new street car. Although Nat was by far the bigger man, his hands were devoted to the more delicate task of painting the company logo on the driver's side door.

A boy named Jeffrey who lived by the canal was attracted by the ruckus of the sledgehammer blows and came running up the road to say to Allan, "What're you doing?"

"Smashing a car."

"Why?"

"So I can get rich."

"Why?"

Jeffrey kept asking questions while the two men went about their chores. "Where'd you get that funny-looking microphone? How come you're putting it on the hood? Is the paint dry yet? Is the microphone you put in the painting the same one you put on the hood? Did you know that you forgot to smash that spot over there?"

Allan said, "Why don't you go home, Jeffrey?"

"Because."

The boy watched with great interest while Allan smashed the spot he'd pointed out. "One more question?"

"No."

"How come you're smashing your brand-new car?"

Allan decided that Jeffrey's head was another spot he'd forgotten to smash. "Because when this starts showing up in some little boy's rearview mirror, that little boy had better get out of the way. Now beat it. Scram. Go home."

With Jeffrey gone and the microphone securely in its proper place, Mrs. Shanahan joined them in the driveway as they christened their new car with a six-pack of Michelob Light. After much haggling, the three stockholders of Electronic News Tonight convened a special meeting under BYLAW 1.7 to decide the name of their new vehicle. Mrs. Shanahan combined her 33.3 shares with Nat's 33.3 shares because her son, as usual, had taken her for granted. The majority partners voted to call it Genghis Kar.

4

The Hit on Tappy Shoes

ELMO HAD THE HEEBIE-JEEBIES, SO HE PUT HIS GAME FACE ON:
angry eyes, twisted lips, furrowed brow. These went well
with baggy pants and a leather vest without sleeves. That
way people could see his muscles and his fading blue tatoo
of a snake in league with an eagle. He had a maroon combat
beret on his head and an envelope full of money in his
pocket, babushka money he'd collected back in the neighborhood. He took the hat off. He didn't have much hair
because he'd shaved it off just the other day.

No gun either.

Elmo didn't need a gun. He had Alderman Douglas Smith
for a friend and a tire iron under the seat of his 1987 Chevy.
As the Chevy herky-jerked its way through the streets of the
South Side, Elmo talked to himself because he was the only
person who would really understand.

He said, "I hate this town and that's a fact, especially in
the summertime. You sweat so much your clothes is soaking
wet, and then the dirt and the smog and the burnt rubber
stink gets mixed up with your sweat until it feels like your
underwear's been dipped in butter. You could probably die

from wearing your clothes if you didn't change them once a week."

Talking to himself helped settle down the heebie-jeebies. Elmo said to himself, "The problem with the heebie-jeebies is how everybody's got them but nobody ever talks about it, so everybody thinks about how they're the only one. I bet Doogie even got them when they shot the Nigger King."

The Chevy made a long, thin shadow as it rolled east, into the city and away from the afternoon sun. The car was bulletproof because the alderman rode in the back sometimes. Elmo reached under the seat and brushed his fingertips against the tire iron. The cold, hard steel made him feel a little better. He'd have to get another tire iron. How much would it cost and who would pay the price?

A hot, wet stench rose from the street and from three hundred thousand other cars as if the city were doing a slow boil in its own toxic juices. Elmo patted the envelope in his pocket and thought about the things that ten thousand dollars could buy if it wasn't wasted on some freakin Rican punk: a better car, another beret, a brand new pair of combat boots, and a date with a girl who did it with a smile. Someday, after Doogie was mayor, Elmo would have these things, especially the smile. Or at least that's what Doogie had said, and Doogie never lied to Elmo—not yet, anyway.

The people on the street changed as Elmo passed through the neighborhoods: white to black to brown to black to yellow to white to brown again. With so many people in so many cars, Elmo was glad his own was equipped with steel plates and a tire iron. You could never tell when some crazy person might come up and ask you for a dollar and shoot you down if you didn't have one, or shoot you if you had one and didn't give it up, or shoot you if you gave it up without being nice about it. That's what the Street Crusaders were for, stepping on people like that and protecting people like Elmo.

He parked on the 1600 block of Elston Avenue and walked the last few blocks to Lincoln Square just in case things didn't go right and he had to get away from it fast.

Elmo had learned that it's easier to escape from cops or crooks on foot than in a vehicle. He had learned this at an early age before Doogie started playing politics.

They'd been working on a caper that didn't go right. The owner of the store was a cheap son of a bitch who'd rather get killed than pay his taxes, so Elmo fired a shot at the mirror to put the fool on notice. The laws came on real fast after that, with their siren on "scream" and their party lights flashing. Doogie ran down an alley and got away. Elmo went for the car and got caught. He would have been convicted except Doogie got to the owner of the store and settled it up somehow. Doogie was already a genius back in 1981 when they were still a bunch of punks instead of politicians and the Street Crusaders were known as the Bebop Bangers, a gang that was so small and so white that even the cops didn't care.

But that was then and this was now, and Elmo wasn't a punk anymore. He patted the money and squeezed the tire iron that was now tucked in his pants as he marched past a tavern called *El Rincón,* which smelled of sweat and beer, then past a place called Beepers and Pay Phones, which was the communications center for most of the narco-killers in Lincoln Square. Elmo noticed that people stopped talking when he walked by. He liked it that way because silence was a sign of fear or respect. Both would be nice. Either would do. He could only expect so much from a bunch of freakin Ricans since they were out to get him and he was out to get them. So far the score was Elmo 3, Ricans 0. Elmo was sure to win because when they scored, the game was over.

Unlike Elmo, Popeye blended into Lincoln Square like a plant blends into the jungle. His skin was the same color as the brownstone wall of an all-night bowling alley known as *Jugar el Boliche.* The red throb of a neon bowling pin matched the color of his baseball cap. Popeye was a Cardinals fan otherwise dressed in baggy pants, a dago-T, and Nike basketball shoes. Elmo walked up.

Popeye said, "What's the word, Mo?"

Elmo nodded and tapped his tire iron against the brown-stone. "The word is money, Mr. Eye. I've got some for you, and I've got the name of a guy to sell you the tool you need."

"I'm packing. That's my tool."

Elmo shook his head as he handed Popeye the envelope. "If you want to get away and if you want to do it right, you'll need some techno-death: smart bombs, laser guns, a precision-guided shitstorm. That's how it's done in modern times."

"I got no problem with that. So how'm I gonna get me some?"

"You go down to Little Egypt and talk to this guy over by this boat they call the *Connected Yankee*."

Popeye shrugged and rubbed his glass eyeball. The one eye he didn't have hurt a lot more in the summertime. He said, "Where's that and who's this guy?"

Elmo said, "Let's slow down. Let's have some showtime first. If we have a little showtime then you'll know what I'm about. What I'm all about is this. Don't try to steal the money or otherwise mess with me. You think you can handle that?"

Popeye adjusted his baseball cap. He could handle anything for ten thousand now and another twenty later when the job was done. He said, "Whatever."

So together they leaned against the brownstone, watching the world go by and the sun go down. At dusk, the anti-crime sulfur lights started to make a low buzzing sound that got lower and louder as the sky got darker. The street was bathed in a strange yellow light that was brighter than the stars or the moon. Car radios and a dozen ghetto-blasters all played the same station with fast-singing salsa and lots of percussion from the Sound Machine.

'Spanic bowlers drifted in and out of *Jugar el Boliche* while Elmo proudly waited for something. For a while Popeye couldn't figure out what it was, but as their shadows got longer and were swallowed by the night, he realized that Elmo was waiting for the dark to hide what he intended to do. It made him nervous and curious. Elmo was a creep, but he had the money, and Popeye was a man with a plan.

They waited until well past midnight, until Armando "Tappy Shoes" Calderone came by walking the pimp. All of the bangers from Lincoln Square knew how to walk the walk. They looked like a flock of flightless birds with their heads pushed forward and their wrists curled back and their legs as stiff as stilts with feet.

Elmo called to the bird named Tappy. "Say, son. You got some toot?" He had tucked the tire iron into the sleeve of his shirt, so Tappy wouldn't see it.

The boy thought it over. The dealers from Beepers and Pay Phones gave some smoke and some money to any kid who found them a new customer. Tappy asked Elmo, "How much toot you looking for?"

"Get me a gram for the going rate and quick."

Tappy agreed to do just that and ran away into the night. Elmo said to Popeye, "Drugs are bad. He should've said no."

Popeye thought about this, and he thought about some smart remark that would let Elmo know that he wasn't anybody's fool.

Before he could think of one, Tappy returned with his fist wrapped around a fold of paper. He offered the drug to Elmo and said, "Now gimme my money, man."

Elmo grabbed the drugs and looked both ways, like a responsible motorist. When he didn't see any traffic, his hand shot out like a bullwhip, grabbing the boy by his hair. He held Tappy's head in place as the tire iron landed with a splat.

Tappy's knees buckled.

He died right away.

Popeye leaned back into a shadow and hushed, "Why you do that, you crazy mutherfuck?"

"Shut up, punk, and watch what I do."

He pulled his maroon Street Crusader combat beret out of the side pocket of his leather vest and walked over to a telephone booth. He motioned at Popeye to follow along, so he could hear what Elmo had to say to Emergency 911.

"My name is Elmo Givens, and I'm the executive vice president of the Crusade for Safer Streets. I'd like to report a murder over by Lincoln Square. Looks like another drug dealer got killed by another narco-punk."

He hung up the phone and leaned over the fallen body of Tappy Shoes. He used the boy's T-shirt to wipe a spot of blood from the business end of his tire iron. Then he stood up and said to Popeye, "The thing you need to know is if you try to fuck with me, I'll crush your skull with a tire iron and then call in the laws to come clean up the mess."

5

Time Is Money

IN THE LONG MOMENTS A LONELY MAN HAS, ALLAN SLEPT TO THE busy sounds of the neighborhood squirrels at work. And his mother slept in the bed she'd shared with Allan's dad before he died from cancer of the everything. And Nat slept in the basement on a couch next to the old coal furnace that had warmed the bones of Diamond-Tooth Eddie, three generations of Shanahans, and now one rootless photographer of Pollarican extraction. The last in the house to wake up was Nat, who emerged from his slumber at 10:57 P.M. That left just enough time to wash his face before news music sounded the beginning of another working night.

Mrs. Shanahan listened to the radio traffic while the two men ate a little food and drank a lot of coffee in front of four television sets. Nat watched Channels Three and Eight while Allan watched some of Four and all of Twelve. Allan always watched Channel Twelve. They took turns with the others, but never with Channel Twelve. Janette's channel was Allan's channel, to be watched with a transfixion of horror and lust as she read the day's catastrophes with those oh-so-kissable lips.

Nat used to tease his partner about Janette until he realized that the poor fool really had been smitten by Her Flatness. Imagine falling in love with a two-dimensional dwarf. What else could you call a women who fit inside a twelve-inch box?

Nat sipped his coffee and took a bite of tuna casserole. That's two good things about Allan, he reminded himself. He knows how to make lots of money fast and he makes me glad that I'm not him. Only a fool would fall in love with a TV woman, because a TV woman can only love herself.

Nat said, "They've got promos for Janette's series on my soap already and the sweeps haven't even started yet."

"The news dee at Twelve's having a nervous fit, " Allan replied. "Channel Eight's got them in a demographic squeeze when you break the audience down by age. Twelve's viewers are all on life support. Here's money."

Nat turned down the sound on the two TVs he was watching so he could hear Janette say there'd been a fire in a duplex on the Southwest Side. Allan clicked on his stopwatch the second her face was covered by the flames and smoke they had captured on videotape. Nat counted up the money in his head as she read the terrible news over fifteen seconds of edited tape, complete with natural sound: two were injured, the cause was unknown, and the damage was listed at two hundred and seventy-five thou.

"That's enough for my next month's rent," Nat announced when the flames and smoke had disappeared.

Janette said it was the fifth major fire in that part of town in the last six weeks. Teenage gangsters were suspected of the crime and please be sure to watch her upcoming series, "The Brotherhood of Death." Allan let out an unrequited sigh and made an entry in the books: Seventeen seconds of video at $50 a second equals $850. He wondered if maybe they should raise the price to $75 per and he wondered if Janette would be impressed by such a display of confidence.

When the news was over they went to work.

Nat tested the new car with mad dashes and quick stops up and down the Irish Democrat expressways that the Irish mayors had constructed before the blacks took over. Up and down the Dan Ryan. Up and down the Kennedy. They slowed down over by Lincoln Square because these days that's where most of the news came from. Nat liked the new company car. It jiggled and wiggled in low gear, and couldn't wait for the race to begin. Allan talked to his mother on the two-way radio.

Allan: Add eight-fifty to the bill for Channel Twelve, okay? That's what they owe us for last night's fire.

Mother: I hope that fireman's okay. His face looked pretty bad.

Allan: The captain said it was arson. I guess they want to build condos over there.

Mother: Who's they? They should make arson legal. It's the cheapest way to—

Allan: The cheapest way to what, Ma?

Mother: The cheapest way to— Hold on, okay?

Nat hit the brakes and angled toward an exit just in case. "Some blues're going uptown on a code red."

Allan grabbed the dashboard as Nat hit the gas. They rushed down the exit ramp. Nat punched the horn as they approached a red light. A brand-new Cadillac ducked out of their way as they blew straight through the intersection and headed for the Outer Drive. Allan saw his life rush by. He was familiar with the show by now.

"What is it, Ma?"

"I don't know. Hang on."

They hit seventy going east on Diversey Avenue. Ahead of them a light showed yellow and a slow car was in the way, so Nat cut around and punched the horn. Some crosstown traffic stopped to let them through.

"Mother!"

The night rushed by at seventy, then eighty, then eighty-five miles an hour. It didn't feel like Shoe Goo Summer any more. The air became light and almost cool, and the speed blew all the bad smells away. Allan screamed. Nat smiled.

Allan's mother said, "Never mind. It's a bogie. I repeat. It's a bogus event."

"Thanks, Ma," Allan said.

Nat slowed down until the Shoe Goo Summer night got hot and sticky again. Allan let go of the dashboard and touched his chest to check out his heart. It beat like an Osterizer. They looked for a place to turn around.

"What was it?"

"A fight. Nobody dead."

"That's great, Ma. That's really great."

They drove for two more hours without getting anywhere. Up and down the Kennedy, up and down the Dan Ryan. They tried the Eisenhower just for a change of scenery, driving past the big factory clock that didn't work and past the Magikist Rug Cleaners sign which read Do you know where your children are? on the way out and Please register to vote on the way in.

Then they went back to the usual routine, through uptown and downtown and midtown, over angry streets and beneath elegant penthouse apartments. Mrs. Shanahan read them a story over the two-way radio, something in the *Reader's Digest* about Eskimo whale hunters lost at sea. Her reading was interrupted by a robbery and a two-alarm fire, but nothing worth taking pictures of.

Nat said, "Read that part again, where the Eskimos think they're gonna die."

Mrs. Shanahan obliged and the night proceeded without event. When the story was over Allan said, "Nothing going on. Let's get a bite to eat."

Nat said that was okay as long as they went back to the 'hood.

6

Little Wimpy

THAT LOST, LONELY HOUR WHEN IT'S TOO LATE TO BE AWAKE AND too early to be alive was the perfect time to mourn a cherished past, whether it existed in fact or only on the perfect streets of an imperfect memory. In this respect Nat was like a little boy who walks around with a wrinkled picture of his dead dog tucked in his back pocket. It hurt him to remember the guys, the girls, the long midsummer afternoons, but the pain itself brought a rough sort of comfort. If his past still bothered him after all these years, it must have meant something after all. What that was, he didn't know.

He slowed down after they turned left on Arlington Street, getting the feel of the place, remembering how it used to be and seeing how time and money had transformed the mean streets into easy streets, and the dowdy apartments into expensive condominiums for people who wouldn't dream of sitting on the stoop and watching the world walk by.

"It's pretty sad, I have to say. This neighborhood used to have people on the street instead of just imported cars. We'd be listening to the radio, talking to the women, and sitting on the stoop just to be outside. Now it's like everybody stays in their own little space because they're afraid of everybody else. It's very sad, and it never used to be like this. You look at it now and the streets are dead."

Allan yawned. "That's because these people have regular jobs, and it's 2:15 in the morning."

It didn't matter what Allan said. Nat wasn't listening to his partner but to the whispering ghosts of his own yesterday. He turned onto Wrightwood Avenue and slowed down as they passed by the silent remains of the Louisa May Alcott Public School. Although the brownstone buildings across the street had been sandblasted on the outside and potted with plants on the inside, the schoolyard had fallen into a state of neglect. The playground that he remembered as his entire world for a Shoe Goo Summer or two was still covered with lumpy asphalt, but nobody played there anymore. The basketball hoops had been torn off and never replaced, and the softball field was overrun with weeds. Worst of all was Mary's Candy Store, which was now the site of a fashionable boutique, The Banana Republic—Clothes for the Adventure of Life.

They started looking for a place to park as soon as they hit Clark Street. The two-way radio was quiet, but Allan was still on edge. He dreaded these excursions into Nat's old neighborhood because they infused his partner with equal parts of philosophy and melancholy, a particularly deadly combination for reasons that Allan could not understand. Nat attributed the destruction of his old neighborhood to an ongoing struggle between brunettes and blondes, basketball and racquetball, ghetto-blasters and Walkman radios.

Nat said, "These people have got no community. You even take the way they are with their music, playing it all by themselves with headphones on and shit. My people always shared their music with a boom box big enough for the world to hear. To me it's pretty coldhearted to be greedy with music, even if it is just some cowboys howling at the moon."

Allan looked out the window at his own memories. He remembered looking for Eddie's treasure and playing with Eddie's sap and listening to his father describe the gangster's sad demise. The most interesting events of his life had happened to someone else. He said, "So where do you want to eat?"

"The Golden Grill, I guess."

They parked Genghis Kar in a taxi stand and didn't bother to lock the doors. At 2:15 on a Wednesday morning, no one rich enough to be in the 'hood would tamper with such a foreboding vehicle.

Allan followed Nat into the restaurant with the two-way radio attached to his hip by means of Velcro straps. They took a booth by the door in case his mother called with some news that couldn't wait. That wasn't likely because she was taking a break too, a half-hour nap and a little bite of food to tide her over until 6:00 A.M., when Electronic News Tonight usually called it a day.

After they had settled into the booth, Nat said, "Tonight's a bust. Let's go home. There's nothing going on."

"Wrong. Our contract says we don't go home until six or until we get some news. That's the company policy."

Nat backed off. He always lost policy disputes, and besides, the policies were making him rich. He said, "Let me ask you this."

Allan braced himself because this was the standard preamble to a question that his partner asked him once or twice a month, usually on a Wednesday while they were sitting in the Golden Grill.

Nat said, "Don't you ever get sick of what we're doing, taking tape of nightmares for fifty bills a click? I mean, I know we're getting rich and that's okay, but it's not the sort of thing a man can brag about."

Allan was going to answer in the same way he always did, but before he could, Emily Philipidapolis passed out menus and banged some water on the table. Emily was already very old when Nat was still very young and had worked at the

Golden since before Nat was born. They talked for a while. Emily said, "I saw Crazy Horse the other day. He didn't look so good."

Crazy never looked good, at least not since that cop from the Youth Patrol crushed his face with a single punch. Emily mopped off the table as Nat told Allan all about it.

"Goddamn Tamburino got him in a corner and Crazy took the punch like a real man who'd already served some time. Stood up straight and didn't look away and told Tamburino he should kiss his ass. We were all impressed. The only thing is, Tamburino had his head jammed against the wall, so there's no place for Crazy's face to go after he laid on the punch, so his jaw caved in. Crazy never did get it fixed up right. That cost too much money. He's pretty ugly now, with a smashed face and getting older."

"And that's what you call the good times, right?"

"Well, I've got some news for you, Mr. TV News Producer. That Tamburino's a big man now, works for the mayor himself as some kind of bodyguard. Makes me wonder about that mayor. I voted for him even if he's black. Might have to vote for an Irish next time, even that alderman from Marquette Park. Is Douglas Smith an Irish name?"

Allan nodded. Emily thought he was nodding at her, but he was nodding at the menu instead, having decided on the Greekburger with fries and a real malted milk. That was the one good thing about Nat's old neighborhood. The restaurants served real malted milks, not those chocolate-flavored chemicals you get from Wendy's McBurger King. Nat said to Emily, "And the word from Crazy Horse is what?"

Emily's answer was preceded by the loud snapping of her gum, which sounded like a small-caliber handgun. Her teeth were falling out, and Allan feared that someday he would find one in his food.

"Same old, same old," Emily said at last. "He still works down at the Greyhound, taking bets on the ponies and selling on the side. When I seen him he was mostly talking about the gangster war by Lincoln Square. Everybody talks about nothing but the war since you two started to put it on the news. The thing I can never tell is if you guys discovered the war or started it. Some of those kids'd probably kill just to get on the late-night news."

Allan peeked over his menu. "What'd this guy say about the gangster war?"

Emily gave him a sincere look as if about to divulge a dangerous secret. She held this look for as long as she could, enjoying the suspense. Then she said in a flat, bored tone, "What'll it be, boys? Denver omelette's on special tonight."

Nat ordered the rib eye steak, Allan the Greekburger Deluxe. Emily hustled away and shouted their orders to her brother, Peter, who squirted some yellow stuff on the grill and smeared it with a couple of pieces of meat.

Nat said to Allan, "Let's talk about the doc. You know it's right. Here's the plan. We start with newsreel footage of Al Capone. Go to his grave in Cicero and talk about gangs all down through the ages. We say Jesus and the twelve were a gang and so were Hitler and his pals. Gangs are like a gun, or even a book, in the way they're good or bad depending on how they're used. Trust me. We do this doc and you'll be so famous Janette'll be getting all wet about you."

Allan listened to their food cooking as he thought about this for a moment. His partner had never made this argument before. The meat sizzled and the malted whirled. Emily plopped some lettuce in a bowl, sprinkled something brown over it, and dared to call it salad.

Allan said, "The thing about you is you've got these romantic notions about the gangs, like they're little boy scouts with hand grenades. Nobody's going to buy that line even on public TV. The problem with you is you think there's justice in the world. We make a doc like you're talking about, and we'll get toasted like day-old bread for glorifying drug-creep losers."

Nat might have been moved by this complaint had he not heard it dozens of times before. He usually responded by listing a number of prominent Caucasian males who had committed greater crimes than any ever imagined by the Stone Cobras or the Doomed Disciples or any of the city's forty-seven other organized, recognized street associations. But before he could recite the familiar litany, Emily delivered their food. She held onto Allan's malted as hostage to his good behavior.

Allan leaned over his Greekburger. The steam made even Shoe Goo Summer seem cool. He poked at the fries with his spoon, making sure Emily hadn't dropped a molar. Nat cut into his steak, making sure it was thoroughly cooked.

Emily said to Allan while looking at Nat, "Horse says there's some kind of shake-out going on, with the younger boys killing the older ones to make some room at the top."

She laid down the malted and said to Nat while looking at Allan, "It seems like a bad business, Little Wimpy. After talking to Crazy, I mean. You're lucky you got on the straight and narrow, or some wild boy half your age would be trying to take you out. Just like Gilligan. Being in the news business, you must have heard about that, I guess."

Allan took a bite and looked at Emily while he chewed. "Did you just call him Little Wimpy?"

Nat changed the subject fast. "Gilligan was this little kid who got real big real quick. Me and the boys used to push him around until this one year he grew five inches and gained thirty pounds. Now he's a thick-necked muscleman, and nobody picks on him anymore."

Emily finally gave up the malted. Allan took a slurp. She said, "You got that right. He's dead."

Gilligan had been shot in the face by a fourteen-year-old member of the Doomed Disciples. It happened on a Tuesday, Emily said, but Nat hadn't heard the news because it had happened during the daylight hours when he and Allan were off the clock. Allan ate his burger and listened. They talked as if he wasn't there.

"That can't be so," Nat said, but he knew that it had to be. Emily smoked a cigarette while the two men poked at their food. Allan ordered some coffee to fight off the sleep. The time was almost 3:00 A.M. He said, "What I want to know is how come she calls you Little Wimpy?"

Nat ignored the question and spoke to Emily instead. "I

can't see Gilligan dead that way. He was a stone-cold gangster, the kind nobody wanted to stand by because he might explode sometime. And a little punk like that. It doesn't make any sense, you know. We've got to do that doc."

Allan thought, *Forget it, Nat. They'll never buy your movie.* Allan said, "Sure. I suppose. But we need to make some more money first. Rich people can afford to be stupid."

Nat looked at his hands but didn't see them. Allan started talking about profit and loss, hoping the talk about the doc was over. He was wrong. When Allan stopped talking, Nat said, "You see, the kids don't follow the rules anymore and that's how it really shows. There are no rules if the gang's got none."

Further remarks along this line were interrupted when the two-way radio scratched Allan's hip with garbled fuzz. He ripped it free from its Velcro straps, pushed a button, and said, "This is ENT remote to ENT dispatch. Your message did not copy, Ma. Could you try that again? Over."

She said a boy had died in front of a bowling alley in Lincoln Square. "Police dispatch says one of the Street Crusaders called it in, so there's a crowd at the scene already. It'll be a circus, so we better roll on this. It's time to go get paid."

7

Elmo Bites the Big One

SHE WAS THICK AND SOFT. HE WAS THIN AND SEEMED TO BE MOSTLY elbows and knees. She smelled of garlic and expensive perfume; he of sweat and menthol cigarettes. She believed in everything and he believed in nothing. She was Sister Delilah Blue and he was Radio Larry.

They stood in the doorway of the bowling alley, huddling together against the oily rain that was splashing down on the corpse of Tappy Shoes, on the paramedics who had been summoned to scrape him off the sidewalk, and on the crowd of 'Spanic bowlers who had gathered to see what was going on. The rain spattered the two dark shapes that watched in silence from another doorway just across the street, the station wagon full of Street Crusaders that pulled up to the curb, and the cops who stood an uneasy vigil, trying to give the impression that they had things under control.

The flicker of a red neon bowling pin put a purple blush in Delilah's cheeks. She liked Radio Larry, and not just because he was everywhere and never seemed to sleep; not just because dozens of other journalists followed his every lead; not just because he used to be a cop himself and was the favorite of every flatfoot in the city; and not just because he had a knack for pitching softball questions that looked like hardballs, which made Willis look even more heroic when he knocked them over the fence. Delilah liked Larry because he made his money off the worst, but always hoped for the best.

She said, "Ever see a jungle without any trees?"

Larry watched the rain come down and waited for 4:00 A.M. That's when he would break into The All-Night Retro Rock Review with a live remote from Lincoln Square. He said, "What're you talking about?"

"I'm talking about trees, Lawrence. You ever see a tree? They use them to make houses and baseball bats. Lincoln Square doesn't have any trees, and I'm trying to tell you why."

"Why?"

"Because of the sulfur lights."

Larry looked at the amber lamp above their heads and at the golden shower that the rain made as it passed through its beam. He snuffed out one cigarette on the light pole and fetched another from his pocket.

Delilah said, "The Irish mayors put up the lights to stop all the crime in Lincoln Square. All they did was kill the trees."

"Do-gooders strike again?"

"Goo-goos gone bad. It never gets dark around here anymore, and trees need their rest too, you know. The dark is our friend, Lawrence. You ever think of that?"

Larry thought about it every now and then because he worked in the dark, and every week or so there came a night in which nobody killed anybody else, and he had very little news to do. On nights like that he thought about things, and sometimes he thought that the dark might be his friend. He said, "I better go get ready. I've got this remote to do. Thanks for the tip, Delilah. There's a guy named Elmo who's working for Doogie. I'd say he's your best bet. Got a criminal record and a bad attitude. He might wiggle if you poke him where the sun don't shine."

With this he blew out a cloud of smoke that mingled with the light and the rain. Delilah said, "How come you smoke so much?"

Larry looked at his hand and seemed a bit surprised that a cigarette was smoldering in the V between two fingers. "That's where I get the gravel in my voice. I'll tell Allan to come see you."

He started to move away, but Delilah grabbed him by the elbow and pinned him down. She hoped he would try to grab her back, but instead he went as limp as an overcooked noodle. She said, "I could be wrong but probably not. Every now and then I get this little vibe from you that's almost like sympathy, like sometimes you wish the killing'd stop even if they pay you by the story."

His noodle arm became uncooked, became tense, stiff and unyielding. Larry had been keeping count. Three years before, 178 kids had been killed by teenage gangsters. This year, 376 had died already and the cops expected it to hit five hundred before the year was done because the best of the gangsters figured it was better to die a violent death than to waste away quietly in a crumbling city with no way in or out.

He said, "The ones in the gangs are the clever ones, the ones with smarts and energy. They want to improve themselves and they figure they've got to take some chances. Entrepreneurs with Uzis, if you know what I'm talking about."

Delilah let go of his arm. As he drifted away she said, "You don't need to worry. Your secret's safe with me."

"And what secret is that?"

"About you secretly being sensitive. I bet you even cry at the movies."

She stopped talking and thought for a moment, decided she was going too far. "I don't want to mess with you unless you want to mess with me. How about it, Lawrence? You want to be friends with me?"

Larry was glad it was raining because it washed the

expression off his face. He said, "I don't have any friends, Sister. I'm a broadcast journalist."

Officer Edwards was having a pleasant fantasy about the divorced woman who lived upstairs. He was about to demonstrate his imaginary charms to her imaginary gratitude when he heard the tooting of an imported car in distress. The rain beads on his windshield flattened into ripples when he turned on his party lights and gave chase down Wrightwood Avenue.

"This is five-niner blue. I'm westbound in pursuit of a—I'm in pursuit of a—"

The dispatcher waited for a moment, then said, "This is central, five-niner blue. Talk to me, Eddie. Are you okay? Over."

He had eased his foot off the pedal a bit. No longer sure he wanted to catch the vehicle he was chasing, he was still in pursuit but losing ground. "It looks like it used to be some kind of blue but not like any cruiser I've ever seen. It's been in a blender, like, but I can still see the marks and the city seal and—hey, what's that? There's some kind of doings in Lincoln Square. What's the situation? Over."

Nat and Allan beat him to the situation by a good seventeen seconds, time enough for Nat to slip into the street while Allan slid over to the driver's seat and retrieved the 8½-by-11-inch Press card they used to avoid parking tickets. Nat had his camera out of the trunk and was already checking the white balance by the time Edwards screeched to a halt and jumped out of his patrol car. The officer didn't notice the rain at first. He was too busy marveling at the bowlers and the noise and the lights and the fact that one Plymouth Fury's high-speed chase of another had led him to the scene of a really important and exciting crime.

The patrolman leaned against Genghis Kar, pulled out his ticket book, and flipped it open. Allan pulled out his reporter's notebook, flipped it open, and recited the usual lines, showering the officer with spittle as he spoke. His teeth were so big and so poorly organized that he couldn't close his mouth without great effort. He produced a spray when excited, but the rain was coming down so hard the cop couldn't tell the difference.

"I know we were going a little fast, but we're Electronic News Tonight. You want to get on TV?" Allan squinted at the policeman's nameplate and scribbled Edwards in his reporter's notebook.

Officer Edwards adjusted his chest so the nameplate stuck out a little more. He said, "Yeah, sure. Why not? I don't know anything. Let me just call the station. This place needs some crowd control."

Allan picked his way through the bowlers. He was looking for Radio Larry, but he saw Nat first. The photographer danced between the raindrops while sucking in all the sight and the sound. It looked like another exclusive. Nat was the only shooter at the scene.

Allan admired his partner's technique, which had all the grace and strength of a professional wrestler. With the tape deck on his back and the camera on his shoulder, he circled the tragedy as if it were both his lover and his foe. Sometimes he hunched down and other times he stood up on his tiptoes and held the camera high above his head so he could shoot over the taller people who had gathered around the last remains of Tappy Shoes.

The dead boy looked like a squashed spider with twig-thin limbs jutting out at crazy angles from a wet, sticky mess. His blood and his brains had spilled onto the sidewalk, mingling with the water and the grime until the rain that was washing the blood away slowed to a drizzle and then stopped altogether. Heat rose from the street.

Nat wiped mist off his lens, then scanned the crowd for a wide shot before zooming in for a close-up shot of a young Hispanic boy who was crying into his hands, mourning the loss of Tappy Shoes. He adjusted the setting on his microphone to be sure to capture the muffled sobs. That's why they called him Nat, short for Natural Sound. He never missed a beat, never lost a bite.

Allan whispered into his ear. "Take a shot of the cop, okay?"

Nat nodded, but just as he leveled into the shot, his sun gun produced an electrical hiss and started to send out its hot white light in eerie, erratic bursts, like the light of a dying sun. Officer Edwards, who didn't know what this meant, put a little bounce in his step and tickled a bystander with his nightstick, a move that might have made the early morning news had the camera been functioning properly.

Allan said, "You seen Larry?"

"He's over by the Currency Exchange."

Nat lowered the camera and rested it on his knee. He fiddled with the battery pack, but the bursts of hot light became fewer and farther between until they stopped altogether.

"Damn," the photographer said. "I've got to go get another battery pack and then I'll have to white balance again. Damn! We need some new gear. How is it we made four hundred thousand last year and I have to work with this piece of junk?"

Allan adopted the condescending tone he always used when discussing money. "New gear's not in the budget until the second quarter of next year. Don't smash the equipment and it won't break down."

With that he was off to the Currency Exchange. He found Larry talking into a pay phone under a sign that read Offenders Will Be Prosecuted. There was no indication who the offenders were or what their offense might be. Larry nodded into the phone and said, "Well what about this crack thing? Uh huh, uh huh, uh huh." Larry became quiet, and picked his nose for solace. For a long time he stood very still, like one of those cardboard cutouts of movie stars you get your picture taken with. He said, "Got it? Okay," then hung up the phone.

Allan pulled out a fifty-dollar bill and waved it under Larry's nose. "In a minute, Shanahan. I'm doing a remote in ninety seconds."

In no particular hurry, and betraying no hint of excitement, Larry stepped out into the street. Allan waited a decent interval before tagging along.

The street was fuller and louder now, a rhythmic, throbbing thing. Still, no other TV cameras had shown up, which was good news for Electronic News Tonight. A clean sweep of the three affiliates could be worth $150 a second, not counting the secondary rights to "Crime Time Prime," "Police Beat," and the other syndicated cop shows. Allan thanked God for those network budget cuts as he watched Larry begin his routine.

Within moments Larry had transformed his briefcase into a remote radio transmitter, complete with blinking lights, an antenna, and knobs he would twist for various arcane radio purposes. He dragged this contraption with him under the chassis of his four-wheel-drive Bronco, which rode on oversize tires so that he could crawl underneath it without too much trouble. Allan flopped down on the curb, so he could listen to Larry file his report in the hard, cynical tone of voice he had stolen from Walter Winchell.

"This is Radio Larry Melville with news live at the top of the hour. I'm hiding under a car right now because the bullets could start flying any minute. In Lincoln Square you never know when your number's up. Death could come from an AK-47, or it could come from a cocaine overdose. For Armando Tappy Shoes Calderone, it came about an hour ago from a blunt instrument wielded by a person or persons unknown. That makes 377 gangster murders this year—377 and counting. On the Northwest Side of this troubled town, this is Larry Melville reporting for WDM Radio, 'News Live at Fifty-Five.'"

Larry extracted himself from his hiding place. "The magic of radio," he said. "They should give me combat pay."

"They won't. One of these days we'll get your little routine on tape and blackmail you with the late-night news."

Larry nodded grimly as if blackmail was something he thought about a lot. "I saw you waving some money around."

Allan retrieved the fifty. It disappeared into Larry's wallet. "What we got here is more of the same, excepting for the blunt instrument. Haven't seen it done like that more than two or three times all year. The little shits must've run out of bullets, or maybe we got us a weirdo who likes the sound a club makes when it smashes into an empty head. Kind of like cracking a coconut, only it's hollow instead of wet. How's that for sound effects?"

Allan waited for more, but that's all there was. Allan said, "That's it? That's not worth fifty bucks."

Larry looked hurt. He wasn't. "Maybe not, but there's something else I know because a birdie told me so." He'd dropped the Walter Winchell bit and sounded like he was trying to breathe through a mouthful of pasta.

"Would this be a fifty-dollar birdie or a hundred?"

Larry shook his head. "This'll be 10 percent of what you get, no matter when you get it. Especially if you get it right away—like tonight, for instance."

Allan changed the subject in order to give himself a little time to think. "There must be something else about this kid. You say his street name was Tappy Shoes."

Larry listened to the question but didn't answer it. Instead he jumped up on the bumper of his Bronco to get a better look at the situation. Every time the police pushed at one bulge in the throbbing throng of all-night bowlers, another bulge would press against the small clearing where Tappy Shoes lay. People who tried to walk away were hemmed in by a squadron of Street Crusaders, who had formed a ring around the crowd.

Allan looked for another bumper so he could jump up, too, and had to settle for one attached to an ancient Oldsmobile with corroding mag wheels, riding cinder blocks instead of tires.

From this vantage point he could see the paramedics wrap up Tappy Shoes and he could hear the crowd work up to the gurgling it always made when the city stuffs a dead boy into the back of one of its ambulances. When the gurgling subsided, Allan said, "Ten percent of what?"

Larry didn't look at him. "Ten percent of nothing if you don't want the job. I'll go tip Jeffries from the *News*. He's a real news gigolo. Charges by the column inch."

The bowlers made another noise, like gurgling in reverse, as Alderman Smith's armored car pulled into the spot just vacated by Tappy Shoes' ambulance. After a little scuffling, the crowd started to change shape as the curious assembled around Smith and the uncertain were herded into position by the phalanx of Street Crusaders, who cheered their leader's every word.

"People of Lincoln Square. You don't have to put up with this. You don't have to see your boys die in the street and you don't have to live in fear. What you do have to do is protect yourselves from the narco-killers and their criminal friends at City Hall. You need to know that the mayor is the biggest gangster of them all and on primary day we need to kick his butt right out of town if we're going to do what's got to be done!"

The Street Crusaders hooted their huzzahs, joined by bowlers who had been aroused to one passion or the other. Allan noticed that there was one Crusader who hadn't yelled, a heavy man with a shaved head and a thick neck who was standing next to a smaller form in a shadow across the street.

Douglas continued. "You need to learn to defend yourselves because I'll tell you something: the cops won't do it because the cops are working for the other side. Only you know what? There's safety in numbers. I bet if that young man had been a Street Crusader he wouldn't be dead right now. A Street Crusader's never alone when the pushing comes to shove."

Douglas nodded. This meant he was through and it was a signal for his loyalists to break ranks in such a way as to push the bowlers in the general direction of the currency exchange, between two tidy Crusaders handing out simple but effective brochures. Most of the people threw them away, but some gave theirs a cursory glance. Most returned to their homes or their lanes, but a few loitered for a while, wondering what to do next.

Radio Larry said to Allan, "The guy's a whiz. I'll give him that. You ever notice how he's got this thing he does with his hat? He always takes it off when he lays it on too thick, holding it real respectfully, like we caught him praying in church."

They watched without comment for a moment until Nat came over, holding his camera at ease. "Now what?"

Allan thought about it for a few seconds and then told Larry that 10 percent would be okay. Larry rubbed his hands together, savoring the score. "Deal. What you do is take a nice juicy bite of that skinhead creep over there."

He gestured at Elmo who had watched the entire spectacle while standing next to a jittery Eye. Allan looked at Nat and shrugged. "Let's go bite this guy. I'll lead the way with the mike. You keep rolling tape."

Popeye disappeared when the sun gun illuminated their little corner of Milwaukee Avenue. Elmo was paralyzed like a raccoon that had strayed into the beam of headlights on the road. Nat handed the mike to Allan. They both got ready do some dancing if things turned as bad as it looked like they might.

"Back off, jackoff," Elmo said.

Allan yanked on the microphone and filled his lungs with air. "What happened to Tappy Shoes?" he screamed, loud enough to be heard by Elmo, Popeye, Alderman Smith, and everyone else who had gathered in the neon glow of *Jugar el Boliche*.

The hot light of the sun gun broiled Elmo's face as he backed against the brownstone wall. He shuffled to the left. The light followed him. He shuffled to the right. Again the light followed him as if he was some vaudeville dancer doing the old soft shoe.

Allan screamed again. "What happened?"

When the TV camera had advanced to within ten feet of the Street Crusader, a softer, calmer voice spoke. It was

Douglas Smith. "Tell them what happened, Elmo. These people are on our side."

Elmo squared his shoulders, shaking his fist at the light. He remembered one of Doogie's favorite lines. "What you need to know is Doogie Smith and the Street Crusaders are the only thing keeping more kids from getting all shot up, and I'm not just saying this because he's a friend of mine. The mayor has got to be the one to blame for selling us down the river to the narco-killer street gangs that really run this town."

Douglas clapped his hands, and the Street Crusaders started to cheer. Nat turned off the sun gun. The night swallowed Elmo and coughed up the radio man, who had watched the interview with that special combination of envy and disgust with which journalists working in the other media regarded TV news reporters.

Allan said, "The magic of television. Where do we go get paid?"

"Do I get my 10 percent?"

"Ten percent. Just like you said."

"Okay. That woman over there wants to talk to you."

He pointed at a doorway that was tucked between the tavern and the bowling alley. Nat turned on his sun gun and the dark disappeared into the skin of a tall, wide woman of color. Sister Delilah Blue pretended not to notice the light as she fanned herself with a brochure entitled "Alderman Douglas Smith for Mayor."

8

Male 'Spanic Tears

CHANNEL TWELVE WAS QUIET AT 5:47 A.M. The morning anchor had disappeared into the ladies room to work on the fluff in her hair, and the emergency radios emitted a contented hum typical of the early morning hours when even killers, rapists, junkies, and thieves were resting from their labors.

But there was no rest for Jerry Parker, who worked in a part of the TV newsroom where the hot lights never shined. As the station's assignment editor, he worked behind-the-scenes to perpetuate the illusion that at Channel Twelve brains and beauty entered into a common cause through the efforts of clear-thinking journalists who cared more about the Republic than about their multi-year contracts for personal services.

The truth of things was less sublime. Janette, Carl, Ernie, and Pete rarely composed the stories they read and left most of the writing and all of the thinking to Parker and his homely crew of backstage newshounds. This allowed the on-camera talent to devote their wits to the all-important question of who sat on which side of the Channel Twelve anchor desk. Janette and Carl both preferred the left sides of their faces and so both wanted to turn to the right during two-shots and cross talk. Carl had a bigger deal and better chemistry, so his profile prevailed.

Parker liked his job because it gave him the opportunity to feel superior to good-looking people.

Parker hated his job because the July sweeps were pending and because, sweeps or not, he had to swallow a daily dose of the envy that is produced in those who work closely with *it,* but do not possess *it* themselves. *It* was that certain something that many want, few have, and no one can define. Those who had *it* were paid hundreds of thousands of dollars to be admired by strangers. Parker was paid very much less to start work at 4:30 A.M., talk to fakers on the phone, and decide which of the day's many events qualified as news. The phone rang. Parker answered.

"This is Allan," said a voice made groggy by too little sleep and testy by too much coffee.

"What's up, Shanahan?"

Before getting down to business, they consoled each other with unkind remarks about the people with *it.* Carl's bald spot was already outgrowing his new toupee, and Ernie had hurt himself water-skiing and couldn't do his weather dance for the next six weeks. Allan listened with mock horror to Parker's account of the news director's behavior at the latest news meet.

"He says he'll bang-bang some pretty pricey people if things don't turn around."

"Who's he going to bang?"

"Everybody. Carl for sure. Maybe Janette."

"Why would he bang-bang Janette?"

"Better her than him, and besides, her series on the drug war sucks."

Allan tapped his pen against the kitchen table, marking time he no longer had. "If the numbers go south, you assign her to us. We'll get you some fire and blood like that tape we've got of the kid that got killed last night."

Parker checked the log that the night editor kept of major incidents. "Oh, yeah? Which dead kid is that?"

"Over in Lincoln Square."

"No kidding. There's always a dead kid in Lincoln Square. Call me back later when you've got something that hasn't already happened fifty thousand times."

"It only happened to this kid once. Name—Armando Calderone, a.k.a. Tappy Shoes, age 14. He was a member of The Brotherhood until about 4:32 A.M. He's DOA at Children's Memorial."

Allan paused, hoping the assignment editor would fill in the silence with a dollar amount. Parker knew that trick, so he paused too, looking at his clipboard as if the night man's scribbled observations were more interesting than anything Allan might have to say. A good fifteen seconds of dead air followed during which the morning anchor returned from the makeup table and began the never-ending chore of adjusting her hair. Parker watched her walk across the room.

"So?"

"So we've got a body and a crowd and some natural sound."

"So?"

"So this is news. Young boy dead in streets of uncaring city. His friends can't save him now, and the drug lords rule the night, blah, blah, woof, woof, et cetera, et cetera. The words don't matter. This is TV."

Parker didn't hear this because his attention had drifted to the backside of the morning anchor. Her hair sprayed and her makeup on straight, she was now leaning over the latest edition of the *Chicago Tribune.* She was an ambitious woman who worked hard to keep herself informed.

Parker said, "We had nine dead kids last week and forty-two dead last month. Go find some kid that isn't dead and maybe that'll be news."

Allan crunched his Bic. A sliver of plastic got caught between his teeth. "I've got a sound bite with a Street Crusader who said it's Mayor Cleveland's fault and Doogie Smith will save the day."

"And?"

"And bowlers who feel bad about the whole sorry mess."

"And?"

"And tears, Parker. We've got tears."

"Hey, if I want tears I can cry my own. All I have to do is look at my budget for tape from you."

Allan tried some more silence. This gave Parker time to think about the relative merit of various tears.

Allan said, "These are male tears I'm talking about. Male Hispanic tears: salty salsa, blubbering machismo. A sensitive person of color. I'll take him to Channel Eight. They love a good cry over there."

In the first blush of that hot Chicago morn, Parker imagined his own tears staining a pink slip with the smeared letters of his own name upon it.

"Male Hispanic tears? That's another story. Can you get them here in thirty minutes? The next hour's got a hole in the local break."

Nat got the tape there in twenty-eight minutes and thirty-five seconds, well under his average time of thirty-two minutes, fifteen seconds. He sipped coffee while Parker supervised the edit. They chopped off Elmo's sound bite and the establishing shot of Officer Edwards, but kept the closeup of the bloody sidewalk, the wide shot of the ambulance, the tears, and the muffled sob. The morning anchor did a seven-second story on the death of Tappy Shoes before kicking it over to Del, who did his morning weather dance in front of a blank blue wall on which the control room superimposed colorful maps. Then it was back to New York and the "Today" show with Bryant, Willard and Katie.

A news toady asked Nat to stick around for the aftermath of a hurried conference. Although only Nat cared to look, anyone could see the conference in pantomime through the glass partition which separated the bosses from the rest of the Channel Twelve cast.

The pantomime was a lively one. The producer and the news director yelled at Parker. Parker yelled back. Nat was glad he didn't work at a TV station anymore. Right out of college he did just that. First it drove him to coffee and then it drove him to drink, but that's where they started to call him Nat. Nat was short for Natural Sound because the half-Polish, half-Puerto Rican photographer had a gift for sucking crisp sound bites out of the background noise caused by a house fire or a drug bust or a domestic dispute involving a gun. First he'd get the pictures and next he'd get the sound. In the editing bay he would mix it altogether with two-shots, cutaways, and other tricks that made Nat's pictures more real than the events themselves. The magic of television.

Parker emerged from his meeting looking pissed off and pissed on. Nat followed him into the soundproof glass booth where the assistant assignment editors tuned in to the radio traffic of the police and fire departments. Parker flicked his thumb at an assistant and said, "Out."

The Hot Room, it was called. The walls were full of equipment and the air was full of noise as five emergency radios blurted out the familiar litany of trouble—murder and mugging, robbery and rape, each in a numbered code. One radio announced that a fifty-seven-year-old female had died on the Near North Side. Parker turned down the volume, and the woman was allowed to die in peace.

"I don't want to say it, and you don't want to hear it, but we got these network budget cuts. They want us to make more with less. We're maxed out on shooters. Half of my people're out doing fluff and half're out doing nothing. I can't even go bang-bang because Channel Eight is trying to steal our talent and the news director doesn't know what a big favor that would be. There's one camera at the Sox game for a story about the organist and one in Milwaukee for a story on pretzels. This is National Pretzel Week. Did you know pretzels make you regular and they also make you drink more beer? Advertising is working on a deal with this brewery in Wisconsin. So sue me. I'm a whore. There's this news doctor in from L.A. who says we need more people news before the September sweeps."

"What's the shoot?"

"Deep Tunnel?"

"Come on. Don't be cruel. You call that people news?"

"I call it politics. Like the mayor would say, we've got some extended circumstances."

"Like what?"

"Like the mayor. His people are griping in a serious way that Doogie's been getting all the good publicity. They're right. So sue me. The only good pub the mayor's got going is that goddamn tunnel of his."

"I stopped doing sewers a million bucks ago."

"It's a tunnel, not a sewer, and they haven't even used it yet. How about a fiver for some B-roll and a bite?"

"I don't know, Parker. I usually sleep in the afternoon, and we're pretty busy these days. We're up all night chasing fires and murders and stuff like that. There's no time left to go crawling down into some sewer, even if it's never been used."

"Okay, six hundred."

"And I also have a philosophical problem here. It's a pride question for a person of my station to go walking around in a sewer just because the mayor's flak wants good pub."

"Seven."

Barbados seemed so close Nat could almost smell the salt and feel the sun. "The other thing is I'm not sure any amount of money is worth spending more time with Allan. You've got to understand I spend all night with the guy, driving from one nightmare to the other, and the man just will not shut his mouth with all these theories he's got."

Parker looked at the newsroom and hated it. He looked at the journalists loitering over the morning *Trib*. He hated them, too, with their overtime and their bonuses. He wished he could bang-bang the whole sorry bunch. "Eight-fifty. That's all I've got." -

Nat opened the glass door, and the sound rushed in, typewriters and excited voices. Janette Baylor had arrived and was in her usual tizzy. Nat noticed that her nose and chin protruded too much. She looked a lot better on television, when her face was flattened.

"Eight-fifty should cover it, but only because we like you, Park."

9

Effluence Under Pressure

AS DELILAH PACED BENEATH THE ARCHED CEILING OF THE DEEP Tunnel, she imagined what the enormous tube would be like after they opened the spigots and it became the cold, wet passage through which coursed the fecal matter of three million folks. It was not the asshole but the colon of a city with severe digestive problems. She listened to the echo of her own spiked heels, waiting for 3:15.

When possible, the mayor's press secretary scheduled photo opportunities for 3:15 P.M., so the TV reporters would have time enough to write but not enough to think. She had learned early on in the Cleveland administration that docile reporters could became a menace when allowed the luxury of thought.

Memories of those early days echoed in her head as she paced the width of the Deep Tunnel Project. Back then, the Irish incumbent had written them off as little threat but they had worked hard and were helped by a freak flood that annoyed the voters, backed up the sewers, and created breeding grounds for a particularly bloodthirsty generation of mosquitos. After a year marred by water damage, lawsuits, and untold numbers of mosquito bites, Willis had scored a narrow victory in the Democratic primary and then performed a ritual slaughter of the Republican nominee.

They had taken office on a wave of optimism and joy. That's when the trouble began.

During the campaign, the mayor had promised to take some sort of stand against crime, to deliver some sort of message to the street gangs that controlled vast sections of the city at night. To this end, key members of the new administration had started discussing publicity stunts and the various sound bites which they might generate on this subject. They had eventually decided that the mayor and his family would move into the John Tinney McTavish Apartments.

John Tinney McTavish, the man, was a cartoonist whose style was to depict the planet as a head with migraines splitting the various and sundry hot spots of his day: the Crimea, the Balkans, the Philippines. At the turn of the century he collaborated with his fellow Scot, Colonel Robert R. McCormick, to make the *Chicago Tribune* the undisputed voice of American conservatism.

John Tinney McTavish, the apartments, would have made the man turn over in his grave. If the bleak gray towers provided low-cost housing for thousands of low-income people, they also provided a hiding place for the criminals who preyed on them. A young girl could not live at the McTavish without being molested by pimps. An old man could not live there without paying protection money to younger men. Mothers could not live there without fearing for their children. Children could not live there without feeling pressured to steal or fight or shoot up drugs, to kill or to be killed.

It had been decided that the mayor and his wife would live at the McTavish for a month or so, and by so doing, honor his campaign pledge and silence Alderman Smith. They had hoped that somehow this would make the housing project a better place to live or, at least, remind the lakefront liberals of just how bad things could be. Delilah had called a press conference to announce this heroic gesture, and scheduled it for 9:00 A.M. so that the television reporters would have plenty of time to gather and think about the news before their 6:00 P.M. broadcasts. By noon, she had known she had made a terrible mistake.

Radio Larry had broken the story on the 10:00 A.M. edition of "News Live at Fifty-Five." This was before Delilah had discovered a redeeming aspect to his nature and, perhaps, before that aspect had asserted itself in him. At Larry's prompting, the deejays at WDM had spent the rest of the day making wisecracks like "What will the neighbors say?" and "There goes the neighborhood."

The TV stations had given maximum coverage to the story, but most of it had been of the wrong kind. For the 5:00 P.M. early report, Channel Eight had an exclusive interview with a nine-year-old McTavish resident who carried a gun to school for self-defense because his ten-year-old brother had been murdered by a twelve-year-old addict. Channel Twelve had led its 6:00 P.M. newscast with a live exchange between Janette Baylor in the studio and Alderman Smith on the front porch of his home in Marquette Park.

JANETTE: You've taken a hard line on safe streets, Mr. Smith. What's going on here?
DOUGLAS: I'll tell you exactly what's going on here, Janette. You are seeing the actions of a desperate man, and we're about to see just how big a mistake we made in this election. I'm telling you that when the mayor moves in, the only part of the McTavish that'll be safe is the apartment he's living in. He can't take it for a year. What about the good people who aren't surrounded by cops and cameras? Who's going to protect them? Willis Cleveland won't protect them. It'll be the Crusade for Safer Streets.

The shorter the word, the bigger the type, especially if it's bad. McTavish's own *Chicago Trib* had nosed around for an angle it could call its own, something new to say. Douglas had provided one. Under a story headlined CLEVE LEAVES KIDS BEHIND the paper had reported that while the mayor and his lovely wife were moving into the McTavish, their lovely children were not and would continue to attend an exclusive private school in the University district.

Mr. and Mrs. Cleveland had spent three bitter, sullen months in an apartment on the twentieth floor of Building G in Complex One. Seven of their neighbors were murdered during that time, and the mayor's name was closely associated with each and every one. The couple's eventual return to their home in the University district was the occasion of a final flurry of stories about how Douglas was right after all, that the mayor couldn't take it for a year even though he'd never promised to.

In the aftermath of this calamity, Delilah and the mayor had decided that things had gone sour because the TV reporters had been given time to think. Then and there, they had vowed never to give them time to think again by scheduling all their press conferences for 3:15 P.M. This allowed the reporters just enough time to rush back to their respective studios and slap something together for the six o'clock news. Delilah and the mayor stuck to this rule even when the topic was as seemingly impervious to negative spin as the Mosquito Abatement District's Deep Tunnel Project.

At 3:17, Willis said, "Thank you all for coming. You know, good news is hard to find in this town because good news is made of sweat instead of blood, and sweat doesn't make such a pretty color when you're watching it in your living room."

A photographer dropped his tripod, making a clattering sound that was amplified and multiplied as it echoed back from a darkness too vast for the TV lights to penetrate. When the noise died down, Delilah distributed one-page statements describing the mission and dimensions of the tunnel. A congressman named Brodsky cut the ribbon and the mayor turned the spigot. Pictures were taken and natural sound was captured on half-inch strips of magnetic tape.

Willis said, "I saw Brand X on the TV just the other day when that boy got killed by Lincoln Square. Next time you put Doogie on the news you should ask him what he's ever done. The answer is nothing, by the way. Douglas Smith doesn't even have a real job, which how come he's like this *dis*ease that's spreading *dis*harmony and *dis*cord. Well, I say *dis* has got to stop. The baditude of his attitude has got to be adjusted and Congressman Brodsky here is the man going to help me do it. He's one of the most effectible congressmen we've got, starting with all the money he got for this tunnel we're standing in. Get over here, Eddie, and tell these folks what you've got to say."

The reporters chuckled into their notebooks as Congressman Brodsky emerged from the tunnel's gloom. Mayor Cleveland was much loved for his verbal innovations. He was always elevating the elevator, preserving disorder and bragging about his own work ethnic. There was much whispered debate of whether this was by clumsy mistake or sly intent. In either case, he was much loved for these flights of verbal fancy, not least because of the confusion they caused among the scribes. How was one to report his position on the distribution of free condos to high-school students?

Brodsky made the mayor look even better by comparison. He was a thin, angular fellow with nervous eyes, a receding hairline and a safe congressional district conducive to the quiet accumulation of honoraria and bribes. He'd been indicted once and then cheerfully reelected by voters comforted by the notion that at least he was their crook and could be trusted to steal from the other guy. His coat was a size too big and he seemed to be sweating a lot, as if he used to be a much bigger man who was fretting the pounds away.

"You can get your sound bites from Brother Cleveland here. I'm here to say that the U.S. Congress . . ."

Nat adjusted his microphone and zoomed in for an

extreme close-up while the congressman talked at great length about effluence under pressure. When he pulled back from the extreme close-up for an extreme wide shot, the corner of the frame caught Delilah pulling Allan aside. He wished he could mike their little chat.

Delilah gave Allan an auntlike hug. "It seems like everywhere I look, there you are again. When can I see some tape?"

"You want broadcast quality?"

"What's the difference to you?"

"It's a hundred more per second."

Delilah laughed so loudly she disturbed the press conference. A man from the Mosquito Abatement District was talking about how insects breed. Delilah said, "You guys are doing a number on me, but I'm not a girl to fuss over nickels, especially when they're not my own."

"Then stop by the studio. Nat'll make you a dub."

"What's that?"

"A copy. If you like what you see, then we'll sell it to you for one of those attack ads you do so well."

10

Run Scared, Win Big

THE DOORBELL SOUNDED LIKE AN OLD TELEPHONE FROM THE DAYS before rings and dials were superseded by buttons and beeps. Mrs. Shanahan was having a private bathroom moment with Marv, the gelding cat that Frank bought her when he knew he was going to die.

Marv followed her to the door, getting ready to cling like hell if she tried to leave the house. Marv was made nervous by the seemingly organized labor of the squirrels moving in upstairs.

Marv, if nervous, was neatly groomed. Mrs. Shanahan was not. One of the advantages of working for her own son in her own house was the opportunity to not get out of one's bedclothes for several days at a time. With her lips wrapped around a smoking butt and her terrycloth robe open down to her navel, she still didn't show off the sagging tips of her formerly perky breasts.

"Just a minute," she told the caller as she slipped off the chain, slid back the bolt, and opened the door a crack. Marv started rubbing his empty sack against the back of her bare feet, but jumped when the missus sucked in some smoke

70

and coughed out some surprise. Her lungs had become congested with the jealousy that the old feel for the young, the guilt the white feels for the black, and the disdain that the thin feels for the thick.

"Yes? What can I do for you," she said, her voice in tune with the sour look on her face.

The mayor's press secretary had been too young, too black, and too thick for too long to worry about it anymore. She adjusted her hat in a just-us-girls way. She spoke in a soft and kindly way which made Allan's mother feel even older, guiltier, and thinner.

"I am Sister Delilah Blue. I preach to the people and sing to the Lord. I'm here to see a Mr. Allan Shanahan of Electronic News Tonight. Excuse me if I've been knocking on the wrong domicile."

Allan's mother opened the door a little more and thought about it a little longer. Delilah furrowed her brow, so the old woman would think she was confused. She wasn't. Her voice still soft and her manner still polite, she backed away from the door and adjusted her hat again. "My apologies again if I've been bothering you."

"Wait a second. He's inside," Mrs. Shanahan said. She punctuated her statement by banging the door shut. The squirrels in the attic scrambled for cover, then kept still for a moment. They had resumed their chewing by the time their landlady unhooked the chain and let the visitor in.

Marv attached himself to Delilah during her walk down into the basement. They found Nat asleep on the company couch and Allan reviewing the company books. He said, "Have a seat, Sister. Right over there."

Delilah cleared away a stack of $\frac{1}{2}$-inch videotapes from a leather chair which the company had purchased from the estate of a dead physician. The leather made a hissing sound as she sat down. Allan poured some coffee. Delilah didn't want any.

"Coffee is proscribed by my religion," she said with clear remorse, "along with cigarettes, alcohol, pornography, and drugs. We are allowed as many sweets as one lost soul can eat. That's why I am so abundant."

Marv planted his ass on Delilah's pumps, then emitted a contented purr. Allan said, "Out ringing doorbells, huh? Must be an election year."

"That's a hazard of the profession. The voters get to speak their piece every four years and sometimes they even make sense. Most times they need a little help, which brings us to Alderman Smith. He is talking some dangerous shit. Excuse me. My religion proscribes strong language, too, but sometimes my religion is wrong."

Nat produced a snore that sounded like a gargle, rolled over, and snored some more. Allan apologized on his behalf. "I still don't see why you're all worked up. Doogie seems a little too crazy to get himself elected."

"These are crazy times, child. At the moment he's just a wannabe, but that's how a person gets to be a be." The leather hissed as Delilah shifted her weight around. "Anything can happen. This is America. The main problem with that is the anything could be bad."

"We don't do a lot of politics. This is a cash-and-carry business."

Delilah nodded as she pulled a folded envelope from her purse. Allan reached for the envelope, but she pressed it to her chest. "This is city business, so I'll see the merchandise first. This is an election year. I've got to guard the public coin."

Allan shook Nat awake and told him there was work to do. The photographer rubbed the sleep from his eyes as they all filed into the editing bay, a remodeled rumpus room where Allan and his pal Billy Paulson had smoked their first cigarettes many years ago, when life was simpler and black politicians didn't pay thousands of dollars for a few seconds of electronic wizardry. In the center of the room were some swivel chairs and a large table with two television monitors on it that were connected by a confusion of wires to a computer console featuring a keyboard and a joystick.

Allan selected a blank tape from the end of a rickety shelf

and handed it to Nat, who pushed a button and yawned while the equipment beeped. When the monitors blinked on, he plugged in the tape and wiggled the joystick until the static snow gave way to a fury of many colors.

They watched events go by in fast forward: Keystone Cops scurrying about directing traffic as it broke the sound barrier; the bowlers buzzing at high pitch and throbbing like a heart about to explode; the flashing of nothing as the sun gun popped off; and the flashing of hot light as it popped back on. They saw the gathering of the Street Crusaders and an extreme closeup of a bloody patch of sidewalk; they heard the falsetto wailing of the crowd as the paramedics loaded Armando Tappy Shoes Calderone into the back of the ambulance. There was the careful manner of Radio Larry, who even at fast forward stood perfectly still; the quieting of the crowd as the ambulance drove away with the young boy's corpse; the jostling for position as Alderman Smith began to speak; the sound bite with Elmo; and the sound bite with the cop. In fast forward they all sounded like Alvin and the Chipmunks, a 33-rpm record played at 45.

Delilah tapped Nat on the shoulder. "Now back it up to the part where Doogie starts talking. That's the part we need right now."

Nat grabbed another videotape from a box he kept under the editing console and plugged it into the second monitor. He used the joystick to back the original tape up to the beginning of the speech and then pressed one button marked PLAY/RECORD and another marked REAL TIME. Alvin and the Chipmunks slowed down to normal speed. Douglas said, "People of Lincoln Square. You don't have to put up with this. . . ."

When the alderman's speech was over, Nat rewound the second videotape, removed it from the editing machine, and gave it to Delilah. The mayor's press secretary handed the envelope to Allan.

"It seems like you make an awful lot of money for such a little bit of work." She paused a moment so they could reflect on this. "If you want to make some more and promise not to tell anybody, I've got a deal that should do us all some good. How about it? What do you say?"

Nat turned down the volume and put the joystick in reverse. The original tape rewound in a high-speed, reverse-action pantomime that made the death of Tappy Shoes seem like a merry escapade. "Maybe, if you tell me this one thing. How come you've got that Tamburino hanging around?"

Delilah pretended ignorance. She knew all about Tamburino and what had happened to Crazy Horse, all about the dozen or so others who had been beaten, maimed, or killed by the renegade policeman. Delilah made it a point to know all about everything.

"I don't know what you're talking about. I don't know any Tamburino."

"Sure you do," Nat said. "His neck is so thick it looks like he doesn't have one."

Delilah pretended a glimmer of recognition in her eyes. "You mean the bodyguard?"

"That's right."

"His name is Tino Padilla. He's a bad cop, I'm afraid. A man of violence. That's why we got him for the job. He's supposed to protect the mayor, and he might have to stop a bullet sometime, so we need someone who's mean and—expendable in the eyes of God."

Nat wasn't convinced, but he grunted his approval anyway. "Okay, so what's the deal?"

Sister Delilah Blue folded her hands together and closed her eyes for a moment. She spoke not to the men but to the deity that presided over their affairs. "Our plan is to run scared and win big. To do that we need to get some dirt on Doogie Smith, the kind to make good and sure he won't be winning any election. Not this year or ever again."

Then she opened her eyes, unfolded her hands. This time she addressed herself directly to Allan and Nat. "If you boys think you can handle that and not be flapping any jaw about it, then you can make some pretty good money. The not-talking part is very important. We're prepared to pay extra for that."

11

Raw War

SUPPORTED BY CONTRIBUTIONS OF MONEY FROM BABUSHKAS, THE deeply pessimistic, and the merely trendy, Douglas Smith had surrounded himself with all of the accoutrements of a modern political campaign. His headquarters were in the empty shell of a Ma and Pa store that had been run out of business by the 7-Eleven down the street in a neighborhood on the Far West Side where two-bedroom bungalows cramped against one-way streets. Windows that once advertised homemade sandwiches and fresh asparagus had been papered over with posters, photographs, and newspaper clippings that advertised the alderman's numerous accomplishments.

As the political season approached, Doogie let his hair grow out to a conservative length and encouraged his Crusaders to do the same. On Wednesdays he ate lunch at the Hancock Center with a consultant from the National Front, a political group that had had success electing thugs in England. The consultant had all sorts of good ideas about how to use TV commercials, telephone banks, and 3-by-5-

inch postcards with a flattering photograph on one side and Doogie's positions on the issues listed on the other.

Douglas was reminded of the postcards when he looked at his reflection in the bathroom mirror. With the beret, without it, with the beret again. He squared his shoulders, adjusted his tie, and spoke as if the whole world were listening, with his eyes in a righteous frenzy and the fist of one hand smacking the palm of the other.

"There'll be a bungle in the jungle and a riot in the streets, just like how it happened when the Nigger King got killed."

He said this again without the beret and without the extravagant gestures, in an even, conversational tone. For once in his life, he couldn't decide to whom he was speaking and what he wanted to say. Was he bringing consolation to the people or terror to the bureaucrats? Was it the carrot or the stick? The fire or the ice? Was he the echo of a better past or the herald of an uncertain future? Whatever it was he wanted to say, he would not be able to say it. The consultant from the National Front said that it would not be politic. He would have to say something else, but nothing else would ring so true.

"Get in here, Elmo."

Elmo wedged into the bathroom and stood at attention by the toilet which hadn't been flushed. Douglas nodded at the toilet. Elmo flushed it. Douglas took one more glance at the mirror before looking at Elmo.

"I bet you don't remember when the Nigger King got killed."

Elmo shook his head. He was only three years old in 1968, and he didn't much care for ancient history. The more Douglas talked about it, the less Elmo cared.

"Well, I remember," Douglas said. "I'm never going to forget." Douglas saw the mirror as the window of his memory, reflecting the better light of life before AIDS and crack cocaine, when Chicago was run by white men and the video wizards hadn't invented fifty-seven channels of cable TV.

* * *

Douglas mostly takes the bus to school, all the way in from Marquette Park. He rides with bums and businessmen on the regular city bus because Xavier is a Catholic school and doesn't have any buses of its own. On his first week out as a freshman, this sophomore says to him that there's a Gypsy whorehouse upstairs of this tavern up by Kedzie, so the highlight of every school day for the next four years is almost twisting his neck off to see if he can see Gypsies screwing up on the second floor. He looks up once in the morning and again in the afternoon.

The other highlight is when he rides past this playground that's covered with broken glass, where a bunch of little niggers play football anyway. That's how come niggers're strong, because the weak ones all bleed to death from the broken glass before they're old enough to breed.

He hears about it first in history class. Mr. Buchman is the teacher, and they're studying World War I. Buchman has this old newspaper with a headline on it that says RAW WAR! He wants to know what's so special about the headline, and Doug is the only one who raises his hand because he is the only one who notices that raw war spelled backward is still raw war, only before he says so, the proctor gets on the intercom to announce that the Nigger King is dead, thanks to some white guy with a pretty good rifle who must have been a pretty good shot.

They cancel all classes and send all the students home, which is no big deal unless you've got to go past a Gypsy whorehouse and a playground full of little nigger kids so tough they play football on broken glass.

It's like the air is made of gasoline fumes waiting for a spark to set it all on fire. Everybody on the bus is nervous, and somebody says the niggers are having a riot someplace. The passengers can see smoke coming from the West Side and most of the cars are driving around with their headlights on in the middle of the day. That's how niggers grieve when one of their preachers gets called back to God. He hears somebody on the bus say that the niggers might beat you up and steal your car if you don't turn your headlights on, so then the bus driver turns the headlights on.

Douglas is so nervous that he forgets to look up at the second-story window of the Gypsy whorehouse, or maybe he looks but doesn't see anything. Or maybe he's thinking in a crazy way of fifty different things like RAW WAR!, dead preachers, and jungle bunnies out on a tear. He doesn't see anything when the bus stops by the playground, but the kids who play there must think he is seeing them because the biggest one screams out, "What you looking at, Fuckface?"

That's what they call him, Fuckface. It seems as if all the times that he was watching them, they were watching back, and had given him their own nickname. He says he doesn't mean nothing, that he isn't looking at anything, but they don't hear him because he doesn't say it very loud. The bus pulls away from the curb, and the football players start running after it. Some of them kids can run real fast because they make it to the next stop before the bus does. They get on the bus, and the driver's so afraid that he doesn't even make them pay the child's fare, which was only twenty-five cents back then.

Then Doug is surrounded by a half-dozen kids who can outrun a city bus and play football on broken glass. They punch and kick and spit and scratch while the other passengers look the other way, so they won't have to testify if somebody gets arrested. His mother calls the cops when he gets home, but they don't get there for three whole days because the niggers really do have a riot. But it's nothing like what Doug plans for twenty-five years later: a bungle in the jungle and a riot in the streets, just like how it happened when the Nigger King got killed.

The memory let go for a while, and Douglas was looking at an older, smarter image of himself. He squared his shoulders, adjusted his beret, and looked himself right in the eye.

"Well, what do you think?"

Elmo took a moment to figure out what his leader wanted him to say. What do I think about what? The riot? The election? His speech? His cologne? Whatever it was, Elmo knew what to say. "I think it's great, just great."

Douglas took the beret off and looked in the mirror one more time. He scowled, sighed, put it on again. "Wrong again, Elmo. I can't wear this anymore. Makes me look like the Hitler Youth and there's still a few geezers that remember who he was. Not many, but enough to matter if the race gets tight. Now get me some coffee and go over the schedule one more time."

Mario Luchesi had parked his Real Italian-ice stand on the outskirts of a field that separated the two grim towers of the John Tinney McTavish Apartments. The stand was spangled with colorful plastic figurines that his granddaughters had made from old juice bottles and hung up like ornaments for some Christmas that would never end. With steady hands and a practiced smile, the old man served up lupine seeds and Italian ices to the handful of black people who had clambered down from the projects to see what the commotion was all about.

Most of the commotion was about the tight knot of newspaper, radio, and television journalists, including Ken Barney of the *Trib*, Melissa Wells of the *Sun-Times*, and Radio Larry of WDM, who huddled together for protection, sweating a lot and sucking on various flavors of Italian ice. Nat and Allan were there on Delilah's expense account, and Channel Twelve was represented by Janette Baylor, who was wearing the sort of spiked heels that made her ass rotate with every step she took.

Delilah circled the gathering of reporters with a rolled-up copy of the alderman's schedule. She unrolled the schedule and started folding it into smaller and smaller squares. When the paper wouldn't fold anymore, she unfolded it and used it to fan herself, stopping to glance at it from time to time. Willis had scratched in his own notes with a blood-red, felt-tipped pen.

8:15 to 9:45	Convoy to Bureau of Elections	*Hope he hits a pothole.*
9:45 to 10:00	File for city mayor	*And lose your ass, chucklehead.*
10:00 to 10:15	Stop by Marina Towers for photo opportunity	*Maybe he'll get in a crash.*
10:30 to 10:45	Convoy to McTavish Apts.	*Damn!*
10:45 to 12:00	Announce candidacy, answer questions	*Question: How come you're so ugly?*
12:00 to 1:00	Convoy to fund raiser	*Follow him, Sis, and find out where the money's coming from*

Mario sold all his lupine seeds and almost ran out of Italian ices before the alderman made his appearance. The summer heat was good for business as it bounced off the air-conditioned glass towers of the downtown business district and became trapped in the crowded neighborhoods where people of all shapes, sizes, colors, and beliefs jostled against one another while getting stickier and angrier by the day. No one was stickier than the reporters who had gathered at the McTavish Apartments for the big announcement, and that was okay with Mario, too. Sticky people were thirsty people, and nothing was better for a parched, Shoe Goo Summer thirst than a large cup of Italian ice with real bits of fruit mixed in. Nat ordered the cantaloupe, Allan the lime. "I think I'm going to die," he said.

Nat didn't glance up as he was counting the pieces of cantaloupe swimming amidst his Italian ice. He knew without looking that Allan was staring at Janette. "How soon? I mean how come?"

"Because she's standing right there sucking on a microphone with her butt sticking out. She looks pretty good in three dimensions, but I guess her nose is pretty big."

Nat walked over to Radio Larry, who was slurping on a cup of watermelon as he held court near a gushing fire hydrant. A gang from the McTavish had opened the hydrant for the benefit of the dozen or so half-naked children who splashed in the small lake it had made. Allan watched Janette watch Radio Larry. He wondered if she liked him and hated Larry if she did.

Delilah jotted down some notes on the back of the alderman's schedule. She looked at Allan, nodded at Nat, and listened to Radio Larry brag about yet another of his exclusives for WDM Radio "News Live at Fifty-Five."

"I had this story a month ago. See, I knew Doogie when he was just another little punk instead of the important punk he's getting to be."

A particularly dim reporter from Channel Eight took out her notebook and pried it open with a purple fingernail. "How's that spelled?"

"L-A-R-R-Y."

"Not you. Smith."

Larry spelled Smith with a Y so the reporter wouldn't bother him again and then launched into a long dissertation on granny babushkas and narco-killers. The reporters traded stories about Douglas while the news photographers jostled for position in front of the portable stage that his supporters had set up on the sidewalk. Mario dished out the Italian ice while Delilah counted the familiar faces and tried to predict who would write what about Doogie's announcement. Ken Barney would get it straight, and his editors would play it down because the *Tribune* was a big paper with bigger ambitions. Melissa would write as if this was the second coming of the last resort and her editors at the *Sun-Times* would play it up big because they knew the *Trib* would play it down. Nat and Allan would play it the way she told them to play it because they were on the city payroll. As to Radio Larry, he would play it first and then move on to some other catastrophe, poor dear.

Delilah knew that Larry would scoop them all because radio is quick and as quickly forgotten as the lies little boys tell to little girls. Fifteen minutes after the announcement, Larry would be on the air with his breathless Walter Winchell way of spreading rumors in the wind. Then he would disappear into the murky shallows of his private life, not to surface again until someone else was killed or another press conference was held. In the meantime, the hundreds of thousands of people who listened to the morning news would think they had heard something about Douglas Smith but not be sure what it was until they saw it with their own eyes on the TV news that evening.

TV news, Delilah sighed. She knew that TV news had too much reach and not enough grasp, that it touched everything and understood nothing. But she also knew that this election, like the last two, would be won or lost on television. And she knew that of all the politicians who scrambled for power in this power-mad city, only Doogie could rival the mayor at playing the TV game. The mayor used a big smile and a warm heart to reassure frightened white people that there was at least one black man who wouldn't beat them up, steal their jewelry, or marry their daughters. Doogie used hate and fear and an army of Street Crusaders to reassure these same frightened whites that here was one man who would protect their lives, their property, their gene pool, and kick some butt while he was at it.

Delilah tried to imagine the next day's headlines and tried to think of ways to put the proper spin on things, to make sure everybody knew the mayor's side of the story. At the end of the alderman's press conference she would cozy up to Radio Larry and look as if she knew something. The TV guys would fall in line behind their guru and she would answer the questions the mayor wanted her to answer even if Radio Larry neglected to ask them.

She checked her watch again and looked at her copy of Doogie's schedule. It was 10:25 A.M. She was pleased. He hadn't yet learned to schedule his news for 3:15 P.M. She sighed. It might not matter, though. The problem with reporters was they almost never asked the right questions. Delilah tried to imagine some of the stupid questions they might ask her. Is it true that the mayor has hired a New York advertising firm to handle his TV commercials? Can you tell us his position on capital punishment? What about the alderman's allegation that the mayor promised to take it easy on the gangs if they helped him get elected? Much reach, but little grasp. Delilah sighed again, checked her watch, and folded the schedule back into a tight, sweaty tube.

At 10:35, right on schedule, a battalion of Street Crusaders marched down the street and set up ranks in front of the portable stage from which their leader would make his announcement.

At 10:43, right on schedule, the alderman's Crusade Cruiser, a souped-up Chevy van with bulletproof windows and reinforced steel panels, turned off Halsted Street and eased to a stop in front of Mario's. Elmo jumped out of the front passenger seat and studied the reporters and the crowd. He quickly counted the bystanders and the Street Crusaders before his eyes got stuck on Delilah. She was the only person in the whole crowd who dared to return his glance. Elmo laughed at some joke that chuckled from the dark part of his brain, then turned back, and knocked twice on the back-door window of the Cruiser. Douglas stepped out and followed his companion onto the portable stage.

A smattering of applause came from the Street Crusaders as Douglas said, "I'm forty-five seconds late. Sorry about the delay."

No one laughed. Douglas didn't expect them to. He expected them to listen to what he had to say and then write their little stories. "If everyone is ready, I'll get right to the point. You want to know why there's no kids in that playground over there? Because the narco-gang in that one building is having a drug war with the narco-gang in the other one. They shoot guns at each other out the windows, so any little children going out to play are taking their lives in their hands. That's why I'm running for mayor while you media people with your fancy hairdos are all sucking on Mario's Italian lemonade. This morning I filed a petition with twenty-five thousand signatures that is going to get me on the primary ballot for mayor. I'm starting my campaign right here because the crime in those two buildings is worse than ever, and the welfare moms are having so many welfare babies that the workingman doesn't have anything left to feed his own. My first promise is to tear those two buildings down. They're so full of narco-killers, pimps, and thieves that real working people don't have a place to stay. I'll take your questions now."

Radio Larry screeched out a question in his weary, cynical Walter Winchell voice. "The people in those projects are all black, Mr. Smith. Isn't it true that when you talk about killers and pimps and thieves you're really just using code words for unemployed blacks?"

Douglas stuck out his chin as if he were spoiling for a fight. "I don't care how black they are. The mayor cares, but I don't. You've got to face the fact that we've got a problem here. My little sister can walk around Marquette Park way after ten o'clock at night and never have to worry that she'll be raped or beaten or shot up with drugs. But if she walked around the McTavish, she'd be dead before she got to Halsted Street. The people who live on my street take care of their community. If the people who live around here don't clean up this place by the time I'm elected, I'm going to clean it up for them."

Nat took a wide shot of the housing project. Laundry was hanging out the windows, and gang graffiti was sprayed on the bricks. He panned down to the street as the reporters barked out the same old questions they barked at every candidate.

"Do you support a tax increase for the Deep Tunnel Project?"

"What's your favorite food?"

"Are you in favor of binding arbitration?"

"Have you ever had an affair?"

"What's your position on downtown development?"

"If you were a piece of art, what piece would you be?"

This last question was shouted from the back row by Janette Baylor of Channel Twelve. Allan imagined himself to be chiseled Greek marble wearing nothing but a fig leaf while the alderman thought it over.

"Now that's a real good question, Janette. I've never thought about it much, but I guess I'd be that 'Thinker' thing. Isn't that the one where the guy's sitting there with his chin on his hand and his elbow on his knee, worrying about tomorrow? Or maybe I'd be one of them stone lions guarding the door of the Art Institute. That's me, a stone lion. Next question, please."

Allan tried to ask the question Delilah had paid him to ask, but was drowned out by Endell of the *Daily Defender*, who was interested in the political dynamics of certain obscure campaign contributions. The alderman's answer was a masterpiece of artful obscurity, which the reporters recorded in great detail.

When Smith was done, Allan and Nat approached the stage joined at the microphone. Nat rolled tape while Allan said, "Is it true that in 1983 you worked at a neo-Nazi book store and earned $16,689 selling books like *Mein Kampf, The Klansman,* and the *Protocols of the Elders of Zion?*"

On a signal from Douglas, Elmo quickly dropped a coin into the pay phone he'd been guarding. The alderman smiled the crisp, professional salesman's smile that he'd developed along with his confident commander's voice. He adjusted his tie and ran his hand over the soft brush of his conservative hair.

"What's your name, sir?"

The reporters all looked at Allan. The ones who weren't wondering about the neo-Nazi books were wondering why Allan hadn't taken better care of his teeth. Allan identified himself.

"Well I'll tell you this, Mr. Allan Shanahan of Electronic News Tonight, I'm not one to forget my mistakes or pretend they never happened. I used to be younger than I am now, and I'm not afraid to—"

The first shot was like the first drop of a heavy rain. The alderman stopped talking, and everybody froze, hoping it was just a firecracker or the sound of an engine with mechanical difficulties. The second shot was like a bad dream, and the third like that dream come true. After that came general confusion as the McTavish projects erupted like two towers made of lightning and stone. Most of the reporters dropped to the ground, but Radio Larry ran for his Bronco with the oversized tires, carrying his briefcase like a football and his microphone like the Olympic torch. He dived under the Bronco and started broadcasting a remote to the crackling sound of small arms fire. Nat checked his audio levels and made sure there was sound coming in, then shot video of the towers, the street, the reporters, and Mario's Real Italian Ice Stand, which had battened down the hatches and started rolling away from the mayhem.

"Now what?"

Allan pointed at the podium, so Nat shot video of Douglas standing tall against the trouble like some comic-book hero whom bullets could not harm. He signaled to the Street Crusaders to form a protective ring and started talking to Elmo. The firefight faded in intensity, and the reporters jumped to their feet and rushed to their awaiting vehicles in a general stampede. Trailing the pack was Janette Baylor, her spiked heels clicking and her soft parts all jiggling madly in every possible direction. Up and down, to and fro, all around the town. Allan was so astonished by the display that he moved left while Nat moved right, which had the effect of unplugging the microphone from the camera.

"How much would it cost us to get a camera where I don't need a grip?"

"Too much. How come?"

"Because I'm tired of trying to do my job with you hooked on me like a baby whose doctor forgot to cut the cord. You're cramping my style."

"This isn't a fashion show."

Nat didn't have a smart reply, so he let it go at that. By the time they got their gear squared away, the gunfire had died down to a few sporadic shots beneath which could be heard the sorrowful wail of approaching police sirens. Delilah came out of hiding and checked her watch again.

12

Mrs. Shanahan's Nitz

NAT AND ALLAN SLEPT THROUGH THE EVENING NEWS BUT CAUGHT the late-night shows, videotaping three programs and watching the fourth one live. Channel Twelve devoted two stories and three minutes to what had happened on the street connecting McTavish Tower East to McTavish Tower West.

The first story was about a beautiful white woman whose passing Subaru had crashed into a light pole after her radiator caught a stray bullet from the firefight. The camera lingered on her cheek, which was bruised, and her lips, which were both full and trembling.

Janette followed with a breathless report from the scene that employed the usual emotions: the horror, the anger, the sad disbelief, and the alarmed gratitude that Douglas Smith and the Street Crusaders had been there to do something about it.

Although Janette's hair was a little mussed up from all of the excitement and the running around, and although her cheeks were a little flushed, and although the live feed was blemished by technical difficulties, Allan noticed that she had stopped jiggling long enough to say, "Police officers arrived fifteen minutes after the first shot was fired. Until then, the McTavish was an urban battle zone with brother pitted against brother and mothers shedding familiar tears. Back to you, John."

John read a shorter story about the alderman's announcement that he would be a candidate for mayor in the September primary election. The usual disclaimer followed about the Republican candidate. He would surely be a stiff because only a stiff would seek an office he could never hope to obtain. Then it was back to the alderman for one final bite which was crisp, to the point, and of the perfect length.

"The real criminals are over in City Hall, where victims are punished and monsters are given coward laws to hide behind."

Channel Four used the same sound bite and so did Channel Eight. When they had finished reviewing all four newscasts, Allan turned off the television and settled back on the company couch.

"This guy's good. He's got this rhythm to his speech where he gives it a little jolt every four or five syllables. 'Where *vic*tims are punished and *mon*sters are given *cow*ard laws to *hide* behind.' Sounds like a goddamn anchorman."

"Better than that," Nat replied. "He's got this light in his eyes that makes it look like he knows what he's talking about, and he knows what sound we're gonna bite on. Who cares about Nazi books when he's hammering home about the *mon*sters and the *cow*ards and all the rest. The only thing he didn't do is throw in some Jesus to make us all feel better."

Allan's mother yelled down from the kitchen that Sister Delilah Blue was on the phone. That's how she said it, with her full name and title, only Mrs. Shanahan had had one glass of wine too many, so it sounded more like sick the lie law boo. Allan took the call.

"You seen the bulljive on the TV?"

Allan said yes, he'd seen the bulljive four times on four different channels, and wasn't it a shame.

Delilah mumbled something Allan couldn't hear, then mumbled something he could. "I think Doogie's got that wanton woman from Channel Twelve tucked in his trousers now. I think the pocket's got a hole in it and she's yanking on his thing."

Allan felt the hot blush rush through his body. His scalp tingled where the blush leaked sweat. "What woman is that?"

"Janette Baylor, the one with the nose. Doogie's got her cheering for the cause. You know how I know? In her stories she always calls his boys the Crusade for Safer Streets. The only person I know calls them that is Doogie Smith himself. Everybody else says the Street Crusaders because that sounds more like what they are, a bunch of gangster punks."

"I'm sorry, Sister. What can I say?"

Nobody could say anything that would make Delilah feel any better. She was angry because the entire press corps had fallen for a cheap, sleazy setup. She was angry because Janette was rooting for Douglas. She was angry because the mayor was angry and had yelled and screamed at her about it. Mostly she was angry because Douglas had reminded the city of the mayor's public-relations disaster at the McTavish Towers.

"What you can say, Brother Shanahan, is that you shot us some tape that'll make it all right."

"Nat's working on it now," he said. Nat wasn't working on anything. He was watching a rerun of "MASH" on cable.

"Then drop it by my office in the morning."

They drove all night without getting anywhere. The city was quiet. It was a tight, nervous quiet like a phone call that hasn't happened yet or a courtroom before the verdict where everybody except the killer knows he's going to fry. The night was cooler than the day, but it was still too hot for chasing down the news. Nat drove as fast as he could, making a breeze of sorts from the heavy air trapped in the hollow of Lower Wacker Drive, but it was used air and the breeze was like a southern wind, which only served to propel the heat into their every pore and make it harder to breathe. The two men were soaking in their own sweat, listening to Allan's mother ramble on the two-way radio.

"You boys need real jobs with regular pay where you get up in the morning. It's not healthy that you should stay up all night and sleep all day, except for watching soap operas and baseball games. And another thing is it's not right that you two young men should always be chasing after dead people. You should be chasing after girls instead. Over."

Allan thought he'd heard a nitz. A nitz was a sound his mother made by clapping her tongue against her teeth. Sometimes it meant she disapproved of something. The rest of the time it meant she disapproved of everything.

"It's what we do for a living, Ma, so let's not talk about it. If you don't like it, we can move our office someplace else. Over."

Allan's mother nitzed again. As amplified by the two-way radio, it sounded to Allan like the noise made as the lobes of her brain became unhinged from one another. Nat thought her nitz sounded more like the snapping of wet fingers. But on one point the two agreed. The older Allan's mother got, the more she nitzed, just like her father had done during his last few lucid years before old age had destroyed his brain and he had forgotten who everyone was. Allan's mother had not yet forgotten anyone or anything of importance to her life or the life of her son. However, she did nitz a lot and was subject to increasingly frequent morbidities.

"Did you ever notice how everybody thinks they're never going to die? Even Mrs. Carter and she's almost dead already. Did you ever notice that? Over."

Just before dawn they shot pictures of a jackknifed semi that nobody wanted to buy. After dawn they took a late break at the all-night Wendy's on Michigan Avenue. It had been Allan's turn to choose the place. They read the paper until 8:00 A.M. when City Hall was opened to the public.

A big cop with bad breath asked them a bunch of questions when they got off the elevator. Name? Address?

Social Security number? The air conditioning felt like a dry-martini drunk, outside in.

The cop said, "What you got in the paper bag?"

"It's a videotape," Allan replied.

The cop took the bag and looked inside but didn't hand it back. "And your business here is what?"

Allan explained. The cop called somebody on the telephone, nodding slowly while giving Nat a tough-cop look. Then he handed back the videotape and pointed them down a beige hall with a green carpet permeated with the clean, chemical smell of a good scrubbing down.

Delilah was running a little late, so they sat on a couch outside her office and occupied themselves with old magazines displayed in a rack on the wall. Nat read a diatribe in *Time* magazine against politically correct hip-hop thinking while Allan thumbed through a vintage copy of *Cosmo,* lingering at length on the advertisements for sexy cigarettes and women's underwear. When the mayor's press secretary showed up, he wondered if she smoked and what she had on under a power-blue business suit that was too tight at the waist and too loose at the hips and chest.

"You boys're up awful early on me. Come on in."

They followed her into the room with mahogany furniture, music by Bach, and a display case full of African thingamabobs. Delilah tugged on the hem of her skirt, which kept bunching up at her derriere and showing a bit of slip.

"So you got me some tape for those heavy negatives? The alderman's up four points from that little TV show he put on yesterday. He'll lose two back by next week, but that'll still put him near 25 percent, give or take whatever it is that pollsters give or take."

Allan looked out the window at the huge, rust-brown Picasso standing in the square across the street and at the pigeons perched on the womanly curve of what might be the figure's hips or wings or breasts or cheeks, depending on the beholder's eye.

"We rolled a little tape, but there's not much to it that you didn't already see on TV."

Delilah sat down, folded her fists together, and placed them on her mahogany desk. Nat felt as if he had been called into the principal's office.

"I'm not paying you for not much tape. I'm paying you for some heavy negs and to make our guy look good."

Allan couldn't take his eyes off the Picasso, so he spoke without turning around. "So, do some kind of feel-good media buy. Surround him with a bunch of kids and go skip a few stones on the lake. The stuff in the tunnel is boring. So is government."

"What was that?" Delilah said. Allan turned around and said it again, this time loud enough for her to hear.

The mayor's press officer unfolded her fists and tapped her knuckles on the desk. "That's the problem with being mayor. The good stuff'll put you to sleep. Doogie's the other problem, the one that worries me. Let's roll tape."

Nat hit PLAY on the office VCR while Delilah dimmed the overhead lights. Allan turned away from the window as the countdown went 5—4—3—2—1—

It was 10:45 A.M. at the McTavish, and Douglas was announcing his candidacy; the scene included the speech, the questions, the excitement, and the image of Douglas standing tall amid the chaos of the fire fight. The microphone picked up everything, including the part where Nat and Allan talked about what they should do next and decided to point the camera at the stage. Then Allan moved one way, Nat moved the other, and their microphone became unplugged.

They watched the silent screen for a moment, until the frame was filled with Elmo. That's when Delilah said, "There's our guy again. We need to take a TV time-out here."

Nat pushed a button and the tape stopped moving. Delilah pinched a bit of ear and gave it a little tug. "That guy with the cue-ball head is the same guy we saw over by

Lincoln Square on that first tape you charged me too much money for."

Delilah pulled her copy of that tape from a drawer and handed it to Nat. They watched with interest as the countdown went 5—4—3—2—1—It was 4:00 A.M. in Lincoln Square and a neon bowling pin flickered its red light on the last remains of Tappy Shoes. A crowd of all-night bowlers had gathered, and the Street Crusaders came on down. Nervous cops directed traffic as they carried Tappy Shoes away. Doogie gave another speech. When they got to the sound bite from Elmo, Delilah reached for the phone.

"Stop it right there for a while and go back to the part where he starts talking. Put it on hold while I go get the law." Nat fussed with the TV set while Delilah told her secretary to track down Sergeant Padilla. Then she and Allan talked about poll results and spin control while Nat remembered the day that Crazy Horse got crunched.

It's a lazy day in August and he's marking the time until school starts up again. In the morning he rides around the 'hood on an undersized bicycle with an oversized banana seat and gooseneck handlebars. In the afternoon he's at the playground, hanging out with the gangsters and listening to the music on China's boom box. Gilligan, Rowdy, Screwball, and Crazy are all talking about this caper that China's figured out.

A newsstand over by the corner of Fullerton and Clark sells every kind of paper you can think of and every kind of dirty magazine. The plan: Rowdy hangs out in a telephone booth down the street until China and the rest come driving up in his vehicle. They pull over and flash some money, like they're buying a dirty magazine only they can't decide for sure which one. What about the one with lots of cheek? Or the one with all the lesbians? While they're talking it over with the guy that runs the stand, Rowdy comes up from behind with a knife and says to the newsstand guy, "Get in the car or you're gonna get stuck," and he gives him a little poke in the ribs to make sure he understands.

China and the rest drive away with the guy lying on the floor in back. They take his money and anything else, like his watch and his keys and his ring and what-have-you, and dump him off on the West Side so he has to walk back through a neighborhood full of angry blacks. Rowdy cleans out the newspaper stand, and then they all meet back at the playground to smoke a little dope, drink a bunch of beer, and read some dirty magazines, especially the one with all the lesbians.

"Let's do it," Nat says.

Everybody laughs and Crazy says to Nat, "Yo mama."

"What about her?"

"She might give us a whupping if we did a caper and you got caught. You and me gonna stay back home and keep an eye on the 'hood."

Nat starts complaining and Crazy says if he doesn't stop he's going to get his lights punched out, so China, Rowdy, and Gilligan drive off to do the caper while Nat and Crazy talk about sports and girls for two hours straight. Crazy talks about Puerto Rico, and Nat talks about how someday he's going to be an artist and sign his name to a painting that's worth a million bucks.

Crazy says, "But you won't forget your friends then, right?"

"No, man, I won't never forget."

Then all of a sudden this Plymouth Fury pulls up to the playground and two city cops get out. One cop stands back with his hand on his gun while the other one starts talking trash.

"Where's all your little glue-sniffing pals?" the one cop says. His name is Tino Padilla, but everybody in the neighborhood calls him the Tumbling Tamburino.

Crazy says they must be someplace else, and Tamburino wants to know if they heard that some freakin Ricans knocked over this newspaper stand over by Fullerton and Clark.

Wimpy says, "No shit?" and Tamburino says, "That's right."

Then Tamburino makes a move for Little Wimpy but before the cop can get physical, Crazy calls him a cocksucking pig.

The rest is pretty much a blur because Little Wimpy turns his eyes away. Tamburino grabs Crazy by the throat and throws him against the brick wall of the Louisa May Alcott Public School. His head bounces against the bricks, and he calls Tamburino a faggot, and Tamburino puts his weight behind a short punch that leaves a fist-sized dent in the left side of Crazy's face. Crazy spits out blood and teeth and bone as the two cops walk away. Nat takes Crazy to the hospital, but all they do is give him some drugs and sew up this hole in the roof of his mouth so his brain doesn't leak out when he's eating potato chips. They then go back to the playground where the boys are all smoking dope, drinking beer, and fighting over the dirty magazine with all the lesbians in it.

"How's it going, Little Wimpy?" Tamburino said.

Nat adopted his old punk attitude almost by reflex. His head tilted, he gave Tamburino the cold stare he'd learned when he was but a boy. His fists curled back toward his wrists, and his legs got stiff at the knees. He would have started to walk the pimp, but he didn't have anyplace to go. "I'm doing what I'm doing, Mr. Tamburino man."

The officer's paws were tangled together, like one huge hand with two sets of knuckles. He'd put on twenty pounds of mostly muscle with a little more mean mixed in. But what bothered Nat more was that Tamburino didn't look surprised to find himself in the same room with a reformed Cobra. Sister Delilah Blue explained. "Sergeant Padilla and Radio Larry recommended you for the job."

The cop untangled his hands and extended one to Nat. Instead of shaking it, Nat examined a button on his shirt.

"Wimpy and me got history," Tamburino said. "He used to be a punk and I used to do my job."

Everybody but Nat laughed at this remark. Allan got the distinct impression that no two people were laughing at the exact same thing. "How come you called him Little Wimpy?"

Tamburino thought it about for a moment too long. Before he could reply, Nat hit PLAY on the TV set and the video Elmo started to talk.

Allan had heard it all before, so instead of looking at the TV set he looked at Delilah's rear end. It looked big but not too big, soft but not too soft. It was the sort of rear that caused Greeks to make Earth a fertile woman and the Sun a potent man. Allan dreamed about soil and seed while Elmo droned on about Douglas keeping the city safe and things getting out of control, about how another teenage kid got killed and Mayor Cleveland is the one to blame.

After the bite was finished, Tamburino picked up the phone and whispered something into the receiver. He hung up the phone and said to Delilah, "I'm sure we got a sheet on him with just the highlights on it. First I'm looking at the tattoos and the way he shaves his head. That boy needs a spanking. I can tell you that for sure."

Myron hit the buzzer and said there was an officer outside. Delilah said to send him in and moments later a computer printout was delivered by a young cop in a crisp blue uniform. The others watched in attentive silence while Tamburino looked at the sheet. He recited the particulars as if they were items on a laundry list.

"It's mostly just chickenshit criminality as far as I can tell. We got armed robbery, extortion, and dealing in the wrong kind of mind-altering buzz. He robbed a liquor store and got two years, suspended. Assault with a deadly weapon, dropped. Disturbing the peace, dropped. Concealed weapon, suspended. He was a person of interest in the murder of some guy from Marquette Park. The investigation continues. That was thirteen years ago."

Delilah pretended to be more disappointed than she was. "We need to do better than that."

They talked in circles for quite some time, reviewing the tape over and over and studying the criminal file. Tamburino described a person of interest as a suspect without any evidence, and Delilah asked Nat why the raw tape they'd just reviewed was so much rougher than the final product she'd seen on television.

"What happened to all the ahs and ums and you knows?"

"Low-velocity sound."

"What's that?"

"The ahs and the ums and the you knows, sound that doesn't say anything. We splice them out and use cutaways and two-shots to cover up the seam in the tape."

"A two-shot? What's that?"

Nat spoke a little louder since he knew what he was talking about. "You shoot the subject from the back, at the face of the person asking the questions. That gets the talent's face on the tube while you cover up the place where you chopped away the sound."

Allan interrupted with a shrill complaint about the high cost of editing bays. When he was finished, Delilah said she had another job for Electronic News Tonight.

"We're going down to Little Egypt for this to-do they're having down there. We need for you to come along, with all expenses paid, of course. Doogie will probably be there, too, and Willis thinks you can help us do a little job on him. May the Lord have mercy on my simple soul, and you can cut out all the ums and ahs."

CHANNEL EIGHT

JULY 24, 6:12 P.M. LEDE INTO WEATHER OUT OF FIRST NEWS BLOCK CAMERA TWO: MEDIUM CLOSE-UP/JIM

JIM: Downtown workers and shoppers were buzzing with excitement this afternoon thanks to Gerald Philby of Los Angeles. (ROLL FLY TAPE) Philby is better known as the Human Fly. Wearing black tights and suction cups, he started climbing the Sandburg Center to the amusement of passersby and the irritation of the police. Philby was arrested at the Center's penthouse apartment following a short press conference. Here's the buzz:

ROLL PHILBY SOUND BITE/OUTCUE: ". . . at McCormick Place and the show starts at seven."

CAMERA THREE: TWO-SHOT/JIM, BILL

JIM: Philby was charged with trespassing and is in Cook County jail right now, with bond set at $250. I hope he makes bail before showtime.

BILL: Sounds like a swat on the wrist to me, Jim.

JIM: The whole town's buzzing. It should be a pretty hot show.

BILL: Well, if you want a hot show, you don't have to go too far around here. It was another sizzler out there today. The mercury hit 103, and that's the thirteenth record high so far this year. (ROLL WEATHER MAP) As you can see on our satellite map, there's not a cloud in the sky, and we're starting to see some dust bowl conditions down in Little Egypt.

CAMERA ONE: TWO-SHOT/BILL, MARCIA

BILL: The chances of rain are slim to none for the next week or so. I'll be back a little later with the five-day forecast. Marcia—

CAMERA TWO: EXTREME CLOSE-UP/MARCIA

MARCIA: Thanks, Bill. When we come back, Brad Richter has a story about a neighborhood activist who wants to take his crusade off the street and into City Hall. And our commentator Harding Porter asks the burning question, "Will the real mayor stand up?"

NEWS MUSIC TO COMMERCIAL WITH FREEZE-FRAME OF ALDERMAN SMITH AND PRINT OUT: Streetwise candidate.

13

The Food Chain

BILBO CHEWED ON HIS CAGE IN THE GLOVE COMPARTMENT WHILE Popeye turned left and headed for the lake. The gerbil was trying to escape. Hammerhead wished he would but didn't dare say so. Instead he looked out the window and tried to think of something else. The sound of tooth enamel scraping at steel was driving him insane.

Popeye said, "You'll watch Bilbo if I croak, right?"

"Yeah, sure. Why not?"

"Because you hate the little fuck. That's why."

Hammerhead had to be very careful here. "You won't croak."

"That's right. So if anything ever happens to Bo, I'll find you and make you pay the price."

Hammerhead said that would be okay. If he got charge of the gerbil he'd also get charge of the car, and he could do a lot worse. It had mag wheels in front, racing slicks in back, and a little something extra under the hood. The inside was decorated like a fine apartment, with rabbit-fur upholstery, a plastic Jesus on the dash, and a pair of polished oak karate sticks dangling from the rearview mirror. Popeye kept food in a dry-ice cooler, condoms in the ashtray, and a cheap handgun under the driver's seat. Someday Bilbo might chew right through the glove compartment and get run over by a truck or something. Funny how cars had glove compartments when rich old ladies were the only ones he ever saw driving with gloves. They and the gerbils must have a lot of pull.

Popeye turned on WRCO-FM, Radio Free Puerto Rico, cranked it up loud, and opened the windows wide so everybody on the Northwest Side could hear the drums do battle with the horns. Popeye drove slowly, taking his own sweet time as they went over the river and under the overpass of a train that didn't run anymore, past the angry neighborhoods, and into the thin strip of high-rise apartments along the lake that clung to the city like a fur collar to a threadbare coat.

They parked on a side street and walked along a wall that was built against the tide; only the tide wasn't there anymore. Hammerhead was only seventeen, but he could remember summers when it seemed like the tide would never stop and the world would never get old. Now he wasn't so sure. The water had receded in the last few years as Lake Michigan boiled away, as the sun got hotter and the city smelled as if it were deep fried in dirty motor oil.

He took off his Reeboks when they reached the dead brown grass and put them back on when the grass ran out. This summer the wall on the lake was too hot to walk on in bare feet, which was another thing different from when he was younger. As the lake retreated from the city, it left behind a hundred yards of littered beach dotted with white people working on a tan. Hammerhead couldn't figure out why white people wanted color because brown people were usually poor and drove old cars from Detroit while white people had more money than they could use and drove fancy new cars from faraway places he'd seen on TV one time.

They walked around Diversey Harbor, where all the rich

white people who wanted to be brown parked their boats while they were baking in the sun. Out on the lake, a hundred gliding sails reminded them of all the things they could not have. As the sun broiled a little more lake, the two young gangsters talked about the future as if they had one and tried to imagine what it was like to glide on a lake as big as a sea in a boat without a motor.

Popeye said, "What's for food?"

At first Hammerhead wasn't going to answer, but the silence only reminded him that he was hungry too. "We could go fishing for carp."

"What's for bait?"

"How about Bo."

Popeye didn't think this was funny, but he pretended that he did. "Fuck you. The Eye needs beer. You got any green?"

Hammerhead said what he always said when he didn't know what else to say. "Sheeet."

Popeye popped out his glass eye and gave it a thoughtful look. "We better go scope out the pidge."

The gun club's catapult made a metallic twang as it launched its cargo into a gentle arc from shore to lake. With the glass left eye cupped in his greasy right hand, Popeye followed the trajectory of the clay pigeon. The gun club sounded a muffled bang, and the pidge turned into black plastic dust that drifted onto the water like the sooty snow of Gary, Indiana.

"Nice shot," Popeye said. He looked at the gun club with his real eye and pointed the glass one at Hammerhead.

"Come on, blood," Hammerhead said. "You're giving me the wiggles."

"The Eye needs food and beer."

"Then the Eye's gonna have to wait. This sucker's a dead shot that don't want to miss. Put the damn thing away so's I can concentrate on my business here."

Popeye forced the eye back into its socket but pointed the pupil in the wrong direction. Now he looked like a zombie.

Hammerhead wiggled some more and said, "Turn it around so it's looking at me instead of that shit you've got for brains."

Popeye adjusted his glass eyeball while the catapult launched another clay pigeon into the sky above Lake Michigan. Another shotgun blast destroyed this target too, sending another shower of black plastic snow drifting onto the lake.

A clean miss was worth a quarter if they could fetch the undamaged pidge. Catapult twang, pidge in air, shotgun bang, plastic snow. In an hour Hammerhead had retrieved seventeen clay pigeons. One more and they could cash them in at the club for enough money for a bologna sandwich from the Korean, a quart of beer from Armanetti's, and a gallon of gasoline for Billy the Bopper's car.

Hammerhead said, "Talk about the Place."

Popeye laughed. "I swear you boys are all the same, thinking the Place is cool. The Place is a roof, a guard, and three square meals a day with a bunch of losers telling the same boring stories over and over again."

"Stories about their capers, right?"

Popeye tried to remember one of the boring stories, but before he could recall one, an important event intervened. The catapult twanged, the pidge flew, a shotgun blasted, and the pidge flew some more. No black snow this time. A miss.

Popeye said, "Better be quick."

Hammerhead was. He took a running start off the retaining wall and dived into Lake Michigan without so much as a splash. Popeye had to imagine the dive because he couldn't see that far. Little by little, day by day, his nights were getting longer. The doc had said they would, and it looked like the doc was right. As Hammerhead raced for the pidge, Popeye remembered the day the doc had laid it on the line.

There are six hundred men in the yard with nothing much to do. Some are waiting by the two hoops for a chance to shoot one of two basketballs. The others are talking or walking or sitting in the sun. Popeye smokes a cigarette and dreams about Miami. There's lots of Latinas there, especially the lady from the Miami Sound Machine, Gloria Something-or-Other. Popeye's in love with her, or with the smaller version of her that he saw on the TV one time.

He is thinking about Gloria and walking by some of the Black Galabeyes when one of the gangsters says, "The good thing about being Muslim is you can have as many wives as you want. The bad thing is they all be ugly. That's why the Arabs make 'em wear them veils."

Popeye thinks this is funny, so he laughs. He is going to go over and say how ugly women are better in bed, but before he can the biggest and blackest of the Galabeyes says, "What's the chuckle, Jose?"

Popeye swallows his own words. They feel like gravel going down but he spits them back up anyway. There are five other Black Galabeyes around, but none of them are laughing.

The biggest and the blackest speaks again. "You think our women's ugly?

Popeye opens his mouth but never has a chance to talk.

"Then listen to this, Jose. You gonna be a woman pretty soon, and your man'll be the Dick of Death. His johnson's 'bout as long as a baseball bat, and he got a dose of the AIDS from junking up. The Dick knows he's gonna die, and it makes him real mean. How come you not laughing anymore?"

Popeye doesn't know how it happened, but one week later he moves into another cell. The Dick's name is Freddy. He's as tall as a house and as wide as a truck. Freddy's in love. He says, "Gonna rip you a new butthole that's big enough for me."

The Dick of Death is big and strong, but Popeye is quick and motivated. They play catch-me for an hour or so, until the Dick runs out of gas. He says, "Fuck you then, Jose. You got to sleep sometime. I'll wake up as soon as you do, and then you'll be squealing like a pig."

The Dick falls asleep and starts to snore. Every now and then he rolls over and opens his eyes a bit, but Popeye stays

awake by thinking about Gloria from the Miami Sound
Machine. One time Popeye dozes off, but the Dick makes
some kind of noise that wakes him up just in time. Other
than that, Popeye stays awake for five long days and nights
until he collapses in the yard and is carried off to the
infirmary. When he wakes up he sees this doctor has
removed his glass eyeball and is holding it up to the light.

"Where'd you lose your eye?"

He remembers when it happened and how the pain
seemed so unreal, so sharp and deep that it couldn't have
been possible. Hot blood and eye juice oozed through a hole
in something he didn't even know he had, getting sucked up
by a big gray sponge that wasn't really a sponge but his
brain. It reminded him of the time he got shot in the thigh,
and at first he thought he'd peed in his pants, only the pee
was red and it wouldn't stop. That's what happened to his
head that day when his brain became a sponge. It felt like
he'd peed in his head, and since then he hadn't been the
same. They fixed him up and sent him to prison for an old
burglary he'd forgotten all about, but he doesn't tell this to
the doctor. All he says is, "Lost it in a fight."

And all the doctor says is, "You see that chart over there?
The one with all the Es?"

"Sure I do," Popeye says. "What the fuck's an E?"

The doctor examines Popeye's good eye and seems
pleased with the result. "You better find a new line of work,
mi amigo."

"How come is that?"

"Because you're going blind."

"That right?"

"That's right. Sometimes it happens to people, especially
when they get one eye poked out. What happens is the eye
that's left works so hard that it burns out after a while, gets
tired. You better stop watching television and get a new line
of work, so you don't get sent back here. Come back here a
blind man and you'll be bending over for every punk that's
too sick to get it the hard way. A good-looking kid like you,

you'll be wearing diapers in a week. Your farts'll sound like a tire with a leak."

Hammerhead climbed back onto the retaining wall with a black clay pigeon clamped between his teeth. With one rolling motion, he plopped down onto the concrete and added the pidge to his pile. Wet and out of breath, he said, "Let's go get some food."

They knocked on the back door of the Diversey Gun Club and exchanged eighteen clay pigeons for $3.75. At twenty-five cents each, they had another seventy-five cents coming, but neither gangster had mastered multiplication tables, or even knew what they were.

They made their purchases with care, choosing the ripest bologna sandwich the Korean had to offer. They removed the meat and ate the rest on the way to the Logan Park Lagoon. While waiting for some carp to take the hook, Hammerhead said to the Eye, "What's it like in the Place?"

Popeye thought about it, but before he could answer, a carp nibbled on his line. He sank the hook, reeled it in, and slapped on some more bologna. He said, "A lot like this lagoon, I guess. It's where they dump the goldfish when they get tired of feeding them and cleaning up the turds. The big goldfish eat the little goldfish until you got yourself a carp to fry in the chair. Smear him all up with barbecue sauce and he tastes as good as trout."

Hammerhead had a fish on the line, but he was so intent on Popeye's words that he didn't know it until the fish and the bologna were gone. "I think you're thinking on a caper."

"That's right. But it's just between us, okay? There's not enough taxes to go around, and I got ways to spend it. You want to go on a ride with me?"

14

The Kankakee Get N' Go

BILBO'S EFFORTS TO CHEW A HOLE IN THE GLOVE COMPARTMENT were interrupted only by his efforts to replenish himself for more chewing by eating and sleeping. Everything else was either done while chewing or not done at all. Hammerhead tried to think of something else, but he could sooner stop the beating of his own heart than block out the sound of tooth against steel.

"Fuckin' A," Hammerhead said. "Didn't even stop to take a dump. I swear he just keeps right at it while he's squeezing one out."

Popeye nodded with a ritual smile, as a father might do at the lesser accomplishments of a talented son. "You just be sure he don't get out."

They crossed the old ship canal twice on their way out of town and once again near Lockport, Illinois. It was in Lockport that Popeye kept the engine running while Hammerhead walked into the public library and walked out with Volume L of the *World Book Encyclopedia* tucked into the front of his pants. A magnetized bookmark set off an alarm at the door, but the librarians in Lockport were so unaccus-

108

tomed to the theft of books that Popeye and Hammerhead were back across the canal again by the time anyone figured out that the alarm had not malfunctioned.

When they had passed the place where the canal pours into the countryside, Popeye turned to Hammerhead and said, "Break it down for me now."

The movement of the car, the chewing of the gerbil, and Hammerhead's neglect of his studies made for a difficult read.

"It says here that Little Egypt is in the delta. The delta—I don't know what delta means—'The delta where the Miss —Mississ,' I don't know what that is. It's Miss Pee or something kind of like that, only longer. Anyway it's where it gets together with the Ohio River. 'It is famous for its rich farmland and a—' ac—ac—something. 'The name comes from a number of small towns named after—named after the great cities of ancient Egypt.' This book needs more pictures."

"What does ancient mean?"

"It must mean big. If this is Little Egypt, then the ancient one must be big."

"But if they're small towns, how come they named them after big cities? What does the book say about that?"

"I don't know, Eye. How about you let me read? 'Among these cities are Thebes, Karnak, and Cairo.'"

By chance he pronounced it Kay-row, just like the people who live there. "'Cairo is the county seat and spec—' spec—something, 'in river transportation and the manufacture of playground equipment.'"

"What does it say about the *Connected Yankee?*"

"*Connected Yankee?* What's that?"

"Some kind of boat that's on the river down there."

Hammerhead scanned the article, but he didn't find any mention of Yankees, connected or not. It had lots of stuff about boats on the river and a few words about the riverboat trade, but no *Connected Yankee.* Popeye seemed disturbed by this.

Hammerhead put the book down and waited for his

partner to say something. The Eye was thinking, and it didn't feel so good. His glass eye always hurt when he thought about things he couldn't see. "How far is it from where we are now?"

Volume L had a map with a little line that said, "100 miles." The line was about as long as Hammerhead's thumb was wide. He measured three thumbs and a little more, then said, "It looks like about three hundred and fifty miles or something close to that."

Popeye cursed. Hammerhead laughed. "We can maybe trade Bilbo in for a cup of gasoline."

Popeye shook his head. His glass eye was starting to throb again, but then he figured things out. "Listen, Hammer. I been thinking and here is what I thought. We're doing the people a service here, so we ought to get us some taxes on the way."

As the scalding heat of the city gave way to the scorching heat of the plain, Bilbo took a little nap, storing up the energy to chew on steel all night. Hammerhead watched the corn rush by. "Tell me about the caper, Eye. How's it going down?"

Popeye hadn't told him much, just what he needed to know. That was part of the plan, in case it turned out bad. "We meet a guy and we make a buy. You drive and I cut the jive. You think you can handle that?"

Hammerhead shrugged and made a face that Popeye couldn't see. Hammerhead was sitting on his blind side, so he stopped shrugging and gave him the finger. "What's the money like?"

"It's like having all the women all at once."

"That's not what I mean. How much money is there?"

Popeye thought about it for much too long. "Enough to have us a lifetime party and maybe even buy that restaurant where me and my uncle used to work."

"How much is that?"

"Enough."

"What about mine?"

"You get one in ten. That's five hundred greens. You still in?"

"Five hundred?"

Hammerhead figured Popeye was lying about the money, but he didn't know how much. Still, he'd never seen five hundred dollars before, and where would he sleep if he didn't go along? That was another bad thing about living in the back seat of the Bopper's car. You never knew where you were going for sure. Yesterday they were going to the lake, now they were going to Little Egypt. Hammerhead picked up the L book, and read a little more. Things went a bit more smoothly now that Bilbo was asleep.

" 'Cairo was a hotbed of Southern sentiment during the Civil War, and the home of several secret'—something— 'sympathetic to the rebel cause. Cave-in-Rock was the hideout of river pirates'—I guess that's guys like us—'who lured innocent victims into a sandstone cave with the promise of women and drink and then robbed them of their possessions.' I guess that means they collected taxes. 'The population'—I don't know what peaked means, but it— 'peaked at 15,203 in 1920, and now stands at 4,800 thanks to depressed economic conditions.' Why would anybody want to thank depressed conditions? Still don't say a thing about this *Connected Yankee* of yours. How's that fit into the caper anyway?"

Popeye didn't answer. The day was turning gray, and he wanted to fill the gas tank before the sun went down. "Next place we come to, we got to go to work."

Popeye had it all figured out, and it worked just like he said it would. "You got to steal a lot or you got to steal a little. It's the capers in the middle that'll get you put in jail."

So they cruised into the East Kankakee Get N' Go and acted as though they had lots of time on their hands. Hammerhead filled up the tank while Popeye pretended to make a telephone call. Popeye grabbed a few groceries while Hammerhead pretended to take a leak. Hammerhead snuck back to the car while Popeye distracted the clerk.

"You got some Pepto-Bismol?"

"It's over in aisle three."

The clerk was wrong because Popeye had hidden it behind the Kellogg's Corn Flakes. He said, "I just checked aisle three. There ain't no Pepto there."

"Then we must be out," the clerk replied.

Popeye clutched his stomach and swayed from side to side. "I'm in a bad situation, got the runs that just won't quit. We need to make it to Chicago by tonight, but we're stopping every five ticks or so so I can be squatting by the side of the road and pinch out some stuff that looks like—"

The clerk held up his hands, begging him to stop because he'd rather leave the counter unattended than hear about the fluids produced by someone else's bowels. "Hang on. I'll go check. You just wait right here."

Popeye didn't wait. He and Hammerhead were well down the road by the time the clerk returned. They drove away at an easy pace. That was the hardest part. Hammerhead watched in the rearview mirror and jumped when they passed a state trooper hiding behind a billboard that advertised the South Kankakee Motel 6. Popeye munched on a bag of barbecue-flavored potato chips.

"There won't be any cops," he said.

"How's that?"

"Because we only stole about thirty bucks and none of it was greens. So a cop's got to drive out to the Get N' Go and then he's got to talk to the clerk. Then he's got to do a report and then he's got to call the station. And then what's the station gonna say? Be on the lookout for two Puerto Ricans with a bag of chips. Chow down, Head. Destroy the evidence."

Hammerhead relaxed a bit since the Eye was making sense. He settled back in his seat and held the wheel like a feather. They drifted back and forth across the centerline, but that didn't matter because Billy the Bopper's car was the only one on the road to Cairo. After a while the sun disappeared, and the air cooled down a bit. They were free and easy with a head of steam, a fill-up of gas, and no sign of trouble for miles around. Then Bilbo stirred from his slumber and announced his presence by kicking some sawdust out of the cage and onto his master's basketball shoes. Popeye fed him some pellets which he downed in a few quick gulps before getting down to the serious business of turning the pellets into turds and scraping his teeth against steel.

Get N' Go was a statewide chain, so they robbed franchises in Gilman, Tuscola, Effingham, and Carbondale. It was 4:00 A.M. of the next day by the time they came to a stop in Mound City, near the place where the Ohio and the Mississippi rivers formed the delta that gave Little Egypt its name.

Mound City was surrounded by the burial mounds that the Illinois Indians had built on the flat plains where corn grows when it's not so hot and dry. Some mounds were in the shape of great coiled snakes and some mounds were in the shape of birds in flight. The mounds were a mystery to many men but not to Popeye and Bilbo. They didn't even know the mounds existed, although they parked Billy the Bopper's car in the shadow of a sixteen-acre mound in the shape of a barking dog. They climbed up the dog's tail and slept on his haunches.

Before they nodded off, Hammerhead said, "Hey, Eye. Check it out. It's like we're watching a movie show."

"What you talking about?"

"I'm talking about the stars, blood. The sky's full of stars."

Popeye looked up at the night, but he didn't see anything. To him the stars looked just as black as the space in which they were suspended. "Yeah, just as you say. Like watching a movie show."

In the morning they collected some taxes from the Mound City Get N' Go before traveling the last thirty miles or so to Cairo, the gateway to Little Egypt.

The town had seen better days. Cairo had once fancied

itself to be the very heart of America, barging grain and beef down the Mississippi for export to England and barging ore and coal up the Ohio to the steel mills of Pennsylvania. But trucks and trains had happened to Cairo many years ago, and these days the rivers were mostly used for flushing out the waste produced by the people who lived upstream.

Half of the buildings were boarded up, and the other half were occupied by people of little hope. The few citizens who were on the streets weren't doing very much, just ambling from one place to the other with none of the sense of urgency that propels people through a vital town. Structures had been left to decay because there was no need to fix them up or reason to tear them down. No new tenants would rent the space and no new buildings would take their place.

The only sign of commerce was displayed by a withered old woman who had piled old clothes and shoes onto tables set up in front of her shop, as if she knew that her customers lacked the energy to venture inside the place. The rest of the street was quiet except for a group of old black men shuffling around a parking lot uncluttered by even a single car.

Hammerhead said, "You're saying we drove two days for this?"

Popeye rubbed the socket with the glass eyeball in it. "I see the river okay, but I don't see no *Connected Yankee*. That book said this is Cairo, right?"

15

Living Important Lives

AFTER THINKING ABOUT IT STEADILY FOR THE LAST EIGHT YEARS or so, Elmo had decided that he mostly liked politics except for the parts he didn't. He liked the excitement and the attention, the money and the way women looked their way when they walked into a room. And he especially liked the idea that a yo-yo like Doogie Smith could stir things up and be the talk of Toddle Town by getting his face on the TV news.

Politics was like a Pete Ward pop-up with the Sox trailing two to one and the bases juiced in the bottom of the ninth. The attempt to defy the laws of social gravity by brute force was no less heroic for the fact that the rise must eventually end, and the humiliating fall into Zolio Versailles's mitt must eventually begin. Until that happened, they might as well enjoy the view and hope against hope that the shortstop dropped the ball. The difference between Doogie and Elmo was that Doogie believed in pop-ups that never came down.

It started with the Mill Road Tavern softball team and the keggers they would throw after they'd lose a game, which were lots. A few of the guys got to talking about the neighborhood, and Doogie said the best way to make sure no nigger shortstops ever moved in was to form a welcoming committee. The committee's efforts were appreciated by the people because the committee created the illusion of safety, and by the police because the committee did all the dirty work.

Then they got to talking about wearing hats like Stallone wore in *Rambo* and Doogie said why not honey up some of the old women into putting on a smorgasbord and maybe even raffle off a couple of tickets to Wrestlemania III. One smorgasbord led to another and another, all of them cooked by granny babushkas and attended by their spandex progeny. Pretty soon everybody in the crew had not just a snappy hat but green fatigues, Street Crusader T-shirts, and iron-toed combat boots, so Doogie said maybe they should branch out into other neighborhoods with other granny babushkas. After a while, Street Crusaders were all over the Southwest Side, and Doogie was becoming the most famous local product since the Nazi that led the march on Skokie. So Doogie said why not open up a storefront and get a 1-900 number, and maybe even run for alderman from Marquette Park.

They learned an amazing thing as they worked their way up from granny babushka smorgasbords to brie and chablis with high society. Chicagoans of every station were mesmerized by the grinding cavalcade of corruption and blood they saw on the evening news. They learned that Toddle Town needed a man of action, preferably one with a noble chin and a way with words—words like narco-killers, phrases like "city fall, not hall," or sentences like "The mayor and his mosquitos better take a look around because the people of this city want more out of life than a new tunnel. They want to be able to walk down the street at night without thinking they're going to get killed by some narco-killer who's going to be crazy mad until he gets more drugs."

"Certs, Elmo. Now."

Elmo pretended he wasn't listening until Doogie said,

"Elmo, I'm talking to you. Don't be a bonehead when I'm talking to you. If you want to be a bonehead any other time, you go ahead and that's okay, but don't be a bonehead when I'm talking to you."

Elmo was on his way. The thing he didn't like about politics was the way it was turning Doogie Smith into a big asshole. He liked him better when they were just growing up and Marquette Park was still a white man's neighborhood, when women kept to their own kind, when they didn't have any 7-Elevens or breath mints either that he could remember.

As he strutted down the street, Elmo nodded at people he knew and glared at people he didn't. He was stopped in his tracks by the flashing red warning of a DON'T WALK, DON'T WALK, DON'T WALK sign. For one of those crazy, nonsensical seconds his brain had every now and then, he thought it said DON'T TALK, DON'T TALK, DON'T TALK. He had been thinking of Little Egypt and had remembered what Doogie had said.

"Don't talk about it to anybody, especially me. If you don't talk about it, then things will be okay."

Not talking was the hardest part, especially when he was not talking to himself. Sometimes when Doogie wasn't around, Elmo would talk to himself because he had to talk to somebody. He figured that didn't count as talking, and besides, since Doogie didn't know, it probably didn't count, and Doogie was a jerk, so fuck him.

So he talked to himself while walking to the 7-Eleven. When he was safely on the other side of the street, he sniggered, which is how he laughed at jokes that other people wouldn't understand. He thought about the better times, when Marquette Park didn't have any niggers or Ricans or any of that Asian bullshit, either, like this Chinaman in front of him in line at the 7-Eleven who was slowing him down. Marquette Park still didn't have any niggers, although some dagos had moved in and that was close enough.

When the Chinaman finally coughed up the money for his

pack of Lucky Strikes, the clerk greeted Elmo with a nervous smile. That was another thing Elmo liked about politics. People like the clerk showed him a lot more respect these days.

"What'll it be?"

"Certs."

"What kind?"

"What kind of what?"

"Certs. We got spearmint and peppermint."

Elmo thought about it for a while.

What does Doogie want? I don't know. Just pick one. But if I pick the wrong one he'll yell at me. Then take one of each, you sap.

"You okay?"

"Yeah. I'll take one of each."

On the way back to the HQ, Elmo thought some more about the good old days when hot summer nights like this meant a game of softball and maybe they'd cruise down to Old Town to shake down the faggots who were looking to gobble some tender young pud. This was back before the softball team when they were called the West Side Rangers. Doogie was the leader, and Elmo was the guy who beat up guys who got out of line. And then for a while they were called the West Side Brotherhood, until Elmo made the mistake of killing this new recruit for stepping out of line. Doogie told Elmo to forget all about it. He did. After that came the softball team, and after that they started calling themselves the Crusade for Safer Streets.

Things started happening fast after that—meetings and speeches and being on TV, and every time just to talk about street gangs and drugs. Elmo didn't understand why drugs were such a big deal, since when he and Doogie used to shake down faggots they'd do it so they could buy some toot. Now they did whiskey instead, and it was down to suits, ties, and breath mints, so Doogie could breathe all over rich women who lived on the forty-third floor of Marina Towers North.

"Marina Towers," Elmo sniggered as he laid the breath

mints on the kitchen table in their apartment, upstairs from the HQ.

Doogie wasn't listening, but Elmo kept on talking anyway. "Used to be if we'd go to a place like Marina Towers they'd call the cops on us. Now we go and they give us money just because we ask for some."

Elmo talked to himself because Doogie had stopped talking to him, which was another thing Elmo didn't like about politics. Elmo had figured out that whenever Doogie talked to him now, he was just practicing the lines he used on the TV or on the chumps from Melrose Park or the rich ladies in the big buildings who gave money to the cause and then fucked Doogie's brains out while Elmo waited in the car. The rich women never talked to Elmo or gave him money or fucked his brains out, which was another thing he didn't like about politics.

His thoughts were interrupted by the sound of Doogie swearing under his breath. He pointed his chin at the mints. "What's this?"

Elmo cringed and looked away. Doogie was mad and he didn't know why. "What's what?"

"You got stock in Certs? I tell you to get me a pack of breath mints and you go and get me two. You've got a problem, Elmo. The problem is you don't listen to me."

Elmo watched Doogie unwrap the peppermint Certs and pop one in his mouth. He chanted "peppermint" over and over again, and from here on, any time Doogie wanted breath mints, Elmo would make it peppermint Certs.

"Here's the thing," Doogie said, sucking on both the words and the mint. Elmo relaxed because Doogie never yelled when he said, "Here's the thing." All Elmo had to do was look impressed and say, "Uh huh," because Doogie was really talking to himself, like Elmo did when he went to get Certs. That was another thing he didn't like about politics. At least when Elmo talked to himself, he did it when nobody else was around.

"Here's the thing, Elmo. Elections get you nothing but mediacrats. Mediacre people voting for mediacre candidates they see on the media. The really great leaders take their power through the barrel of a gun."

"Uh huh."

"Napoleon, Hitler, George Washington. Here's the thing, Elmo. If the people give you the power, they can always take it away, but if you're strong enough to take it by force, the power's all yours until you meet a stronger man."

"Uh huh."

"We're taking a chance by working with this Popeye punk, but I think it'll all work out. We'll get the Africans and 'Spanics kicking out the jams until the cows come home. What time is it anyway?"

"Uh huh."

"What did you say?"

"Uh huh?"

"You're being a bonehead, Elmo, when I already told you not to be."

The two tube towers of Marina City presided over the dense sludge of the river that connected the lake to ever bigger rivers until they reached the Mississippi. Each floor of each tube had been carved into dozens of condominiums, and each condo was shaped like a slice of overpriced, overdecorated concrete pie. Amanda Holcomb, a longtime supporter of the Crusade for Safer Streets, was rich enough to own two slices. One had been made into a large, wedge-shaped reception area where she hosted magnificent social functions at which people got drunk enough to give money to her idea of worthy causes: family planning, animal rights, Douglas MacArthur Smith.

By the time her guest of honor arrived, Amanda's living room was already full of sweet-smelling women from the Downtown Preservation Society, a group of Marina City residents devoted to good deeds, champagne lunches, and unkind remarks about their absent friends. The organization's stated goal was to clean up the Chicago River so the water that passed beneath their powdered noses would not smell so foul. The organization's actual goal was to make the city a better place for people like themselves, of which there were but a precious few.

They filled the room with glitter and noise, with hair spray and invective. Black and red were their colors of choice, although much was made of the print dress worn by the wife of an advertising man. Gossips flitted from one cluster to another, like bees pollinating willing ears with news of the latest infidelity. Husbands loitered by the cocktail wienies, trying not to look so drunk.

Elmo's job was to look real, carry the money, and smile every fifteen seconds or so, whether he felt like it or not. For a while there, he just sniffed it all in: the Georgio, the Obsession, the Preference by L'Oreal. And another smell lurked just beneath the perfume, the smell of all that hot patootie working into a lather. That was the smell Elmo liked.

Smiling is pretty boring work, and after a while the scents became so mixed together that his nose could no longer sniff any difference between the underfed women wearing jasmine and musk and the elderly women wearing flowers in a bottle. Soon after that, he lost the rhythm of his smile and started to look around instead of just sniffing. Nice tits. Fat ass. He followed one particularly long pair of legs to the hem of the much-talked-about print dress. The garment was kind of like a bag belted tight at the waist, as if the wearer didn't mind that her hips were wider than the rest of her form. Those hips were getting the hairy eyeball from the thin women in black and red who were always slaving it up to exercise videos. Elmo regarded exercise as a way for girls to get hips like a boy and guys to get big muscleman tits. Who needed muscles anyway? That's what tire irons were for.

Elmo ogled her for a moment, measuring the way her flesh shifted around beneath the soft print folds. When his eyes got up to her face, he noticed that she was talking to some guy who was ignoring her and ogling Elmo instead.

"Faggot," he whispered to himself.

Doogie, meanwhile, was talking to a flat. That's what Elmo called the ones with hips like boys that were dishing out the talk about who's got the flattest butt. That's why they called it flattery. The one Doogie was talking to was a little runt who must have weighed less than a hundred pounds, with rusty red hair and freckles. She looked like a sawed-off two-by-four.

Doogie pushed her at Elmo and said, "This is my chairman, Mr. Elmo Givens. He'll take care of you."

She used Elmo's back to write out a check, then left him to the cloud of scent she had produced. He looked at the check before putting it away. The bottom line was a thousand green; the memo line read, "Meet me later?"

"Shit," Elmo said.

How could these women not know that Alderman Douglas MacArthur Smith was a first-class yo-yo. Sure, Elmo liked the guy. They'd been friends for years, which was how come Elmo knew that Doogie was a secret squish. He couldn't fight his way out of a wet paper bag, and the reason he'd poked a million women is because not a single one ever wanted him back for a second time. Now, there he was, wedged between these two flabby flats. That's what Elmo called it when age won out over exercise and the two-by-fours started to sag into empty little bags at the elbow and chin.

One of the flats was wearing so much jewelry she could hardly stand up, while the other was drunk and almost stuck Doogie in the eye with a swizzle stick. Doogie gave them the high hat when the print dress started talking politics to a bunch of drunk husbands who didn't give a rip.

Elmo joined them. He was working on a plan based on two sure things: One of the flats wanted Doogie; so did the one with the print dress and the hips.

Elmo figured he could nail the reject if he played the angles right. These rich ladies were tougher than the girls back in Marquette Park, but he'd been watching Doogie work the flats for the last four years and he was starting to figure out that it must have something to do with nothing. Nothing was the only thing that Doogie ever did, but these women just kept acting like he was their last crack at the Second Coming. Elmo had asked Doogie about women one time and the alderman had said that they love it when you treat them like shit.

Maybe so, but the print dress was different. Doogie was bragging about saving all those granny babushkas that ride the city buses, but the woman with the hips wasn't buying. She wanted to know why the Street Crusaders wore combat boots and combat berets, and was it true that Doogie used to work in a store that sold Nazi books and tapes? Doogie changed the subject.

"There's a war going on down there, and you don't even know it because you live in a tower and drive to the opera in a Mercedes-Benz. You should ride the bus for once like one of those little granny babushkas that live in my neighborhood."

This was greeted by a smattering of applause, the loudest of which came from the husband of the woman in the bright print dress. The woman pressed her case. She said the Street Crusaders were a lot like the Hitler Youth, and Doogie said Hitler got a bad rap and would have been the greatest German ever if he'd stopped after Czechoslovakia.

She said the trouble in the streets was caused by trouble in the home and Doogie said, "These narco-killers have no home. They have nothing left to lose. That's what makes them dangerous. You are quite a piece of work."

Elmo didn't say anything. He just smiled every fifteen seconds, like Doogie had told him to, and listened to the flabby flats.

The one with too much jewelry said, "I want you to know our organization has been very kind to colored people, but I do not always feel that our work is appreciated."

The other one sucked on her swizzle stick. "I admire what this scruffy alderman has done. I always feel safe when I see these young Crusaders of his. When they're around, women of means are not accosted by young ruffians."

Elmo couldn't understand how people who were so dumb

could have so much money. He thought about this and smiled on schedule until Doogie said in a voice he intended to be overheard, "I'm sorry, Mrs. Hayes, but that's just not enough. I wouldn't take anything less than a thousand from a woman as rich as you. It's a pride thing with me. I bet you spent a thousand just on that fine black dress of yours."

Elmo thought he was going to puke. The gathering had too much talk and not enough air, too much wine, cheese, and perfume and not enough action and beer. The loud drunks were getting louder while the quiet drunks became more sullen. Some woman cackled at the top of her lungs at a joke that couldn't have been that funny, and another dropped her cigarette case into the bowl of punch. The occasional husband waited patiently, while the servants walked around with superior attitudes.

Doogie and the hips kept barking at each other over how to save the world until he said something that made her ears turn red and her lips quiver with unexpended rage. Before she could reply, he spun around on his heels and started talking to her husband, buddying up the guy just like he used to buddy up the homos that they ripped off over by Logan Park.

Elmo laughed so hard he forgot to smile. Those were the good old days. Doogie and the homos would get to talking about this and that, and just when they were getting to the part where the fag would grab for Doogie's pud, Elmo would jump out of the bushes and crack the sucker a good one. Only one time Elmo got cornered by a cop, and he didn't get there in time, so Doogie's pud got grabbed real good by this faggot as big as a house. Doogie got pretty mad. Elmo thought it was pretty funny, but he didn't dare laugh. That was the first time he figured out that his friend was really a yo-yo in disguise.

"Your boss is quite the jerk," the woman with the hips announced. All of a sudden, there she was with a glass of wine and this real funny look.

"Yes, ma'am," Elmo said. "The streets can turn a man to stone."

The hips sipped wine and asked him all about it as if she really cared. Elmo tried to treat her like shit but was intoxicated by that hot patootie smell.

Elmo waited out in the car while Doogie did it to the woman with the hips in a second-floor apartment on the Near North Side. The squish turned out to be her husband, who cared a lot less than Elmo about the happenings in his second-floor apartment on Chicago's Near North Side. He walked around the block six or seven times, making a silly smile every time he passed by Elmo's car. He stopped walking after a while and stood there rubbing Elmo's outside mirror as if it were a black plastic tit and he cared about that sort of thing.

"Women," he said.

"What's that?"

The husband stopped rubbing and leaned a little closer. "I admire you fellows. I think you live important lives. I'd like to be important, too."

Elmo started to tremble, caught between his own fear and Doogie's instructions on how to deal with rich people. Over and over again, he had said that you can do just about anything if you're smart and rich enough, and that you can still do just about anything if you're smart enough to give someone rich enough exactly what he wants.

"You seem pretty important to me," he said.

The car started to sweat as soon as the husband slammed the passenger door. Maybe it was his hot breath, or the hot night, or the hot flash of anger that made Elmo want to explode. In any event, a moist film began to coat the windshield of the car. Elmo became very afraid until he managed to calm himself by escaping to the second-story bedroom of his dreams.

The print dress was in tatters and the hips were even more

superb than they had first appeared to be. They rolled like whitewall tires down a bumpy road as he took her from the back. Skin trembled and fluid flowed in the second-story bedroom of Elmo's dreams until Doogie knocked on the window of the car.

"I don't mean to be interrupting, but we got things to do."

16

Killing by the Numbers

THEY PARKED THE BOPPER'S CAR ON COMMERCIAL AVENUE and took a walk along the black asphalt levee that protected Cairo from the water where the rivers of Middle America meet. From the north came the waters of the wide Missouri, the Wisconsin, and the Illinois, while from the east came the Ohio and its many tributaries. To the south it was all just more Mississippi, a lazy float for a steady stream of barges laden with ore and food. Popeye was worried.

"Those boats don't look connected to me. This better be the place."

"The building says Cairo. That's all I can say."

Hammerhead was talking about the Cairo Customs House, a red brick building that was being sandblasted in the unhurried way that seemed to distinguish all activity in the riverfront town. A burly man in goggles and gloves was trying to clean the motto above the Customs House door. Hammerhead was anxious to know what the words would say.

"I don't see where there's anyone to pop around here," he

127

said. "It's like everybody's dead already, only they ain't stopped moving yet."

Sand from the blaster spilled over the levee and started that long and slippery slide down to the Cairo docks. The river was at low mark, taking a rest from the raging floods of the year before. Popeye was having doubts about the caper, but he did not dare to speak of them for fear that to do so would help to make them true. That's how he felt about cops, death, and bad luck—that they would happen if he talked about them. He talked about their contact instead.

"The man with the money said he'd be along at noon. You go see what time it is."

Hammerhead yelled at the sandblaster, who was taking a break from his chores. The sand cloud had settled to earth. Letter by gritty letter, the secret words were revealing themselves: I N G O

"It's half-past eleven almost. Where'd you two guys come from?"

"The city."

"Which one?"

"There's only one."

"Chicago, huh? Gamblers, I suppose. That's something that I could never understand, betting money when you could be drinking it instead. You better take a few steps back, or you'll be sucking stone."

The worker turned on the blaster, and the sand cloud swirled again. He was mucking out a D when a man in desert combat fatigues climbed onto the levee and started walking their way. He was almost as short as Popeye, with almost as many muscles, but his skin was clear and smooth and tanned, like clay that had been worked by hand and left out in the sun to dry. He had still blue eyes, light brown hair, and a toothpick clenched between perfect teeth.

"Tech Sarge is my name," he said, making Popeye figure this meant his name must be something else.

Tech Sarge was a demolitions expert who had blown up the Cong in Asia, the Cubans in Africa, and Muslim fanatics from Tehran to Tripoli. He had made a pretty good living until the Contra money dried up. "I know you must be Popeye, but who's your partner here?"

Hammerhead introduced himself, and Popeye asked the mercenary where the *Connected Yankee* was supposed to be. Tech Sarge laughed, but not the sort of laugh that anyone else was likely to join.

"Connecticut Yankee, you mean. You sure you guys are up to this?"

Popeye said, "No problem," and Hammerhead looked up at the sandblaster and the letters that had been scrubbed from the stone: I N G O D W E T. What seemed to be an R and three more letters remained to be revealed. Sarge shifted his toothpick from one corner of his mouth to the other.

"I don't want to talk right here. There's a place in the trees with a little more privacy. Follow me there, and I'll show you what I've got."

They followed him past shacks and shanties and down a gravel road that dropped into bottom land about five miles north of town. They found themselves in a clearing with a few rotten buildings surrounded by some woods.

Hammerhead said, "This place makes the 'hood look good, like all the stories my mama used to tell about the island where she growed up, with old men sitting on a coconut stump waiting for nothing to happen."

Popeye asked the eternal question. "So what about the *Connected Yankee?"*

Sarge examined his toothpick for evidence of gum disease, then pressed his lips together into something like a smile. "You mean Connecticut?"

"Yankee. Right. That's where the caper's going down."

Sarge unclenched his lips and the half-smile disappeared. "It's a riverboat, like I said. Stops in Cairo twice a week and spends the rest of the time going up and down the Mississippi to East Saint Loo. They don't spend a lot of time in Cairo because it's such a pit."

"Solid. Let's talk about the caper," Popeye said. "You got us a popcorn machine?"

"What's that?"

"A gun."

"Why do you call it a popcorn machine?"

"Because of the sound it makes. Pop-a-dop-pop. Eating popcorn means you're getting killed."

Tech Sarge considered this. A faint twinkle flickered in his still blue eyes until the glacial cold extinguished it. "So you guys must be gangsters."

"That's what the blues would say."

"Well, I don't sell popcorn. And I don't sell popcorn machines. I sell techno-death. Let's take a look at what we got."

The double back doors of the panel truck were sealed with a combination lock that popped open after number right, number left, and number right again. Sarge opened the doors on a portable arsenal, describing the contents in crisp detail.

"We've got a Phrobis knife that'll slice a tomato and saw through steel, just like the knife on late-night TV. We got an HK MP5 submachine gun that the German GSG-9 anti-terrorists use."

Popeye stroked the barrel with a tenderness most men save for their private parts. "Check it out, Head."

Sarge smiled. "Gives you lots of whacking, 700 rounds per, without too much kickback. How many people you want to send to God?"

"I'm only getting paid for one."

"What's his name?"

"What's the difference?"

Tech Sarge took a deep breath and squeezed it hard. The assholes were the main problem with sales. Smart assholes he could stand. Dumb ones were another story. He let the air out and forced a casual tone. "We service special needs. The reason people come to us is that we have the right tool for the right job. What's the job?"

"Elmo didn't tell you that?"

"I don't know who Elmo is, but he didn't tell me a goddamn thing. I just met a guy who gave me some money and said he'd give me more if I came down here and met you at the place where we just met. We can save a lot of time and trouble if you just detail the operation so I can help you pick the proper tool."

Hammerhead watched the rivers while they talked about the caper, and about the man, and the money, and the *Connected Yankee*. The rivers were always moving but never getting anywhere, and the city was stuck between a past that never was and a future that would never be, a past and a future very much like his own. But then he remembered the Old Customs House, and the words of wisdom above its door. IN GOD WET and a word that began with R. Why was God wet? And what word began with R? Was it right or rong or rich or rican, or some other word that began with R but meant much more than he could ever know? Hammerhead knew that if he could solve this puzzle, he could live among the gringo wizards in their downtown towers of glass and steel. Tech Sarge was saying, "All you do is pull the trigger, and it does all the thinking. That's how people get killed these days."

Tech Sarge and Popeye were looking at a stubby black gun that looked like an oversize tommy gun. Popeye listened carefully while the salesman explained. "This is the MM-1—the Street Sweeper, it's called. The laser sight gives you pinpoint accuracy, so if you can point at something, you can hit it, too. Fires a 37-mm, high-explosive bullet. You see that outhouse over there?"

He pointed at a small structure about two hundred yards away. It was tilting at a precarious angle, the wood gray with weather and neglect. Popeye nodded.

"Go ahead. Give it a shot."

Popeye raised the weapon to his shoulder, turned on the laser sight, and slowly squeezed the trigger. The outhouse exploded into smithereens.

"Nice hit, Eye," Hammerhead said.

"He's just the mule," Sarge said. "That's the thing about

techno-death. The mule doesn't need any brains. All he needs is legs to carry the system, a finger to pull the trigger. Any fool can be a killer when you're talking techno-death. You thought about beating a hasty?"

"Beating a what?"

"A hasty retreat. Making an exit. Doing the skedaddle."

Popeye shrugged. "I can run faster than anybody."

The mercenary leaned into the back of his truck and came out with a small canvas bag about the size and shape of a loaf of Wonder Bread. "There's no place to go when you're on one of them boats unless you can run on water. That's why you need one of these."

"What's that?"

It was a self-inflatable, self-propelled, self-sufficient Zodiak raft used by the Navy SEALS. All Popeye had to do was hang on tight, jump overboard, and pull the string. A Zodiak would materialize from the box, and Popeye would be on his way.

"We're killing by the numbers here," Tech Sarge said. "Get the numbers right and you can't go wrong."

17

Bringing Home the Hate

ELMO FELT A BEAD OF SWEAT COLLECT ON THE TIP OF HIS NOSE, then drop into the black puddle that was collecting at his feet. At high noon of Shoe Goo Summer there wasn't a cloud in the sky. Birds were making noise among the manicured elm trees as he waited for Doogie in a parking lot filled with cars that cost more money than his father's house. Elmo leaned against his own dowdy vehicle, feeling bored, tired, and angry because there were too many rules and not enough women after Doogie was done. Doogie was doing all the women, getting all the money, and having all the fun. Hemorrhoids were the only thing Elmo was getting, having to wait in the car while Doogie did something exciting to someone important in some place made of cold gray stones, like the Harrington Hills Country Club. Through a tall window, he could see cool shadows slide through a world he had dreamed about when he was a child. Softly he whispered to himself a single discouraging word, "Shit!"

Things weren't supposed to be like this. When he and Doogie were kids, everything looked different from Marquette Park. Places were made of trees or steel, as seen through television. And people were either very rich and beautiful and talented and funny, or very sad and poor and ugly and unfortunate, as seen through television. The rich ones laughed and danced and lived in houses made of big gray stones and had wacky next-door neighbors with amusing personal problems. The poor ones had either beaten or robbed somebody or had been beaten or robbed by somebody else. If they ever made it on TV, the reason was they were dead in some jungle or on some street, as seen through the single unblinking eye of the television set in Elmo's living room.

Now Doogie lived in televisionland with all of the beautiful people and their wacky neighbors, but Elmo was still a member of the viewing audience. Doogie had consultants and pollsters who helped him make fancy political commercials where he looked sincere, and he attended news conferences and gave interviews where the cameras were always rolling and the reporters were always impressed. Elmo was getting a close look at the wonderful TV world, but he was still stuck in that other world where the women weren't interested and the men were a lot like his father, beer-swilling louts who'd started voting for Roosevelt, Stevenson, and Kennedy, but switched to Nixon after that goddamn Johnson gave it all away to the niggers. Men like this thought Doogie was the greatest kick-ass son a father could ever have, but they didn't think about Elmo at all. Fuck 'em.

He thought of the money. The mercenary would get some for his truck full of techno-death. And Popeye would get some for pulling the trigger. The advertising man would get some for making commercials where Doogie looked sincere, and the TV people would get some for putting them on the air. The pollster would get some for knowing how to count, and the political consultant would get some for smoking his pipe and nodding his head every now and then. The 7-Eleven would get some for supplying the breath mints, and Doogie would get the rest. Elmo would get to wait outside by the car while Doogie talked to some old codger at the Harrington Hills Country Club. Elmo shook his head in disgust, and another bead of sweat flew off his nose and plopped into the puddle at his feet.

Sister Delilah Blue felt the power of the Lord coursing through her veins as the poor in spirit filed into her church, black mamas with plenty of kids and old folks with the look of holy hope in their eyes. Her sermon was all about them, about faith, and growing old. She said faith was like "Hanging on to a trembling vine, a trembling vine of life everlasting. Oh, Lord, we need You to help us hang on tight, hang on tight to the foreverness of Your victory over death, and if You give us Your forever faith, we shall not die, we shall not die. We shall not die a forever death but will come to see the glory of Your shining love for us. Sing it to the Lord, Brother Ishmael Jones."

After church, she shook some hands and counseled some sinners before hurrying away to the mayor's condo on the Near North Side. They sat at the kitchen table on either side of a pot of black coffee and talked about the mayor's chances, about the negs and the positives, and about how they were going to start turning things around real soon.

Willis said, "There's never no hope, but the baditude of his attitude has got to be adjusted. We need to take him out."

They talked about Little Egypt and the Illinois Conference of Local Governments. They'd have dozens of mayors, hundreds of aldermen, and a U.S. senator trapped on a riverboat loaded for food and frivolity. Delilah figured it was a good place to roll some tape, to start popping Doogie with those heavy negs about the Nazi bookstore. Willis had a little hope and a lot of worry.

"I guess I'm going to have to say amen, but there's the law of unextended consequences. There's people in our fair city who'd take a Nazi for a nigger any day."

Delilah refilled his coffee cup and fixed the blinds so the light wouldn't shine in his eyes. She secretly took a guilty pleasure in providing such comforts to the man who, for nearly eight years, had given to her what all other men had not. He had given her a strong shoulder to lean on, and a soft reproach for her tendency to eat too much in times of trouble; a reliable set of sensible beliefs; and the thrill of the unknown brought about by his governance of a city of three million people.

She said, "We've got to jump on Doogie's negs and pump up your own positives."

The mayor laughed. "Like what? The Deep Tunnel Project? I got everybody's problems but my own. Garbage don't get picked up and people blame the mayor. Bus is late and it's the mayor's fault. Same goes for when the snow falls and the bugs bite and the Chicago River springs another leak. You remember what happened to that last Irishman? The only worry Doogie's got is when he should start flapping jaw about city pay hikes and narco-killers, and all the rest of what have you. Hell, I might even be voting him in myself if he wasn't always bringing home the hate. He can have this goddamn job."

Alderman Douglas MacArthur Smith waited in a chair that was more like a throne in a room that was more like a hall. There was a fancy coffee table with a fancy silver bowl filled with chocolates he couldn't pronounce. Something German, he supposed. There were several portraits of grim people hanging on the walls and a huge tapestry so faded with age he couldn't quite see the details.

He grabbed a chocolate and got up to get a better look. The chocolate, like the room and its appointments, had the quiet, confident smell of money that he had detected in everything he saw and touched at the Harrington Hills Country Club. Douglas was learning a lot about money in his quest for control of City Hall.

As his standing in the public-opinion polls improved, he learned that real money belonged to people who never had to prove or improve themselves, to people who knew exactly who they were and believed that they were rich because they deserved to be. He had lately been trying to duplicate in his bathroom mirror their look of tranquil superiority. He thought it might come in handy someday.

Douglas took a bite of the chocolate and looked at the tapestry. The candy tasted sweet and pure and sure of itself, just like their money would taste if you could eat it. The tapestry was something else altogether. Old and tired, it depicted people in funny outfits playing music and dancing in the woods. The boys looked like girls, and the girls looked like angels, and everybody seemed to be having lots of fun, except one girl who sat on a rock and looked at a fallen leaf as if the leaf knew the answer to a riddle.

He regarded the leaf with curiosity while thinking about a riddle of his own. He'd just seen a poll that had shown him to be losing most of the ground he had gained in June. Yes, the people were angry and afraid, and yes, they were tired of seeing the bloodbath on television, and yes, they thought that city life was a nightmare, but no, they didn't think that he had the answer to any of this. Douglas wasn't the answer. Mayor Cleveland wasn't the answer. Money wasn't the answer, and neither was God. Nothing was the answer. That's what the majority of the people believed. A minority disagreed. Douglas had paid $25,000 to a consultant from the National Front to tell him what made that minority tick.

The consultant had said, "If you break things down according to an issue/attitude coefficient, we can detect a positive correlation between two negative perceptions."

Say what?

"The worse people feel about themselves, the better they feel about you."

This riddle was perplexing Douglas when a servant came up to him and said, "If you'll please come this way, sir."

He was led through two tall double doors into a room in

which five old men were arrayed in a crescent around a round table cut in half. The sawed-off side of the semicircle contained only a single chair, just like the one outside on which Douglas had been contemplating his June poll results. A man with white hair and liver spots told him to sit down, make himself comfortable.

"Thank you for coming, Mr. Alderman. We appreciate your joining us."

Douglas noticed that the man's hands were trembling and decided that he couldn't be nervous so he must be sick, sick of what, he couldn't say. Maybe too much fancy food.

"We've conducted a survey of public opinion," the man with the liver spots said. "We don't live in the city, but we do have certain investments to protect. So we work together when the cause is right. We've followed your career. Is your cause right?"

"Yes sir," Douglas began. "I believe it is."

They talked about issues for an hour and a half. About the disturbing trend in this or that and about the utter foolishness of something or other. The nation was being destroyed by easy credit and subsidized malingering. Welfare moms were being paid to have children, and welfare dads were dealing drugs to welfare kids who killed each other at an alarming rate but were taking over the country anyway. The old men did most of the talking and Douglas mostly agreed.

"Our genetic pool is being polluted."

"You're right."

"The kids are crazy and the schools are turning into lunatic asylums."

"That's just what I'm talking about."

"The workingman doesn't work anymore."

"You're right."

"We need to save more and spend less."

"That's just what I'm talking about."

Douglas smiled at all the right things and scowled at all the wrong ones. He didn't laugh at anything because that would have violated one of his most important rules. Don't make jokes around rich people because they never give money to comedians. When the interview was over, the man with the liver spots propped up his hands into a trembling steeple. Polished fingernails made the spire glisten.

"Thank you, alderman," he said. "You'll get a large number of small contributions, and we trust you'll spend it wisely."

Mrs. Cleveland had to bang the pan harder and harder before her husband noticed that she was there.

"What's for dinner, hon?"

She said she didn't know yet, that she was torn between chili and stew. Willis said he loved her stew and then listened to Delilah run on and on about constituent profiles. Mrs. Cleveland hated profiles, polls, and public relations because they reminded her that while she got all the sex, Delilah got all the conversation. Mrs. Cleveland had long since passed the point where she preferred sex to conversation, but her duty to her people and her city and her man required that she accept her lot without complaint. Eavesdropping was allowed, however.

Her husband said, "What you're saying is we got one poll says Doogie's stuck and another one says he's on the move. We need to leak the one that says he's stuck and worry a lot about the other one. That's the one what's true. Talk to me about the paid media."

Delilah didn't want to talk about the paid media. The subject was too depressing. One commercial showed the mayor wading through a stack of papers on his desk. Another showed him walking through the Deep Tunnel Project while a narrator recalled the summer that mosquitos had infested the city. A basso profundo made it sound like one of the plagues that God had wrought through Moses. "Now he's facing tomorrow with a five-point program to put more police officers on the street." With that he turned the spigot and the Deep Tunnel rumbled to life. The sun set over the Hancock Center and all was right with the Near North

Side. The lakefront liberals could sleep in peace and Delilah still had her apartment on the thirty-second floor.

"Mosquitos won't win this thing," she said. "We'll be killing bugs while Doogie's killing us. I heard he's bought about a gross of 30-second prime time for the first week in September. That's when the stations'll all be juiced for the sweeps."

Willis sipped his coffee and watched his wife chop away at some food. She was stuffing the stew with vegetables so he wouldn't have a heart attack. He'd spend half of dinner poking through the greens and looking for a piece of meat.

He said, "How much time we got?"

"We can match him three to one on the thirties and still have a bunch of those fifteens left."

"That's the one with the family?"

Mrs. Cleveland chopped on a carrot so hard that the fat end made like a sling shot across the counter and into the sink.

"Nice shot," Delilah said. "We got all the time we need. What we need is something to say."

Another carrot top landed in the sink. Willis knew she was getting mad, but he couldn't quite figure out why. He said, "It's not a good year for that feel-good stuff. Folks're too mad to start feeling good. That's where Doogie be hitting us hard. The poor trash'll think he's one of them, and rich trash'll think he can keep the peace while they go on vacation."

Willis pushed himself away from the table. His knees felt like rusty hinges as he stood up, walked across the kitchen, and poked his nose at the stew. He gave his wife a little squeeze.

"The people listen but they do not hear," she said.

"Thanks, hon. I'll remember that. What about the TV dudes?"

Delilah shrugged. "I'm sadly disappointed. I'm afraid I've got to say that all they got is some well-done tape of Doogie on a roll: helping kids, helping grannies, talking tough, looking good. We already spent about ten on them. We can dump them if you want."

Another carrot top shot across the counter, but Willis grabbed it before it hit the sink and scraped out a little bite of orange carrot meat. "We can wait on that for one more week while we go down and do this paddleboat thing. Rumor and insinuendo. That's what'll win it this time."

18

Cabbage with a College Degree

ALWAYS CHANGING AND ALWAYS THE SAME, THE RIVERS OF MID-
dle America converged and disappeared, converged and
disappeared. Where did the water come from and where did
the water go? How did a town like Cairo get to be at such a
place and why was it such a dump? Hammerhead suspected
that the answers to these and other questions had been
sandblasted out of the stone above the door of the Old Cairo
Customs House.

IN GOD WET RUST. Hammerhead said it to himself over and
over again, like one of those decades of the rosary his Mama
used to pray when she needed God in a hurry.

"What's that?"

"Nothing, Eye. I didn't say shit."

Popeye let it go. He was too busy watching the water to
talk about something with the Head that the Head didn't
want to talk about. The kid was getting to be a little punk, so
breaking up was going to be best for all around. Popeye
would get to keep all the taxes, and Hammerhead could keep
the car and Bilbo, too. That was proper.

"Check it out, Eye."

Popeye couldn't see most things because the sun had been swallowed by a southeast Missouri cornfield, but he could see the glimmer of a light on the river of dark that flowed before his eye. When closer, it produced the first faint sounds of the uneasy kind of noise white people make when they're working on some fun: shrill laughter, twangy music, loud voices trying to impress. It sounded as if all the light and joy that Cairo didn't have had jumped aboard a big old raft and paddled north against the flow. Now, after many adventures, the raft was coming back home and bringing the magic along.

Nat and Allan hitched a ride on a plane chartered by the Association of North Suburban Democratic Mayors. As most of the mayors and councilmen of the north suburbs were lifelong Republicans, the plane had plenty of room for Nat, Allan, and the boxes full of TV monitors, cameras, and editing gear they had brought along for the ride. They had packed their equipment in Styrofoam peanuts, but nothing could protect them from the constant chatter of their fellow passengers.

"What a place to hold a conference."

"That's why they call it a political *party*."

"I've never been on a riverboat before."

"I heard everybody dresses like people in a book."

"What's a book?"

"It's television with pages."

"Government should *not* be in the gambling business."

"It's a way to get taxes without any pain."

"No pain for who?"

"For the mayors, of course."

"I heard the Peanut isn't laughing much."

"Who's that?"

"Mayor Cleveland, I mean. Haven't you ever seen his head? It's like a peanut that grew some hair."

"Come on."

"You check. Take a look. Like a big black peanut that was left out in the sun too long. Ha! Ha!"

"So how come he's not laughing?"

"Because Doogie Smith's gonna be there too. I heard he's been racking up the points, that one poll has him at 32 and another at 38. It's all over if he hits 45 because the momentum will take him home from there."

"Doogie can't win. No way."

"He might. You can never tell about no-man's-land, and that's where the swing votes are."

"That's true."

"You're right."

"You can never tell."

"I'm just glad I live in the burbs. The worst we got is Republicans. Ha! Ha!"

In the sluggish heat of an August morning, the *Connecticut Yankee* looked like a calliope that had run out of steam. The huge rear paddle was still and the brass band was taking a break. Politicians loitered around a banner that read WELCOME ILLINOIS CONFERENCE OF LOCAL GOVERNMENTS, but their conversation was muted, as if they were discussing public business they did not want the public to hear. A tall man with a long white coat, a big white hat, and a short white beard advertised the historical flavor for which the stern-wheeler was becoming famous. He tipped his wide-brimmed hat at the passersby and regaled them with his wit and wisdom.

"Welcome aboard the *Connecticut Yankee*. We have all the modern inconveniences. Be good and you will be lonesome. Cauliflower is cabbage with a college degree. Man is the only animal that blushes and the only animal that needs to. You can't pray a lie. When in doubt, tell the truth. My name is Samuel Langhorne Clemens, but you can call me Mark Twain. The reports of my death are greatly exaggerated."

Allan fussed over the boarding passes with a ticket agent dressed like Huckleberry Finn while Nat supervised the handling of the peanuted boxes that contained their fragile television gear. Most of the heavy lifting was done by a large black porter dressed in a straw hat and tattered clothes. He wore thick nylon slippers meant to give the impression that his feet were bare.

They followed the porter onto the boat where they were greeted by Tom Sawyer and directed to their room by his girlfriend Becky. They walked past a cleaning woman dressed as the Pauper and a blackjack dealer dressed as the Prince. When they reached the confines of their room, Allan scarfed down the chocolate mint that was resting on his pillow and read out loud from a brochure with a picture of Twain on the cover and emblazoned with letters made of glossy brown logs.

WELCOME ABOARD THE
CONNECTICUT YANKEE

A limited historical gambling permit, authorized by vote of THE ILLINOIS LEGISLATURE, gives our guests the chance to see the Mississippi as it used to be. Harken back to simpler times when the river was the backbone of America and Cairo was the place where East meets West. This riverboat is dedicated to a young pilot by the name of Samuel Langhorne Clemens, who navigated these waters many years ago and went on to write classic stories of comedy and adventure under the name of Mark Twain. Meet Huck and Jim, the Prince and the Pauper, Tom Sawyer and his girlfriend Becky. See midnight performances of *Showboat* in the Pudd'nhead Wilson ballroom. Enjoy your stay and remember that, even if you lose your shirt, it's a contribution to the ILLINOIS STATE TREASURY.

Allan blew out a lungful of air to let Nat know it was his turn to say something. Nat didn't speak for fear it would only encourage Allan, who was encouraged anyway.

"I think I've finally got it figured out. Women, I mean, and how it is they're always so mad all the time. At men, I mean."

He blew out another lungful of air. The carbon dioxide

mingled with the heat and made it hard to breathe. The heat was different in Little Egypt, not as oily as the city heat. But the air was so dry it made his tongue feel as if it were going to crack. Even talking to Allan was better than thinking about the heat.

"Okay, Allan. You tell me. How come women are always so mad?"

Allan had crumpled the brochure into a sort of martinet's baton, which he waved under his partner's chin.

"Because we give them everything they want and it still doesn't make them happy. First, they wanted careers, but all they got was work. Then they wanted sensitive guys, but all they got was weenies. I don't know what they want next, but that won't make them happy, either."

Nat stuck his head out the porthole and took a whiff of river air. It smelled of moss and fallen leaves, of life and death on the Mississippi. He spoke softly, so Allan couldn't hear. "You know, you could be right. I'll have to remember that."

"What's that? What did you say?"

"I said I'm going out for a walk. Be back in a little while."

They drove all the way to Thebes to rip off that town's Get N' Go in the middle of a Tuesday afternoon. The clerk was more astounded than frightened and thought they must be stupid or crazy or both. He offered to split the cash and give them a half-hour start, but Popeye said no, that cash and a partner were not part of the caper. They drove back to Cairo with a full tank of gas, ten microwave submarine sandwiches, and an entire stand-up display case of Hostess pastry products, minus the Twinkies. Those had been sold out.

Hammerhead said. "The man's got it right to think you're crazy. We're sitting here eating Ding Dongs when we could be collecting some taxes. Maybe even a hundred bucks."

"We don't need the money."

Popeye saw the worry on Hammerhead's face. "Hey, I'm just kidding, little blood. We always got to get our taxes.

Money's the dick that fucks the world, but we need to lay low until the caper happens."

As they drove in silence between fields of corn, Popeye watched a TV show in the back of his head. Fat guys with big cigars sat at a big table in a golden room telling each other how rich and powerful and lucky they were until one of them exploded and then all of his rich, powerful, lucky friends tried to brush the mashed and bloody bits from their other otherwise unsoiled lapels.

Hammerhead also thought about death, about Popeye's and his own. He dared not talk about it until he saw the vast expanse of the river delta and the cornfields beyond that wouldn't quit. "It's like you can see forever, but there's nothing there. This place gives me the creepies."

Popeye didn't reply because he didn't want Hammerhead to know that he had the creepies, too. They drove in silence to the parking lot above Cairo Dock and then walked to the levee, where they watched and waited, waited and watched. The paddleboat was just like the Cairo Customs House. The letters on it made words, but the words didn't make any sense.

Hammerhead said, "So that's how you spell Connecticut. Doesn't look right to me."

"How?"

"What?"

"Do you spell Connecticut."

"C-O-N-N-E-C-T-I-C-U-T. That guy with the gun called it the *Connecticut Yankee*. What's that?"

Popeye shook his head. "Shit, man, I don't know. You're the one knows how to read. Maybe he was lying. Still looks like it's Connected to me."

"What you going to do with your taxes?"

Popeye thought about it but didn't say a word. First, he figured to go to Florida, blow it all on getting high and getting laid, and dancing to some of that Miami Sound Machine. Then he figured that didn't make much sense because if he was really going to be rich he might as well act like it. So he decided he'd take his nineteen thou, five hundred and buy himself that restaurant where he and his uncle used to work, and if any money *was* left over after that, he'd buy himself a brand-new car that didn't still smell like Billy the Bopper. But he didn't say any of this to Hammerhead. All he said was, "I'll be spending mine on me. That's what taxes're for."

Hammerhead looked at the *Connecticut Yankee,* but instead of a paddleboat, he saw a world full of things he couldn't afford and people he couldn't understand. "When do we go to work?"

"We're not going anywhere. I'm going down to the river, and you got to stay with the car. Wait for me. If I don't come back for five whole years, that's how long you wait."

"Where do I sleep and what do I eat? I don't have any green."

"You don't need any green. You got a case of Ding-Dongs and some sandwiches. When they run out, you got a gun and a car to go rob stores. Just remember how you never take any money. You take some food and gas, and they don't care, but the police are very serious about people who steal money. So what are the other things I told you about stealing?"

Hammerhead remembered his lessons. Use a gun and never go back to the same place twice. Hammer figured that if the Eye didn't get back right away Little Egypt might run out of Get N' Gos pretty quick and he'd have to drive all the way up to East St. Louis.

They traded some punches and called each other names in one of those awkward good-byes said by men who like each other but are afraid to show it. Popeye headed down to the dock while Hammerhead parked Billy the Bopper's car out behind an old house that had been left to rot. He made his camp in a field of corn, watching the day turn into night and listening to Bilbo eat, shit, and chew steel. The corn was hot, dusty, and in need of rain, almost popping on the cob. Parched corn husks crinkled every time he moved. Crinkle, crinkle, crack. Crinkle, crinkle, crack. Like the sound of a big fire snapping in the dry still of a nowhere night.

Shortly after midnight, a big wind rolled over the river

and blew all the clouds away. The sky wasn't empty anymore, but full of all those stars the Head could never touch.
So he munched on another submarine sandwich and
mushed down some more Ding-Dongs, thinking all the time
about the things to remember when robbing an all-night
grocery store.

Belowdecks was the last place Nat thought to look for that
special someone to be found in every large gathering of
strangers. This particular gathering was around gaming
tables set up in a large room without any windows. It was so
pumped up with oxygen and indirect lighting that the mind
took flight while the body cast no shadow, as if the throng
had ascended into heaven.

She was sitting at the roulette wheel, her elbows prying a
space between a pair of dark blue suits who seemed oblivious to both her beauty and the wheel, as they babbled on
over her head about local zoning problems. Her eyes became
like big brown BBs when the master of the table spun the
wheel and launched the pea on its way. Scratch at the felt
with one hand. Rattle the chips with the other. Grit your
teeth. Chew your lips. Hold your breath. Relax.

"Seventeen red's a winner. Red seventeen."

Nat lost sixty-eight dollars at the blackjack table before
the blue suits gave it up. He made good use of the time,
working out exactly how he wanted to proceed. This was not
the right place for the Caribbean diplomat routine. Too bad.
He had found successful women to be particularly suscepti-
ble to one-night stands with suspected communists. A lot
like screwing the devil, only they could walk away in the
morning and didn't have to go to hell. Not tonight, dear. He
decided to be himself, and when the time came, he moved
with the same gangly ease he displayed while shooting video
at the scene of a crime without getting any blood on his
shoes.

He said, "The Russians are the ones that got this figured."

"Will the players now place their bets?"

She smiled, but he couldn't tell if it was at her luck or his remark. "When they play, the odds are better and the loser's troubles are over. My name's Nat Puchinski."

She seemed fascinated, but again he couldn't tell if it was at his remark or at the chances of winning a ten-dollar bet on forty-two black. She pushed a chip onto that square and waited for the spin without saying a word. She neither moved, blinked, nor breathed, but her eyes followed the progress of the pea as it rolled, then bounced, then spun for what must have been forever. Only when it became perfectly clear that the ball had not landed on forty-two black did she turn to Nat and say, "Okay. So go play Russian roulette."

She lost four hundred more dollars and drank two more glasses of wine. Nat drank more but lost less. The more charming he became, the more repelled she was by the easy confidence with which he was making love.

"You remind me of what the philosopher said."

"Which philosopher was that?"

"Allan Shanahan and he's an is, not a was."

The man spinning the wheel made a last call for bets before launching the pea. They lost.

"What did he say?"

"Who?"

"Allan Shanahan."

"He said modes of female hostility are a consequence of interpersonal frictions resulting from disappointment at the results of a well-documented but henceforth futile male indulgence in various vicarious female aspirations."

"What?"

"He said women are mad at men because we give you everything you ask for and it still doesn't make you happy."

While the mayors climbed aboard the *Connecticut Yankee,* Popeye hid behind a newspaper and sat on a suitcase that contained the laser-guided gun with exploding bullets and the Zodiak inflatable raft. He'd never seen so many smiles on so many white guys having fun with their skinny ties and their fat guts made soft with age and easy living.

The suits were being helped aboard by an old man with a white goatee who kept shouting things that didn't make sense, things like "It's a difference of opinion that makes horse races," and "Nothing so needs reforming as other people's habits."

Off to the side was a black guy dressed in ragged threads who seemed to be in charge of the luggage. Popeye watched him closely and waited for the mayor, who arrived in a hurry just after dark in a long black car driven by some freakin' Rican cop.

Rican cops were the worst of all. This one took his orders from a thick black mama with torpedo tits. Popeye knew he was a cop, but he didn't know why he knew. Maybe it was the cheap sunglasses, or maybe it was the baggy suit or the forty-weight oil he put in his hair, or the way he sneered at the funky old man in the white suit who wouldn't shut up.

"Soap and education are not as sudden as a massacre, but they are more deadly in the long run."

The mayor thought this was funny, but the woman thought it was stupid. So she shooed the two men aboard the boat and left the black guy in ragged threads to worry about their bags. The old white man and his black companion followed them onto the boat. They were greeted there by cheers, applause, and the kind of noise that Pollacks love, where fat tubas do musical battle with happy accordions. Popeye took this distraction as a chance to drag his suitcase over by the boarding ramp and set it in a pitch-black shadow formed by its juncture with Cairo Dock. There he waited some more as silent lights slid up and down the great black rivers which converged in the night somewhere.

The boat wouldn't leave until 3:00 A.M. That's what Tech Sarge had said. Popeye couldn't read, but he could tell time and something was creepy about 3:00 A.M. He thought of the three in "three's the charm" and the three in the Holy Trinity, like the priests used to say in Puerto Rico. Three in the morning was the point of no return, when it's too late to go to sleep and too early to collect any taxes because the chumps are all asleep. The other thing that was creepy about 3:00 A.M. was the way the big hand stands on the little one and does a slow-motion tumble to 3:15.

Popeye checked his popcorn machine. It was digging into his back, making it sore. He switched it to his side pocket, and it started digging into his crotch, so he held it in his hands for a while, like a loaf of bread for mama. Give a boy a fish and he'll eat tonight, but give a boy a popcorn machine and he'll eat until he points it at some crazy Korean with terminal cancer and nothing to lose but his pain. All gangs start with a gun. It is both their confession and their communion because guns are what raise gangsters above all the other poor chumps who take it lying down. Guns are a deal you make with yourself: I will die young, but with the proper respect.

The voices in Popeye's head were silenced by the voices moving down the ramp. Two white men dressed like Huckleberry Finn were pushing a cart full of ashes and dirt and empty beer bottles. They dumped the trash into a bin, shared a few puffs from the same cigarette, and then climbed back onto the boat. They repeated the ritual several times over the next hour or so until the party quieted down and the suits stopped making a mess. They were making one final trip down the ramp when Popeye picked up the suitcase and stepped out of the shadow.

"There's this bag you forgot over there. Looks like it goes with a very rich dude."

The two Hucks looked at one another. "Give it here then," the smaller one said.

"Wrong," Popeye replied. "I figure there's a reward and that it belongs to me. I'll have words with the man in charge, and then I'll be on my way."

"Well, let's go then and don't be slow. We're leaving in fifteen minutes and you got to be off the boat by then."

The big paddles at the rear of the stern-wheeler churned a thick backwash from the black water of the muddy Mississippi. The white foam captured the moonlight and trailed the boat with the persistence of an imperfect memory, always churning up new bubbles that were always disappearing into a past that wouldn't quit.

The woman was like a just-opened bottle of well-shaken beer, crazy with foam that could make your head spin. She regarded the sleeping Nat through the blue smoke of a cigarette that never touched her lips. She remembered the other men she'd known, the tax lawyer from Toledo and Edward C. Vaugh of the FBI. She remembered the systems analyst with the slightest lisp and the drugstore clerk who was really an actor in search of the perfect role. Mostly she remembered the economist she'd met in school, a callow boy smitten by stats who attempted to quantify orgasms as if they were a key indicator of the gross domestic product.

"That was a nine," he used to say or, "That was only a six. Honey, are you okay?" She remembered the economist best because they had been married for seventeen years until she dumped him for the lawyer, who dumped her for a law clerk fresh out of school.

With his olive skin and radical views, Nat was everything they were not, and nothing that they were. He was part of that happier world in which people loved to sing and dance and laugh and screw and the real fun didn't cost a thing. She pressed her lips around the cigarette and used a few strands of her hair to tickle the tip of his nose.

When he was awake she said, "Let's get one thing straight right now. You didn't get away with anything. I *chose* to be seduced just like I *chose* that dress over there."

She nodded at a crumpled pile on the floor, where she had dropped her clothes in haste several hours before.

"Yes, mum," Nat replied, forgetting for a moment that he wasn't a Caribbean diplomat this time. "I'll be off now, then."

The cost accountant snuffed out her cigarette. "Not so fast," she said. "I *choose* to be seduced again."

19

Bulljive with a Mensch

DAWN CAME TO THE RIVER AND PUT ALL THE BIRDS IN A TIZZY AS the *Connecticut Yankee* paddled north against the southbound current. The early business of a country morning started in earnest when a company of Hucks and a platoon of Jims began moving food and flatware into place for the mayors and alderman from all around the state who were waking from their slumber. As gray dawn gave birth to shimmering day, the officials came to roost on wrought-iron tables that had been painted white and bolted to the main deck under pale yellow canopies that fluttered like buttercups in the breeze.

Aldermen of every size and shape milled around the deck and jostled for position along the rail to watch the river chew at the high bank on the Missouri side. Mayors of every opinion and disposition collided with one another while waiting for the food to be served.

The abundance of politicians who had gathered for the conference established a strange chemistry on the main deck. Before long each of the wrought-iron tables had been turned into a mini-city of sorts, each with its own elected official, its own protocol, its own cadre of hangers-on. Alderman Smith presided over a table attended by Elmo, who said, "Goddamn!"

Douglas was poking at a stack of flapjacks. Elmo had finished his own meal and was coveting the alderman's leftovers. Douglas said, "What's your problem now?"

"This boat. I'm glad I'll be getting off it soon. Where's my stop again?"

"Some jerkwater town called Thebes. Sarge'll meet you there and drive you back to Pilot's Point. You can watch from there."

"Good. This boat gives me the heebie-jeebies."

Douglas speared some flapjack on his fork but didn't eat it right away. "You were born with the heebie-jeebies. I mean sometimes I think you *are* the heebie-jeebies. It's all that coffee you drink."

Elmo looked at his cup. It was empty. "You saying this boat don't bother you? You got all these niggers dressed in rags, and it seems like we're hardly moving. Going against the river like this, the boat's got to bust a nut just to stay still. That bother you?"

With a slow but steady motion, Douglas lifted the fork to his mouth and loaded some flapjack in. He watched Elmo's reaction as he chewed. "The only thing that bothers me is the way you're always looking at my food."

For a while Elmo looked at the river instead, and then he looked at the riverbank. He looked at the politicians shuffling around the deck, and he looked at the puffs of smoke that the riverboat's engine was launching into the early morning sky. He looked at the endless grind of the paddle wheel and at the trail of foam it left behind. But no matter now many things he looked at, his eyes always came back to the leftover flapjacks on the alderman's plate.

He said, "The clothes are the thing that really bothers me. Like that old codger that's always walking around and talking to himself and the girls all dressed as boys and what about these dudes waiting on tables in straw hats, rags, and shit."

Douglas put his fork down and pushed himself away from his plate. Elmo stopped thinking about the crew and started thinking about the flapjacks again.

"Read a book, Elmo. Read a book for once."

"Why would I want to do that?"

Douglas didn't have an answer to that. Before he could make one up, a young man dressed as Huck's friend, Jim, came over and asked him if he was done with his meal. Douglas smiled at Elmo, whose heart sank when his friend nodded and the waiter carried the leftovers away.

"Because you're dumb as a breadstick, Elmo. That's why you should read a book. If you read a book you'd know what's going to happen when the dirty deed gets done. Niggers like to riot when they get mad, and if they don't we'll start it up ourselves. Torch a few cars, kill a Jew or two, and beat up some little Korean sap with a grocery store where all the jungle bunnies live. Don't take that much to make it look like the whole goddamn city's on fire. TV takes a little bit of trouble and spreads it everywhere. Speaking of trouble, there's that woman with the fat behind that does all the mayor's thinking. I wonder what they're talking about. My ears are burning, so it must be me."

Willis was the only mayor on the boat whose assembly of hangers-on included other mayors. At his table were the black mayors of Oak Park and Maywood and the Jewish mayor of Lincolnwood, an aging mensch with a schoolboy crush on the mayor's press secretary.

"I really like your media."

Delilah pretended to like it too. "We're trying to avoid the heavy negatives. Don't want too much bitter in the bile. Makes it hard to govern."

The mayor of Lincolnwood nodded at her chest. "My biggest problem is the stop sign on Touhy Avenue. I don't even have to campaign anymore. Haven't had an opponent since 1978."

"Maybe Doogie'll move to Lincolnwood after we kick his butt."

"There's people with money saying that won't happen."

"We'll find out at the League debate. We've got a month to go to B.J. Day."

"B.J.?"

"That mean's bulljive. Some of that nigger talk."

This got the attention of the black mayors of Oak Park and Maywood, who had been filling Willis's ears with muck about west suburban enterprise zones. They were anxious to see if the word nigger would cause the *mensch* to squirm.

He didn't squirm but neither did he take it all in stride. With a great flurry of manicured hands, he flagged down a Huckleberry Finn and ordered Bloody Marys all around, then launched into a Jewish parable about the man with the broken mandolin.

Willis didn't listen to the Jewish parable but sipped his drink and watched the river flowing by. He could imagine all that mud floating south to make a big impression on New Orleans and leaving the country with its insides hollowed out. Where did all the mud come from? Someday, some way, the country would have to run out of that Mississippi mud and the only thing left behind would be the stones and the mountains the river had sucked clean.

"You know what scares me about that town?"

The parable was finished, and the mayors were talking about Cairo now, each making much of how its dreary condition compared with that of their own communities. "Used to be bigger than Chicago, back when the barge was king. That was 1840 or sometime thereabouts, but then they built the railroads and Cairo took a slide."

He stopped for a moment and the other mayors laughed, albeit nervously and without a lot of gusto. Each depended in his own way upon Chicago's fate and was anxious that its mayor should not become depressed.

"So talk about my day."

Delilah took her time fetching the schedule from her purse. This gave the suburban mayors a chance to bolt down their drinks and start saying their good-byes.

When they were gone, she said, "It's pretty much whatever you want it to be, with a certain couple of things where you don't have any choice. The dinner won't start until 7:00 P.M. I've got us tickets for the matinee of *Showboat,* and I'll be going to the seminar on how to buy time on cable TV. You should do the photo op."

"Which photo op is that?"

"Shaking hands with Mark Twain. We can send some laser photos to City Hall and run them over to the papers in time for the morning edition."

Willis made an ugly face. "I need to think about that. Wasn't it just when we was in school that *Huckleberry Finn* was racist. I'm concerned about the author's political correctitude."

"Mark Twain's okay. The black pundit over at the *Trib* just wrote how Huck was really this little black kid from Hannibal, Mo. Nigger Jim's a hero and Mark Twain's okay."

"Maybe. Only things're always changing lickety-split. Next year Twain'll be incorrect again, but that photo'll still be around. No. What else is going on?"

"Your speech?"

"What about it?"

"The senator will give his speech first, and you're on after him. Try to be nice, okay?"

"That could be a problem."

It almost always was. The mayor and the senator did not get along, thanks to a personality conflict that was exacerbated by their respective positions as the two most powerful Democrats in the state.

Delilah sighed, but Willis didn't notice, so she sighed a little louder. "We don't need another tussle right now."

Willis drained his drink and crunched his celery stalk. "Man gets elected on the family name and then puts them all to shame. It's a sad commentation on the democratic process. You can put that in my speech."

"I can but I won't."

"You will if I tell you to."

"Maybe but I've got something that's better than that."

Delilah dipped into her purse for a yellowing copy of a

speech Douglas had given years before to the West Side Community Action Council. In addition to the usual stuff about crime and drugs, the speech contained passing praise for one Marshall Robertson Hill.

The mayor looked up from the speech. "I know I heard that name, but I can't remember where."

Pleased with herself, Delilah smiled. "He led the march on Skokie."

Willis squinted at the river, but he was looking at the past instead. Skokie was a northern suburb inhabited by thirty or forty thousand Jews, many of whom had survived the Holocaust. In 1977, the American Nazi Party asked for a permit to march down its streets. The ACLU came to their rescue when the city denied them a permit. An unconstitutional abridgement of the freedom of speech, they said. Even Nazis have a right to be heard, they said. The truth is its own best defense, they said, and a lie is its own worst enemy.

Willis said, "You are the straw that stirs the drink. The pot that cooks the stew. Write me up a few remarks and make it some of that hellfire hollering you be doing at the faithful on a Sunday afternoon."

20

You Got to Be Invisible

THE RIVERBOAT PADDLED INTO THEBES SHORTLY AFTER NOON, and twenty minutes later it paddled out again, minus one passenger and another load of trash. From Popeye's hiding place behind a crate of canned semisweet chocolate, the *Connected Yankee* appeared to be an engine for churning things that smelled good into things that smelled bad. Grumpy Hucks and bitter Jims would deliver Hefty bags of garbage into a trash compactor and take away carts full of shrimp cocktail or Jell-O or pie or cans of semisweet chocolate, which the cooks made into a dessert listed on the menu as mississippi mud.

Popeye remembered the whole routine from that restaurant where he used to work before he decided he'd rather be a thief and live in a car than clean up the gunk that old men cough up from their lungs. When he was in charge, he wouldn't let anybody spit in the ashtrays, and the cigar smokers had better show respect, or they'd be out the door.

He checked the disposable watch he'd stolen from the novelty rack at the Effingham Get N' Go. He'd have to make a decision soon, but both of his options were wrong. He looked at his hands, but that didn't help. The Hucks were too light and the Jims were too dark and the Beckys were out of the question. A man needed to have some pride. He'd learned that much in the restaurant where he and his Uncle Willie used to work.

Martino's, it's called. Suits eat there all the time, and Wilfredo is a waiter who gets him a job setting up tables and cleaning them off when they're done making a mess. The brown hockers are the worst part, great gobs of rubbery spit from the lungs of suits who smoke cigars, but for as long as it lasts, he makes three twenty-five an hour and another five dollars a day in tips.

Then he makes the mistake of laughing at a joke made at a table full of suits who work at American Federal Savings and Loan, which is the kind of bank that does business with companies instead of people because people are unpredictable. The suits are all just sitting there with their red faces and their big cigars and their rubbery hockers when one of them says, "So Mikes pulls out his hose and takes a pee on Paddy's grave and while he did it he says, 'Only I hope you don't mind if I strain it through me kidneys first.'"

He doesn't really laugh at the joke, but at the laughter itself. Their laughter is so loud and uncontrolled that it infects him with hysterics, which last until he notices that the suits have all stopped laughing and are staring at him in a curious way. He doesn't get many tips that day.

Later his Uncle Willie explains, "You don't laugh and you don't talk unless they're talking to you and then you say yes or no or Thank you, sir. You don't say anything else, and you never look them in the eyes. If you talk to a suit, you look at his shoes, and you don't talk until he talks first. That's the invisible thing to do. You're a good boy, but you got to be invisible. You work real hard, and you don't be laughing, and you might even get to be waiter someday."

He tries it for a week or two, looking at shoes and moving among the drunken suits with a towel draped over his arm until he's assigned to the table of an angry man who sits alone and stares at something that isn't there. The man drinks three martinis and smokes a pack of cigarettes, but he doesn't touch his food, so Popeye comes over to wipe up this big brown hocker from an ashtray full of butts and dirt.

"What the hell you doing, boy?"

"I'm cleaning the table, sir," he says with his eyes fixed on the angry man's shoes. "You didn't eat your lunch, sir. Maybe I could put it in a doggie bag."

He stresses the words doggie bag, which is a busboy's way of treating the customers like the customers treat him. The angry man doesn't like it much.

"Maybe I'll put your face in a bag and feed it to my goddamn dog."

Popeye nods at the man's shoes and moves on to the next table. After work he tells Wilfredo all about it and his uncle says that he'd done a good job and that some customers are trouble and there was nothing much a busboy could do.

Popeye figures if that's the best a busboy can do, he'd rather be a punk, so he joins the Alone Unknown. His mother becomes very upset, but he thinks Wilfredo understands. After that come the capers and the taxes; the ice pick and the glass eyeball; the respect of kids and the funny nickname. And after that comes the joint and the Dick and the doctor who says he's going blind. And after that comes a friend of a friend of a friend from the joint with a job, a caper that'll make him rich if he's not afraid to die.

Shortly after 3:00 P.M., a Huck made the decision that Popeye couldn't make by walking his way with a crowbar and instructions to make a vat full of mississippi mud. He began to apply the crowbar to the crate that Popeye was hiding behind.

After a quick check to make sure no one else was coming through the kitchen door, Popeye jumped on the Huck with a karate kick in the gut. The gangster stepped aside while the busboy threw up something that looked like too much chicken-fried steak. The Huck started coughing and tried to

catch his breath, but before he could Popeye dragged him
behind the crate.

"What's your name?"

He could have done worse. This Huck's hair was straight,
but at least it was black, and his skin was more yellow than
pink, which was as close to color as some guys got. He
coughed out some puke and sucked in some air.

"Eddie Gravas."

"Gravas? What kinda name is Gravas?"

Before the Huck could answer, Popeye stuffed one sock
into the busboy's mouth and tied it in place with the other.
"Take off your clothes, Eddie, unless you want to die."

When the Huck had removed his straw hat and his
uniform rags, Popeye tied him to a pipe with his own
shoestrings. Then he gave him the glass-eyed stare he'd
learned when he was in prison. The Huck squirmed at first,
like most people do when they're stared at, but then he held
his breath and became very still as he realized that the eye
looking at him couldn't see a thing. Popeye removed his
own clothes and put on the Huckleberry rags.

"Who are you?" somebody asked as soon as he stepped
out of the hold and into the kitchen. The questioner was a
woman dressed like a sixteenth-century boy of noble birth.
Had Popeye been able to read and had he read Mark Twain,
he would have recognized the garb of Edward the Sixth of
England, the prince in Twain's *The Prince and the Pauper*.

As it was, he merely said, "I'm Ernie Gravas. Eddie's
cousin. He asked me to work his shift. He's sick."

The kitchen was hot and confused, which worked to
Popeye's advantage. If the Prince didn't quite believe what
he'd said, she was too tired and busy to worry about it very
much. Instead she returned to the task of packing the yolks
back into deviled eggs while Popeye walked out the kitchen
door and into the river of humanity that flowed through the
hall.

No one paid much attention to Popeye, or to the suitcase
under his arm as he worked his way past Princes and

Paupers, Hucks and Jims and even Mark Twain himself before he reached the main mess hall. The room was still and quiet but loaded for dinner like a gun resting on the dashboard right before it's time to go get paid. Long tables covered with white tablecloths waited for the suits; flags of every possible design were posted all over the place; and light came from a crystal chandelier hanging from a cable fixed up to look like twisted rope. In the front was something Tech Sarge had called the speaker's podium. That's where the hit would happen, where the caper would go down, where the corn would pop. Popeye would wait in the back of the hall near a well-stocked bar and more tables piled high with stuffed mushrooms, smoked oysters, every sort of cheese, crackers, and meat. There was also a large plate of glazed salmon chilled by an ice carving in the shape of Illinois past which flowed a river of blood-red cocktail sauce. His restaurant would have sauce like that some day if he didn't spend all his taxes on women and getting high.

21

Blood on That Mississippi Mud

NAT AMUSED HIMSELF BY SHOOTING TAPE OF ALL THE FLAGS, starting with the Stars and Stripes, which presided over the other flags from cables strung up by the chandelier. Smaller and hanging from longer cables was the state flag, which had an eagle with a shield in its talons and a banner in its beak. Smaller yet and planted on the tables, were the eye-catching city flags, a riot of color and municipal pride. They reminded him of a room full of adolescents trying to be different in the very same way—with a plain field of some primary color and a circle of oak leaves, wheat, or some other vegetation wrapped around an object of local importance. In the case of Cairo, the object was a barge; in the case of Skokie, an Indian with a prominent nose. The mayor of Lincolnwood sat next to a red flag with green olive branches arranged around the famous profile of its namesake, while Willis presided over the blue bars and golden stars of Chicago.

The managers of the *Connecticut Yankee* had equipped the hall with huge fans so the flags would flutter a bit. Nat took a wide shot, then put the lens cap on. "When's it supposed to happen?"

Allan checked his schedule, then he checked his watch. "My guess is after the salad but before the main course. During the soup, I guess. Dinner starts at seven o'clock, and he's the second speaker."

"This is a waste of valuable time."

"That's why they call it work. That's why they pay us money. They'd charge admission if it was fun. Look at all the women."

Not that there were so many women in the hall, but Allan had looked at them all and at the way that each engaged in the usual competition of which their male partners were but dimly aware. Who had the highest heels? The finest clothes? The richest man? Delilah had the widest butt.

She sashayed over to them and said to Nat, "You ready to roll some tape?"

"There's nothing to be but ready. When's it going to happen?"

Delilah checked her watch, thought about it for a moment, and said she didn't know for sure. "Once these boys start talking, you've just got to sit and listen. You need a bladder as big as a beach ball to succeed in politics."

Willis Cleveland had his happy face on as he picked his way through the crowd to a table at the front of the dining hall. As the mayor of the state's largest city, he was accorded the grudging respect that little powers pay to bigger ones. The other officials were Mayor This from There or Mayor That from Where, but Willis was simply the Mayor, much as Wayne was simply the Duke or Ruth was simply the Babe. Although many of the incumbents in the hall would have their own primaries late that summer, Willis's campaign was the one that everyone was talking about. What were his latest numbers? Where was the money at? Would he agree to debate his opponent? When would he start playing rough and how rough would he play?

The man with all the answers reached his table just as Delilah was swallowing a deviled egg.

"You must need a raise in pay," he said.

"I've always needed that, but why're you saying so?"

"Because you're eating up all this free food like it's going out of style."

Delilah looked down at what had been a plate of appetizers. But for a puddle of cocktail sauce and a crumb of Swedish meatball, she might have licked it clean. "Must be all the stress," she said. "I've put on fifteen pounds since Doogie announced. Make that twenty."

"Then we better knock him out of the box before you choke on a chicken bone."

The mayor sucked on a rum and Coke and crushed an ice cube with his constant smile. He saw Doogie step into the pool of light that Nat's sun gun produced, then watched as Nat circled the alderman. Dirty dancing with the lights turned on. Disgusting. He turned to Delilah and said, "How's my speech?"

Delilah handed him three pages held together with a paper clip and went to get some more food while he looked it over. When she returned, he greeted her with a thin smile that meant he wasn't pleased. "It's good but it's not me," he said.

"My speeches never are. How come you make me write them anyway?"

"Because you showing me what I'm not helps me figure out what I am."

"And what are you tonight?"

"I am the vengeance of the Lord, Sister. I am the trials of Job and the plagues of Egypt all wrapped up in the fires of hell. I am the flood that got Noah to build that ark for the animals and the whale that swallowed Jonah on the way to Ninevah. I am Joshua's horn and the lion in Daniel's den."

"Amen. Just save your roar for Doogie and leave the senator alone."

* * *

Popeye could see the senator's shoes from his hiding place beneath a table loaded down with all manner of hors d'oeuvres. He could also see the shoes of the many supplicants who pestered the senator for favors and advice while he balanced a plate full of stuffed mushrooms on his second martini of the night.

Popeye saw every kind of shoe in the store: the heavy work shoes of the farmer who was mayor of Rushville, and the Hush Puppies favored by the bunions of the DuPage county clerk; the Birkenstocks of the councilman from South Peoria and the stiletto heels worn by Sister Delilah Blue.

Popeye heard Delilah say to the senator, "I hope you're not causing any trouble tonight."

"What kind of trouble is that?"

"The kind where you start talking trash and Willis starts talking back. Do me the favor of being nice."

Popeye heard the senator take a sip of his second drink. "Okay, but only because I owe you one. It's your own fault if you lose this thing."

"You're right, but tell me how come."

"I think Willis made a mistake when he got them to push the primary back."

"But it saves money if we have it later on."

"That's not why he did it."

"Why?"

"He did it because he figured white folks take vacations when it's hot and colored folks stay home and vote."

"Well, they do, and we need them since it's looking real close."

"But if the vote were still in April, it would all be over now, and he could be taking one of those vacations that colored folks can't afford."

Popeye looked at his weapon, weighed it in his hand. He didn't understand how it worked, but he knew that it would because it was easy and hard at the same time. Just like flashlights and TV sets, elevators and automobiles. They were all easy to operate. Push a button; turn a key. The hard part was knowing how they worked. People gave you money if you knew how things worked, lots of money and lots of respect. If you didn't know you were just a punk, but every dog has his day, and every punk has his caper. He peeked at a pair of wing tips and waited for the speech.

Silent Hucks and invisible Jims circulated among the conventioneers with carts of food and condiments as the senator climbed up on the portable stage, took his place at the podium, and began his speech with a joke about the president and a few kind words about the Illinois Conference of Local Governments.

The senator was not like the other politicians who had gathered in the ballroom of the riverboat as it paddled its way upstream. He lacked the rough, raw edge most had acquired as they clawed their way to the top over the bodies of more scrupulous men. He had the pleasant demeanor common to those born to comfort and wealth, who never doubted for a moment that this was the way it was meant to be. He calmly pursued modest ambitions and had entered politics at an early age for lack of anything better to do. Duty required that he defend the interests of his family, and his mild manner qualified him for nothing else.

Sometimes he didn't have very much to say, but he always said it in a cultivated way. In person he sounded like the sweet voice of reason itself, but his was one of those personalities that are shrunk rather than magnified by the television's unblinking eye. When played against the hysterical clamor of televised discourse and debate, he sounded so meek that even his most thunderous speech came off like an apology.

Using the well-polished vocabulary for which his ancestors were so famous, he talked, over the crunch of salad fresh from the crisper, about the moral decline of the nation and the spectacular scandals of the idle rich. His remarks on the banking crisis were punctuated with the sound of two hundred elected officials slurping their soup. The best material he saved for the main course, which didn't make as much of a racket. The two hundred officials loaded up on broasted chicken, mashed potatoes, and green beans while the senator lectured them on a subject with which he was familiar—the decline of liberalism in America.

Nat was rolling tape although he had no hope that it would generate any revenue. He checked the sound level every now and then, but the senator never strayed from the pious, melodious tone with which his family had lectured voters for more than a hundred years. Allan tried to pay attention, but his thoughts kept drifting to this new theory he was developing concerning the role of women in broadcasting. He thought about the mocking laughter in Janette Baylor's eyes and tried to figure out how she knew that men were idiots.

He said, "Hey, Nat, you catching this?"

"Yeah. So what?"

"I think he's saying something new. Maybe we can sell him some tape of himself or sell it to the GOP. I never heard him say this before."

Nat zoomed in for an extreme close-up, just in case Allan was right. Political consultants always liked to use an ECU when their clients or their clients' opponents said something new.

What the senator said was this, "We are correct in a tentative way while the rad-reacts—the radical reactionaries—are wrong in spectacular fashion. The proof of this is in the obscene plenty possessed by the few and the hopeless future waiting for everybody else. But the rad-reacts who set this table have the blessings of their spiteful God and the courage of their misbegotten convictions. The fault is not with them but us. They, at least, believe in what they are doing while we liberals hem and haw, ponder and wander, vacillate and equivocate. It no longer matters that we're right in our belief that the establishment of a better society is the only way out of this wilderness. As it stands now, the worst thing we liberals can do to a good idea is to propose it in a public forum. The rad-reacts will oppose it with all their sinister skill, and the public will believe that if liberals want it, then it will never be."

The officials erupted into applause at the conclusion of the senator's speech, although Willis Cleveland believed most of the appreciation was directed at the carts full of mississippi mud that the crew of Hucks and Jims was pushing around the dining area. He didn't stand up until the clapping died down because he didn't want his own applause to be confused with that directed at the dessert or the senator.

When he got to the podium, he said, "That was a mighty fine accolation, but you don't have to clap for me. I won't be telling any jokes tonight, and I'm not going to get into the subject of liberal wimps and what have you. The extinguished senator covered all that and he knows more about it than me.

"What I'm going to talk about is people who sell Nazi books and about people marching through Skokie when they're not invited. I'm going to talk about people who are bringing home the hate, which means I'm gonna talk about Douglas MacArthur Smith. I hope you pay attention and write it all down because I'm not going to talk about it twice."

Willis removed the microphone from the podium so that he could walk around the stage. The crowd was getting sleepy now from too much wine, too much food, too much soaring rhetoric. A few of the mayors were looking at Cleveland, but most were looking at their mississippi mud or staring off into space. Willis wanted them to hear what he had to say, but they weren't his real audience. He was talking to Nat's TV camera and to the thousands of voters in his fair city who needed to know that Doogie was a dirty dog.

"I want to talk about a man who's trying to tear my town apart, about a man who don't give a good goddamn who gets hurt while he's doing it. You all know who I'm talking about because he's sitting right over there."

He walked back over to the podium and looked out at the crowd, which glanced his way every now and then between bites of mississippi mud. He wanted them to feel his pain and share his despair, to know what it was like to get up every morning and wonder if this was going to be the day that the whole thing fell apart. He wanted them to know that the biggest city in their state had arranged an uneasy truce among people with nothing but place in common. He wanted them to understand, but they wanted him to stop talking, so they could get back to the gaming tables or have enough time for another drink or two before the midnight performance of *Showboat*.

He thought he saw something move by the pile of crumbs that used to be hors d'oeuvres. He thought it must have been those Huckleberry Jims moving around in the back of the hall, and it gave him the hope that his words were maybe being heard. He decided to speak to the Hucks and the Jims and forget about the others. He tried to establish eye contact and bellowed a little louder so the help could hear him, too.

"Growing up on the West Side, I remember when the sun went down, and we could look over east in the direction of the lake and see the last rays of another hard day bouncing off all the glass towers we got downtown, and I'd be thinking that someday, that's where I want to be. Now that I'm there, I'm not so sure because the problem with being in a tower is you can see the whole damn mess. Looking up from the ghetto, there's a better world far away but looking down from the tower, all you can see is how the city's falling apart at the seams. That's the way it'll always be if'n we don't give those folks something to love instead of hate. There's some people driven by hope, and there's others driven by fear. I'm the former, and Alderman Smith is the other kind, and I guess what this election is about is finding out which way the people want to go. I used to think I knew, but I'm not so sure anymore."

That's when the love turned to hate and the hope to fear. He thought he saw a thin hand peel back a fold of tablecloth and he thought he saw a hollow tube poking out of the murk. He thought he saw a spark, and he thought he heard a boom, and before he knew what he was doing, he had jumped away from the podium and onto the polished oak floor of the stage. The spark was followed by a flash that poured a hot, bright light into every pore of his skin. Sharp pain came at him from everywhere at once until a firmament was made of which all things were divided into dark, left, cold, numb or light, right, heat, pain. There was light up ahead on the right, pitch black behind on the left and nothing in between, as if the universe itself had been divided into its two most basic elements. From the light came the hectoring voices of Sheryl Cleveland, Delilah Blue, and the 3.2 million other people in his city who wanted Willis to guide them into a brighter tomorrow. From the dark came the unspoken promise of a better world in which the weak were strong, the poor were rich, and the right was easy. So many voices were clamoring from the light that Willis could not tell what anyone was saying. But those were the voices he knew and loved, and those were the people who needed him, so he stepped away from the dark and the cold and the numb toward the noise and the heat and the light and the pain.

22

Techno Death

FROM HIS VANTAGE POINT AT PILOT'S POINT, TECH SARGE COULD see the twinkling lights of Cairo huddled next to the dark expanse of the place where the two black rivers converged. He imagined the confusion that now reigned there as people heard the first reports of what had happened aboard the riverboat. The exploding bullet was a challenge to the courage of many men, of many Hucks and many Jims. Between now and the coming dawn, heroes would step forward and cowards would be known. This was the next best thing to war itself in a world obsessed with peace.

"Do it now," Elmo said.

"Where's my money?" Sarge replied.

Elmo fetched a shoebox full of twenty-dollar bills while the mercenary examined the river through the green glow of his night-vision goggles. The water looked like the night had taken liquid form and the party boat looked like a new moon celebrating a new month with a spectacular fireworks display. In his mind's eye, he could see how it all went down. Three dozen hot bits of exploding bullet shooting off in

174

three dozen directions through flesh and bone and wall and door to kill a dozen people and start a dozen fires.

Sarge picked up the remote control. The light was off and the beep was silent. "You sure all the money's there?"

"Sure I'm sure. Let's do it now."

The mercenary looked at the remote control while he thought things over. When the light flashed on and the beep sounded, it would mean that Popeye had jumped in the water and inflated the Zodiak. Then it was a simple thing to launch a rocket and let the technology guide it to the homing device he'd planted in the pontoon. The waiting was the hardest part, the waiting and the fact that he couldn't see the target he was going to destroy.

"I'll count the money first," he said.

"Maybe he'll get away."

"And maybe you'll try to save a few nickels by cheating me out of my pay. I'll count the money first."

The harsh white light of Nat's sun gun was like the pallor of death itself, blinding and turning the faces it touched into a ghostly white. The frightened officials had already heard the explosion and seen the blood and tasted the smoke. Now they cringed from the television camera that made it all official. Allan ran interference as his partner sucked light, noise, blood, and smoke into the tape deck strapped to his hip. He kicked an overturned cart out of Nat's way and deflected a mayor who stumbled into his path. He held the microphone high above his head so Nat would get plenty of natural sound.

"We're rich," Allan said to Nat while the videographer plugged in a new battery pack. Nat was exhausted, drenched with sweat.

"You disgust me, Shanahan. How rich is that?"

"Hard to say for sure. Very. Did you get the blast?"

Nat shook his head. "I don't think so. I don't know. We got the sound, of course, and maybe some of the flash, but not the explosion itself. I was taking a wide shot at the time, so we've got the reaction and that might be just as good."

"We're still rich," Allan said. "Shoot as much tape as you can with lots of different faces. As soon as we get back to Cairo, you charter a plane to the city, and I'll start working the telephone. You go ahead and start cutting tape while I make a few telephone calls."

Amid all the smoke and confusion, all the moaning of the wounded and the screaming of the merely splattered, Popeye looked like just another Huck who didn't know what to do. The suits and the Jims and the Princes and the Paupers were running in every direction at once. A man dressed like Tom Sawyer held a woman dressed like Becky in his arms while Mark Twain looked befuddled and dozens of officials wandered in a daze. Popeye made sure that he didn't move too fast or too slow, that he was just another part of the general confusion. He talked to himself a little. It helped him settle down.

"Take a chill pill, Eye. The trick to doing a caper like this is you've always got to be chilling like your blood's gone cold."

Popeye worked his way to the back of the boat, toward where the paddle wheel was churning the river into foam with slow, smooth, hypnotic purpose, oblivious to the calamity that he had wrought in the Samuel Langhorne Clemens Memorial Dining Hall. Under the roar of the wheel, he could hear two Jims straining themselves in a shadow where the river moon did not shine. He hid behind a deck chair and listened to black men in a black shadow in the blackest part of the night.

"Give it a push, come on."

"I'm pushing."

"Push harder then."

"I can't."

"You better."

"Ugh!"

"Come on, blood. Hurry it up. The goddamn boat's on fire."

The harder they worked, the longer it took to do whatever

they were trying to do. Popeye thought things over. If he jumped now, they might see him and then tell the cops all about it. If he waited too long, some more Jims might wander by, and the trouble would just get worse. If he headed back to the front of the boat, no telling what would happen, but the chances were it would be bad.

The Jims made a determined grunt, and Popeye saw that their labors had produced a small boat, which they proceeded to lower into the water. One Jim climbed into the boat and directed it forward on some important mission having to do with the fire. The other Jim stepped back into the shadow of the paddle wheel and started wrestling with something that looked like a boa constrictor but must have been a fire hose.

Popeye decided it was time to make his move, but before he took three steps to the railing, the second Jim said, "Over here, Huck. Come give me a hand."

He stopped in his tracks for a moment too long. This gave the Jim time enough to step out of his shadow and get a good look at Popeye's face. Eyeball to glass eyeball they stood there, each taking measure of the other. Popeye was looking at the same Jim that had let him on board the boat the night before.

Popeye pulled out his gun and said, "Okay, mutherfuck, here's the way it is. I'm a crazy Puerto Rican with a big-ass gun who's gonna use it to blow your head off if you don't do like I say. Do a face plant on the floor right now."

The startled Jim did just that.

Popeye looked at the back of his head and listened to the fear. The smart thing, the simple and easy thing, would be to pull the trigger and put poor Jim out of his misery. Then he could sound no alarm and give no testimony. He wouldn't have to get out of bed in the morning and spend all day cleaning brown hockers out of ashtrays used by suits that smoked cigars. He wouldn't have to grow old, get sick, and spend his last ten years dying of cancer in a place that wouldn't let him alone until his last penny and the last pennies of those who loved him had been spent to pay his medical bills. And those were but a few of the many things he wouldn't have to do. Popeye had many other reasons to pull the trigger, but before he could think of them all, he heard the sound of excited men running toward the back of the boat. So instead of pulling the trigger, he cracked open his metal suitcase, removed the bundled Zodiak, held it to his chest, and jumped overboard.

"I've got a signal," Tech Sarge said.

He held up the remote locator so Elmo could see what he was talking about. The light was flashing, and the beep was beeping.

"Let's do it then," Elmo said.

The mercenary smiled. The condescending smile was one he had once used on his raw recruits.

"Easy, Elmo. Give it time. He's not going anywhere. Better if he puts some distance between the Zodie and the boat."

Elmo clenched his fists and started pacing back and forth. He tried to distract himself by thinking of all the excitement the next few months would hold. Doogie said there'd be riots like when the Nigger King got killed. Elmo was too young for that riot, so this would be his first. Gunshots at four in the morning, Jews in the emergency room, and gasoline bombs crashing through the windows of Korean grocery stores.

"Elmo?"

The Ricans'd ice the niggers, and the niggers'd ice the Jews, and the Jews'd take all their money and go back home to Skokie. When it was all over, Doogie would be the only man left who could protect what's left from all those jungle bunnies with knives. Douglas MacArthur Smith.

"Elmo?"

The best thing is they wouldn't have to worry about the mayor anymore. He was always causing trouble, always getting in the way.

"Elmo, I'm talking to you."

"What?"

The mercenary was smiling again, offering Elmo the remote control with the flashing light and the beeping beeps. "It's time to do it now. It's your party. Go ahead."

Elmo took the device. It was heavier than it looked and produced a faint vibration. For a brief moment, he was afraid that if he pushed the button it would explode instead of the raft. It didn't. Far off, a small burst of light marked the water, followed some seconds later by a gentle, almost apologetic boom. Then darkness and silence and the uneasy relief that comes when somebody else gets killed.

Tech Sarge said, "So what'd you do about the other one?"

"What other one is that?"

"The other Puerto Rican that was hanging out with Eye. Hammerhead was his name, I think. He was Popeye's partner when I gave him the techno-death. What'd you do with him?"

Elmo felt the hot rush of shame rising to his face and was glad that he was standing in the black cranny of Pilot's Point. His scalp started to itch and his palms started to sweat. His brain started to hum, and his ears started to ring.

"Damn!"

"What's wrong?"

"Damn! Damn! Damn!"

That was the only word he could say. And the only thing he could think about was a warehouse full of peppermint Certs. He had bought them all at the 7-Eleven and carried them all back to Doogie, but it was never enough. Everything was never enough.

"Damn! Damn! Damn!"

CHANNEL THREE

JULY 31, 6:30 P.M. LEDE INTO FIRST BREAK WITH
NEWS MUSIC FADE
CAMERA ONE: TWO-SHOT/BEV, MILLER
  BEV: Good evening. I'm Bev Majors.
  MILLER: And I'm Miller James. Tonight's top story: More
  exclusive pictures of last night's attempted assassination of
  Mayor Willis Cleveland, and an exclusive interview with his
  press secretary, Sister Delilah Blue. (ROLL TAPE OF CON-
  VENTION) The blast occurred about 9:45 last night, just as
  officials of the Illinois Conference of Local Governments
  were gathering on a Mississippi riverboat for their annual
  convention. It was just another election-year event when
  the guest of honor took center stage.
(ROLL SENATOR SOUND BITE, WITH OUTCUE: ". . . the
only way out of this wilderness.")
  MILLER: But somewhere on the *Connecticut Yankee* authorities say an assassin lurked with murder on his mind.
  Officials believe he used an advanced weapons system.
  (ROLL TAPE WITH NATURAL SOUND OF BLAST FOL-

180

LOWED BY SCREAMS) Some of the officials ran for cover. Others were wounded by flying bits of bone and glass. Seven received serious wounds and were taken to Cairo Memorial Hospital. The target of the assassination attempt is said to be in stable condition tonight. (ROLL FREEZE-FRAME OF MAYOR CLEVELAND) Cleveland is nearing the end of his second term as mayor of the state's largest city. He still controls a powerful political coalition of black, brown, and white voters that has dominated local politics for the last eight years. But tonight the mayor is fighting for his life and the coalition he built is on the verge of falling apart. Emily Jones has this report: ROLL JONES PACKAGE WITH OUTCUE: ". . . Emily Jones reporting."

CAMERA TWO: MEDIUM CLOSE-UP/BEV

BEV: Scuba divers are searching the river for information about a second explosion that occurred about fifteen minutes after the attack on the mayor. As Ralph Young reports, authorities are looking for clues.

ROLL YOUNG PACKAGE WITH OUTCUE: ". . . Ralph Young reporting."

CAMERA ONE: TWO-SHOT/CHUCK, BEV

BEV: We'll have more on this explosive story later in the news. But first we turn to Chuck with the weather. (TWO-SHOT/BEV, CHUCK) What's the story, Chuck?

WIDE-SHOT/CHUCK, WEATHER MAP

CHUCK: Bev, the short version is only two words long: greenhouse effect. The National Weather Service came out with a White Paper on the heat wave that has damaged crops and dried up rivers all across the state. We'll have more right after this.

ROLL ANIMATED WEATHER MAP WITH LOCAL TEMPS; CUT TO LOTTO BREAK

23

Urban Disturbances

THIS WOULD NOT BE A GOOD DAY. PARKER WAS CERTAIN OF that, and he was supposed to know because TV assignment editors must be able to predict events. How else could they get a TV camera in the right place at the right time without much help from the hair-spray set. For Parker, this sixth sense was a function of instinct, experience, and a determined effort to always expect the worst. The worst didn't always happen, but anything less than the worst was rarely worth forty-five seconds on the evening news.

He looked at the city outside the single window that he shared with the sixty-seven other journalists who worked for Channel Twelve News. It was hot but quiet, sweaty but still. A few early risers had tried to beat the dawn to work, but mostly he saw outside that window the uneasy promise of a day that hadn't happened yet.

There was a different city on the TV set, on which he was viewing an air check of Channel Three News. Their city was in a state of seige. Their city was having a race war between the people who loved the mayor and the people who thought they had something to gain if he died from his injuries.

182

Their city had caught on fire, and arson was suspected. Their city was being destroyed by a prowling riot that could break out at any place in any of a thousand ways: The broken glass on the sidewalk in front of Phil's Kosher Deli and Sweets; the curious sight of a blue and white police cruiser that the mob had flipped over on its back, looking as helpless as a bug with its wheels still spinning in the air; flames rising from the naked frame of the St. Luke's Settlement House; disconsolate fire fighters who had stopped trying to extinguish this fire or that and contented themselves with hosing down the buildings on either side.

The pictures didn't bother Parker much. His career was devoted to tape like that and the clips he had gathered for Channel Twelve were just as good or better. What bothered Parker were the numbers he had seen on a memorandum that was waiting on the desk of each and every reporter, photographer, editor, and producer who would be straggling into the newsroom between 4 and 11 A.M. The numbers were the ratings from the summer sweeps, two weeks of frenzy toward the end of July. Unless there had been a horrible mistake, a typo, or sabotage, Channel Twelve had been knocked out of the top spot by those sleazeballs from Channel Three.

There would be hell to pay and Parker would have to pay his share. The news director would take another look at his people so that some of the more expensive and least effective talent could be relieved of their duties. Next would come an emergency meeting for the purpose of giving a pep talk to the survivors. Reference would be made to a long tradition of making money hand over fist and the reporters would be inspired thereby. The editors would pore over the *Chicago Tribune* in search of tomorrow's trend and Parker would be directed to concoct a special series that would reengage and reinform the tens of thousands of loyal viewers who had switched to Channel Three for reasons he could only guess at. Maybe it was Janette's profile or Channel Three's series on lipstick lesbians. Whatever it was, it had to stop before the September sweeps began.

But first must come the business of the day, assigning stories to the electronic news gathering or ENG teams that would soon file into the newsroom. This was an assignment editor's reason to be, the thing that made it all worthwhile. A chance to exercise power over those blessed with talent and beauty he could only dream about. He punished reporter Bob Ripley by assigning him to cover the governor's prayer breakfast and punished videographer Betty Shelson by assigning her to shoot with Ripley. He rewarded the ENG team of Ed Walker and Donald Jacobi by assigning them to the DuPage County Food Festival. So it went through the usual assortment of staged news events: press conferences by guys with ties, photo ops with visiting celebs, and the opening of a new art gallery devoted to comic book illustrations.

That done, he picked up a manila folder in which he stored the yellowing newspaper clippings that passed for ideas at Channel Twelve. A short story on weight-loss hypnosis from the Sunday edition of *The New York Times* and a longer piece on household pollution from *The Wall Street Journal.* He glanced at a story the *Trib* had published several weeks before.

BOX-DWELLER LOOKING FOR LOVE
by Jessica Whitcomb-Hill
Tribune staff writer

A man who has been living in a cardboard box for the last fifteen years says he'll marry someday if he can find a woman who'll sleep with him and his dogs.

Bowser Hillman is one of the street people who lives in the alley behind the Martha Hollins Detox Center in the city's Uptown district. But unlike many of the other homeless men and women who frequent the area, he is addicted neither to alcohol nor drugs and rarely eats the free meals served every day at noon in the basement of St. Damien's Catholic Church.

The only thing Bowser's hooked on are Bill, Bob, and Bette, the three mutts who never stray far from the doggie treats he carries in the pocket of his coat. He calls the dogs his kids and says they need a woman's touch.

"Me and the kids have been thinking about getting us a new box when the cardboard market improves," he says.

(Continued on page E-8)

Parker didn't read the rest. No sex, no guns, no numbers. No series on homeless people. Viewers didn't like stories that made them feel sad. Afraid generated big numbers, and aroused made people want to spend money on the advertisers' products, but sad made them want to turn off the set, go to bed, and maybe make love to their wives. Parker needed a series that wasn't so sad, so he picked up the phone, dialed, and listened. The old lady answered.

"Electronic News Tonight, Helen Shanahan speaking."

"Helen, this is Jerry, the A.E. at Channel Twelve."

"My, we're up bright and early. What can I do for you, Parker?"

He told her what she could do, hung up the phone, and waited for her to do it. About ten minutes later, Allan was on the line.

"Hey, Park. What's up?"

"Not up. Down. The latest book puts Three at number one."

They shared an awkward silence, like two friends pretending to grieve for someone they secretly despised. "I'm sorry to hear that. I really am. Anything I can do? The meter's running, of course."

"Ten bucks a minute, just to talk about it?"

"We've got expenses, Parker. If you want to talk about my budget and all the vehicles Nat smashes up, I'll be glad to tell you the grim details, but I'll have to charge for that time too. It's a great story, by the way. All about this crazy videographer and the cost of used cop cars. Is that why you wanted to talk?"

There was fifty cents' worth of silence while Parker

gathered his thoughts. "I need you to do a series but I don't know what it is. We need new ideas fast. It's bang-bang time."

"Bang-bang? What's that?"

"That's how we get the sack around here. When the news dee cans somebody, he pulls the trigger on his thumb and always goes 'Bang-bang.' The news dee's a jerk. I guess that's redundant."

Allan chewed his lips, and thought about it for a dollar's worth of time. "I'll even give you a real good price. We're working on a project that's already got some tape. Give us Baylor for the talking head."

"Janette? You're kidding. How come?"

"She's got the pipes. She's got the lungs. She's got *it* and she smells nice too."

Delilah shared the results of the latest tracking poll with the rest of the mayor's staff, who had huddled in his office for protection from the fire storm their city had become. His empty chair and spotless desk commanded their attention, as if his essence still lingered in the place and was sending them a message that they could not understand. A city planner spoke for the group.

"Forget the numbers and talk about the man. What's his condition?"

"Stable."

"He was stable yesterday. When can we go say howdy?"

"Not today. He's resting. The mayor needs his rest, and he needs for us to take care of business. Let's talk numbers."

"The numbers don't mean a goddamn thing. It's who tried to do him."

"That doesn't matter half as much as the fellow who's putting it all to work, so here's the numbers I'm talking about: Cleveland 44, Smith 41, Undecided 15."

She let the numbers sink in for a moment but they didn't seem to have any effect on the stunned gathering.

"It all breaks down like this: The brothers and sisters are all on board and the whites are mostly for Doogie, excepting for the lakefront liberals, of course. God bless their wine and cheese. The 'Spanic browns in no-man's-land are mostly waiting to see what happens. The one getting them will win this thing."

She stopped talking for a moment and looked at the gathered bureaucrats. They were looking back at her with the dull glaze of fear in their eyes, a fear for their own skins that they dare not articulate. She said, "The good news is that Willis is holding his own—hasn't been under 45 percent since the day before he was born. Our problem is the undecideds will be deciding pretty soon, and he's too beat up to do the Kiss N' Shake."

The planner loosened his tie as if it was choking him. "His condition's too 'stable,' right? Isn't there some kind of sympathy vote, seeing as how he could have got killed?"

Delilah shrugged. "And Doogie's got his own kind of negatives, but these are negative times. There's folks thinking there's a nigger with a butcher knife hiding behind every willow tree every time they go out at night. Oh, why did the good Lord make the night so black?"

This produced a general grumbling from the group. They all looked at the mayor's chair, missing him more than they ever had before. The planner started losing it. He looked up at the chief. "So tell us what happened to that bonehead bodyguard. That Tamburino fellow that you dragged out of some cage. None of this would've happened if the cops had done their job."

Chief Dreyer blew his stack at that and called the planner a toney-assed fuckhaid from the Near North Side. The city attorney agreed with the planner, and the fire chief agreed with the chief of police. They all started shouting at the same time, with Delilah the only one listening. They were still going at it when she slipped out the door, and they kept it up while she took a taxi to Walter Reed Memorial Hospital, where the mayor was listed in stable condition.

She looked with sadness at the stricken form of the man who had once persuaded her that sweet black Jesus was setting his people free. He had been the only man in her life since he walked into her storefront church and showed her how to pray in the ways that really counted: on the street, with the dollar, in the ballot box. They'd never had sex or even kissed or even whispered sweet lies to one another, but she was his lover, in any case. Everything she did was for Willis, and all she wanted was for the great man inside him to break out into the clear.

They had started with nothing and worked until they had it all. He had a wife and kids and a dog with fleas, and she always took her vacations alone and spent Saturday nights with a bottle of wine and a tub of Carnation Rocky Road ice cream with real marshmallows and some kind of nuts. Now they were going back to nothing, less than nothing when you thought the whole thing through. She had a city on fire, and he had the kind of life you suck from plastic tubes.

His vital signs were indicated by blinking lights, ragged graphs, and the rhythmic beeping of a heart-like device. Ba-be-boop. Ba-be-boop. Ba-be-boop. Ba-be-boop. Sometimes it seemed like the machines were alive, and he was dead, that he was the witless life-support system and they were the feeble but intelligent being. If she pulled the plug, the machines would become still and quiet and dark, while his condition would remain the same, stable.

He'd suffered damage to the corpus callosum with collateral effects on the cerebellum. The diagnosis was a split brain, the prognosis was unsure. That's what the doctor had said. Three other doctors agreed. They also agreed that he was incoherent while awake and that he was beset by sleeping fits of increasing duration and frequency. He was never alert for more than fifteen minutes at a time, and when he spoke he mumbled and moaned about things that didn't make any sense.

"This is a very mixed bag," the youngest of many neurologists said. Dr. Bartholomew was his name. He seemed to be a callow youth with clear blue eyes and rosy cheeks, but having just graduated from Northwestern Medical School, he was up-to-date on theory and procedure. For this reason, his elders regarded him as a prodigy of sorts and were anxious to share the credit for his future accomplishments. He also had a painfully uncertain manner, the peculiar features of which were slender, busy hands that inspired more pity than confidence, and a halting pattern of speech that encouraged listeners to attempt the completion of his excruciating sentences.

"Part of the problem is . . ."

"Mental?" Delilah suggested.

"Psychological," he replied. "And the other part is . . ."

"Physical?"

"Yes. Of course. That's right. The primary disconnect is between the speech center and the right frontal lobe. That can be quite problematic."

"And problematic is what?"

"Problematic is—well—problematic is a . . ."

"A problem?"

"Exactly. The right frontal quadrant of the medulla is the part of the brain that is most closely associated with . . ."

The young doctor seemed to be searching for words that did not exist. He wished to illuminate but not to offend, to inform but not to alarm. As there was no simple layman's term for what happened to the mayor's corpus callosum, he didn't even attempt an explanation and moved on to another issue.

"We have a psychological component here. That might be why he's sleeping so much. Sleep is a great escape and the mayor has been . . ."

"Iced?"

"Well, he's certainly been through a lot. He's *rem*ing up a storm, so he must be dreaming all the time. His pulse is steady, and his metabolic functions are normal, so it seems to be a pleasant dream. I think part of it is sleep's a lot more fun. Can't say I disagree with that."

The doctor began adjusting one of the mayor's tubes, giving Delilah a moment to think things over, to figure out for herself what this may or may not mean. She touched the mayor's flaccid hand and listened to the ba-be-boop of his heart. The rhythmic beeping had a hypnotic effect that lured her into daydreams of a better past, before the reality of power had shattered their illusions of what good it might accomplish. She remembered all the hellfire speeches and the way he would bring her words to life and make them march on to greater glory like an army of vowels and consonants. Pretending she was writing one more speech, she listened to the words he could not say.

I'm talking to you, Sister Delilah Blue, because you're the one who knows how to hear. I don't know who done it to me, but I know who got it done. I know what you're thinking, and that's okay. It could've been one of them Nazis or one of them Black Galabeye dudes. It could've been some greaser creep from Oakwood Park what drank too much of the wrong kind of wine. It could've been lots of maniac people with all sorts of angry on their minds. They're confused about stuff that ought to make them laugh and afraid of some tomorrow that's never gonna come. If they're the one, then all's forgiven, as long as we can pin it on Doogie Smith. I am the Fire and he is the Ice. The Fire melts the Ice and the Ice turns to Water. The Water drips on the Fire and the poor flame flickers out. Then everything is dark and dry as a bone when the whole to-do gets done.

The doctor's hands flitted into Delilah's consciousness, breaking the spell that possessed her. Theories and procedures needed to be discussed, and the mayor's wife must, of course, be informed of something, although of what he still didn't know.

Nat blew at the pinwheel he'd fashioned from the July spreadsheet. "You know you might look kind of goofy, but you're still pretty slick."

Allan covered his mouth, but he still looked goofy. "How's that?"

"You got Channel Twelve paying us to do what we're already doing for Delilah. We'll be rolling in it when you add in the payout from the riverboat."

According to the numbers on Nat's pinwheel, the incident

aboard the *Connecticut Yankee* was proving to be a bonanza of heroic proportions. Their videotape had been the object of frenzied bidding due to the nature of the event, the quality of the tape, and the lucky coincidence that it was available for the last two days of the July sweeps. They sold the local broadcast rights to Channel Three for $15,000. ABC purchased the national rights for $50,000 plus royalties of $1,500 for every second of tape used after the initial broadcast. A Japanese conglomerate purchased the overseas rights for $150,000, in part because the blood and the panic could be used to illustrate the moral decline of the American foe.

For Allan, this was like quenching a thirst with salt water. The more he drank, the thirstier he became until dementia took hold.

"How about this? We get Geraldo to be our talking head for a special on cable TV. I see it as a cross between that TV show 'Crime Time' and that special he did on Al Capone's vault, only this'll be a lot better. We call it 'America's Colors: Blood, White and Blue,' or something along those lines. I bet we make two million. One for Geraldo and the other one for us."

"Let's take care of Janette first, and then we'll do Geraldo."

Allan was struck dumb by the very mention of her name, which conjured up the swell of her hips and the cut of her hair in his mind's eye. She was a constant scratching in his head, as if an uneasy thought was trying to escape. As he thought about the moist parting of her lips in smile, he convinced himself that she was smiling at him and that he was smiling back at her with the straighter, more neatly organized teeth he sometimes imagined himself to have.

24

The Big Lonely of Gloria Cantrell

TECH SARGE AND ELMO DROVE A WONDER BREAD DELIVERY truck into Lincoln Square at a leisurely pace, parking on a side street just outside the chain-link fence that encircled the patch of crumbling asphalt claimed as home by the Alone Unknown. The fence had several holes cut in it for easy access and surrounded a playground on which money was collected and order was maintained according to the same principles that prevailed outside the fence. The young were deceived by the old; the strong gave orders to the weak; the wise were outwitted by fools.

The sudden and unannounced departure of Popeye and Hammerhead left a void that a gangster by the name of Grog had filled. Tech Sarge and Elmo watched with interest as Grog strutted across the yard to a group of toughs doing nothing on a flight of concrete steps beneath a sign that read: Jean Baptiste Pointe du Sable Memorial School. Because school was out, the playground belonged to the Alone Unknown. When school was in, the gangsters hung out at the little park across the street from Liberty Bank, where all there was to do was watch a three-foot-tall Statue of Liberty do 360s in a little glass tube.

Tech Sarge said, "So who's this du Sable character?"

Elmo thought about it. Sniggered. The snigger became a chuckle, and the chuckle became a belly laugh. Sweat streamed down his face as he struggled to compose himself.

"We read about him when I was in school. It's about the only thing I remember because it was such a load of shit." He paused to laugh some more, take a deep breath, and wipe some sweat away.

"He's the guy that discovered this place. Chicago, I mean. Shee-ka-goo. Bad onion smell. My teacher said he was a trader, but she never did say what he traded. She said he lived here for twenty, thirty years and then sold out to a guy named Kedzie."

Sarge was waiting for the funny part, but Elmo didn't say any more. After a sweaty silence, Sarge said, "That's very amusing, Elmo. You should be a comedian. Las Vegas is full of guys like you."

For a moment Elmo imagined himself standing on a stage bathed in light. He was wearing a green suit that glittered, and he was telling jokes about his mother-in-law. That meant he'd have to get married. The audience laughed at his every word, and chorus girls waited offstage for a moment of his time. The fantasy disappeared when another thought intruded.

"Oh, right. But I forgot to tell you the funny part. This du Sable was a nigger, one of these caramel-colored kind you get when races breed. My teacher used to brag about it because she was a nigger, too. And you want to know why this town's a mess? Nigger at the start. Nigger at the finish. Nigger teachers in between."

Elmo laughed some more. He looked for Sarge to do the same, but had to settle for a thin smile that could have meant a lot of things but nothing that was fun. Maybe Elmo didn't belong in Las Vegas after all. When he finished laughing, he got down to business.

"How about it? What do you say?"

Sarge shrugged. "I guess. But I don't understand you people. Here we are doing doo-doo duty on a couple little punks when if you'd asked me in the first place the target would already be destroyed, the election would be a sure thing, and we wouldn't have any doo-doo duty."

Elmo thought about peppermint Certs or maybe it was spearmint. He still couldn't get them straight. "Trust us. Doogie's a genius. It makes sense if you step it all out. Doogie's a man of many steps."

"So step on it," Tech Sarge said.

"All right. White man kills the mayor, then the mayor's like a dead Kennedy and his best black soldier slides right in. The chief of police is our best guess, or that woman with all the smarts. But a brown man kills the mayor and the coloreds start up a gorilla war. These people still live in tribes, you know, with fifty thousand cousins and no old man."

"What if a black man does it?"

"Does what?"

"Kills the mayor."

"Nothing. A brother does it, and it doesn't do anybody any good or any harm, either. Except for the mayor, that is. But we're not killing him anymore. We're killing Hammerhead. Doogie wants it to look like a brother did it for revenge. It needs to be sloppy with some voodoo on the side."

"We need to talk about that. You think he's coming back for sure? I'd rather do him on the road."

They watched the gangsters who had gathered on the steps of the school. They seemed to be waiting for something to happen. Not a good something or a bad something. Just something. Anything. Maybe they were waiting for their next drug deal, and maybe they were waiting for Hammerhead. Sarge didn't notice and Elmo didn't care.

"There's six different roads he could be on, but they all come back to here. Punk like that's got no place else to go."

* * *

Hammerhead wasn't going anywhere because he and Bilbo were still waiting for Popeye in the alley behind the building with the mysterious message on it. The gerbil kept scraping at the glove-compartment wall while the gangster tried to figure out what the message meant by looking at the rivers and the sky. IN GOD WET RUST. The rivers were about as wet as wet could be, and the sky looked a little rusty sometimes, especially in the evening when the sun was going down.

He was running out of food, running out of gas, and running out of places to rob. He'd already done the only Get N' Go in all of Alexander County and had to drive as far as Metropolis to rob a place called Harvey's General Store and Video. He'd filled up the tank there, grabbed a bag full of food, and pointed his gun at the clerk with the usual warning. It was only later that he figured out that the clerk must have been Harvey himself since he acted like it was his own gas and his own junk food that Hammerhead was trying to steal. Instead of being scared and nervous and calling the state patrol, Harvey produced a shotgun from behind the counter and gave him both barrels. The buckshot sounded like a rock storm and turned the back window of Billy the Bopper's car into a million slivers of cut glass. Bilbo stopped chewing for five whole minutes before getting back to work.

Afterward, Hammerhead reviewed this particular caper over a meal of smoked wienies, nacho chips, and cheese in an aerosol can. Then he went over Popeye's rules of robbing all-night grocery stores and was rattled by the realization that the rules didn't always apply. He had done everything right, and it had still turned out all wrong.

Karnak Gas and Goods was just as bad in its own way. The caper itself went off without a hitch, and he made it back to Cairo without getting shot at by some crazy guy named Harvey. But when he had parked behind the building where he and the Eye were supposed to meet and had dumped his stolen groceries out on the passenger seat, the

sight of all that quick-stop food made his stomach growl like
an angry dog. He looked at the gerbil and for a passing
moment Bilbo looked good enough to eat. None of that
microwave stuff that's wrapped in cellophane. More like the
extra-crispy chicken thighs from the Kentucky Fried on
Milwaukee Avenue. Too bad.

"Shit," Hammerhead said to himself.

"Goddamn," Hammerhead replied.

Bilbo stopped chewing long enough to take a dump.
Hammerhead stuffed himself with chips and salami,
Twinkies and pop, until his belly strained against the fabric
of his shirt. When the bag of chips was empty and the cold
cuts were all gone, when he had licked the last bit of cream
from the wrapper that the Twinkies came in, Hammerhead
made the alarming discovery that the more he ate, the
hungrier he became, and that the longer he waited, the less
he expected to ever see Popeye again.

The next day he followed Get N' Go signs all the way to
Memphis, Illinois, only to discover that it had been devas-
tated by the latest flood. Hammerhead watched the waterlogged ruins cook in the sun for a little while before driving
back empty-handed to the Cairo riverfront.

He left the car in the alley behind the Old Customs House
and started walking around the block. Once, twice and
again. His stomach complained every time he walked by
Steamboat Annie's, a slice of life wedged between two
abandoned buildings. He was thinking about Popeye and
the worst that could have happened, but eventually the
growling of his stomach commanded his attention. On the
fourth time around the block, he paused in front of the
restaurant and read a mimeographed menu taped to the
door that advertised soups and salads, chicken and fries,
chili by the cup or bowl and every sort of burger under the
sun. He didn't bother to look at the prices because he had no
intention of paying for his meal, or money to do so if he
wanted to.

He walked in and sat down at the counter next to a man
with a newspaper who needed a shave. The place smelled of

tobacco, boiled fat, and lazy summer afternoons during which old men with nothing to do talk about the weather and other things they cannot change. The man was gnawing on a toothpick in a strangely determined way that reminded Hammerhead of Bilbo's unending efforts to escape. Hammerhead glanced over the man's shoulder at a story about the price of corn until the waitress came over.

"Menu?"

"What?"

"If you know what you want, tell me what it is. If you don't, I'll get you a menu."

Hammerhead had been living in his own head for so long that he couldn't answer right away. He opened his mouth but did not speak, moved his lips but did not make any noise. The waitress took this to mean that he wanted a menu and deposited one on the counter.

"Coffee?"

This time he managed a mumble which sounded enough like yes to bring the waitress forward with a pot. After a half-cup of coffee, he was able to speak in sentences and he ordered the chicken and fries with soup and salad on the side.

He was finished with the salad and halfway into the soup when the man he was sitting next to left the restaurant without his copy of the *Cairo Daily Scroll*. Hammerhead picked up the paper and started paging through the familiar headlines: TWO KILLED IN BOATING ACCIDENT; ARABS PROTEST WEST BANK SETTLEMENTS; BOARD REVIEWS ZONING APPEAL; IMPORTS CHALLENGE U.S. AUTOMAKERS. Anytime or any place, the headlines never changed. Hammerhead didn't understand why people didn't just buy one paper and carry it around in their pockets until it fell apart.

Somebody said, "Excuse me, sir."

Hammerhead turned around and saw a Cairo policeman in cheap sunglasses. Behind him was another policeman who had taken his glasses off and was chewing on the part that wrapped around his ear. He was a big man with a face so hard you might hurt your hand if you punched it.

"You driving that Cutlass parked in the alley behind the Old Customs House?"

Hammerhead slurped some soup and shook his head.

"Is your name William Cruz?"

"No. Who's that?"

"His street name is Billy the Bopper. He owns the car I'm talking about."

"Like I said, it's not my car."

The one cop looked at the other, exchanging some meaningful information in the twinkle of a quick cop glance. "What's your name?"

"Ed Rivas."

"Where you from, Ed?"

"The city."

"Which city is that?"

"This state only has one city. Cairo's just a town."

"Then what're you doing down here?"

"Looking for a job."

"Then you better go home because we don't have any jobs. Where were you on the night of 30 July?"

Hammerhead picked up a thigh, which reminded him of Bilbo. He figured he had better eat fast. "I don't remember for sure. Probably on the road."

"Driving that car in the alley, right?"

"No. Like I said, it's not my car. I don't have no car and I never heard of no Willie the Whopper."

"That's Billy the Bopper. What're you driving if it's not that car?"

He stuck out his thumb and gave it a shake. "I'm riding on other people's wheels. Trucker picked me up coming out of the big town and dropped me off over by the dock. You mind if I eat my food?"

The cops had run out of questions, but they hadn't run out of time. In the lumbering manner of big, strong men, they planted themselves in a booth by the door and slurped up coffee from a pot of their own that the waitress had placed on the table between them.

After sucking the meat off the thigh, Hammerhead picked

up a chicken wing and broke it at the knuckle. He sucked the meat off the chicken wing and picked up his final piece, a drumstick. He turned it over and weighed it in his hand. Before he was eating too slow, now he was eating too fast because now he needed time to think, time to wait for the cops to leave. He nibbled at the drumstick and counted his fries, picked up the paper and bided his time, tried to figure out how he could bolt without paying when there were two cops between him and the door.

Starting back at the sports page and working his way to the front of the paper, he read more carefully this time. The Sox were on a winning streak and the Cubbies were in a funk. Hip-hop fashions were the order of the day, with baggy trousers for the guys and spandex tights for the gals. A church that Hammerhead couldn't pronounce, the Presbyterians, was having some kind of funky do about sissy boys and whether or not God thought it was okay to be like that. The editor of the *Daily Scroll* had strong opinions about things that Hammerhead didn't even know existed and his horoscope provided the following advice: Individual who spreads gossip means no harm but causes trouble. You get second chance and surprise those who thought you missed the boat.

"No shit," Hammerhead said to himself.

The cops stopped slurping long enough to listen for more. The waitress wandered his way. "Anything else you need?"

"No. I'm fine."

"You want me to take this away?" She was looking at his plate, which now held three naked bones and a handful of cold french fries.

"No, not yet," Hammerhead said. "Maybe some coffee if that's okay."

She refilled his cup, and the cops settled back in their booth. Hammerhead still didn't have a plan, so he wasted a little more time. On page five was a story about Russia and on four a story about bugs that would have made him laugh if he wasn't so afraid.

That's when he saw page three, and a small story he'd

missed altogether on his first run through the *Daily Scroll*. His heart sank and his pulse raced. He knew before he'd read a word that the story was all about Popeye, and he knew that Popeye was dead already and that he and the gerbil were on their own.

SEARCH OF RIVER CONTINUES

The Alexander County Emergency Rescue Unit continued to search Tuesday for evidence concerning the blast that rocked the *Connecticut Yankee* last week. Although no new clues were found, officials are increasingly confident that the river holds the key to what caused the explosion that seriously injured eight at the recent Illinois Conference of Local Governments.

So far, divers have retrieved the shredded scraps of a rubber raft, a few pieces of what is believed to be some sort of weapon, and a basketball shoe containing a severed foot. Officials believe that the foot, the raft, and the weapon may have all belonged to an unidentified man who detonated some sort of explosive device around 9 P.M. on July 30.

Police Chief Raymond Hart is now discounting earlier theories that the explosion was an accident.

"We're talking attempted murder, and you can quote me in the paper on that," he said.

Divers began dragging the river on Sunday in response to eyewitness reports that a second explosion occurred on the river about twenty minutes after the original blast. Officials speculate that the second explosion may have been caused by a malfunctioning of the weapon used in the attack. Willis Cleveland, mayor of the state's largest city, was the presumed target of the attack. He is listed in stable condition at a hospital in Chicago.

Hammerhead stopped reading but kept staring at the paper. A steady heat rose and collected in his ears, as if his blood had begun a slow boil that hadn't produced any bubbles yet. Maybe the air conditioning had broken down, and the relentless sun had stopped pounding the two rivers and was pounding the restaurant instead. Maybe it was the flush of shame we feel when left alone to contemplate some of the things we have done. Maybe it was caused by the sizzle of the griddle and the steaming of the coffeepot and the way the one cop looked as he chewed the tip of his cheap sunglasses.

What really caused the heat didn't matter nearly as much as what Hammerhead believed the cause to be. He thought the burning sensation in his skin and the ringing in his ears meant that the *Daily Scroll* was telling the truth, that Popeye really was dead and that his spirit had found a resting place in the darkest part of Hammerhead's heart. He checked his eye to see if it was now made of glass, and he looked at the waitress to see if she was now looking back at him like women used to look back at the Eye. She was.

"Coffee?"

"You."

"What?"

This was Popeye talking now, even if his eye wasn't made of glass. "I suppose you got a man or two because you're so pretty, but if they don't ever treat you right then you can always come to me. I know how to treat a lady."

Popeye couldn't have said it better. The waitress put down her coffeepot and wiped the counter for a moment. Her husband worked the barges all day, and they only made love on Saturday nights, unless there was a televised football game. He didn't know how to treat a lady. He didn't even know what a lady was. Hammerhead, on the other hand, was young, brown, and sweet. She put down her mop, picked up her pot, and said, "No," wishing she'd said yes.

Hammerhead said that was okay. Popeye would have never said that. His spirit was slipping away, leaving Hammerhead to worry about Bilbo and the cops on his own.

They had stopped talking, stopped slurping, stopped

breathing almost. The one chewing on his sunglasses had listened closely to Hammerhead and the waitress talking and now hated the little creep that much more.

Hammerhead remembered the gun. He had it tucked into the belt of his pants, digging a barrel-shaped hole in his thigh. Should he or shouldn't he? What would Popeye do? He decided that if Popeye were there he would pick up his plate, chicken bones and all, and fling it at the cops as if it was a Frisbee. That's what Hammerhead did. While they were ducking away from the eruption of bones, fries, ketchup, grease, and nasty slivers of shattered plate, he jumped over the counter and crashed through the swinging doors that opened onto the back.

Waiting for him in the pungent steam of the kitchen was a raw-boned man with rotten teeth, his apron spotted with beef blood. In his hand was a carving knife. Hammerhead pulled out his gun.

"I need out of here."

He could hear the scrambling of the cops and the scratching of their radio as the man pointed with his knife at a metal door that had been painted three different shades of green: forest for the knob, kelly for the dead bolt, and lime for everything else. Hammerhead went through it and found himself in the same alley in which he had parked the car.

The car was waiting down behind the Old Customs House with gas in the tank, a gerbil in the glove compartment, and all the speed that Billy the Bopper could put in a car that was fifteen years past its prime. Hammerhead knew he should take care of Bilbo but he had to take care of himself first, so he ran the other way—down the alley, through a gangway, across an empty parking lot, and into the musty husk of a shuttered building that used to be the headquarters of Browning Cartage Company.

He sat on an old apple crate in a room full of empty wine bottles. Through a knothole in one of the boards that had been nailed over a broken window he watched the activity on Commercial Avenue and waited for cops who never came. One officer was cruising the streets, but it wasn't either of the two who had questioned him in the restaurant. The cop had his window open and his shotgun at the ready, but he kept his eyes locked in a straight-ahead direction, as if to make sure that he wouldn't see a thing.

Bilbo hadn't eaten in quite some time, longer still since he'd had one of those gerbil pellets that kept his jaw loosened and his teeth sharpened for the all-important task of chewing his way to freedom. He'd almost cut through one wire and had made a serious gash in another, but he was running out of steam. You couldn't expect a gerbil to survive on slobbered-over bits of stale bread and the occasional Twinkie crumb, but Hammerhead seemed content to let him waste away. Bilbo missed Popeye, although he lacked the wits to know it.

All Bilbo knew was hunger and thirst and the broiling heat of a downstate summer day until two cops pried open the driver's door of Billy the Bopper's car and started looking for guns and dope.

"Hey, what's this?" the one cop said.

"It's a glove compartment. What do you think?"

"Never seen one like that before. Covered with chicken wire, I mean."

"That must be where they keep the drugs. You check while I call the station."

Bilbo squeezed himself into a corner and shivered with fear while the cop with the cheap sunglasses peeled back the wire of his cage. He peed all over himself when the cop stuck his hand in the cage and started to feel around for guns and drugs. When the cop's fingers poked at his back he would have pooped all over himself, too, if he'd had any food in his guts. As it was, all he could do was take a big bite out of the clumsy thumb and scramble his way to freedom while the one cop screamed and the other one wondered what the problem was.

Nothing much was happening on the street, but Hammerhead stared at it anyway. The only other thing to look at was the last remains of the Browning Cartage Company and that was only wine bottles, rotting wood, and the stench caused by men and women who didn't mind peeing in the same place they slept. The street was like a movie by comparison—a dog trotting around as if he owned the place; scraps of paper chased by gusts of wind; people walking back and forth from no place to nowhere. His heart beat a little faster every time the cop drove by, but the cop never stopped, never slowed, never looked to either side.

After a while the street seemed as boring as the room he was sitting in, so Hammerhead's mind started to wander in unfamiliar directions. He thought about things that he had never thought about before and remembered things he hadn't remembered in years—the picture his mother had of two little boys in perfect white suits with jet black hair and scrubbed brown smiles, of Hammerhead and Raoul, the brother he had lost to the time and distance of sunny California.

The picture had been taken in Puerto Rico, which was one of the other things that Hammerhead never thought about. He remembered it as a place where all the people were as happy as he and Raoul seemed to be in the photo their mother had always cherished. Their father remembered Puerto Rico as the place where he had lived his better days. He used to suggest that they should go back, but Mama would have nothing of that. She was tired of being poor. They were poor in Chicago, too, but it was a different kind of poor. There they were TV-set poor and old-Buick poor. The kind of poor where you ate meat all the time and died of heart disease instead of the rot. The city was an easy, well-fed poor, and you could go to a movie every now and then. After Puerto Rico, that was good enough for Mama.

Papa didn't see it that way. To him, being poor in Puerto Rico meant that four million people shared your misery, like a great big party that didn't cost a lot. Everyone was poor in Puerto Rico, and Papa felt a lot better in thinking that he was not alone. But in the city almost everyone was rich. A big house, a new car, and a closet full of clothes—all the things that Hammerhead's father could never provide for his family—were the only real measure of a man in the north. Being poor in the city meant you had to eat shit five times a day and then go home and watch it on TV. The commercials kept telling his father to buy all these things he couldn't afford, and the news kept showing him what happened to Puerto Ricans who tried to improve themselves by illegal means, which seemed to be the only means available. After a while, Hammerhead's father gave it up and went back home. Mama went on welfare, Raoul left for California, and Hammerhead was recruited by the Alone Unknown.

The sun went down while Hammerhead was thinking. When he stopped he noticed that all the noise and light of the day had been sucked into a small building with a flashing neon sign in front. He couldn't quite read what the sign said, but he still knew what it meant. Behind it was the smell of beer and the sound of music from a jukebox full of that howling jive white folks like. He knew the air inside would be thick with smoke and the parking lot would be crowded with cars that the owners were much too drunk to drive. Popeye had told him about cars like that.

Hammerhead waited until it was almost closing time, which is 2:00 A.M. in Cairo and the other little towns of Little Egypt. By then there were only three cars left in the parking lot, including a Toyota 4x4 that looked brand new and big enough to live in for a while. He hoped the tank had plenty of gas because he didn't want to have to rob a Get N' Go right away. Stealing a car would be robbing enough for one night, but no big deal if the owner stumbled by with the keys.

The heat was close and hard to breathe. His throat was parched, and his lips were cracking, and he found himself hoping that the driver of the 4x4 would bring a beer along when he walked into the parking lot.

He didn't. He wanted another beer, but the bartender wouldn't sell him one.

"Go home, Bunker," the bartender had said. "Get yourself some sleep. Whatever happened to Gloria? Maybe you should let her drive."

Bunker started swearing and calling the bartender names, but he still wouldn't give him another beer. He almost knocked a table over as he wobbled to the door, and he almost dropped his keys as he tried to unlock the door to his vehicle. The keyhole was acting like a moving target, and his aim was a little off. Hammerhead offered to give him a hand.

"Fuck off," Bunker said.

Hammerhead drew his gun and pointed it at Bunker, who was too drunk to be afraid or even to know that his life was in danger. He pointed his key at the moving target and gave it another try.

"Give me the key," Hammerhead said.

"I said fuck off," Bunker replied. Those were two of his favorite words.

Hammerhead heard the brief crescendo of hillbilly music followed by the thick slur of drunks on the move. He recognized these as the sounds of someone else leaving the bar and knew that they would soon be around the corner and in the parking lot.

"How come you're talking to me like that."

Bunker was going to reply, but before he could, the gun came crashing down on his wrist. The drunk fell one way and his keys fell the other. Hammerhead swept them up off the ground and hit the keyhole on his very first try. He was driving out of the parking lot just as the other drunks were walking in.

The heat didn't seem so hard to breathe now that he was on the move. He drove by the Old Customs House to see how Billy the Bopper's car was doing. It remained there, still waiting for Hammerhead and still being watched by a cop in a squad car who seemed more interested in something he was reading. He hoped Bilbo was still chewing away at steel and wondering where Popeye was in the dim sort of way that gerbils wonder. In the morning they would tow it away and sell it for scrap to some local guy who bought plenty of tickets to the Policeman's Ball. Hammerhead hoped the buyer would be kind to Popeye's pet.

He was well on his way out of town when Gloria woke up from her drunken slumber in the back seat of Bunker's 4x4. She rubbed the stupor from her eyes and tried to wet her lips with a tongue as dry and stale as yesterday's beef jerky.

"Pull over, Bunkie. I gotta take a pee."

Hammerhead hit the brakes. The 4x4 slowed to a halt, and the air became thick again. The moon spilled a beam into the back seat. It landed on an older woman who was round all over—round face, round hips, round breasts straining at the buttons of her blouse. She looked at Hammerhead with weary eyes, confused but not yet frightened.

"Who are you?"

Maybe it was the alcohol that clouded her senses or maybe it was the moonbeam. Maybe Hammerhead was becoming a man or maybe the living spirit of the dead Popeye really was resting in his best friend's heart. In any event, Hammerhead said the right thing, just like Popeye would have done.

"Bunkie got arrested. He said I should drive you home."

Gloria Cantrell sat up straighter and looked outside. She was still confused, but she wasn't afraid. "What's your name?"

He decided not to lie about that. He told her his name was Eduard Rivas and then told a different lie instead. "I guess I got lost. Maybe you should tell me where you want to go."

Gloria thought about it. She thought about how she started out with Raymond and ended up with Bunker. Raymond had left her for a girl half her age, and she didn't know which part hurt her more, Raymond leaving or being thirty-eight. The more she thought about it, the less she worried about Raymond and the more she worried about forty.

That's when the big lonely started. A little lonely had always been there, even when she was with Raymond and he wasn't being a jerk. But it got worse after he left, and Gloria found out there were only two cures: dying and fucking. One cure was permanent, the other temporary. For the time being she preferred fucking.

That's where Bunker came in. He didn't have a clue, but he did have all his teeth that day when he flashed a big smile at Gloria in the River's Bend Saloon. The Bender it was called. She asked Bunker for a light and he asked her for a cigarette. Three hours, seven beers, and two dances later, they were going at it hard and fast, like he was pounding nails. Bunker was a carpenter. Gloria squealed and talked dirty, hoping this would slow him down. But the carpenter would not be distracted from the orgasm he was constructing like one of those cheap houses that is half-built already before it gets to the construction site.

Bunker wasn't much, but he was all she had, and Bunker wasn't here. A kid named Eduard was. An Indian kid by the look of him. Gloria didn't mind. A young Indian kid—like the kind that built those mounds in the shapes of snakes and birds and dogs—but that was okay, too. Besides, it was four in the morning, and she had the big lonely again, like her gut was a hole that she was falling into.

"I'm not going anywhere until I take a pee. How about pulling to the side of the road?"

Hammerhead thought about leaving her as she squatted in the bushes. But something in her eyes, or something in his heart, or something that Popeye's spirit whispered from the back of his brain persuaded him to wait until she came back to the car. He was glad he did, because she came back naked as the day she was born, carrying her clothes in a wrinkled ball.

She climbed into the 4x4 and said, "Sit back."

He did as he was told. She told him to relax while she rubbed the hot lump between his legs. She told him she was going to suck him and then she did just that. Steam rose from the river and the light of an August moon bathed their bodies as they rested.

When Hammerhead was ready again, they did a slow belly roll to a place in the heart they'd never been before. He was sweet to her and gentle, but strong. Not the old, cruel strong, like Raymond, Bunker and all the rest, but a lithe, eager strong. He was to her like the ever-swelling, never-ending tide of some ocean in her soul. She was to him like the gift of life itself, the door to a world he'd heard about but didn't believe was real. His younger brown body came to her older white one, and they both felt a warm shiver in which everyone is new and everything is possible. Every time he pressed his soul deep into hers, she wanted to keep it there forever, and she also wanted to let it go so he could press it home again. Theirs wasn't the angry sort of fucking that she and Raymond used to do because she knew that this boy worshipped her and would do whatever it took to get her where she wanted to go. When she got there she started to cry, and then Hammerhead exploded too, with a hot burst that filled her up and leaked all over Bunker's imitation rabbit-fur seat cover.

25

Smaller Bites

THE COOLING SHADOWS OF THE EDITING BAY REMINDED NAT THAT the dark could also be a place of sleep and peace, forever making him the promise of something like love. As if in a trance, he sat for a while staring at all the throbbing dots. That's what they looked like if you put your nose right up to the tube and could forget the illusion of two-dimensional reality that the dots combined to produce, the illusion of which Nat was both master and slave. He nudged the joy stick and continued his review of the videotape he'd captured of the city drifting into anarchy. It didn't seem to matter that tears and fears, fire and blood were common-place in no-man's-land before the mayor was shot. People now hung on tightly to the notion that the mayhem had meaning for once. He wiggled the joy stick until he found the piece of tape he was looking for.

"The mayor is still in stable condition, whatever the hell that means. What we need here is some law and order, but I've got to say I have my doubts. Our mayor was cut down at a public meeting in a public place, but the police still can't find who did it. That's because they're all hiding behind their ironclad pension funds and their fat city union contracts. When's the last time you seen a city cop on the unemployment line? Public servants don't serve the public anymore because we're too busy serving them."

Nat turned the volume down and let Doogie speak in silence for a while. He'd been slicing and dicing tape all day, taking a quick nap on the couch so he'd be able to work some more. The work was boring in large part, boring and precise, like stitching a quilt out of electronic blips. The patches were shifting shapes of cathode color, and the thread was modulated natural sound that could be booted or muted, depending on the situation and the effect Nat wanted to produce.

When he finished the job, it would still be a mess, but a smaller mess than before. The work reminded Nat of those poor ladies down in Central America who sew baseballs for a living. If they didn't sew the stitches tightly, the pitches would curve all over the place and the high-priced sluggers wouldn't get their hits. Baseball as we know it would soon cease to be, and the Republic would be imperiled thereby. The Big Leagues paid only two cents a ball, but those ladies had better get it right.

Plenty of loosely stitched curve balls were in the eighty hours of raw tape they had gathered for their various clients. Organizing the material into something coherent would not be an easy task. To this end, Nat was making two lists of the footage they had captured, one list for Delilah Blue and the other for use in the five-part series they were producing for Channel Twelve. The bits and pieces of videotape for sale included: Doogie and the mayor and lots of other people talking about crack cocaine and how it hurt the city; Elmo with and without hair, and the sound bite they got from him the night Armando "Tappy Shoes" Calderone was killed; crude black and white photographs of other teenage victims of teenage gangster violence; plenty of videotape from the assassination attempt, with some particularly gruesome pictures of the astonished mayor of Alton bleeding at the jowls from a wound caused by a flying sliver of podium.

Channel Twelve liked that one, so Allan would write it into the script, and Janette would read it into the mike. During one of a never-ending series of never-ending meetings, Parker had insisted they use it.

He had jumped up from his seat and said, "Maybe Janette can do that bit where they say, 'The pictures you are about to see may be too strong for some viewers.' That always wakes them up."

Nat looked at the monitor. Doogie was still speaking in silence. He made a third list in his mind of the tape they still had to shoot to fill out the five-part series. This task was complicated by Allan and Jerry not being able to decide what the series was going to be about. Part One would be about the Crack War and Part Five about the Street Crusaders and the politics of gangsterism. The parts in the middle were up for grabs and would be assembled according to the requirements of scripts as yet unwritten.

By the time they were done they would have enough raw material to say just about anything in as many parts as they wanted to say it. The list of sights and sounds already filled two oversize legal pads: sound bites with gang bangers and their grieving mothers; experts employed by the President's Commission on Urban Youth Crime; charts and graphs tracking trends and data; an interview with a skinhead who had a swastika tattooed on his forehead and was proud to be a citizen of white America; tape of Doogie's election campaign and of the ongoing disturbances.

The sound bite with Elmo was the hardest part. He had that nervous look in his eyes that people sometimes get when they speak the truth by mistake, and the sound track was cluttered with the ambient noise of the street pressing in on him from all sides as the authorities cleaned up the mess that had been Tappy Shoes.

And in the statement Elmo had made Nat detected rich currents of meaning that rose above and flowed beneath mere words. The trembling voice held something that went deeper than the usual unease suffered by people when the camera turns their way. He played the bite over and over again, juicing up the ambient or toning it down a bit when Elmo said it was Willis's fault that the city was destroying itself and Doogie would save the day.

"It's too long," Allan had said.

Nat disagreed but didn't say so right away. Parker wasn't sure and Janette didn't care. Nat looked at another slice of tape, but kept going back to what Elmo had said. There was something in the eyes he could not see, something in the words he could not hear. He thought about it when they were driving around with Janette and when they were setting up for her latest interview. He thought about it before going to sleep and as Doogie's pantomime speech penetrated the cool shadows of the editing bay. It was there that Nat began to think about a shorter sound bite that would say much more with less.

Alderman Smith watched the drugstore blonde give the wheel a whirl. Somebody bought a vowel and the blonde flipped some e's. It was a phrase: To e or ot to e. Doogie talked to the TV set. He said, "To be or not to be, you stupid piece of shit."

Douglas liked this game show a lot. He had decided it was popular because the contestants were dumber than the average American, which made the average American feel superior to himself. He called into the kitchen. "Come get me some Certs."

When a commercial came on, the alderman's thoughts drifted back to the press conference at Haymarket Square. He tried to imagine how it would look on the six o'clock news, with grim ranks of Street Crusaders and testimonials from people who'd been injured or robbed during the "ethnic disturbances" that had followed the events in Little Egypt. Trouble looked good on the news, like a cop show that had run amok and blundered over the shifting line between TV fact and fiction. It made a spectacle of red blood and golden fire reflected in broken glass. A made-for-TV riot. Eat your heart out, M.L. King, who never got to see the riot he'd caused.

Elmo came in with some peppermint Certs. Douglas popped one into his mouth and sucked on it while they played the theme to the "NBC Nightly News," with the orange glow of the western sky and the Statue of Liberty spinning on her heels.

The national news was mostly about Russia and the weather. The Romanovs were making a comeback, and Hurricane Leonard was picking up steam. A long, sad story followed about a farmer who had to kill all his cows because the drought had destroyed his feed crop and dried up the aquifer. Their tortured mooing was more than the farmer could stand. They finished with a story about the world's biggest hairball and the cat that had produced it. NBC gave the Statue of Liberty one more whirl, and the Republic rested easy for yet another night. Cut to commercial.

"Let's go, Elmo," Douglas said. "It's almost time already."

Elmo brought in the beer and chips, which they slurped and crunched to the relentless drumming and wall-to-wall horns of the "Channel Twelve News" music. Pictures exploded from the night skyline of a city made of light—pictures of John and Janette, sports with Bill, Pete with the weather and a comic commentary. Elmo liked that Carpinski. He was a funny guy. The announcer got excited as he started things off with his usual line:

"And here's Chicago's top news team."

The news music faded and the never-ending tale of woe began. Old people were dying from heat stroke and young ones from AIDS and drugs and guns. Then came sports, weather, a movie review, and a little politics before the break just to keep them honest.

Janette's lead-in was flawless. She punched the right words and punched them hard: alderman . . . poverty . . . working . . . blame. Elmo stopped chewing although his mouth was full of uncrunched chips.

Crumbs spilled out when he said, "I'd like to fuck her face."

"Shut up, Elmo. My sound bite's coming up here."

The candidate listened to himself on television, admiring his own ability to say it all in ten seconds. The 2-D Douglas said, "That's where we must put the blame, my friends, and that's where we must start to rebuild our city. The labor riots of the last century and the ethnic disturbances of this one are bred in the same rat's nest of governmental corruption."

The 2-D Douglas gave way to a story about a homeless man who lived in a box with three devoted dogs. The 3-D Douglas hit the mute button, turned to his bodyguard, and said, "They need to find the body quick. Good things'll happen if they find the body and bad things if they find this Hammerhead guy. How come you haven't popped him yet?"

"He could be dead, too, maybe, or too scared to come back home. We've got people watching the roads and watching the yard where he does hang time, but he hasn't showed up. Not yet, anyway. We'll pop him when he does, okay?"

Douglas hit the mute button in time to hear Janette and the gang at "Channel Twelve News" say good-night to their loyal listeners. The camera lingered on her as the news music swelled into a fanfare of excited horns.

"I think she likes me," Allan said. "What about you?" He didn't have to say who she was. She was long and lean, dark and delightful, and had a face that looked great in two dimensions. In the way that men once believed that the crescent moon was but the bend in Diana's bow, Allan had come to believe that if only Janette could overlook a few protruding teeth and his tendency to spray, she would come to love him for his mind, his money, and his news judgment. Janette encouraged this delusion.

Nat said, "I never liked you, Allan. I think you're a chump. I'd quit this thing if it wasn't for money. What's the money at right now?"

"That's not what I mean. I mean, do you think *she* likes me?"

"No. What's the money at?"

They counted up the money from the mayor's office and the money from Channel Twelve. To this they added the money from the blast seen round the world. Francs from France, marks from Germany, and yen from the Japanese. They were rich but not rich enough. Not yet, anyway.

Nat said, "Let's talk about my doc."

"You don't have a doc. Let's talk about Jan."

"Wait a second. Here's our tape."

For the fifth day in a row, Channel Twelve used some of their explosion footage to illustrate a story about the assassination attempt and its many and varied aftereffects. They were trying to get some mileage out of the one week of secondary rights they had secured after Allan lowered the price to $100 per.

Nat turned down the sound after Janette reported no new leads. Allan jotted down 13 seconds in the logbook, the length of the tape they'd supplied for Janette's report. Thirteen seconds, thirteen hundred dollars. The news director at Channel Twelve didn't like the deal much and wanted a meeting to thrash things out. Allan thought maybe Janette would be there.

He said, "You want to make money or you want to make a doc? You can't do both." His eyes drifted back to the TV set and the flattened image of his beloved.

"All right," Nat said. "You be that way. Forget about the doc. Let's talk about the series and see how much we've got—two years' worth of all the dead gangsters we covered for local stations. Most of the gangsters are still in their teens and most of the tape is from the Northwest Side so our opening shot is Logan Park. There's people having fun with music in the background. Somebody plays an acoustic guitar that breaks out into the blues. We do some quick edits of the dead kids on the low notes. A long freeze frame on the last mug shot and Janette says something that's not too dumb and very short. You hear what I'm trying to say?"

Allan chewed his lips. "I hear that you're shooting a doc and calling it a series. It's not going to happen. This is TV news we're doing. Ninety seconds and then you go sell soap."

Nat stomped off into the editing bay, shut the door, looked at the tube. Elmo's face was just where he had left it, frozen in a video moment that had happened weeks before. Nat pressed the button called REAL TIME and Elmo's 2-D image started to move and speak.

"What you need to know is Doogie Smith and the Street Crusaders are the only thing keeping more kids from getting all shot up, and I'm not just saying this because he's a friend of mine. The mayor has got to be the one to blame for selling us down the river to the narco-killer street gangs that really run this town."

Allan came in without knocking, sipping his coffee and rubbing his eyes. Face puffy, hair unkempt, attitude adjusted. "Give it up, Nat. It doesn't work. You're trying too hard and it shows."

Nat put the joy stick in reverse, retreating to the part where they loaded Tappy Shoes into the ambulance. "Fine. Whatever. Forget the doc. Where we going to put this bite?"

When the two men had reviewed the sound bite one more time, Allan said, "No place. It's too long for a news format. We're back to the doc again if we start using bites like this."

Nat picked up a pencil and threw it against the edit bay door. The lead tip shattered, and the fragments tumbled to the floor. "But the Street Crusaders are part of the story, and all we've got is Doogie. We need a bite from the troops, and this is the only troop we got."

"Then let's go interview somebody else, some other Street Crusader."

Nat punched the REWIND button and watched the rapid unhappening of events. Seeing the death of Tappy Shoes in reverse was like rewinding back to his own childhood. "I've got a better idea."

"What's that?"

"We talk to this guy I know. Crazy Horse is his name, and he knows all about the gangs. He'll give us a good talking-to and maybe get us back on a better track. We'll pick up

Janette after the ten o'clock show so she can hold the microphone."

That got Allan's attention. His eyes opened wide and the blood rushed through his veins at a somewhat faster pace. He put down the empty coffee cup and started looking for a comb or brush. He couldn't find either and used his fingers instead.

"Okay. It's a shoot. But that sound bite's still too long. Trim it down with a jump cut, and maybe we can splice it in someplace if it means that much to you. Part Two or maybe Three, the stuff that hasn't been mapped out yet."

Allan called the station while Nat started fussing with various techniques to cut the sound bite down to size. First he chopped off the last sentence, but that left a bite that didn't make sense. Next he chopped off the first two sentences, but then it became just another attack on the mayor. Allan looked at the edited bites.

"I don't think so. Correct that. We can't say bad things about the mayor with all the money he's paying us. Even if he is a veggie, I'd rather not piss Delilah off."

Nat loitered in the newsroom while Allan dickered with the night editor over details of their expense account. Janette slipped a thumb under her brassiere and gave her boobs a tug, then glanced up from her newspaper to make sure Nat was watching. He was. She said, "Where we going?"

"Downtown."

"Why?"

"To talk to this guy."

"You mean a source? How exciting. You must enjoy your work."

Nat glanced over to the glass radio room, where Allan and the night editor were haggling over mileage and meals. "I like the money is all. I'll be getting out when I get enough."

She put down her paper and hitched up her skirt on the pretext of scratching an itch on her knee. Nat looked at an idle battery pack instead, wondering if it was more reliable than his own.

"Your partner is a bit of a dweeb," Janette said, "if you don't mind my saying so."

"I don't mind, but he might. Allan's a little sensitive."

Janette shrugged, as if she'd heard of sensitivity once but didn't believe it really existed. "So how come you photographers are always so artistic? I noticed that about the shooters here. They read books and have liberal opinions. They're mostly all artists and these weird Bohemian types. Sometimes it seems like you are, too, so it must be some photographer deal."

"I think you're imagining things," Nat said.

Janette smiled. She was imagining things. She was imagining Nat lying naked on his bed and becoming sexually aroused by her reading of the late-night news, especially the bloody parts. Death and sex. Sex and death, the yin and the yang of TV news.

"I can have a good imagination too," she said. "Sometimes when I'm reading the news, I pretend that the TV looks both ways and I try to imagine what 350,000 people are doing at 10:00 P.M. on a weekday night. Think about it. Some are drunk and maybe crazy, and some are having sex with the television on. Then we have all the guys that masturbate while I'm reading the news. You wouldn't believe the mail I get, the things these weirdos write. I'll show you my letters sometime. Thursday, maybe. What do you think?"

Nat didn't say what he thought, just that he was busy on Thursday and busy on Friday, too. "I'm working on this project, and I've got to get it done."

"That's what I mean about photogs. Artistic Bohemian types."

219

26

Talking to Crazy

THE CLOSE QUARTERS OF THE CAR ENHANCED THE EFFECT OF Janette's perfume. Allan thought she smelled like bottled spring and snorted big loads of her scent as quickly as he could. Nat thought that when combined with the smog and the sweat and the already breathed air of Lower Wacker Drive, she smelled like a funeral.

She said, "So where's this source of yours?"

She was talking to Nat, but Allan answered. "Down at the Greyhound Station."

Again to Nat, she said, "How exciting."

She didn't look excited, tried to yawn but couldn't. They had interviewed a number of street gangsters in the week since her assignment editor had hired these guys to save his neck, and all of the gangsters looked like they needed a bath and they all said the same thing: "Gangs is the power of the people, mon. Gangs is the slow-mo revolution against the oppressive power of fat."

They drove around for three long nights before she figured out that fat meant money in that hip-hop talk the kids were doing now. Fat was too much money: specifically, the kind that TV journalists had.

She said, "Where'd you get this car?"

Nat replied by punching the accelerator. Allan answered at great length, for which Nat was grateful. It allowed him to ignore them both and watch the street. Janette didn't listen because she was too busy looking at herself in the rearview mirror.

She liked what she saw, and believed that she was the only reason that thousands of people kept themselves informed about current events. Last year she read the news about the AIDS epidemic, and this year she was reading about teenage gangsters. Next year she would read the news about something else. It didn't matter what it was because Channel Twelve's 350,000 regular viewers tuned in for her, not the news. The news was like the condo market at a cocktail party, something for boring people like Allan to talk about at length.

Allan was her willing slave and that was all well and good. She would have preferred a slave with a little less tooth, but he would have to do. She had a place in her life for mindless devotion. Nat was more perplexing. He wanted her, of course. All heteros did. But he seemed unwilling to pursue any of her carefully disguised invitations. Maybe he was gay, but she didn't think so. Maybe he was stupid, but she doubted it. Maybe he had been wounded in one of those nasty little wars she read on the late-night news. This seemed more likely, but she had to know for sure. In the hot flush of that Shoe Goo Summer night, she vowed to find out what his problem was and to solve it if she could.

Nat stuck his head out the window and breathed in some city air. The scent of Janette and the noise of Allan was starting to make him dizzy. His partner's familiar chant was like the hopeful murmuring of a monk at prayer, and caused him to think about all the churches he'd stopped going to. His defense against these unwelcome thoughts was to daydream about Barbados and the woman he'd met in the gaming room of the *Connecticut Yankee*. After a while this was worse than church or Allan because it reminded him how bad things were and how good things could sometimes get. So he tried to think about city politics and all the money they were making, and about his documentary and various theories that purported to explain the heat. He tried to think about lots of things, but his thoughts kept drifting back to the time he'd spent riding the Greyhound bus.

Poor people go Greyhound. They didn't put that on the TV ads, but that was the truth of things. Nat didn't like to think about it because he used to be poor when he was a kid. Every now and then he would have to take the Greyhound from one dusty city to another, mostly during the holidays when he was a college student. He'd go north to Milwaukee for school, and then back south to Chicago for Thanksgiving and Christmas and Easter and one more Shoe Goo Summer with Crazy and the boys from the old neighborhood, who didn't understand him anymore.

College had done him a lot of good, but it had also done him some bad. His world was smaller before he went to college, small enough to understand. Before college, his horizon was the fence that enclosed the playground of the Louisa May Alcott Public School, and the neighborhood was a place of gritty hope, where Jews and Germans and Ricans and Africans and Italians and Poles and Ukrainians struggled with one another for a piece of the rock. They mostly got some of what they were fighting for, only to have it turn sour later on when their children became white-collar trash, entangling themselves in mixed marriages consummated in Downers Grove.

Before college, the back-alley nights were ruled by gangs that hadn't yet discovered crack cocaine and hadn't yet become big business. The playground was ruled by tough guys who wore leather coats and combat boots in the winter, T-shirts and high-top basketball shoes in the summer. The girls all did crazy things to make their hair look special and screwed around at an early age because it was cheaper than going to a movie at the Biograph. On Saturday night they would pump up the volume on Crazy's boom box so that everybody in the 'hood could share the noise. They'd all pitch in for some Schlitz Malt Liquor and watch the moon rise over the four-story parking garage at the corner of Wrightwood and Clark.

He knew it wasn't much, but he liked it a lot until he left, when years and years of his parents' labor paid off all at once. His mother had worked nights at the hospital, and his father had worked weekends at Fred's Retreads so that when Nat graduated from Waller High School, they could pack him off to some college in Milwaukee run by guys all dressed up in black—Jesuits.

College meant the Greyhound, and the Greyhound was a drag. Nat remembered sitting next to an old black grannie with fat elbows and knitting needles; next to a retarded boy with his destination pinned to the collar of his coat; behind two young lovers who seemed to be doing it, or something very much like it, in the dark of the drive between Kenosha and Racine; in front of the most noisy, most squiggly family he had ever seen.

Those were the things about the Greyhoud that he liked. The thing he hated was that it reminded him of how poor he was. That was okay now that he was rich, but it also reminded him of Crazy Horse and the thing that he had done for Nat that Nat could never do back.

At 11:00 P.M. on a Friday, the Greyhound was the busiest place downtown, a great shell of a building filled with people who couldn't afford to be someplace else, some with purpose and most without. Three sailors from the Great Lakes Naval Base huddled around a pay TV and scrambled for another quarter when their time ran out. As Electronic News Tonight glided down the escalator, a fat woman with too many shopping bags glided up. Travelers waited in line for their tickets and waited in line for their buses. They waited in line for their luggage and waited in line for cafeteria food. A few strays unattached to lines wandered around the place. An old man who smelled of Newports and whiskey asked Allan for a match and seemed offended when he gave him one. A security guard with nervous eyes presided over an uneasy peace, trying not to notice the pimps, the whores, the drugs, and the sailors who were looking for same when they weren't looking at one of the pay TVs attached to every black vinyl chair.

Janette Baylor caused quite a sensation as her spike heels clacked against the linoleum floor of the departure area. The sailors whispered among themselves, the pimps gave her appraising glances, and the security guard averted his eyes. The whores were merely annoyed. Nat and Allan could be mistaken for bums-in-luck or drug users looking to trade a stolen camera for a fix. But Janette was a distinctly alien presence with her Marshall Fields' wardrobe and 2-D smile. Everybody stopped doing nothing and then did it again when she was out of sight. Janette didn't mind. It was just like reading the late-night news.

Crazy Horse was the overnight man at a shoeshine stand tucked among a row of shops that rented space from Greyhound. He also sold newspapers, magazines, candy, and tobacco, but the real money came from selling cocaine to executives and making book on just about anything. His shoeshine chair was a fancy leather piece mounted on a platform of felt and plywood like the throne of some penniless king. He was reading the *Racing Form* with the serene attitude that his station in life required when the TV journalists surrounded his stand. He didn't look up.

Nat said, "Shine, boy?"

"Go away, asshole," Crazy Horse replied.

Janette was amused, and Allan merely alarmed by the long silence that ensued. Crazy was still looking at his *Racing Form,* but he wasn't reading it anymore.

Allan finally said, "Is your name Crazy Horse?"

Everyone exhaled at once, as if the silence itself had sighed in relief. Crazy set down his *Racing Form,* uncovering a broken bridge of flesh and bone that used to be his left cheekbone. One by one and piece by piece, his teeth had fallen out until that side of his face became like an empty bag, soaked with the moisture of rotting gums.

Allan swallowed a gasp he dared not utter. He felt as if he were choking on a tennis ball. Crazy nodded at Allan and spoke to Nat.

"Who's the muscle you got with you?"

Allan coughed up the tennis ball. He felt pretty good about being called muscle until he realized it was just a joke. Then he felt pretty bad about it and felt a rush of roiling blood rise to the surface of his cheeks. Janette introduced herself. Crazy Horse was impressed.

"I seen you all the time with that goofy weatherman."

That eased the tension because they all could agree that the weatherman was indeed goofy. Nat and Crazy Horse hugged each other and performed a handshake of remarkable speed and complexity. The side of Horse's face that still had teeth seemed as proud as it could possibly be. Nat was almost blinded by the light in his eyes. Crazy took full credit for what Little Wimpy had become, Mr. TV Kool.

"I watch the TV every night before I come to work, with the lovely lady here and all the rest. Sitting back sucking on a cup of coffee, I got my remote control all ready to watch all the gangster news about how this punk killed that punk and they all be cracking with the rot cocaine. The gangsters never would be killing like that when Wimpy and me was in the 'hood. Our get-high was reefer and beer. So gimme some news, Little Wimpy. What you doing here at the midnight hour? I thought you only did gangster news. I'm a civilian now."

Allan and Janette waited with strained patience while the two old friends remembered old times. Nat told Crazy about the money and the women and Crazy told Nat about all the gangsters who had finally gotten too old to hang around the playground at Alcott Public School. China got a job with the Winnetka Parks Department and Klacker married a Ukrainian girl who kept him in get-high and groceries. Thumper was a three-time loser at Joliet State, and Earl the Girl had turned faggot for sure and danced at this place where the strippers were men. The rest had died or disappeared.

Crazy said, "You heard about Gilligan, right?"

"Sure I heard, from Emily over by the restaurant. She said he got popped by some kid too young for the Place."

They talked about Gilligan for a while, remembering some of the funny things he'd said and the stupid things he'd done. How he always said everything was stone, blown, or thrown to the bone. How this one time he ripped off this delivery truck and got stuck with twelve dozen electric razors he couldn't even give away. When they ran out of old times, Nat sat on the stool at Crazy's feet and told him why they'd come.

"We're working on a job, this TV thing. I can retire if we do it right and start doing something else that makes more sense. Like get myself a shoeshine stand."

Allan laughed, but he was the only one. Janette had wanted to, but was clever enough to restrain herself.

Crazy said, "Okay. So what's the story?"

Before Nat could say any more, a well-groomed man with a heavy gauze of sleep on his eyes came over to place a few bets. Crazy shined his shoes and carried his action on a number of propositions: Cubs over the Giants, Sally's Girl in the eighth race at Maywood Park, and a crazy eight dollars on Crazy's daily double on the Dow. This was a gentleman's wager based on the last two digits of the Dow Jones Industrial Average at the closing bell, a numbers game favored by his more affluent customers. The banker wanted to know what kind of points or odds he was giving in the mayor's race.

"The books like the alderman, and I can't disagree. Got the talk and the walk and the squawk right now. Big question seems to be the 'Spanics, like my friend Little Wimpy here."

Nat checked the available light around the banker's shoes. "You mind if I take some pictures of your feet?"

Not only did the banker not mind, he adjusted his tie in

case Nat wanted his face too. The TV lights caused a brief sensation among the other occupants of the station. Nat leaned over Crazy as Crazy leaned over the banker's shoes.

"I can't find any money on the mayor with any kind of odds," the banker said.

Crazy suggested that he bet on the weather instead. The banker took the odds on rain and departed with a brand new shine once they had settled on a modest sum and agreed to a reasonable definition of rain. Crazy watched the escalator carry him into the night.

"That was the street right there, Little Wimpy. You listen and it will speak."

"What does it say about the Street Crusaders?"

The question hung in the air for a while as Crazy climbed into his shoeshine chair. The left side of his body, the side with the broken face, sagged a little as he moved. It appeared that all the pain and humiliation the wound produced had taken some solid form that weighed him down when he was weary.

"The Street Crusaders is known to the bone. That's what Gilligan would say if he never got iced by that little punk. The Street Crusaders is God's own gangsters, kicking that righteous criminal butt. Regular gangsters don't like it much, being the butts that're getting kicked and seeing as how the Crusaders is getting all the pub."

Allan wrinkled his brow. "That's publicity, right?"

"Way to go, Muscle Man. Pub is how gangsters get a righteous reputation, and the Street Crusaders been getting it all by saving old ladies and shit like that, but the pub's just lies for the TV news. How come the news got so many lies? You think you'd maybe get something right."

The journalists looked at one another but didn't say a thing. Like most people who ask a lot of questions, they weren't prepared to answer any. Crazy wouldn't let it go.

"It's almost like if it's on the news you know it can't be so. Gangs is the only news I know, and I see how they always get it wrong. Gangsters be loving their neighborhood. It's all the policemans that don't give a shit."

227

Nat tried to explain. "I just take the pictures. Those two write the words. The thing about TV is you open your eyes and shut your ears."

Crazy Horse weighed the words and weighed the pictures in the split-second way a gambler measures things and decided that the odds were that this was true. Odds were what Crazy had learned to go by.

"The talk around town that I been hearing is all about the troubles and how it's the Street Crusaders making it happen. Them and the Black Galabeyes. You go and put that on your TV news."

Nat set up his tripod, and Janette fluffed up her hair. Allan prepared a list of questions and counted backwards, "Three, two, one," during the microphone check. Crazy sat on his shoeshine throne while Janette asked him about his face, the odds, and the troubles. She asked him about the Street Crusaders and about the gangs that ruled the city at night.

Crazy replied with passion. He said the gang was better than a family because it didn't get drunk and beat you up without sharing you a sip from the bottle too. The gang was better than a country because it gave you a chance to live with respect and make a little money on the side. The gang was better than a prayer to God because it wasn't afraid to show its face. The gang was better than nothing. That's where gangs came from.

Nat kept the camera rolling while Crazy did business with some more customers. He sold a magazine to a rumpled man headed for a Greyhound bus and took a wager on the fifth race at Maywood Park from a cleaning lady who knew just enough English to understand the odds. He complained to her about the men's room, and she replied with bitterness in a language he did not understand. A sailor asked him for a shine, but Crazy told him to go get lost.

By then Nat had the tape he needed and started to reel in the microphone. Janette was dragged along like a mermaid who had swallowed the hook. Allan grabbed the microphone. "Hold it up a second. There's one more question we forgot to ask. How come you call him Little Wimpy?"

Crazy dusted off his shoeshine chair. The half of his face that could smile smiled. The eye that couldn't see straight and the ear that couldn't hear right seemed to be seeing and hearing something that had happened long ago, something that made Crazy proud and made Nat wish he was someplace else. Crazy sat back in his chair, turning his good side to Allan.

"You never done a crime?"

"No."

"Never killed a man?"

Silence.

"Never know a man been killed by a man or even been in the Place? Never done a garbage-can barbecue?"

After more silence Crazy leaned forward and whispered so only Allan could hear. "You got to pull a caper if you want to understand. Soon as you do, you come back to me, and I'll tell you what his mama done."

27

Finding a Float

IT STARTS AS A TRICKLE IN MINNESOTA, AS IF THE SKY HAD SPRUNG a leak. For a hundred miles or so, it can't decide where it wants to go—north, then east, then south, then east, east, east, until it gets to Grand Rapids. There it makes a right turn and begins at last its epic journey south down through the swollen belly of a nation that stretches from sea to shining sea, with smokestacks rusting in between.

A hundred streams and a thousand creeks empty their waters into the mighty Mississippi as it carries all things before it like the passage of time itself. It rolls like a life-giving god through land that hasn't changed at all since the days of Huck and Nigger Jim. It passes through the waterlogged towns left behind by the latest flood, and it passes between St. Paul and Minneapolis, cities devoted to the manufacture of calendars and the unimpeded passage of trucks from east to west and back.

As the river rushes through the belly of the land, it collects souvenirs of its travels: chemicals of every sort and urine of every kind; cigarette butts, fast-food wrappers, and the leaves of a maple tree; dead bugs and gray mud, twigs, and sticks; the full issue of the Chicago Sanitary and Ship Canal and of the older canal that replaced; the eggs of fish that thrive in such conditions; and the last remains of Popeye.

The corpse had become snagged by the limbs of a willow tree that was slowly sliding into the river north of Caruthersville, Missouri, which is just across the river from an empty part of Tennessee. Fish nibbled at the extremities while smaller organisms worked to churn protein into gas until Popeye's guts were inflated like a cheap balloon. When a heavy rain in Iowa caused the river to rise, the corpse became dislodged from the tree, rushing downriver like a cork in a storm.

A boy fishing on the Saskatoolie Bridge couldn't believe his eyes. A loving couple from Caruthersville thought they'd been visited by an alien Elvis so it was left to the captain of a barge named *Louise* to call up the Blytheville River Police and report that a body was proceeding south at a speed he described as lickety-split. The Blytheville coppers didn't catch it but the Bricksville coppers did.

"Smells a little ripe to me."

"Looks like a balloon what's made of man."

"You bet. Like one of them floats in that Macy's Parade you can get on the cable from New York City."

"Wonder what'd happen if we hooked him with this gaff?"

"Go ahead. My guess is he'd splatter, but I been wrong before."

28

Newshounds

THE FORM OF THE JAIL FOLLOWED ITS FUNCTION, THANKS TO THE practical nature of the nineteenth-century architect who had built the stolid cube on the ashes of the Chicago fire. In keeping with its grim mission, the walls were made of poured concrete blocks knitted together with steel beams and coated with a plaster that had the pallor and texture of a dead fish broiling in the noontime sun. It had no windows on the first five floors, but the next twenty were perforated with hundreds of narrow slits. The slits allowed in a beggar's portion of air and light, but even the most desperate criminal could never hope to escape through them to the sort of freedom that follows a plunge of fifty feet or more.

Some years after the jail was completed, another nineteenth-century architect built the police headquarters a few blocks away. This fellow had the idea of keeping unsightly prisoners out of the view of respectable folk by connecting the two structures through one of the old supply tunnels that crisscross downtown Chicago like the filament of a subterranean web.

Though as practical as the first architect, the second was

less competent. Months after remodeling was complete, the tunnel started sweating a brackish soup of rainwater, smog, salt, and mud, seasoned with the spit and pee of bums who gleaned the alley between the police station and the jail for half-eaten doughnuts and unwanted prison food. A puddle collected in the part of the tunnel nearest to police head-quarters.

Since the Columbian Exposition of 1893, the city had battled the puddle with a crew of maintenance men and women assigned to the police department. This continued for ninety years, but then municipal tax revenue started to decline in the same term that Willis Cleveland promised to increase the number of uniformed officers fighting crime in the city. The maintenance crew was cut in half and the tunnel abandoned to the puddle on the pretext that, since it was used to move thugs about, it didn't need to be clean. After time, a particularly intrepid species of fungus climbed out of the puddle and toward the high-intensity ceiling lamps that illuminated the end of the passage that emptied into the basement of police headquarters.

This was the tunnel into which Sister Delilah Blue now stepped. She was hoping to avoid the knot of reporters who staked out the front door of police headquarters on the chance that something bad might happen to someone interesting. She clutched Chief Dreyer's arm as they approached the puddle, afraid that if she slipped on the fungus, the damp stink of the place would get all over her gray banker's dress.

"This place needs a good scrubbing," she said.

Chief Dreyer chuckled. The fungus was after the lamps now, choking the light with its rancid embrace. "What this place needs is another fire, so we can start all over again."

When their progress was stopped by the puddle in front of the far door, the chief mumbled at his radio, and the door was shoved open by an officer with one pair of galoshes on his feet and two more pairs in his hands. He marched across the puddle with a purposeful stride, handing one pair of galoshes to the chief and offering his arm to Delilah as she climbed into the other.

Thus shod, they splashed through the puddle, squished into the steel-cage elevator the cops used to move their prisoners, and squeaked through a squad room thick with the smell and sounds busy men make when crowded together with a few intrepid women: phones ringing, pencils dropping, somebody laughing someplace; hard voices barking at one another over the steady background noise of wheezing smokers, feet shuffling, and an untold number of electric typewriters clacking away. Their progress across the room was noted by all because galoshes in that place were regarded as an unambiguous badge of accomplishment, as the habit was to deliver a collar through the tunnel after the suspect had been hauled in for red tape and questioning.

Chief Dreyer closed his door behind Delilah and started to peel the galoshes off, his old cop heart set to racing by the stir their entrance had caused. It had been some years since he had been through the Drink, as the tunnel was called.

"The report should be coming in by fax pretty soon. It should be like I said."

Delilah walked over to the window and looked at the jail across the street. The narrow windows on the upper floors looked like air holes punched through a cardboard box in which some unlucky hamsters were trapped. She wondered what it felt like to look at a slice of freedom six inches wide. "Where'd they find the body?"

"Maybe ninety-five miles south of Cairo. Place called Bricksville. Country folks fished him from the river. The FBI is checking his teeth, but I think we got him marked in a general sort of way."

"General—meaning what?"

The chief looked out the window too. The Place held 3,568 yahoos tonight. He checked the prisoner count every morning. It never went below 3,565. "He's a member of the Alone Unknown. Had AU tatooed on what's left of his arm. That means 'Spanic and between age eleven and thirty-eight. We don't know his name but my guess is the feds will.

The dentals will mark him if he's served any time. Some of these people have real bad teeth."

Delilah turned away from the window and toward the door. "We need to play this exactly right. What're we going to say?"

The chief started cleaning his glasses with a silk handkerchief, working hard at a spot that wouldn't go away. "We say he's Italian instead. One of those blooded kind from Sicily. The dagos'll understand."

"Tell me about the gang."

"Twelve soldiers strong, maybe fifteen if you count all their little brothers that're still in kindergarten. They hang out in the playground of du Sable School."

The name echoed out of their shared past like the blabbering of an unloved teacher. The black preacher and the black chief paused a moment to remember the black man who had founded their city two hundred-odd years before and then left it for St. Louis as soon as he got the chance.

When the moment was over Delilah said, "The feds won't say he's Italian if he's not. How much time you think we got before the story's out?"

Chief Dreyer considered this carefully. He was hoping to leak the news himself to Radio Larry, so the reporter would owe him one. "A day," he said, looking at Delilah to see if she'd flinch.

She didn't flinch. She didn't move a muscle for what seemed like a very long time. Instead she pretended a careful nod with eyes closed, which is what she usually did when either forgiving sins or committing them. "No way. It'll be on the wire before I get back to City Hall."

"Not for a couple of hours at least."

"A couple of minutes, maybe, with all the gossip around this place."

The chief shrugged. Gossip was such an unsavory word, with its connotation of frustrated biddies blathering at tea. He preferred the more manly scuttlebutt.

"We need to be making plans," he said.

"For what?"

"For if we lose. I've seen the same numbers as everybody else. Doogie's going to win this thing, and we all got mouths to feed."

Delilah put on her sweetest face, which was also her most dangerous one. The chief backed off. She said, "Don't even think about it, or you'll be sucking scum in that tunnel downstairs after we win this thing. I wonder."

"What about?"

Delilah didn't say. She had an idea, but it wasn't one she cared to share with the chief, a vigilant protector of his own reputation. "I need a telephone," she said.

"You can use mine right over there. I'll go check on the fax."

Nat emerged from the editing bay with the red eyes and slack jaw that are the side effects of watching too much uncut video. He'd been scanning a box full of raw tape in search of a sound bite Allan needed for part three of the series, in which Janette plumbed the emotions of various women whose young men had been killed. The precise work of manipulating tape with joy stick and keyboard had left his hands weary but unsatisfied. He felt like smashing something—Allan's nose, for instance.

"When the election's over, I'm out of here."

Allan looked up from the legal pad on which he was writing the part three script. "Barbados, huh? You deserve it."

"Forget the Barbados. I mean out. We're done."

"How come?"

"Reason number one is you, and reason number two is money. With all the money we've got coming in, I'll be able to do my doc."

"What money is that?"

"I don't know, Allan. You're the one that counts the beans. How many beans we got?"

From a peg next to a dusty coal bin, Allan fetched the very blackboard that his father had once used to instruct him in the painful geography of Ireland. He checked the numbers on the back page of his clipboard and used a stub of chalk to outline the various "income flows," as he titled the lesson in great chalky blocks.

JULY CASH FLOW ANALYSIS

Client: Week	Mayor's office	Channel 12	Other
#1	$18,000— Cleve vs. Doogie.	$1,200—Kid dead w/tears and residuals.	$5,750—Video press release on bald cure.
#2	$23,075— Cleve vs. Doogie.	$525—Strike at bratwurst factory.	$17,255—Various fires, crashes, murders, etc.
#3	$15,110— Cleve vs. Doogie.	None.	$350—Resale of strike at brat factory.
#4	$123,000— Cleve vs. Doogie; river- boat blast.	$10,000—First installment of sweeps contract.	$250,525—Blast residuals and various.

Allan flashed back to his father while Nat studied the figures. His father was obsessed with Ireland's sad situation but had vowed never to go there until the English had left it alone. Allan's mother applauded this since her husband's mood must surely be affected by the gloomy temperament of the place. Toward the end, when the cancer had spread from his bones to his guts, he attempted to infect Allan with the Irish bitterness that had been both his weakness and his strength. Allan's contemplation of this bitterness was interrupted by Nat.

"So what's August looking like?"

Allan did a quick calculation about August but spoke about his father instead. "You know a funny thing my father used to say?"

Nat didn't know.

"He used to say that Ireland is full of stupid people

because all of the smart ones left. The crooks went to Australia, and the politicians all came here, and Ireland got stuck with the ones that were too depressed to move. That's what he used to say."

"That right?"

"Right. And then he'd go into this long story about the Irish potato famine. He'd use this blackboard here."

"No shit. Makes me want to go sing sappy songs, like 'Danny Boy' except we're talking about the money now. The way it's going, I figure that August will be even better than July, with the campaign heating up and the contract with Channel Twelve and the residuals from the paddle boat still rolling in. So what's the payout look like when you add the whole thing up?"

Nat's share was not a subject Allan was eager to discuss as there were different answers depending on the difference between net and gross as defined in Electronic News Tonight's incorporation papers, under the heading of Capital Equipment Fund. Nat wouldn't appreciate the difference, so Allan made the calculation as slowly as he could and was much relieved when his mother answered the phone and yelled down into the basement that Delilah was on the line.

Delilah and the chief killed time by paging through the rap sheets that the chief's staff had gleaned from an extensive collection. The Alone Unknown Neighborhood Corps had five known offenders among its ranks. They had young faces and old eyes and had committed the usual assortment of crimes: possession, theft, assault and battery, possession with intent to sell. Delilah and the chief joked about their street names and tried to figure out how boys too young to shave had come be called Grog, Hammerhead, Popeye, and the Truth.

The chief said, "The thing you need to know about gangster names is they always make some kind of sense. You take this Hammerhead person here."

He tossed the rap sheet into Delilah's lap. She read the

record carefully and studied the photograph. "Must be the way his nose is smashed."

"Maybe. But the other thing you need to know about gangster names is they're also in some kind of secret code that doesn't mean a thing to you and me, like the Loyal Order of Water Buffaloes and their secret ceremonies. So it could mean this one's got a head bone of stone but if that's what I think, then it must mean something else."

Delilah was looking at the rap sheet on the Truth when a clerk came into the office with a fax from the FBI. Chief Dreyer glanced at the document before handing it over. The fax was a copy of a press release that hadn't been dated yet.

FBI CRIME LAB IDENTIFIES REMAINS

Examination of dental records at the Joliet State Correctional Center confirms the identity of the remains marked 6:37 A.M./AUGUST 8/BRICKSVILLE. Albert Espinosa was a known gang member of Latino descent with a record of numerous arrests and one conviction for theft. He was a suspected drug user and dealer and a known associate of underworld figures. While in prison he was suspected of consorting with Muslim radicals who advocate the overthrow of the U.S. government. He is believed to be responsible for a series of armed robberies in and around Alexander County, Illinois. Traces of sulfur and other residual elements confirm earlier reports that he was an active agent in the incident of 30 July. The FBI would like to thank the law officers of Chicago and Bricksville for local assistance in the resolution of this matter.

"That's it, then," the chief said. "You want I should call out the dogs?"

At this point Delilah told him that Nat, Allan, and Janette were already en route. "Those are the newshounds we're giving this one to."

"How come?"

"Because they won't ask any stupid questions unless we tell them to. They're on the mayor's contingency fund, and they're working some kind of deal with Channel Twelve."

"Sounds to me like they been eating the wienie from both ends, Sister. You maybe should give them the boot."

"Maybe I should but not just yet. The way I see it, the Channel Twelve setup works for us right now. If we get them to break the news on Twelve, and break it the way we want, the other TV channels'll play it down because if Twelve's got it then it can't be news."

Delilah's scheme might have worked if the news had not already been out by the time Electronic News Tonight splashed through the puddle, squished up the elevator, and squeaked across the squad-room floor in three pairs of police galoshes. They reached the chief's office just in time to hear Radio Larry make the announcement in his most urgent Walter Winchell voice.

"Reliable but confidential police sources say that the body was found on the banks of the Mississippi River by authorities in the town of Bricksville. The name of the dead would-be assassin has not yet been released, but our sources tell us he is a member of an Hispanic street gang involved in the traffic of crack cocaine in the Lincoln Square district of the Northwest Side. City Hall is afraid this will aggravate the racial disruptions that have terrified law-abiding people ever since the mayor was injured in the attack of 30 July. Willis Cleveland has not appeared in public since the incident. The one man who could calm the situation is listed in stable condition at Walter Reed Memorial Hospital. This is Radio Larry Melville reporting for WDM Radio, 'News Live at 55.'"

The TV journalists looked at Delilah. Delilah looked at the chief. The chief looked out his window and said, "Whatever else you say about Larry, you've got to say he's fast. I wonder how he does it all the time."

29

CBS

THE CITY HAD A SLOW-MOTION REVOLUTION WITH VIDEO BARRI-
cades patrolled by somber suits with perfect hair who
described the carnage every evening at six and again at ten
and joked about it during the commercial breaks. Stores
were bombed and cars were overturned as the Afterbirth of
a Nation festered untended in the late summer sun. A Jew
who spoke no English, in his late-model Caddy with brushed
leather seats and a cellular phone to Tel Aviv, ran over a
person of color. People on the West Side didn't like this
much, so they destroyed Morganstern's Department Store,
which for eighty-seven years had supplied them with everything from boom boxes to socks.

A black person of color killed a brown person of color
with a carving knife still smeared with last night's roast, and
a brown killed a black for having an affair with his brother's
wife, but the big news was all about the Black Galabeyes and
the Alone Unknown.

Seven hours after the city heard the news about Popeye's
last remains, in the early morning of a muggy August day,
three carloads of black males drove into Lincoln Square

with a crate of molotov cocktails and a gross of Day-Glo spray paint cans. Within moments they had firebombed an empty building and sprayed the following on everything else:

WE GONNA KILL US
SOME SPANICS JUST FOR WILLIS

In the careful confines of Walter Reed Memorial Hospital and with his needs filled and unfilled through an assortment of plastic tubes, Mayor Cleveland slept the sleep not of the dead but of the deeply disappointed. Damage to his corpus callosum and the subsequent loss of blood had taken him into the deep netherworld that separates death from sleep, where all things become what they have never been.

The dark was life and the light was death in the mayor's netherworld. He could climb out of the pit only with great difficulty but had no wish to do so because the world of trance and vision was a great improvement over the world of fuss and fire that waited for him at the top of that climb. His choice was between the dark uncertainty of an unknown tomorrow and the absolute peace that waited through the bright portal of heaven's gate.

The death light was home to beautiful women of every size and color and shape who lived for love and yearned for the mayor's attentions. They nourished him with heroic portions of ice cream and Italian food, but he never got gas or gained a single ounce. They soothed his passion with their own desire and quenched his thirst with sweet ambrosia that made him drunk but never sick and did not contribute to the liver difficulties that his wife believed he would someday have.

The netherworld had its demons too, monsters that preyed on the unsuspecting and pathetic legions of the uninformed who devoured each other because they could not see that the true perpetrators of their rising misery were the monsters gathering beyond the pale. But the legions never ran out of bold young men, and it never seemed to hurt when the monsters ripped his flesh, and the chances were good that sooner or later the monsters would be chased away by giddy women who would caress his temples and repair his wounds with eager kisses and oral sex.

Every now and then he would climb out of the netherworld to see what had transpired in the darker world of fuss and fear. Things never changed, of course, and he always slipped back into the same sweet sleep until he conjured up a demon that no woman could chase away and no drink could obliterate.

He was back aboard the *Connecticut Yankee,* but the paddleboat and its occupants had been transformed into the opposites of themselves. Dark was light and bright was murk, like the negative of a photograph that had somehow become more real than the moment it was preserving. The riverboat that had been a celebration of noise and light in the overworld was now a dark and morbid presence on a shimmering sea set all aglow by the phosphorescent night.

A little black man with orange hair and translucent skin—perhaps it was the sainted X himself—addressed the Sons of Slaves. He said, "The Ice Men gathered in their stone-cold cave to nurse their grudge against the People of the Sun, who sleep under the stars, are warm, and don't need to wear so many threads. And the Ice Men said, 'We will build great cities full of shining towers that sparkle like ice and equip them with running water and cable TV. The People of the Sun will be attracted by these conveniences and dream of living in towers like us. They will leave their tropical paradise and climb our towers of ice, and when they do, we'll pull the plug and freeze them suckas to death. If that don't work, we'll nuke 'em.' That's what the Ice Man said."

Once again Mayor Cleveland climbed out of the netherworld, but after this there was no sliding back. A hospital orderly was adjusting one of his life-giving tubes at the time, and so it was to him that Willis said, "I just had a dream, son, like the Reverend Dr. King. Only this one's more like a nightmare when you get right down to the bone. Where's that Sister Delilah Blue?"

Dr. Bartholomew intercepted Delilah by the elevator, which continued to swallow and disgorge a regular diet of loved ones and healers while they talked about the mayor's condition.

"He's awake now, very alert," the young neurologist said. "He seems to be feeling fine. . . ."

Delilah thought he was finished and took a step toward the mayor's room, but her path was obstructed by an elderly woman in a wheelchair and her progress was further impeded by the doctor's slender hand, which grabbed her by the elbow and tugged with surprising strength.

"—but there seems to be a—"

"Problematic?"

"A problem, if you will. He's not quite—"

"Well?"

"Not quite himself. The damage to the corpus has caused a disconnect. There's some—"

"Some what, doctor?"

"Some undefined trauma. A simple lesion, perhaps. The corpus callosum is a funny piece of work. Do you know anything about split-brain thinking?"

Her arm had gone limp, but he was still clutching her elbow, now more for support than restraint.

"No. What's that?"

The doctor shook his head. "That's part of the problem. We really don't know for sure. The right frontal lobe is the part of the brain most closely associated with . . ."

He paused again, looking for words that didn't exist. Delilah had no idea where he was going and couldn't help him get there. The elevator disgorged some nurses and swallowed an orderly. Dr. Bartholomew said, "It's the part of the brain that seems to govern our sense of—"

"Govern our sense of what?"

"Our sense of propriety. Freud would call it the superego,

although that's not a word a neurologist would use. It's that little voice inside us, the part of the brain that inhibits antisocial impulses. The Little White Lie Department."

After being shaved, drilled, probed, and plugged, the mayor's head looked less like an oversize peanut and more like a blackened light bulb from that mirror universe he'd been dreaming about, where rich is poor and black is white and mayors say exactly what they mean.

"Praise bejeezus, Sister. You are a preachifying, storefront hallelujah hooter, but you always been coming up large for me. You know what I always liked about you? You're not one of these women of color like are passing for black on the television shows: white women dipped in butterscotch with their punctulated rap and the kinks ironed out. I always wanted my women to be just like you, and I'm sorry how it never seemed to work out with us. I know you're lonely and without no man and me continuingly being married and to a splendid gal. I'm thankful for all the things you've done, but there's a lot more we need to do. I feel like Moses after he gone to the mountain and come back."

Delilah hadn't moved a muscle since the mayor first opened his mouth. Now she looked at Dr. Bartholomew, who returned her gaze as best he could, offering sympathy but nothing else.

Willis sat up and raised his hands as if in prayer. He said, "Here's the shining light, and I'm not just talking about attitudes and platitudes. It starts with being black in these United States because it's not just the whites that's feeling guilty. They just like it more because guilt is cheaper than taxes. The wicked truth is the sons of slaves in America got a lot better deal than the sons of princes in Africa. Or if we don't, we think we do and that's even worse, like calories without the chocolate. We've got cars and cable TV, and they got the tsetse fly. Go get me some newsies. I want to give them a piece of my mind."

* * *

Out in the hall, amid the ebb and flow of doctors and nurses, patients and visitors, Dr. Bartholomew tried to explain. "I might even write a paper for JAMA. I'm thinking of calling it CBS, the Charles Barkley Syndrome."

"Charles Barkley? Who's that?"

"A professional basketball player. Black guy with a white wife who says whatever comes to mind, the most quotable man in America."

"Well, we don't want any quotes right now, but we need to get him out where he can smile at all the folks. You got some drugs to shut him up? Keep him happy? Calm him down? We don't need him saying stuff unless it's in the script."

30

Rolling Tape

WITH THE RELUCTANT APPROVAL OF MRS. CLEVELAND, THEY used tranquilizers to return the mayor to a state of oblivion. Every now and then he would come to his senses for a moment and wake up in a hospital room. His bones would ache and his heart would sink when he realized all of the problems that waking up entailed.

Waking up meant the city, the council, the voters, the mess. Waking up meant he'd get attacked in public if the garbage wasn't collected, and waking up meant that distraught mothers would blame him for the death of their unlucky sons. Waking up meant long nights of doubt and uncertainty and press conferences with reporters who asked inane and impertinent questions with a smirk. Waking up meant giving a speech, cutting a deal, begging for the money he needed from the people he most despised.

Most of all, waking up meant campaigning against Alderman Smith, so as soon as the mayor came to his senses, he fell back into a deep sleep. Sometimes he could hear the faint echoes of voices from his waking life.

"All we want to do is roll some tape as soon as he wakes up."

"That would be highly irregular."

"So what? There's folks who think he's already dead and the election is coming up fast. People need to know he's still alive, but they don't need to hear him talking trash."

"But the lights. The excitement. It'll be a jolt."

He drifted in that sweet ether that separates life from death, sleep from stupor, the known dark from the unknown light and his dream world from the one that was slowly slipping away. The women who lived in the ether were as black as the night, and their kisses tasted like licorice. One of the women disappeared into a night blacker than her own skin and promised him that he could speak the truth if only he woke up for a moment.

Willis climbed out of the ether and into the antiseptic closeness of his private hospital room. The machines that needed him beeped and hummed their constant tune as Dr. Bartholomew made notes on a yellow legal pad. Delilah welcomed him back to the world, and Nat started rolling tape. Allan pointed the microphone, and the mayor made a great commotion of clearing his throat, as if it was obstructed with gravel instead of phlegm. He blabbered on for a while about life in the ether, and the firmament of night and day that filled the heavens in the blink of an eye. Then the soft gauze of oblivion slipped from his eyes, and he talked about death as the friend that never leaves us and stays until the bitter end.

Nat checked his white balance and decided to turn his sun gun on, bathing the mayor in a kind of light different from the light that waited on the other side of the ether. This light seared his eyes and intruded on his every pore while the other one was as soft as the moon on a clear summer night. This light meant war, and the other one meant peace.

The mayor smiled and said, "You want us to have racial

harmony; then we need to talk about size. Black men are taller and stronger and faster, besides us having the bigger genitals. This makes white women wonder and white men worry, but that don't mean we can't all be friends. Just be glad that you ain't Chinese. When's the last time you seen a Chinese playing on a football team?"

CHANNEL ELEVEN

AUGUST 28, 7:25 A.M. LEDE TO NATIONAL NEWS
BLOCK

CAMERA ONE: MEDIUM CLOSE-UP/MARIANNE

MARIANNE: After several weeks of silence, Mayor Cleveland has made his first public statement since the attack that almost took his life. Today his press office released edited videotape of the mayor in his room at Walter Reed Memorial Hospital.

ROLL CLEVELAND SOUND BITE/OUTCUE: ". . . to have racial harmony."

MARIANNE: With us this morning to talk about the campaign is Radio Larry Melville, the dean of Chicago beat reporters.

OPEN KOPPEL WINDOW WITH MELVILLE PRINTOUT

CAMERA THREE: TWO-SHOT/MARIANNE, WINDOW

MARIANNE: Larry is a political consultant for "Action News Eleven" during the primary election campaign. He's been helping us make some sense of this dramatic mayor's race. Good morning, Larry.

LARRY: Top of the morning to you, Marianne.

MARIANNE: Do you think the mayor helped himself with that videotape we just saw?

LARRY: The short answer is yes, but it's the kind of help a horse gets when they lead him into the glue factory. He needs to be getting his message out, which is tough to do when you're wearing one of those hospital gowns with air conditioning on the back porch. The only good thing about the gown is, if the mayor feels like spanking himself about now, he can.

MARIANNE: And why would he want to do that?

LARRY: Because six years ago his so-called Election Reform Ordinance moved the local election cycle from the early spring to the late summer, just like in New York. If he'd left well enough alone he'd be reelected already.

MARIANNE: Are you saying that Alderman Smith is going to win?

LARRY: No, but there are two outs in the bottom of the ninth and the mayor needs to hit a home run. He gets one more strike next week when the League of Women Voters has their televised debate.

MARIANNE: Thank you, Larry Melville. Next we'll go to New York for the latest national news and after that we'll be back with the latest numbers from our Pulse of the People Public Opinion Poll.

LARRY: That's about five too many p's for me, Marianne.

MARIANNE: You should give p's a chance, Larry. Thank you once again.

CLOSE KOPPEL WINDOW

CAMERA ONE: MEDIUM CLOSE-UP/MARIANNE

MARIANNE: Radio Larry Melville's city beat reports can be heard every morning at the top of the hour on WDM Radio, "News Live at Fifty-Five." We'll be back right after this.

NEWS MUSIC/FADE TO HILLS BROS. COMMERCIAL BREAK.

31

Can I Get a Few Amens?

EVEN THE VOTERS STARTED PAYING ATTENTION AS AUGUST slipped away. The heat wave continued as the kids got ready to go back to school, and the network affiliates assembled shows for the September sweeps—true crime, football, and situation comedies.

Channel Eight was betting the news farm on a series about breast implants, and Channel Three took a closer look at cellulite and herpes while Channel Twelve cut promos for Janette Baylor's special on the gangs, plugging any gaps with TV tears, poll results, and tape of the continuing disturbances.

A Korean store was set on fire by a person or persons unknown, and a black shoplifter was gunned down with a T-bone steak in his pants. Careful citizens stayed home after dark, and Alderman Smith led the Street Crusaders in a torchlight parade down Michigan Avenue.

Mayor Cleveland made a limited number of public appearances at which his press secretary sought to limit the damage by keeping his mouth full of ethnic food. In key wards throughout the city he ate tacos, gyros, bratwurst,

252

pasta, kielbasa, chitlins, and corned beef and cabbage. Delilah put on five more pounds, but some of that was stress-related.

The Committee to Elect Douglas Smith paid for advertisements in which their candidate walked through the West Side slum while talking about the fears of Joe Sixpack. He never said a word about the narco-killers, but everybody knew what he was talking about. The Committee to Re-elect Willis Cleveland paid for advertisements in which their candidate walked through the resonant void of the Deep Tunnel Project and shook hands with people of all races, colors, and creeds, especially Catholics with Hispanic surnames.

Lawn signs were planted and light poles papered with posters promoting one man or the other. Charges were leveled; retractions were demanded; deals were cut; percentages were played. Nobody really wanted to debate, so they all disagreed about the rules.

Ward heelers put out the word that jobs were at stake and the machine was in danger, while precinct captains made the rounds and operatives worked the angles. Party regulars roamed up and down the elevators of the high-rise apartment buildings where the worried wealthy lived. Alderman Smith addressed small gatherings of unemployed, undecided, understanding factory workers, and Elmo told the Street Crusaders to go get out the vote. Journalists wondered about the meaning of it all and decided that there was no meaning. Political consultants said Smith had won before a single vote was cast.

As the mayor's hopes started to fade, the doctor cut his medication in half, and Delilah stuffed him into a power-blue suit and drove him to a church crowded with people who believed that he was the black messiah they'd all been waiting for. Wearing red satin robes and filling the choir loft, children sang gospel tunes while the faithful settled into their pews. The choir stopped singing when the mayor started to speak.

"I was walking home to sweet black Jesus when I seen a

burning bush just like the one Jehovah used to give Moses a talking-to, and the bush says to me, 'Willis, you cannot die.' I say, 'But Lord, you don't know the trouble I've seen. I've seen negative ads and smear campaigns and my share of downright lies.' Now here's where the bush starts to flicker, like one of them lights where the neon's almost gone, and the bush says, 'I hear you, Willis, but there's trouble coming to a bubble with my chosen people down below. You come home now, and that rapscallion Doogie Smith'll be mayor, and there won't be nobody left to take care of my folks what got a little soul.' How about it, people? Can I get a few Amens?"

"Amen, Brother Cleve. You tell it like it is and say it like it's so."

"All right. That's why I'm here today instead of being dead because Jehovah's got some work for you and me to do. We got to feed the hungry and shelter the homeless and visit folks who got sick in their body and in their soul. Mostly we got to smack that Doogie upside the head, give him a licking 'til he stops ticking, which brings me to the end of the prepared hooey that Sister Blue wrote up for me. See, what happened when I almost died is a fog lifted out of my brain and I could see things clearly for the very first time. What I see is this town needs a little bit of truth and a whole lot of Jesus. Let me hear it loud and strong."

"Amen, Brother Cleve. Amen to that."

"Praise be. Now Jesus you've got to be finding for yourself, but I can help you some with the truth part because I learned the way it is when my brain got scrambled. The problem with black folks is there's Japan that's getting all our jobs and Koreans owning all our stores and . . ."

That's when Delilah turned the microphone off and the choir started singing another gospel song, and though the mayor kept on talking about the naked truth and the shining light, with the sound off it looked like he was singing too.

32

"You're no Bunker Hines"

BUNKER'S 4X4 HAD A TACKLE BOX FULL OF COMPACT DISCS OF some cowboys howling at the moon. The radio wasn't much better. Radio WGRV in Karnak played a little Motown funk, but that ran out of juice as soon as they crossed the Pulaski County line. From there on out it was all white bread and Velveeta about the evils of too much drinking and not enough loving, or maybe it was the other way around. Hammerhead had some cowgirl blues of his own.

Gloria said, "Kidnapping's a federal crime, so you better be nice to me. Otherwise you'll be busting rocks for the rest of your life and touching your toes any old time some hillbilly creep says Howdy. You know what I mean about nice?"

Hammerhead was as nice as he could be under difficult circumstances. For more days than he could remember, they drove among cornfields. They'd rob a place, go have a picnic, and do it on some discarded corn husks three, four, five times a night, until Hammerhead couldn't do it anymore. When the corn husks that they did it on were old and dry enough, it sounded like they were making a fire that would scorch the earth itself.

Hammerhead said, "I got to start being in the 'hood."

"That stinky old city? How come?"

"The music here's driving me crazy, and that's where my people's at."

"I'm people. What about me?"

"It's been nice. You go back to your town, and I go back to mine. I'll be remembering you."

"Excuse me?" Gloria always said excuse me when something startled her. Hammerhead didn't know what excuse me meant, as they never said that back in the 'hood. He thought she was saying, "Accuse me?"

"I'm not accusing nothing. We're too much different is all. You been a proper delight for sure, but it's got to be over now. Forget it."

Gloria didn't want to forget it, and she didn't want him to forget it either. "You want to talk about accusing, then I'm accusing you."

"Accusing me what for?"

"The fact that I was liking those things and the fact that I suggested you do them may or may not come to the attention of the legal authorities. Bunker'll testify how you stole this car with me in it sleeping off my drunk, and then they'll take you back to Little Egypt, and that'll be the end of you. They don't tolerate the mixing of races down there, and the expression of the usual manly desires is frowned upon when the woman is white and the man is of colored extraction. What color are you, anyway? I mean, I know you're brown, but I don't know why. You some kind of Indian?"

Hammerhead kept his eyes on the road and his mind on some distant yesterdays. Every November 19 when he was a kid, his mother and her sister would celebrate Discovery Day by baking a cake, sipping some wine, and telling boring stories in Spanish about the place where they were born. They talked about a fly-infested city on the coast known as Mayaguez where the men went fishing for their supper and the women worked in a chemical plant that supplied the stuff that makes hair spray sticky.

"Rican," he said.

"What?"

"The Alone Unknown is a Rican gang. I'm a Puerto Rican."

They drove in silence for a while, each lost in thought. For her this was a chance to be what she'd never been—older, wiser, and in control. For him this was the end of a dream that had sustained him through many difficult years. Before Gloria, he still believed women to be the keepers of the secret to eternal happiness. Now he knew that this was true, but he also knew that in return they demanded everything he had and everything he didn't.

He thought about kicking her out of the 4x4 in one of the dusty old towns that were as plentiful as the corn in this part of Illinois, but then she'd tell the cops that he had kidnapped her, and he'd get stuck in jail. He thought about tying her up and leaving her under a pile of dried corn husks, but the sun was so hot that she might get hurt or killed, and besides, those big farm machines were always chopping things up into little pieces.

"I've got an idea," he said.

"What's that?"

"I know a place where we can get some real food to eat. Real mashed potatoes with real steak and gravy, fresh vegetables, and hot apple pie with ice cream on the side. We can do it as soon as you get enough of eating this Get N' Go food."

Gloria looked up from the cornfield that had held her in a trance by the sheer force of its golden monotony. The very mention of real food sent her taste buds into a frenzy. She dare not speak for fear she'd drool.

"We'll have to go up by the city, though. Not right to it but up pretty close, if you think you can handle that. I know you're a country girl, and you love that Get N' Go."

* * *

The Ernie Bushmiller Memorial Oasis straddled the interstate, like a prefabricated Colossus of Roads. A constant stream of metal machines rolled between its great bow legs, atop which were assembled the usual shops catering to the basic needs of motorists. The men's room smelled of Burma Shave, and the parking lot sounded like rolling thunder as the huge refrigerator trucks battled the heat with more heat while the drivers refreshed themselves with food, coffee, and air conditioning.

All men are strangers on the always-moving, never-changing road from here to there, but Stewart Karnasecki had decided that some were stranger than others. The night manager gazed up at the larger-than-life portrait of Ernie Bushmiller that presided over the Oasis like the grim visage of a founding father who held his descendants in little regard.

Stewart turned to the waitress and said, "Watch those two over there."

He didn't have to say which two because Hammerhead and Gloria Cantrell were the only two in the place. The other customers were single truckers and single salesmen exchanging news about speed traps and gas prices, the sort of gossip favored by men who travel through a world only six lanes wide.

The waitress said, "The prob is what?" Her name was Honey. She had big hair, flat heels, and a video library that included every movie James Dean ever made.

"They ordered everything on the menu, and they've been sipping coffee for an hour now. What do you bet they bolt as soon as I'm not looking?"

"Then look."

"I can't. There's paperwork. Don't let them out of your sight."

"I wonder."

"What do you wonder about?"

Honey buffed the counter for a bit, stopping when she buffed into a sugar dispenser standing in a puddle of lightly creamed coffee. "I wonder what their story is. She's twenty years older if a day, and he's some kind of colored person, like Sal Mineo in *Rebel*. They're talking like they been doing it for years, but that don't make no sense to me."

Stewart picked up the dispenser and examined the flap where the sugar came out. The passage was obstructed by a coffee-stained clot, so he pounded it with the heel of his hand and the clot dropped onto the pure cane sugar like a turd on freshly fallen snow.

"Watch them. I've got work to do."

Honey buffed her way around the counter while Stewart went into his office to catch the last two innings of the Cubs game on a pocket TV he watched on the sly when Honey wasn't looking. The waitress knew what he was doing since he did it whenever the Cubs were on TV, and it gave her the notion of maybe making some entertainment of her own, live and in the flesh. She made plenty of noise walking to the back, so Stewart would have plenty of time to hide his pocket TV.

"Know what?"

"No. What?"

"I'm thinking that maybe they're Ho-Jo spies."

Stewart looked guilty as hell as he averted his eyes from the drawer where he had hidden his pocket TV. He didn't quite know what to say, so Honey helped him along.

"It's like they're seeing if we smile a lot. What do you bet they stiff me on the tip, and write me up if I squawk about it much? They were fussy about their food, and the girl wants me to tell her about the back roads going downstate. And you notice the way they look at you when you turn the other way?"

"No, I—"

"Trust me, okay? They do. Maybe you better be nice to them just in case I'm right."

She went back to the dining area while Stewart thought it over. Five minutes later, he came out with his tie adjusted and his smile on straight. He became concerned about the sneeze guard on the salad bar and stopped to tell a solitary salesman the only joke he knew that was neither racist nor crude. Then, when it might be construed as an afterthought, he headed for the table where Hammerhead and Gloria were sitting.

If the Colossus had a crotch, they were sitting in it, by a window that gave them a fine view of the traffic surging between the preformed concrete legs. "How you folks doing tonight?"

Gloria looked at Hammerhead, and Hammerhead looked out the window. If he looked hard enough, he could almost see the amber glow of the place that he called home.

Gloria flashed an insincere smile, as if Howard Johnson himself had been her smile instructor. "We're okay. What about you?"

Stewart said he was fine, and they exchanged pleasantries typical of the oases that dotted the interstate. Gloria said the road was sure hot, and Stewart said the Texaco in Calumet had the cheapest gas between here and Kankakee. Hammerhead stared out the window at the constant stream of rubber and steel.

When Stewart was gone, he said, "I think he's got us figured out. So here's the way it goes. You fill up our ride with the motor running, top off the tank real good. Give me a toot on the horn when you're ready and then you count to ten. Then it's quick on the start, quick on the gas, and I'll meet you by that door over there. Got it?"

She got it, and it worked like a charm until she pulled up to the door. Hammerhead never showed up. Stewart did. He insisted she pay for the food and the gasoline and called a state trooper when she couldn't.

"Get your hands up against the vehicle, ma'am."

"How come?"

"That 4x4 you're driving is registered to Bunker Hines of Cairo, Illinois. I'm not a betting man. If I was, I'd bet a dollar that you're no Bunker Hines."

33

Meat Loaf, Again

ALTHOUGH THE TEMPERATURE HOVERED NEAR NINETY DEGREES even after the sun went down, the squirrels in Mrs. Shanahan's attic had already begun preparing for winter. The human occupants of the house where Diamond-Tooth Eddie once lived were slowed to a crawl by the heavy air, but the rodents were becoming furious in their pursuit of acorns, nuts, and other scraps of food.

Allan had had enough. "Call the exterminator. The house'll fall right down on your head if we don't do something now."

His urgency was subverted by the fact that they had had this conversation so many times before and would no doubt have it again before the leaves turned brown. The old woman enjoyed the busy company in her attic, especially during the long nights when ENT was on the road and the dirge from the scanners became too depressing. The squirrels were cute in their way and never dumped their turds on the counter like the field mice who would invade her kitchen in the weeks before Halloween.

"I'd rather be buried sitting right here than pay out money

to a funeral home. Your father made me promise I'd leave you something so you wouldn't be poor like him. So what's with you and that TV girl?"

"Maybe I'm going crazy, Ma, but I saw her looking at me."

"There's no maybe about it."

"Really? You think she likes me?"

"No. No, maybe you're going crazy. You need a woman with typing skills. A TV woman lives off her looks, gets old before her time."

Mother and son ignored each other for the rest of the day as each took comfort in the more dull but more reliable company of their respective TV sets. She watched game shows, and he the colorized version of Bogart and Cagney in the movie *Angels with Dirty Faces*. They slept for a while in the afternoon, although the squirrels continued with their ceaseless labors until the sun went down, the moon came out, and Nat crunched up their gravel driveway behind the wheel of Genghis Kar.

For the second time that week, they ate meat loaf for dinner. This was the cause for some alarm because meat loaf had become a key indicator of Mrs. Shanahan's mental state. As her wits became dulled by age and loneliness, she made more and more meat loaf with fewer and fewer ingredients. Over a dark brown lump of baked hamburger, Nat said, "I'll be cashing out next month. What're the numbers like?"

Allan poked at his own brown lump. When they started eating meat loaf seven days a week, it would be time to send mother to a place where the men bragged about all the Japs they'd killed and the women stared off into space.

"Congratulations, Nat," he said. "You're a millionaire."

"Great. That's great."

"No, that's gross."

"What's gross? What're you talking about?"

After dinner Allan showed Nat the legal papers that established the corporate structure of Electronic News Tonight. He explained the various clauses that set up the three-way partnership, and he explained the difference between net and gross as the difference between Nat being wealthy in fact and wealthy on paper.

"Gross is what you're worth if you stay with the company. The million-plus you get with gross includes your share of the capital-improvement fund. Leave and you only get net."

Mrs. Shanahan started to nitz and complain. Her bones hurt, she couldn't sleep, and her bladder seemed to be shrinking. Worse yet, her meat loaf had lost its zing, and food in general didn't taste good anymore. The two men consoled her as best they could before resuming the discussion she had interrupted.

Nat said, "So what's net?"

"After taxes? Three-fifty, maybe four."

"That's not enough. I need five hundred thousand to shoot my doc."

"Then we better get to working some heavy overtime. Delilah wants us to shoot this debate that's coming up. She's calling it B.J. Day."

"You mean B.J. like in blow job?"

"No. B.J. like in bulljive. You know how funny those black folks talk."

34

The Head in the 'Hood

Bus #11 smelled of unwashed wino as it rolled north up South Shore Drive, but the advertising spaces for rent above the greasy windows conjured up scenes of a happier world. A chilled blonde in a lime green shift had her lips wrapped around a bottle of Bud next to yuppies of color puffing on a pack of Kool Menthol Filtered Lights. A sincere fellow with a winning smile hawked Arlen Donald's Motivation Tapes for the Stress-free Path to a More Productive Life. Hammerhead tried to figure out the meaning of black block letters paid for by the Chicago Education Association. They quoted Epicurus: To be a writer, write.

He'd never noticed the smell of the city until he'd left it for a while. The bum aroma was a sweetened dose of the burnt rubber and wet garbage he'd been sniffing since the hike in from the Ernie Bushmiller Oasis. The funny thing about it was, the closer he got to the city's Gold Coast, the stronger the aroma became, as if the people who lived in the lakefront towers were manufacturing the stuff.

The city had changed while he was gone. The same smelly bus chugged past all sorts of familiar things he'd never really noticed before: a store that sold nothing but neckties; two hard rockers who needed leather and mousse to show how angry they were; a woman with a ring in her nose; a man who wore white gloves while driving a limo as long as a short city block.

Beyond the buildings he could see the flat blue lake and the way it rolled but never moved. It reminded him of the always rolling, never moving cornfields of Little Egypt and what had happened down there. He wondered what was on the other side of Lake Michigan and decided that it must be Detroit. Didn't they always say Detroit, Michigan, when the Lions and Tigers and Pistons played the Bears and the Sox and the Bulls. He tried to imagine a mirror city on the other side of the lake, a big, noisy place where everybody drove brand-new cars because that's where cars come from. He knew that much, at least. He wondered what life was like in Detroit and whether the people who lived there ever thought about him.

Bus #11 turned left on Fullerton and began the long ride into no-man's-land. Hammerhead looked out the window and saw punks strutting into an empty tomorrow and an old woman shuffling along with her past crammed into a plastic shopping bag. Junkies from the detox center bumped into crazies from the mental health outpatient clinic while Bus #11 made trash tornadoes of the scraps of paper and other things dropped on the street since the last time they cleaned it, which was never.

He knew he was home when he saw the miniature Statue of Liberty revolving within a glass cylinder planted by the door of the savings and loan. The statuette was bigger and brighter than he remembered it to be, but it still made freedom seem cheap and small when Hammerhead knew for a fact that it was bigger than the lake and the cornfields put together and it wasn't cheap at all. Some people couldn't buy it at any price.

"Check it out," the Truth said. "Damn if that ain't the Head himself pimping his way back home."

The gangsters stopped what they were doing—nothing—and turned as one in the direction the Truth was looking, and saw Hammerhead strutting up the street as if he'd just ripped off Miss Liberty herself. He moved with the determined stride of those who regard their looks as a weapon: legs stiff, fists clenched, shoulders rocking with every step, chin raised at a defiant angle. His friends gathered around when he stepped onto the playground where the Alone Unknown planned their capers, collected their taxes, and provided vital public services to drug addicts from near and far.

Hammerhead told them about the caper, and they told him they'd heard how the Eye had made them famous by getting his name on the radio and his mug shot on TV. In the days since his corpse surfaced, the ones who could read had gotten copies of all the local papers and read aloud the front-page stories about the amazing things their leader had done in a place they'd never heard of before.

Grog produced a pipe, and they started smoking rot. For a few seconds they all felt like God, and for a few minutes they came to believe that they could do it all. They listened with care and wonder while Hammerhead told them what had happened to the Eye.

"The Eye got popped, fellas, but I don't know who done it for sure. It could've been the cops, but I bet not or they'd already be talking it up big. I think maybe it could've been some lady because there was one time he said to me that if he ever got popped, I should figure maybe a she done it, because women get to be dangerous when they fall in love with you. He always said the way to get popped is be hated by a man or loved by a woman."

As if by some unspoken command, the Alone Unknown huddled more closely together. Grog spoke for the group. "Popeye done a number on us. Working on a caper without his crew."

The others mumbled and grumbled in Spanish and English both. Popeye had done them a number all right. They all agreed about that. Hammerhead nodded and his friends looked away. Nobody said anything for a while, as the gangsters tried to imagine what would happen next. Then the drug wore off, and they didn't feel like God anymore.

From Tech Sarge's vantage point across the street, the playground looked like a thousand points of light, with broken bits of bottle colored the usual hues—green for cola, brown for beer, clear for everything else. He imagined his own reflection in each of those points of light and figured he looked pretty good in a uniform, even if it was only a dark blue jumpsuit with too many zippers and an Illinois Bell Telephone patch. He'd been fussing with that utility pole for more than a week now, pretending to work on the wires and bolts while watching the toughs who gathered daily in the playground to wait for something that never happened. Tech Sarge did his own waiting with more patience but less joy. He had learned in the desert that waiting was part of the fight, that a good soldier kept his game face on when nothing was happening so he'd be ready to move when it did.

The Alone Unknown was a sorry lot with a daily routine that didn't vary in the least: reefer in the morning, basketball in the afternoon, beer, rot, and girls in the evening with lots of hang time in between. Every now and then some cops would stop by with a ration of shit, but nobody ever got busted. Doogie said they were laying off because the brain-dead mayor needed all the 'Spanic votes he could get, but then Doogie said a lot of things that made no sense at all. Sarge had decided long ago that he was working for a jerk. No problem. He had learned how to work for jerks during Operation Desert Storm.

The drugs were the only criminal activity he was able to detect, although he supposed their occasional absences were related to stealing of one sort or another. Every now and then, a fistfight would break out, but it was usually only play fighting of the sort that puppies do when they're bored.

The waiting reminded him of the war games the Army used to play, with Delta Green slugging it out with Red Force over a patch of Arizona desert. A red sticker on your helmet meant that you'd been killed, and the pain of death was a hundred pushups and five hundred jumping jacks. One time when the war games were over and Delta Green had triumphed, Sarge and his team celebrated by loading up with some live ammo and wasting every cactus in sight. The fleshy brown plants looked a lot like Arabs when they burst into shreds, and the fact is the Iraqis weren't much harder to kill when the real fighting started.

Tech Sarge thought about the war while pretending to adjust the same bolt he'd been pretending to adjust all week. All together, they'd toasted maybe a hundred thousand towelheads who never knew what hit them, and the funny part was it would have gone the other way if the towelheads had had all the gear. You didn't have to be a genius to toast somebody with a smart bomb, a laser-guided missile, or any of the other toys that Sarge had stolen and then reported missing. Lock on, press a button, listen to the boom. Soon they'd have it wired so trained monkeys could do the job, as long as the monkeys never got any ideas of their own. The Army didn't need ideas, just eighteen-year-old kids who could learn how to press a button and say, "Yes, sir," with feeling when the brass said it's time to kill.

Yes, sir.

Yes, sir.

Yes, sir.

The Storm made such a pleasant daydream that Hammerhead was back on the yard for fifteen minutes before Tech Sarge noticed. He looked like just another punk with a stiff-legged walk, just another loser getting high on crack and weed, just another pimp in baggy pants and combat boots. But then they started smoking their drugs earlier than usual, and this caused Sarge to take a closer look. That's when he saw that the punk he was supposed to toast had arrived and was talking to some other little punks. Tech Sarge plugged his portable phone into the telephone pole and dialed.

Elmo answered the phone while Douglas regarded his own image on "Channel Twelve News." As the campaign heated up, he had taken to wearing plain blue suits and speaking in a soft, soothing tone of voice, like a friend speaks to the distraught survivors of someone who died with lots of money and unknown intentions. After his own 2-D image did ten seconds on the latest ethnic disturbances, Janette Baylor's 2-D image read the results of the latest *Tribune*/Channel Twelve tracking poll. The numbers were good, but not good enough. Douglas had taken the lead, but the mayor was still within striking distance if he could get enough of those 'Spanic undecideds. Those goddamn 'Spanics.

Elmo said, "It's Sarge. You better talk."

Douglas cleared his throat, preparing to speak like the natural commander he very much wanted to be. Elmo untangled the telephone cord and delivered the receiver into his hand.

"I got him," Tech Sarge said. The portable phone gave his voice a metallic quality that was muffled by the background noise of trucks, cars, and pedestrians milling around on the street below.

"That's good," Douglas said. "What's he doing?"

"Chumming with his pals. I can toast him right now if you want, wrap things up real quick."

"Not yet."

"How come?"

Douglas tried to explain. "It's got to be a knife or a cheap handgun, so it looks like some nigger did it, some nigger that loves the mayor and wants to get revenge."

Sarge tried to do three things at once: cling to the pole, listen to Douglas, and keep an eye on the familiar caravan of unmarked cars that had turned off of Milwaukee Avenue and was heading for the playground of du Sable School.

"You're making things very complicated, just like you did before. You don't seem to understand that killing is hard enough already without trying to be so cute."

Elmo turned down the volume on the TV set, so he could hear Douglas's end of the conversation.

Douglas said, "Here's the thing, Sarge. You're thinking

people and I'm thinking votes. 'Spanic votes to be exact. It's got to look like a rumpus, like a race thing between black and brown. Think of them as votes instead of people, then you'll maybe see what I mean."

Sarge didn't think about it right away because by then the caravan of unmarked cars had surrounded the playground and come to a halt. On a signal from someone in a dark brown suit, the car doors furthest from the gang popped open, and a company of men jumped out. Sarge saw more brown suits and some uniforms, too. Everybody had a gun.

Hammerhead said, "What's this?"

The gangsters turned to look. They had been so involved in the details of Popeye's caper that they hadn't noticed the arrival of the cops. Grog gave the drugs to the smallest of the group, a boy known only as Smoke, and the older gangsters blocked the view of the approaching police while he crawled through a window that opened into the basement of du Sable School.

Grog said to Hammerhead, "They been doing us like this almost every day since Popeye got to be news. The Alone Unknown is famous now, the walk and the talk of the town. We been getting all the gangland pub, thanks to you and the Eye."

The uniformed officers stood back with their guns at the ready while the men in the brown suits lined the gangsters up against the same wall that Smoke had just crawled through. A big cop with rough hands checked them for weapons and drugs. A little cop, who made up in mean what he lacked in size, went down the line and rousted them out one by one, rattling off their priors and putting on a little more squeeze where he thought it might do the most good.

"You boys just need a little fathering is all," the little detective said.

"What're you talking about?"

"There ain't no fathers in no-man's-land, so the cops got to be one-minute dads, put a lifetime of discipline in one talking-to."

He wanted to know about Popeye. Where did he get his money? Who did he hate? Who did he screw? When did he go away? Why did he try to kill the mayor?

Grog said, "You mean Popeye, the guy with all the muscles that used to be some kind of kid's cartoon?"

The little detective threw Grog against the wall and promised to send him to the Place for one crime or another. Then he did the same to Cruiser, Flim Flam, and the Truth. Two other cops took Lupo behind the school and kicked his ass for holding a knife, and the suits had a special plan for Goofball, who was twitching all around as usual.

"We're taking you to detox, son. The hungry'll hurt so bad you'll wish that you were dead. After the election you will be dead when we let the Galabeyes come and pay you back for what Popeye did."

When they got to Hammerhead, the little cop said to the big one, "Who's this we got here? Never seen this one before."

One of the uniformed officers produced a battered brief-case that contained handcuffs, a tape recorder, a confusion of crumpled paper, and a photo album with a vinyl cover blemished by cigarette burns. The officers huddled around the album until they came across a photograph of Hammerhead that was used to illustrate his criminal history which included shoplifting, resisting arrest, and underage drinking and driving.

"He's chickenshit," the big cop said.

"Or smart," the little one replied.

They borrowed a nightstick from a uniformed officer and used it to tickle Hammerhead's ribs. The little one said, "How come we don't have a decent sheet on you?"

"Because I never done nothing wrong. Capers is against the law."

The men in the brown suits thought about this. In their many years of bringing religion to a godless land, they had heard too many outrageous things from too many smart-mouthed punks. But they had never heard anything like this before and didn't know quite how to take it.

271

"Let's run him in," the little cop said.

"I say we kick his ass," his large partner replied. They looked at the photo album again and thought about it some more. After a moment of silent reflection, an easier answer percolated into the part of the brain where fear, confusion, and laziness collaborate in the making of safe decisions. The little cop spoke for the bigger one.

"We're saving you for the Galabeyes, son. They're waiting on the chance to get some revenge. They may as well take it out on you."

35

Hail Mary, Full of Grace

As the sun set, Tech Sarge had a harder time distinguishing Hammerhead from his pals. They looked, walked, and dressed alike in the uniform of their gang: baggy pants, dago-Ts, and Reebok the Pump basketball shoes. He didn't see a bit of difference anywhere in the lot and thought the smartest thing would be to toast them all right now. Doogie wasn't smart. Not about this, at least. Sarge plugged his portable phone into the pole. Doogie answered the call himself.

"What's the news? You do him yet?"

"Not yet. Not never. This boy's bugging out."

"How come?"

"Him and his pals won't split up. By the time I can do it the way you want it done, they could all be in jail already. You want to make it look like a nigger gang did it, then get yourself a nigger gang."

Douglas contemplated his options while clearing his throat of an obstruction it did not have. The Black Galabeyes might do the job, but they were being watched. The other black gangs would want less money but more power, and that would not work out. The chance that Hammerhead might get arrested was a chance he could not take.

"You win."

"How's that?"

"Do it your way. Tonight. Right now. Try a little techno-death."

"You got it."

"There's just one thing."

Sarge looked at the portable phone, afraid for a moment it was about to emit another bad idea. "And just what thing is that?"

"I want you to do it large, so it looks like hell come home to Harlem on a wide-screen television set. You think you can do it large?"

"The larger the money, the larger the do. I need twenty-five cash right now."

"Elmo's on his way."

The Alone Unknown were jaundiced by the yellow light cast on them by the tree-killing sulfur lamps. The Kosmic Kid jumped in the direction of the light when he saw a shadow move. He knew in that moment of truth that happens between two micro-moments that the shadow was going to kill him, and he wanted to die in the brightest light around, so someone would see it happen and remember when he was gone. The rest of the Unknown weren't looking, because they had seen the shadow too and were scattering in every direction at once: to mama, to papa, to an apartment on Elston Avenue that stunk of baby pee that had been cooked at ninety-nine degrees for the last eight weeks or so; to the detox center three blocks away, where a body could get a good night's meal if it was addicted to drugs or alcohol. The Alone Unknown were propelled to these places by the remarkable strength that terror provides, but none of them made it as far as the chain-link fence that separated their world from the larger one.

Tech Sarge said to Elmo, "You see him?"

"I'm not sure. It's dark."

"Fuck it, then, I'll toast 'em all."

Tech Sarge raised his weapon and unleashed a deadly spray. T-Ball caught one in the head and died without pain, but Muffy took one in the belly and watched her guts spill out. The others were hit in other spots, turning the playground into a puddle of their blood. The Truth got the farthest. He was getting ready to jump the fence when the bullets started chopping him up.

They saved the Kid for last, quivering in the golden glow. The last thing he saw was the silhouette behind the flash of the gun that was killing him. Two heads hunched together. Maybe they'd remember him.

Hammerhead would.

While his crew had scattered, he had dropped. He saw it all happen from the dark hollow made by the juncture of the back steps and the school's cornerstone. The concrete block announced that the Jean Baptiste Pointe du Sable Memorial School had been dedicated in A.D. 1923 by Mayor William R. "Bill" Thompson, known to his friends as Big. A small plaque indicated that the red-brick collar around the cornerstone was older than the school itself, having been formerly used to buck up the old Northwest Plank Road connecting Chicago to Milwaukee. The bricks were made of mud and straw and fired in a kiln seven years before the Great Chicago Fire.

Hammerhead had always been impressed by that, and somehow this odd fact scratched at him while Tech Sarge and Elmo started dispatching his friends for good with a single bullet to each of their brains. The plaque reminded him of history class and history class reminded him of mama, who always said that school was his only way of gettin' out of here.

He waited for a break. Muffy Cruz gave him one when Sarge bent over her and saw she wasn't him.

"He must be around here someplace. I'm sure that it was him," Sarge said.

Muffy moaned.

"What was that?"

"I don't know."

"Sounds like Spanish."

Hammerhead made his move. With the speed of youth and the courage of a man who knows he's dead already, he made a blind dive at a window just below the cornerstone. As the grating had been peeled away and the windowpanes replaced by boards, he landed on the floor in a shower of kindling and splinters. He had arrived in the music room. He stepped on a broken tuba and knocked some cymbals over, making it into the art room a moment before Tech Sarge started blasting away.

A police siren sounded in the ever-shrinking distance as an oil slick of summer wind carried the first puff of school smoke up into the clouds. Hammerhead tried to remember where he was as he scrambled to avoid the flashlight that was chasing him up the stairs. Here was where he used to sneak a butt, and over there was where he'd got into a fight with Gilmore over Muffy Cruz. Here was where she kissed him and where Mr. Franklin had a fit over cracking jokes in math class. The square of the hair times the angle of the dangle equals the cube of Muffy's tube. At least Gilmore thought it was funny.

The flashlight was catching up, so he hid in a locker that smelled of girl. The girl smell reminded him of mama again, and mama reminded him of Madonna before she started whoring on MTV. As the flashlight inched past he prayed.

> "Hail Mary, full of grace,
> Get my skinny butt out of this place."

When the flashlight was gone he took the back stairs to the top floor and Mrs. Markam's history class. The blackboard still had a few words on it—something about the Civil War—and the opposite wall still contained cartoonish drawings of the dead presidents assembled around a banner that read LET FREEDOM RING.

Mrs. Markam was always crazy about the fire escape

because one time she caught Muffy going down on Gilmore instead of listening to her rendition of "John Brown's body is a molderin' in the grave." Ever after that, Mrs. Markam made sure the door to the fire escape locked from the outside. The plan now: Turn on the light and make a lot of noise so they follow you into the fire escape. Then you hide behind the open door until they come running by and go out the way you came in, closing the door behind you. It might work. It did.

Elmo said, "That little piece of shit."

"He's dead meat."

"It's getting kind of hot."

"No kidding."

"Let's get out of here."

"Fried meat's fine with me."

36

A Woman with Typing Skills

PARKER COUNTED HIS TROUBLES WHILE STANDING IN THE TANGLE of rootlike cables that separated the anchor desk from the country kitchen set of "Midwest Today," a late-morning program devoted to aerobics and fat-free cooking. The weatherman talked about high-pressure systems while doing his little weather dance in front of the safe-blue wall on which the control room, through the magic of television, superimposed the various maps that Ernie was talking about. Parker remembered the time Ernie wore a safe-blue tie and he did the whole weather report with a safe-blue hole in his gut. Parker had caught hell for that, but nothing like the hell he'd catch if Janette Baylor let him down.

She would. He knew that much for sure. No way in hell could a five-part series on dead teenagers get back even a few of the viewers they had lost to Channel Three. For one thing, dead gangsters weren't news anymore. For another, his agents had informed him that Three was working on a ten-part series that had the wags referring to the September sweeps as Tits N' Cancer Month. His spy said that Three's best-looking female reporter had shot seventeen takes of a stand-up while checking her left one for lumps and that promos giving people a sneak preview would soon be running ten times a day.

As Ernie went on about some high-pressure system, Parker tried to imagine the forthcoming end of his career. His best chance was to hope that their numbers would be so bad that the news dee got bang-banged himself, leaving the smaller fry alone until after the February sweeps.

Ernie's forecast: hot and dry. When the news music trumpets signaled the end of the forecast, Janette removed her clip-on mike and smiled at the dark place where Parker was waiting. She picked her way through the cabled web and leaned against the unplugged refrigerator that decorated the set of "Midwest Today."

"Ernie said you wanted to talk."

Parker didn't want to talk to Janette, but that was his job and his job was on the line. "The series. We need to cut some promos fast. What have you got so far?"

Janette went into great detail about the drugs, the death, the gangs, the tears. Nat knew how to shoot, she knew how to emote, and Allan knew how to write a decent script. She figured the series would be ready for week two of the sweeps, and she knew the whole team was counting on her, so she wouldn't let them down. But before they could talk about possible promos, an assistant editor stuck his head out of the radio room and shouted across the set.

"There's a shitstorm over by Lincoln Square."

Flames leaped out of the first floor and smoke poured out of the second. Spotlights were trained on the roof, as if awaiting the arrival of some rude celebrity who was twenty minutes late. Children had gathered in the street to cheer the destruction of their school and throw rocks at the firemen who were trying to contain the blaze. Paramedics searched for body parts amidst a thousand points of shattered glass that the flames made twinkle like stardust come to earth. The police had set up barricades to restrain the mass of journalists who had gathered to document the mess. Radio Larry was foremost among them.

When Allan arrived Larry said, "The mother of all gang hits here. That's what the lieutenant said. She says there's ten dead bodies at least and there may be more inside. But that's not the kicker. You want to know the kicker? I got bills to pay."

Allan pulled out his wallet and peeled off five twenties. Larry tucked them in his pocket. "The kicker is it's the Alone Unknown."

It took Allan a moment to connect the name of the gang with reports about the body they'd fished from the Bricksville riverfront. It took him another moment to decide that the connection was important. "No kidding?"

Larry listened while the lieutenant bellowed through her bullhorn that whoever was stuck up on the roof was going to fry if he didn't get down pretty quick. "When we bring the net, I'll give you the signal and then you'll jump. You don't want to die, and we don't want to kill you."

"Yeah, sure," Larry mumbled. "That's what prison is for."

The lieutenant showed her best side and shouted another warning when she saw that "Action News Eight" was setting up a live shot across the street. Allan stood up on his tiptoes, looking for Janette.

When he didn't see her, he said to Larry, "Delilah will not be pleased."

Larry nodded. Allan looked up at the roof of the school. Then he looked down at the street and saw that Nat had assembled his gear and was adding the light of his own sun gun to the dozen or so other beacons that probed the night for news.

He took a wide shot of the school and then zoomed in on the flames. He panned the street for a reaction shot of the crowd and followed the trajectory of an empty beer bottle as it left the hand of a young citizen and shattered into pieces near a platoon of firemen fussing with the safety net.

The flames gave a red, gritty quality to the haze that had gathered over the place, so he put on a filter that would bring a little more color out. He zoomed in on a tight shot of a paramedic combing the playground for bits of bone and teeth. Close-up of him looking at something he'd picked up. Extreme close-up of him dropping it into a plastic bag. He turned to adjust the white balance and saw that Janette had arrived on the scene. She had the vaguely amorous look she usually saved for her multitude of viewers. She was waiting for Nat to say something, but he said something else instead.

"You're stepping on my cable."

She looked down. The curly black chord that connected the camera to the battery back was pinned to the pavement by the spike heel of her right shoe.

Nat said, "Where's Allan?"

"Who cares? Parker said I should do a stand-up."

"Okay. Did Allan write it yet?"

Allan had written most of her scripts since they'd started working together, but Janette didn't mind. She wasn't paid $415,000 a year because she could write. She couldn't write, but this time that didn't stop her. "I don't need Allan for this. This one'll be all mine."

Nat shrugged. "Why not? But give me a minute, okay?"

She waited while he collected a few more shots: paramedics looking at a bloody clump of cloth; reporters milling about; the flames climbing up to the third floor; the smoke curling into an overcast sky; the nervous faces of the firemen as they dragged the safety net into place.

When he had all the shots he needed he turned to Janette and said, "Stand-up. Right. Let's do it."

She explained what she had in mind. "Give me the microphone. You take a wide shot of the school and then focus in on that rag over there." She pointed to a bloody shred of what used to be T-Ball's shirt. "I'll start talking and then walk into the frame. What they need to see is the rag at my feet. When I say the words 'authorities declined official comment,' you pull it up to my face. I need a slow pull so there's at least ten seconds between when they see my feet and when they see my face. What do you think?"

Nat handed her the microphone. "Depends on if you say something that sounds better than your legs look."

Through the filter Nat selected, the playground looked like a battlefield covered with bloodstained smoke. The lens found the bloody shreds of T-Ball's shirt and Janette started talking about Lincoln Square, city politics, and the sale of drugs in no-man's-land. The camera followed the swell of her legs and the narrow of her waist. When the lens settled upon her bosom, Nat noticed that the lattice pattern of her black brassiere could be seen through the sheer gauze of her light pink blouse. He felt as if her nipples were looking him right in the eye.

She said, "This summer even the dead can vote. Every act of racial violence gives credence to Alderman Smith's law-and-order appeal, and every gangland killing is another nail in the mayor's political coffin. This is Janette Baylor reporting for 'Channel Twelve News.'"

After a brief pause to allow space for an exit edit, she added, "And this part's just for you, Allan. Listen to your mother. Get yourself a woman with typing skills."

Then she lowered the microphone and held it to her chest. The amorous look she now gave Nat was one her viewers had never seen. "What do you think?"

"It's different. Nothing like it on Channel Three."

Janette's stand-up had an unearthly aspect when seen from the roof of the Jean Baptiste Pointe du Sable Memorial School. Amid all the flurry and hurry of an unfolding news event, she looked like the mother of God herself, standing still and lovely in the anointing glow of Nat's sun gun. The slice of light that enfolded her was like a candle in the gathering gloom where the police officers readied their weapons, the fire fighters dodged rocks, and the deputy coroners combed the playground for what was left of the Alone Unknown.

Not much, Hammerhead figured.

Pretty soon nothing, he thought.

The fire down below was now so hot that it scorched the perspiration off his skin as fast as he could sweat it. Pretty soon the tar on the roof would start to bubble and smoke would begin pouring through the grate by the service elevator. If he didn't boil or suffocate, he'd be around to see what happened when the first bit of roof fell in on itself. If he wasn't standing on the part that collapsed, then he'd see the fire surge through the hole, and then he'd be dead, too, if he wasn't dead already. Hammerhead figured he'd be boiled in tar long before that happened, but one could always hope.

Elmo and Tech Sarge only got as far as the second-floor landing before the heat forced them to turn back up the fire escape. Sarge blew off the handle of the topmost door with few short bursts of his weapon and took the full force of the door in his face when the backdraft of the fire sucked it open with a swift and unexpected violence. The mercenary slumped down on the landing as his weapon rattled down the stairs and into the rising blaze. Elmo stepped over the unconscious man and into the third-floor hall. His search for a way out took him to the window of the life sciences lab. He stood at the window for a moment of uncertainty in the company of a dead frog swimming in formaldehyde and a plastic replica of a human skeleton hanging from a rusted hook. He was mesmerized by the play of light on the playground down below. The probing white lights of the TV cameras clashed with the flashing blue lights of the squad cars and the revolving red lights of the fire engines to make a spectacular display not unlike one of the video games he would sometimes play at the 7-Eleven when there was nothing else to do. Standing in the middle of it all was that TV woman in a hot pink blouse that glistened as in afterglow.

They won't even know my name, he thought, *because Doogie always said I should never carry no I.D. That yo-yo set me up for this. Should have known it would all go wrong since that time he said we could go make money off the*

*faggots by Logan Park. Scrawny little fuck that Doogie was,
with his little weasel eyes and his angles everywhere. I guess
he's got an angle on me, too, with his go get this and go get
that and don't forget the peppermint Certs. Or was it
spearmint? I don't know. All I know for sure is how I'm
maybe going to die while he's sitting back at the HQ
watching it on the big screen TV.*

The female lieutenant had been supplanted by a male
captain with strict instructions from the chief. He used the
bullhorn to pass those instructions on to Hammerhead.

"The safety net is now in place! Turn around and jump
buttocks first by pushing away from the building as hard as
you can! Repeat! Your buttocks first!"

No fucking way, Hammerhead figured. *I'd rather be boiled
in tar,* he thought.

Popeye had told him what would happen if he jumped.
They'd stick you in this building with windows as wide as a
skinny guy's nose, in a cell with the biggest nigger they could
find. They'd surround you with lawyers, pinstriped suits
who'd want you to plead guilty so they wouldn't have to
waste their time, and then give you ten years just for being a
punk, with time off for good behavior. Good behavior is not
complaining when they stick you in the Place with the Dick
of Death and turn out the lights at 10:00 P.M.

He'd stopped sweating by then because the searing heat
rising up from below had boiled all his juices away. Now his
skin would start to blister, and he'd be dead when the
blisters popped. Hammerhead figured he'd rather crash and
looked for a spot to land on that wasn't protected by the
safety net. But before he found a spot he found Janette. She
was wearing pink, staring at a camera, and saying something
important enough to make it on the news. Maybe she was
talking about the fire fighters and the way they wrestled with
the hose, and maybe she was talking about the cops and the
barricade of squad cars they had placed around the fire
fighters to protect them from the crowd. Maybe she was
talking about the guys with yellow gloves and white hats

who were picking up the pieces of his friends, and maybe she was talking about the fire as it flared through the third-floor windows and fought its way to the roof.

Then again maybe she was talking about the Head and wondering why he didn't jump. At that moment he decided to live because then he could hear her say his name on TV and see his own body float into the soft mesh that was waiting for him down below. The rest would almost be worth it if only he could execute a perfect jump and then see it on the TV news. Bubble tar slowed him down as he took a running leap, but he curled his head into his chest and rolled into the nothing like a runaway bowling ball. For a moment there was no weight or sound, just the rush of air and the heavenly glow of the sun guns that had assembled to catch the moment that the safety net swallowed him whole.

By the time Elmo made it to the top of the building the tar used to hot-mop the roof had started to boil off noxious fumes that made his head spin. The safety net was wrapped around the Rican, and the fire fighters were trying to untangle him. They had given up on the school and were mostly concerned with hosing down nearby buildings so that the conflagration would not spread. The reporters were picking up their gear or swarming around the Rican, so there weren't any cameras looking his way when he started waving frantically or crying as loud as his smoke-filled lungs would allow. The only people to notice him were the young children who were more fascinated by the fire than Hammerhead's dramatic leap.

A young boy said in Spanish, *"Mira! Mira!"* Look! Look!

But by the time a weary fireman looked, the place where Elmo was standing had collapsed. All he saw of the Street Crusader was the fire, the smoke, and the red hot ashes floating up into the night.

37

At the Top of the Tower

ALLAN'S BRAIN WAS MAKING SO MUCH NOISE THAT IT TOOK HIM A while to hear the silence and it took him another while to figure out where it was coming from. Not from Nat, who was snoring on the couch and dreaming of successful women on that forever vacation in the sun. Not from his mother, who was upstairs in the kitchen banging her pots against her pans and complaining to her dearly departed husband in what she thought was a whisper about the routine annoyances of married life: pubic hairs in the shower, scuff marks on the kitchen floor, and gastric events at the dinner table. Hers was a life full of better yesterdays, but she wasn't making the silence that put her only son in a sweat.

Squirrels.

Cute rats. Fuzzy mice. Rodents with a sense of responsibility.

It had taken Allan all summer to become accustomed to their incessant pursuit of acorns and their determined excavation of nesting areas amid the eaves and crossbeams of the Shanahans' attic.

Now they were as still and quiet as if they'd never been,

leaving Allan to wonder whether this was real peace or just the calm before some squirrel storm. The only thing worse than their chewing was the silence after they stopped. If they weren't chewing at his house, then the mystery of Little Wimpy was chewing at his brain and daydreams of Janette were chewing at his heart.

Allan wiggled the joy stick back and forth, playing the same tape over and over again. The blood and the smoke, the fire and the noise, the black brassiere showing through the sheer pink blouse.

"Get yourself a woman with typing skills."

That was almost exactly the same thing his mother had said one time. This suggested some kind of female conspiracy, or maybe that dirtball Nat was working on an angle of his own. Maybe he'd done her and she was the best one ever, and he wanted her all to himself, so he tricked her into saying it too. Typing skills.

He thought about the squirrels as much as he could because they did not run for mayor or stage cheesy media events. They didn't have secrets about their Little Wimpy past, and they didn't wear pink and black. They didn't enslave one another with notarized papers of incorporation, and they didn't have to suck the news into a cathode tube or attend press conferences with the chief of police. All they did was collect acorns and chew holes in somebody else's house. They weren't even doing that anymore.

Chief Dreyer's office was carefully spartan, and his manner was carefully gruff because people want their cops to be both stern and sensitive. To be tough on crime, yet soft on the subject of motor vehicle violations. To be stout defenders of the republic, yet emotionally wounded by their struggle with the Dark Forces. To be stern yet sensitive. Over the years Dreyer had been all this and more for three different mayors, but never before had his office held so many people and cameras.

Like the good politician that Dreyer was, he had chosen a small room to make the crowd look big. Radio Larry was at one elbow, and Janette Baylor was at the other. Assembled between them was a heaving mass of reporters and photographers, jostling one another for the best position. Radio Larry asked most of the questions because he had most of the answers.

"Are you suggesting some kind of gang conspiracy?"

"No. I'm suggesting that this individual and the individual known as Popeye knew each other and may have cooperated in certain criminal enterprises."

"Like trying to kill the mayor, right?"

"Now, I didn't say that. What I said was these so-called Alone Unknowns had access to a certain amount of money and they didn't get it from punching the clock at the Lincoln Square Burger King. Whether or not this particular person of interest participated in the attack on the mayor and the nature of said participation is something we don't know just yet. We're trying to find out as fast as we can."

"You do know that there were twelve dead bodies though. Right?"

Chief Dreyer picked up his telephone and told somebody to bring in a report. Reporters and cameras were scattered and squished as a huge lieutenant blasted into the office and deposited a stack of light blue folders on the chief's desk. Larry grabbed one, and Janette grabbed another. Nat zoomed in for an extreme close-up as the other reporters scuffled for their own copies.

Chief Dreyer said, "Make it fourteen for the record. There were two more inside the school that we didn't know about right away. I'm sure you can understand all the confusion, what with body parts scattered all over the place. Never seen a mess like that before, and that includes two years of hang time during the Korean War. This is a very troubled town."

"Does that mean you're throwing your support to Alderman Smith?"

The chief took a deep breath and let it out in a slow leak.

"I'm really surprised at you, Larry. Here we are talking about a gang hit bigger than St. Valentine's Day, and you want to talk about politics. Maybe we should let the other guys ask a few questions for once."

A great howling started. Since everybody asked all sorts of questions at the same time, the chief could choose which one he wanted to answer. He selected a softball from Channel Eight.

"Correct. There has been friction between the Black Galabeyes and the Alone Unknown. We'll be taking a look at that. I think right now you need to recall how the administration cut my budget request for the current fiscal year so he could spend more money on that tunnel of his, but we always do our best with the funds we got."

The howling died down after that, and the questions became more orderly. What kind of weapon did the attackers use? How did the school catch on fire? What was Hammerhead's real name? Have you talked to the mayor lately? The chief said, "I don't know," "I don't know," "I don't know," and "What do you mean by lately?" He stopped answering questions after that.

State Street looked like a three-foot by six-inch slice of insect life from the twenty-third floor of the Cook County Jail. A never-ending swarm of busy little people with their arms wrapped around tiny briefcases, tiny purses, and tiny packages flowed through Hammerhead's field of vision. He amused himself with the notion that he might somehow squeeze through the window and make a bold leap to freedom. He wouldn't survive the fall, but he might smash a few bugs when he landed.

These were ugly thoughts, but they were better than thinking about the Place and better than listening to his cellmate, a crazed Christian who had molested his daughter, killed his wife, and went on about Jehovah all the time.

"Lot gave his daughters to Sodom, and Noah had lain with his daughters. And where the hell did Cain and Abel get their wives from anyway? It was an abomination when she called the cops on me, so I smote her with my mallet. I sell aggregate byproducts."

Worse than the Christian was the fact that Hammerhead never did get to see himself on TV. After he landed in the net, they rushed him to the hospital, even though nothing was broken. Three guys in dark brown suits asked him a bunch of questions about Popeye, their caper, and the *Connecticut Yankee*. Then they asked him how his friends happened to get ripped to shreds. Hammerhead said he didn't know and could he see the tape from the evening news?

"You want tape? I'll show you tape," said a detective who was so fat he looked like a sponge with teeth.

So they showed him super-slow motion of the coroner's office scraping his friends off the playground of du Sable School. He saw the Truth in a black body bag and the Kosmic Kid in several pieces. Muffy Cruz didn't look so pretty anymore, with her dead eyes open and her tits a bloody mess. Hammerhead said he'd rather see the tape of him jumping off the roof. The cop had a fit.

"The only thing you'll be seeing is the inside of the Place and the angry pecker of that killer who's been making eyes at you."

Hammerhead forgot about the insect life, which he had previously decided was better than the Christian but worse than the four stone walls. It had driven him crazy thinking about all those people and wondering where they'd come from and where they were going to and what they had in their briefcases and packages and whether or not they ever looked up and saw him looking down.

The public defender assigned to the case did not inspire Hammerhead with a lot of confidence. He was small man with the nervous habit of tugging on the cuffs of his shirt and coat. His name was Earl Woodbern, and he seemed pretty certain that Hammerhead would be convicted of one thing or another and sent to the Place. This was an election year, and they had all those body parts. The heat from the newsies was very intense. Heads must roll. Hammerhead's would do.

"What they really want is to send somebody down for shooting the mayor. Give them that, and I get you a deal where you don't go to the Place. You know there's Black Galabeyes there?"

Hammerhead said he'd think about it, so they took him back to his cell and the three-foot by six-inch slice of insect life. He'd never been up this high before, never been higher than the roof of the place his mom had with all the cucarachas.

The insects down on the street responded to light, he noticed. His sliver of window was usually empty at night except for the occasional bum weaving from one drink to another or the occasional whore accosting the occasional customer. With dawn would come more general activity, the shopkeepers walking to their counters and the waitresses to their stations. The first crush came about 7:00 A.M., and the insect frenzy would last for an hour or so. Then things eased off a bit, only to surge again at lunchtime and then again in the late afternoon. Things would slow down more surely after that until it was back to darkness, bums, and whores and back to wondering what the other bugs were doing.

As the midmorning light spilled through his sliver of window, the Christian prayed to the God of Noah and Lot. The thin beams of sunlit dust gave him a halo of sorts.

> "The Lord is my Shepherd
> Who leadeth me
> Into the Valley of Woe,
> Where I shall fear no Evil
> But mine own.

You ever heard of this guy in the Place
They call the Dick of Death?"

* * *

Chief Dreyer usually took lunch at the Top of the Tower,
which used to be called The Millionaire's Club before
millionaires became so commonplace. The management
required ties, so Douglas borrowed one from the maitre d'
who always kept a spare. It was a soup-stained thing with a
silver gray background and diagonal maroon stripes that
almost matched the color of the combat beret that he'd
stopped wearing. Douglas smiled at his host.

"I guess this means you still want your job once I get
elected."

Chief Dreyer slurped his soup and crunched his lettuce
while the alderman talked about the future. About how the
police and the Street Crusaders would work hand-in-hand
to rid the city of drug killers and gang violence. About how
family values must be respected and the workingman must
get an even break. About how welfare moms should be put
to work and the street people should have to find some other
place to sleep. About how little old ladies should be able to
ride the bus again without fearing for their lives and how he
intended to turn the McTavish Apartments into one big
prison so they'd have room for all the creeps.

When he'd said all this he said, "The thing I want to know
is what're you going to do for me?"

"I need three hundred and fifty jobs where there isn't any
work to do."

"You got it. So what're you going to do for me?"

"I'm doing something already," Chief Dreyer replied.
"You see that guy over there?"

He nodded at a table in the corner where Radio Larry was
dining alone. "You know who that is?"

Douglas nodded, as did the chief.

"He sees you and me talking over here, and the first thing
he's going to do is put it on the radio. The papers'll pick it up
and after that the TV news, and pretty soon it'll be all over

town that you and me are in cahoots. There's twenty thousand cops in this town, and there's lots of them look to me for respectability. You got a lot of things going your way, but you could still use a little respectability. I got it coming out my butt, me being the chief and all."

"Okay. So they'll respect me in the morning. What else are you going to do for me?"

"I'll also need some budget money to do whatever I want. Two-fifty."

"Thousand?"

"Right."

"Okay. What're you doing to earn it?"

Chief Dreyer didn't answer right away, as his mouth was stuffed with some Steak and Seafood Supreme. It was tricky business, this dealing with amateurs. Douglas thought himself some kind of genius, and he might not play by rules, so Dreyer mentioned that he had a sheet on Douglas with information about that Nazi bookstore and homosexual encounters by the Logan Park Lagoon. These would be leaked to an eager press if Douglas tried to pull a double-cross.

"All right. You're in. Now help me win this thing."

The chief contemplated the remains of his Steak and Seafood Supreme, a chunk of leftover meat surrounded by the stumps of a half-dozen shrimp tails. Eat or be eaten, he thought to himself. He spoke without lifting his eyes. "It's already over as soon as you start that debate. The mayor's been pixilated. That's why they got him under wraps, so he don't start talking like a fool."

Douglas was so startled by this that he almost choked on a scallop. He coughed it up and then tried to wash it back down with wine but gagged again and coughed so hard that wine blew out his nose. The maître d' came over and tried to be of assistance, but seemed more worried about the mash of food and drink that had collected on his tie.

When things settled down, Douglas said, "Just what the hell are you talking about?"

"There's something in his noggin that's not been working right, like his brain's been split in half. The right hand's jerking while the left one's working. You sting him a bit when you do that debate, and the man'll flip out for sure."

The two men regarded their food in silence for a moment, contemplating their prospects to the lilting music of prerecorded violins.

38

Bulljive Day

THEY PARKED GENGHIS KAR BETWEEN A BRAND NEW ACURA Legend and a very old Caddy with a fur-covered steering wheel and Jesus on the dash. The shadows in the parking lot seemed to be alive. On closer inspection they saw that they were occupied by sullen Street Crusaders who smoked cigarettes and talked in low tones while giving the evil eye to the party hacks filing into the Biograph Theater.

Nat said to Allan, "You see that alley over there?"

He was pointing at a narrow gully between the theater and a restaurant that served Hungarian food. Allan didn't look but nodded anyway. "Yeah, sure."

"That's where Dillinger got fingered by the Lady in Red." Now Allan looked. Nat continued. "Rat-a-tata-tat and the feds toasted him. J. Edgar Hoover did the job himself with an assist from Melvin Purvis of the FBI."

Allan stared off into space for a moment, wondering if the director had been wearing lace panties at the time. This phantasm dissolved into one of Janette walking all over his own body, wearing spike heels and leather underwear. He chewed on his anger, swallowed it into a smile, and said, "They say he had a pecker eighteen inches long."

"J. Edgar?"

"No. Dillinger. But they say J. Edgar had it pickled, so he could put in on the mantle like it was some kind of bowling trophy. They say after Hoover croaked they stuck it in this special room in the basement of the Smithsonian. Scientists only allowed. Scientists, presidents, and closet cases from the FBI."

Nat considered this with due gravity as he picked up the battery pack. Their conversation had been overheard and was causing a stir among the Street Crusaders. The thugs stopped talking and smoking as Nat and Allan walked past them on the way to a side door of the theater. Nat was glad they were talking about something besides Janette.

He said, "Who's this 'they' that's saying all this?"

"That's the funniest part because there's lots of people that say it, or they say something else that's close enough. I heard it first in Willow Woods when I was growing up, and then I heard it again in Chicago. I even heard it when I went to college downstate."

"You must like to talk about peckers."

Allan nodded, glad to have the chance to talk about them some more. "Of course, some stories have it as Al Capone's dick, and some say it was Bugsy Moran's, and some say it's only fourteen inches, but the general story is always the same: a dead gangster and a pickled pecker on J. Edgar's mantlepiece. Can you imagine that?"

Nat and Allan set up their gear in the top balcony so they and the other newshounds wouldn't offend the various swells with their rumpled clothes and flinty cynicism. The talk in the balcony was all about paid media and shifting momentum. Douglas was running commercials with tape of the school on fire, and Willis was still in the Deep Tunnel bragging about all the mosquitos he had killed.

The momentum was going the alderman's way. Despite the earnest denials of the various principals, word had spread that Chief Dreyer had joined his camp. Everyone in the balcony was able to agree that this was an important rumor, indeed. Radio Larry said the chief was thought to directly command about seven thousand votes. Another ten thousand or so would be influenced by his endorsement, even if it had been made between bites of Steak and Seafood Supreme in what used to be called the Millionaires Club.

"The votes are nothing," Larry said. "It's the files that I'd be worried about."

Allan contemplated the confusion of stage lights that dangled above a stage on which were set two tables, two chairs, and two sparkling glasses of water. "What files do you mean?"

"The chief's got a file on everybody. He's got a file on you."

Allan tried to figure out what his file might contain. He had lived a boring, if exemplary, life except for a little shoplifting he'd done when he was but a boy. He remembered going into Dominic's Grocery at the corner of Archer and Canal and buying a stick of bubble gum while stealing as much candy as he could stuff into the front of his jockey shorts. The jig was up when he ate all the evidence at once one time and then threw it up all over the living room rug. Alerted by the presence of half-digested malt balls, Mrs. Shanahan conducted an investigation that uncovered a thick wad of candy wrappers Allan had crammed into the toe of an old tennis shoe. Perhaps his file contained a photograph of the tennis shoe, a few yellowing wrappers, and affidavits from Dominic and his mom.

Douglas, too, was thinking about the past as he waited in the wings for the debate to begin. He was so far ahead in the polls that most people thought he was making a mistake by debating the mayor. But this was to be his shining moment, and he didn't want to miss it for reasons of mere practicality. The greatest leaders had always been impractical men, the kind of men who didn't try to sit on a ten-point lead. Great leaders always took risks, always played to win, and always listened, not to their consultants but to the soft whisper of their own inspiration.

He peeked through the curtain where it abutted the wing and felt the power of place coursing through his veins. The Biograph Theater had been refurbished by the Near North Historical Society. The spectacular appointments for which it had been famous in Dillinger's day had been buffed to a translucent gloss.

The high ceiling supported a gilded chandelier of magnificent proportions, and the walls had been decorated with wood panels two stories tall that commemorated important fragments of the city's memory: du Sable's trading post, the Indian attack on Fort McHenry, Pullman's first sleeping car, the fire, the beer wars, the labor riot at Haymarket Square. Then, as now, money and blood were the brick and mortar of history, the stuff of which the city and its leaders must be made.

As he took his place at his end of the table, Douglas imagined a Biograph Theater of tomorrow in which a wood panel devoted to his own regime was hung among the accomplishments of Pullman, Daley, and du Sable. He would stand in the foreground with his tie loosened and his shirt sleeves rolled up to expose forearms that would do a blacksmith proud. A righteous fist would be raised and a friendly hand extended to the teeming masses of simple folk who looked to him for leadership. A phalanx of Street Crusaders, ever-silent and ever-vigilant, would gather in one corner of the tableau while in another would cower a scruffy gang of colored toughs and the welfare mom who had given birth to them. He'd make sure the welfare mom looked just like Sister Delilah Blue and that one of the toughs had a peanut-shaped head reminiscent of Willis's.

He eye-contacted the audience while the lady from the League of Women Voters repeated all the rules. The first five rows of refurbished velvet seats were filled from aisle to aisle with City Hall functionaries like Sister Blue, the hierarchy of the African Methodist Episcopal Church, and other toadies of the mayor. Behind them sat his own team, Street

Crusaders trying to look cool in borrowed suits, rummage-sale ties, and other articles of clothing designed to persuade the inattentive that they were earnest citizens newly committed to his cause.

Sprinkled among the Crusaders were fashionable sorts who had caught the fever, the trendsetters who had discovered rad-right chic and would abandon it as soon as the rabble caught on. Behind them sat the uncaring and the undecided, those who played politics like gamblers play the ponies and those whose livelihoods depended on their cheering loudly for the right person at the right time. Douglas was making a list of people like that, so he could promise them more than they deserved and then give them very much less. The lady from the League began the proceedings.

"Mr. Smith and Mr. Cleveland will each have three minutes to make their opening statements. After that the two participants will have the opportunity to question one another, and then each will be allowed five minutes to make a closing statement."

The TV sun guns were ignited, bathing the speakers in a punishing light that exposed their every wrinkle and pore to the covert scrutiny of an audience left in the dark by the dimming of the gilded chandelier. The mayor spoke about his numerous accomplishments, about his struggle up from poverty, and about his love for a troubled town. Douglas said that may well be true, but Willis was no longer up to the job of bringing peace to a city torn by gang strife and ethnic violence. He looked right into the nearest camera and talked not to the lady from the League or to the few hundred people gathered in the theater, but to the unseen viewers who huddled before the flickering light of the 276,000 television sets that weren't tuned in to any of the multitude of other stations locally available on cable TV.

"I know there's people that's not sure about me because I came up the hard way and never kissed up to the 'powers that be.' I never even had a government job, and I don't belong to any city workers union. I'm just a regular guy from

Marquette Park who's tired of worrying that some drug punks are going to burn down the local public school. There's lots of people afraid of me because they know I won't play ball and I'll rock the boat, and they know that with a guy like me as mayor, people like you will be able to walk around town with your heads held high. You can't do that now, with some gangbanger waiting in some alley for you with a crack habit and a stolen gun who'd rather die for the money in your pocket than go fifteen minutes without his daily drugs."

To the right side of the mayor's brain, his opponent's speech sounded like the babble of frightened animals in the primeval forest of those hoary yesterdays where men triumphed over larger, stronger, faster beasts equipped with claw and saber tooth. To the left side of the mayor's brain, it sounded like every speech he had ever heard and a few he had given himself. He heard the truth honored with a multitude of lies as the selfish were made to seem generous and the craven were made to seem brave. *Shuck this jive,* Willis thought. *Enough is enough already.*

When Douglas finished talking, all eyes turned to the mayor. He didn't speak for a moment so they'd have a chance to think things over. Except for the occasional nervous cough and the low buzz of the television gear, the theater was quiet and still. Paid hacks waited for a cue while the undecideds measured the momentum and counted the votes. Willis looked at the fearful old faces and the angry young ones, and in the only quiet moment a public speaker has, in the artful pause before turning on the talk, he allowed himself a moment of doubt. For that moment he felt ashamed at having never told the people what was really on his mind.

When the moment had passed and the doubts had disappeared, he cleared his throat and said, "The problem with this town is they took a bunch of brothers living in the sticks and promised us jobs, running water, and a late-model Cadillac of our very own. Now we got no jobs, no Cadillac, and no sticks, neither. The water's still running, but it's so polluted we might as well be drinking gasoline. The best thing could happen is a nuclear war, so's we can start the whole thing up again from scratch.

"Maybe you should vote for Alderman Smith because he don't care how many die as long as the dead's not him. Doogie and those Crusaders of his been stirring thing up with the drug gangs, and if I had a million dollars, I'd bet it all that he's the one tried to get me killed so's he could be mayor himself without having to have a real election fair and square. I know the truth hurts, but the lie hurts worse, and if enough of you people vote for me again there's not going to be no more lies.

"I've been to the mountain with Moses, and the Lord saith to us, 'Cut the bulljive, boys.' And now I'd like to say some words about the Mosquito Abatement District. It's hard to posit a negative, but I should be taking all the credit for the mosquitos that haven't been biting anybody since we started digging that tunnel a few years back."

The alderman had jumped to his feet and had started speaking, but nobody could hear what he was saying. His microphone had been switched off by the management of the Biograph, some of those lakefront liberals that had pushed Willis over the top eight years ago next week. Somebody in the audience said, "Hallelujah," and somebody else said, "You crazy sonabitch." Somebody punched somebody else. Pandemonium ensued. Chief Dreyer had a quick change of heart and jumped up on stage to act as the mayor's personal bodyguard. The woman from the League tapped her gavel without effect. Nat started rolling tape, but his inner ear was listening to what Elmo had said so many weeks before.

39

A Little Walking Change

NAT MADE A LIST OF ALL THE THINGS HE'D HAVE TO HAVE TO DO
what he wanted to do, and he thought about the difference
between net and gross as it applied to the revenue from
Electronic News Tonight. The difference between net and
gross was the difference between starting and finishing his
gangster doc. Net would buy him a camera and some time,
then leave him stranded with too much work left undone
and nothing to do it with. Gross would buy him a better
camera, more time and all the other things that went into
the making of a first-class production. No more cheezy
videotape. He'd need miles of high-resolution film, a digital
editing system, and a narrator whose voice sounded like
thunder rolling in from the west. Gross would buy him all
that and more but he was stuck with net. He picked up the
phone and dialed City Hall. Three voices later, Delilah
came on the line.

Nat said, "You really want to win this thing?"

"Yes. Of course, we do."

"How much money have you got?"

"What do you mean, how much? We've already paid you plenty."

There followed one of those uneasy silences, when time travels more slowly and decisions of great and small importance are left to hang in the balance. Delilah used the moment to offer a silent prayer to her African Methodist Episcopal God, and Nat used the moment to estimate the production costs of a full-length documentary that would receive favorable reviews in the specialty press and be shown in claustrophobic art houses to people who drank espresso and pretended movies were important.

When the moment was over, Nat said, "The only way you're going to win is if I fabricate the truth. We charge extra for that."

The hearty aroma of meat loaf was in the air when Mrs. Shanahan answered the door in her bathrobe. She and Delilah chatted for a moment about the weather and the squirrels before Delilah went down to the studio, followed by Marv the cat.

She said, "Name your price."

This chased the sleep from Allan's eyes. "This is against the law."

"Don't give me that," Delilah said. "Worse gets done all the time. I'll give you a hundred thousand and help with any legal expenses."

Allan ran a comb through his hair. "How about making it five hundred, and we'll pay the lawyer ourselves."

"Hold it right there," Nat said. He was speaking to Delilah, but he wanted Allan to hear. "I'm not going for any kind of deal where I get screwed."

They haggled and hassled and then they got it straight.

"Let's chop tape," Nat said.

Monitor One was heavy on the green, so Elmo's maroon combat beret looked a little purple when he removed it from his shaven head. Delilah and Allan watched in silence as Nat wiggled the joy stick until he got to the part where Elmo said, "What you need to know is Doogie Smith and the Street Crusaders are the only thing keeping more kids from getting all shot up, and I'm not just saying this because he's a friend of mine. The mayor has got to be the one to blame for selling us down the river to the narco-killer street gangs that really run this town."

For one thing, the bite was much too long, 22.6 seconds to get from what to town. What he needed was a few cutaways to cover up the edits as he shaved some words away. Fabricating the truth. They did it all the time, and so did everybody else. The viewers never seemed to notice, and the people whose words were surgically removed didn't seem to mind since usually the technique was employed to iron out the ums and ahs, the you knows and non sequiturs that punctuate normal speech but make for unbearable TV. Nat figured they didn't know what was happening or were so glad to be on TV that they didn't dare to complain, or they appreciated the efforts to make them sound a little smarter than they really were. Not that it would matter if they did complain because TV never corrected anything. In this way did TV's multitude of fictions achieve a notoriety denied to facts that take ten seconds or more to explain. Once the news was over, it didn't matter whether things were true or not. Everybody acted as if they were true, which made them as true as things ever got in a time and place where experts said the darndest things. Nat was the expert at chopping tape.

He said, "Elmo won't mind too much if we tighten this up a bit."

Allan fidgeted and Delilah marveled as Nat manipulated the joy stick, punching buttons and sending little flashes of colored light from Monitor One to Monitor Two. It took him only a few minutes to slice up bits of videotape and splice the remains together. The "shot up" was the hardest part because Elmo said it too softly, in a way that implied something less than attempted murder. He solved this problem by running the words through an audio filter that muted the background noise, and then punching up the volume on the sanitized bite. Once he had pumped up the volume, he piped in some crowd noise to smooth out the sound.

"Very clever," Delilah said.

"Reality plus," Allan replied. "TV is life without the boring parts. That's why dull people look exciting on the tube, and TV people always seem kind of slow when you meet them in three dimensions. Anybody can be like a star if a good editor is chopping the tape."

They played Elmo's sound bite again and pointed to the jump cuts, visual jolts suffered by talking heads when unwanted words are extracted and wanted words are spliced together.

As Nat scanned the tape for the perfect shot to cover up the evidence, he explained what he was trying to do. "This is the stuff people never see because guys like me are slick. Jump cuts are up front because they let people know some words have been chopped, but they shatter the illusion that TV is for real. The nets and the bigger affiliates are starting to use slide cuts and dissolves to cover up the jumps, but Allan always buys this low-grade gear, so I can't do anything fancy. A clunky old cutaway will do."

"What's a cutaway?"

"Male Hispanic tears. That's a cutaway."

Nat had found the part of the tape where a young friend of Tappy Shoes Calderone cried about his untimely death. The tears seemed to make just the right statement for a campaign in need of Hispanic votes, so he slapped them over Elmo's talking head and the video jolts disappeared. They played the edited tape one more time.

Delilah said, "Hallelujah!"

"Now all we need is the truth," Nat said.

"The truth? How's that? What do you mean?"

"We can't put this tape out if it's not true. That would be worse than unethical. We'd get caught for sure. If the large part is true, the little lie don't matter."

* * *

Earl Woodbern tugged on the cuffs of his gray suit coat and leaned so close that his words smeared the Plexiglas divider with mist. Hammerhead leaned back and socked him with a stare.

"What kind of deal you talking about?"

"A great deal. The real deal. Better than you ever dreamed. You talk and you walk. Just like that."

"Who am I talking to?"

"Everybody."

But first he was talking to a big black woman who'd been putting on the pounds. Her fingernails were painted silver and looked like dancing coins when she wiggled them about.

Hammerhead had once had a teacher like that who kicked him out of class at du Sable for talking to the girls instead of memorizing the state capitals. Women like that were nobody's fool. Women like that made good friends and bad enemies.

This one said, "My name is Delilah Blue. I am a sister of the Lord."

"If you're a nun then how come you don't got your black colors on?"

Delilah folded her hands together and rested her elbows on the table. The dancing coins came to rest. She said, "Nuns are a Catholic thing. I am ordained in the African Methodist Episcopal Church and do most of my preaching on the South Side of town. You ever been in a church, child?"

Hammerhead shrugged his shoulders. No yes or no, just a shrug. "The guy in my cell is a brother of the Lord. The Lord's got some strange relatives to hear this fuckhead talk."

"The Lord need not answer for his creations, and I don't like that trash-mouth language."

"Then what you want me to say?"

Some of the coins danced to her ear while the rest lay flat on the table, like a reluctant tip left for an indifferent waiter. "I want you to say you participated in a vicious attack on the mayor's life, and Doogie Smith paid you to do it."

"All right. I'll say it. Who the hell is that?"

"Who?"

"This Doogie Smith person."

He nodded while she explained and while she said, "It doesn't really matter what you know. It's what you say that counts."

"If I say what you want, they'll send me to the Place for sure."

Delilah wanted to save him for Jesus right then and there, but restrained herself in the interest of the business at hand. "Not true. We've got a lot of cops and some lawyers and a judge. They all owe us favors, so they'll get your trial and screw it up real bad. Shouldn't be too hard because they're all boneheads anyway. You can maybe even sue them for your civil rights and get out with a little walking change."

40

Allan Gets Hung

MOST OF THE TIME PARKER COULD RELAX A LITTLE BIT AFTER THE newscast began at the butt end of his fifteen-hour day. By then the scripts had all been written and approved, the pictures had all been shot, and the audio tracks had all been cut; the live remotes had already been arranged and the temperatures had already been set for the various weather maps; the anchors' hair had been properly moussed, their ties and shoulder pads adjusted; the pancake makeup had already been applied. A multitude of electronic blips had already been woven into ninety-second packages and assigned to the appropriate blocks of time: before the weather, after the sports, between the commentary and the movie review. If there was any time left, they might double-check a fact or two.

All that remained was the show itself. If things went wrong during the cast, Parker could do nothing about it but watch in horror from the safety of the kitchen where they shot "Midwest Today."

His usual routine was to sip coffee, try to decompress, and start thinking about the next day's news, but this time he had to worry about a meeting the news dee had scheduled for right after the 'cast. Since he didn't know what the meeting was about, his number must be up. Time to get bang-banged.

This suspicion seemed to be confirmed by the unannounced appearance of Allan Shanahan and Nat Puchinski, who filed into the news dee's office fifteen minutes before his own meeting was scheduled to begin. That could only mean that the series was a stiff, and the September sweeps were a disaster before they'd even begun. After a brief review of the cash accounts, the news dee would accuse Electronic News Tonight of ripping the station off. Together they would spin a bogus tale of Parker's incompetence, and since somebody would have to pay the price, the news dee would go bang-bang. He might even offer the job to Allan since the rumor was that he and Nat were calling it quits.

Parker smiled at the unearthly glow of the anchor desk, where Janette was reading the leader to part one of her series, the series that was supposed to save his ass but hadn't. Shanahan could have his job. He deserved it, the ungrateful little shit. It reminded him of that old Chinese curse, or maybe it was voodoo or some other kind of mumbo jumbo. Whatever. The one about how the gods grant the wishes of jerks when they want to punish them. Screw Allan. Screw the gods. Parker could look forward to severance pay, unemployment benefits, and nights unblemished by the misery of those unfortunates whose troubles happened to be captured on tape. He could read books, write letters, go to baseball games. He could go home without worrying if he had missed something, and fall asleep without the assistance of too much alcohol. He could live a normal life and express normal alarm at the horrible things that happened to people every evening at six and ten.

Out on the set, Janette was finishing part one of the series, which segued into a story about the mayor's race. As the campaign entered its final days, the experts were saying that Willis was finished; that his paranoid outburst during the debate was the final nail in the coffin; that we'll be back with the weather right after this. After that came the sports, and after that came some recycled stuff about AIDS and silicone breast implants. After that, the commentary, and after that, the movie review and a leave-em-with-a-smiler about a woman on the South Side who made rain boots out of the rubber from this huge tire pile on the I & M Canal.

After the usual congratulations were exchanged, the anchor team broke up, and the technical crew started to unravel the congestion of equipment that surrounded the anchor desk. Parker watched Janette march from the set to the news dee's office, where she joined the conference already in session. Parker thought it only fitting that she should be there to witness his demise.

The news dee's name was Thomas Nolan, but everyone called him Dr. No unless he happened to be in the room. In that case, they called him Tom. Tom was a short, thick plug of a man who made up in energy what he lacked in size. His sleeves were rolled up, his tie was undone, and his shirttail hung out like a flag at half-mast. As was his habit, he sported a pugnacious attitude that could not hide the fear lurking in his eyes. He gave the general impression of a man en route from one barroom to another.

He said, "This is nuclear. We'll bang-bang Channel Three. We're talking news. Money. Massive promotional possibilities right through the sweeps. We'll break into regular programming and call it a "Channel Twelve Exclusive Focus." I'll send out copies of the script to radio and all the rags. Call a press conference and write a press release. Let them all know we scooped their asses. This is a major coup. Might even win us an Emmy. Who knows? Good work, Jan."

Janette was wearing the same smile she wore when the sports anchor made rude remarks under his breath during the wide-shot that closed the 'cast. Allan came to her rescue after she had mumbled an uncertain "thanks."

He said, "Jan's been a trooper right from the start. Sure she's only talent, but she's also a reporter too, right there

310

with the tough questions every single time, like that time she interviewed the shoeshine man."

Nat grunted in a way that sounded like he probably agreed. He didn't. The best Janette could manage was a quick glance at Allan, followed by an uncertain nod.

Nolan paced back and forth. His legs were short, so he took a lot of steps. He said, "We need to stretch things out, add some Hamburger Helper. I want a long list of follow-up stories, starting with profiles of these hooligans we're biting in the first report. Who's this Crazy person and where did Hammerhead come from? And we need to get right in this Elmo guy's face. You people are on exclusive contract until the end of the month. Where the hell is Parker? We need him in on this."

Nolan stepped outside. Janette took this opportunity to thank Allan for making her look good by suggesting that not only had she already read the script but even may have participated in its preparation.

Allan averted his eyes and turned beet red when Nat said, "Mixing it up with the ladies again?"

This had such a disturbing effect on Allan that he excused himself and rushed from the room, presumably on the pretext of taking a leak.

Janette said, "That wasn't very nice."

"I'm not a very nice person, and besides, he had it coming. He's already stolen about a dozen women from me."

First came the jolt, then the strained snicker from Janette. "Oh, sure."

"No, really. I know Allan's kind of a goof, but he's hung like Dillinger."

"Dillinger? Who's that?"

"You ever been to the Smithsonian?"

Although intensely interested by this exchange, Janette was unable to pursue more details because at that moment Nolan came in, followed first by Parker and then by Allan, whose complexion had changed from beet red to ashen white. When they had all settled into their chosen corners of the office, Nolan resumed his pacing. Turning to Parker, he said, "You hired these people. You trust them, right?"

Nolan waited. Parker did, too.

"Right?"

"Right."

"Good. I want you to approve their script."

Parker was so ready to be fired that he wasn't prepared for anything else and a little disappointed to learn that Nolan wasn't going to go bang-bang. "Yeah, sure. Of course I trust them. What's the story about?"

Nolan stopped pacing when he got to his desk and picked up a clump of the multicolored five-copies on which Channel Twelve reporters and producers typed their scripts. He thumbed through the scripts like a gambler shuffling cards and then dropped the stack in Parker's lap. The others watched in silence while the assignment editor examined the script.

BROADCAST DATE: Sept. X
NEWS BLOCK: Lead
TALENT: Baylor
PRODUCER: Electronic News Tonight
VIDEOGRAPHER: Electronic News Tonight
APPROVED BY: ___

AUDIO:	VIDEO:
ANCHOR LEAD: Tonight this Channel 12 exclusive. A weeks-long investigation by our own Janette Baylor has uncovered evidence that the Street Crusaders were involved in the attempt on Mayor Cleveland's life.	Wide shot of anchor desk.
Although Crusade leader and mayoral candidate	Tight shot of lead anchor.

AUDIO:	VIDEO:
Douglas Smith is not personally implicated, the revelation could affect his chances in next Tuesday's primary election. Here is Janette's report.	

ROLL PACKAGE WITH OUTCUE: ". . . Tuesday's election?"

JANETTE: This was the scene last July when political leaders from around the state gathered aboard the *Connecticut Yankee* for their annual state conference. Shortly after dinner, an explosion rocked the boat and sent officials from around the state scrambling for political cover. The target, Mayor Cleveland, was injured by the blast.	General festivities on riverboat with printout: July 29. Aftermath of blast with printout: July 30.
SMITH BITE: The mayor can't protect this city if he can't protect himself.	Printout: Douglas Smith, mayoral candidate
JANETTE: With the mayor laid low by his injuries, the alderman's fortunes improved. Two weeks ago he passed Cleveland in the public opinion polls, and since then his lead has been widening.	Mayor at the hospital; various shots of Smith campaigning.

AUDIO:

JANETTE: But after a young gang member was arrested in connection with the crime, reports started to circulate that some of Smith's staunchest supporters may have been involved.

CRAZY HORSE BITE: If you want to know who done—it then you look to see who cashes in—That would have to be Doogie and his crew because they take over if the mayor gets popped.

JANETTE: Authorities dismissed these rumors as mere speculation until the suspect himself gave this exclusive interview to "Channel Twelve News." He says the assassination was a hit commissioned by Smith's group, the Crusade for Safer Streets.

HAMMERHEAD BITE: This soldier named Elmo paid us to do it with some kind of techno-death—that does a lot of killing

VIDEO:

Suspect arrested at middle school with printout: Eduard "Hammerhead" Rivas.

Cover jump cuts with wide shot of shoeshine stand with printout: Ramone "Crazy Horse" Pons.

Hammerhead taken to county jail; wide shot of him in interview room.

Cover jump cuts with two-shot of Hammerhead/Janette.

AUDIO:	VIDEO:
without—much sweat. My partner was going to buy himself a restaurant with the coin before he got popped himself.	
JANETTE: "Channel Twelve News" confronted the executive vice president of the Crusade for Safer Streets with the allegations made by the suspect in the case.	Exterior of Crusader headquarters.
ELMO BITE: What you need to know is Doogie Smith and the Street Crusaders—shot up—the mayor—for selling us down the river to all the narco-killer street gangs that really run this town.	Cover jump cuts with Hispanic tears. Printout: Elmo Givens.
JANETTE STAND-UP: Smith declined comment on the allegations. The unanswered question tonight is how will these allegations affect next Tuesday's election?	Printout: Janette Baylor reporting.
ANCHOR WRAP: Thank you, Janette. And here to help us answer that	Wide shot of anchor desk.

AUDIO:	VIDEO:
question is Sister Delilah Blue, the mayor's press secretary.	
START LIVER WITH DELILAH	Open Koppel window.

The script gave Parker the hope that he might well be fired after all, so he initialed it with a flourish and handed the five-copy back to Nolan. The news director separated the copies and made sure they got into the proper hands: yellow copy to the producer so that the anchor lead could be inserted into the TelePrompTer; green copy to the public relations department for use in the preparation of a self-serving press release; white copy to counsel, who would be officially alarmed at the prospect of a libel suit and secretly excited by the legal fees that such a suit would generate; pink copy into his own file so he could blame Parker if it all went sour.

The final copy, colored baby blue, disappeared with Nat and Janette into Edit Bay Five. She cut the audio track, and he began the laborious process of stitching the sound together and covering the stitches with video images of a city on the brink. After a while, when her natural restraint had been overcome by her natural curiosity, she leaned into Nat's ear and whispered, "So tell me about the Smithsonian."

41

The Glass Key

THE CHURCH WAS OVERFLOWING WITH HAPPY PEOPLE IN A FESTIVE mood who swayed to the music of a hip-hop band with a song about how Pharaoh let their people go. The children's choir scuffled to the beat in the Willis Cleveland T-shirts they had formerly worn beneath red satin robes. Their elders breathed a sigh of relief. Somebody turned off the music when Sister Blue stepped up to the mike.

"It's been a long and winding road, but here we are at last. The exit polls are counted, and it looks like we've won this thing. I guess you want to hear from the mayor now because we couldn't have done it without him."

The mayor felt the power of the moment coursing through his veins. It wasn't the power bestowed by voters in this vale of tears but the power of truth and light. The undiluted truth and the everlasting light. Willis had been to hell and back and he wasn't going to lie no more. Now he stepped up to the mike.

"Praise beJeezus, Sister. Praise beJeezus Christ. We've got some work to do, with grandmas eating out of garbage cans and children dreaming on drugs. This city is going down the

317

drain, and we need to plug it fast. Hell, I wouldn't even live here myself if'n I weren't mayor of the place—"

That's when the microphone was unplugged, and the children started to sing. No matter. Willis had won a third term by 7,800 votes out of the 879,000 cast. He was supported by 74 percent of the blacks, 57 percent of the browns, 17 percent of the whites and 13 percent of the yellows; 52 percent of the Democrats and 43 percent of the Republicans; 41 percent of persons ages eighteen to thirty-five, 40 percent of thirty-six to sixty-five, and 79 percent of sixty-five and older; 34 percent of the men and 64 percent of the women.

This last was attributed by pundits to the sympathy excited among women by his narrow brush with death. Quipsters disagreed. They said his success among women was due to their collective delirium at having finally found an honest man. A few thought Delilah might have had a beneficial effect, but Allan disputed all of these common-place observations in favor of a more complicated theory of his own that related to biocurves, menstrual cycles, and a secret longing for nonjudgmental father figures. He tried to square this theory with the available facts as he guided Genghis Kar into the glistening quiet that covered down-town Chicago after a cooling rain.

The heat had broken, and Genghis Kar didn't like it much. Since Nat had quit ENT, the car had developed a habit of stalling during interminably long waits at numerous intersections. Allan suspected that his former partner had engineered this difficulty in revenge for an imagined injustice related to the difference between net and gross. Beneath that lurked a darker suspicion that the engine trouble was but a prelude to a greater catastrophe when Genghis Kar would explode into a shower of rubber, steel, and man.

It sputtered out at the intersection of thirty-fifth and State, just as a small group of kids was preparing to cross the street. Wearing their tent tops, spandex bottoms, and shiny new combat boots, they gathered around the hood ornament in an ever-tightening noose as Allan worked at gear, key, and pedal to get the heap started and make his escape. But the expected surge of noise and power eluded him for a moment as the engine produced a gurgling sound more suited to a washing machine than a ton or two of steel on wheels.

The punks took note of this and started to laugh and joke among themselves about the car and the man driving it, dismissing the one as "a hooptie from hell" and the other as "a snaggletoothed fool."

Genghis Kar gurgled some more, and Allan had another chance to think about another end to his life: not with a boom but a whimper as his blood spilled from a knife wound onto a street that hadn't been swept in years. He tried the key again and Genghis Kar gurgled again, only with more resonance as if what ailed it was moving into its vital organs.

The punks closed in, but instead of pulling guns and flashing knives, they put their heads together, leaned over the vehicle, and started rapping into the vintage 1940s radio microphone that was bolted to its hood. They sang a cappella:

> Let's get down and funky
> Let's all be a junkie
> Let's all get that monkey
> On our big, black back.
> Yes there are no maybes
> That's why we make babies
> It's the only way be-
> sides a crack attack.

There followed some do-wops and oo-bees, some proper jumps and spins. Allan had gone beyond panic into that state of impossible calm noted in soldiers, hostages, and other persons who have endured terrors so sublime that some part of their being has turned numb. His mind had disconnected from the events in and around Genghis Kar, but his body continued with its chores by rote. His fingers turned the key, and his ears heard the engine cough, gag, sputter, roar. He put Kar in gear and stomped on the gas. The punks scattered, and he felt the tangy sweep of city air rushing over his face, but as his thoughts were occupied with squirrels, parents, and Diamond-Tooth Eddie, his escape didn't seem really real until Genghis Kar came to a stop in the fifteen-minute parking zone by the downtown Greyhound Station.

Crazy Horse studied the *Racing Form* as a fortuneteller studies tea leaves, life lines, and the body language of prosperous fools. He knew that somewhere in those long thin columns of handicaps, odds, tips, and records could be found the secret to untold wealth. Having made a small bundle betting on the mayor in his darkest hour, he now wished to turn this into a larger bundle by investing the proceeds wisely. He was considering Kathy Cat in the sixth race at Maywood Park and was studying the *Racing Form* for information about this filly and her nine adversaries. They made much to-do about a long shot by the name of Simon's Son who loved to run in the mud. Crazy Horse put down the *Form* and reached for the section of tomorrow's paper where he would find the latest weather forecast.

It was while between papers that he saw Allan Shanahan sliding down the escalator. Crazy figured Allan must be down on his luck. On the run. Going Greyhound. This was the source of some satisfaction until the escalator deposited Allan on the floor and he turned toward the shoeshine stand, raising his fist in a white man's version of a brown man's salute. Crazy looked down at the weather report. By the time he had made a mental note that there was a 60 percent chance of rain, Allan had reached the shoeshine stand.

Without looking up, Crazy said, "If it ain't the Muscle Man. So how's your muscle, man?"

Allan's muscle was a little sore. He had just broken off a week-long entanglement with Janette Baylor that had left both of them profoundly disappointed. He resisted the temptation to bore Crazy with the long and the short of this sad story.

"I did my crime," he said.

Crazy Horse now looked up at Allan, but all he could see were teeth and the permanent grimace they made in the soft tissue of his mouth. There developed in that moment a brotherhood of sorts, an unspoken understanding between two men afflicted by bad luck and circumstance. Ask either man and each would deny it, but the connection was there just the same.

"What crime you mean?"

"The crime you said I had to do before you'd tell me how Little Wimpy got his name. I'm a criminal now."

"You bite somebody's head off?"

"I lied on television."

This didn't go down right away. Crazy said that TV people lied all the time, from their phony smiles to their overdone concern for unfortunates they'd never even met. Allan agreed but insisted that the truth he and Nat had fabricated was more than your everyday, garden variety, run-of-the-mill TV lie. It had been a whopper of heroic proportions, a fraud that had deceived an entire city into doing what was right.

Crazy was skeptical. "It's no crime if you don't get paid."

Allan described the financial arrangements. Crazy Horse was impressed. "It ain't no crime if there ain't no time."

"Doogie can sue us for everything we've got, and they might even send us to jail. That's if he can prove the Street Crusaders didn't do what we had Elmo say they did. I don't know if they did it, but they can't prove a thing. Hammerhead's playing for the home team now."

Crazy Horse leaned back on his throne and thought things over for a moment. This was not the sort of play that lent itself to odds and percentages. "Your face is almost as ugly as mine. Where'd you get them teeth?"

Allan did not reply because the truth hurt more than the silence. The fact is his dear parents did not think teeth were very important. They had let his grow according to God's plan, and a dental catastrophe was the result. The silence got to Crazy before it got to Allan, so he let the question pass unanswered and told Allan to take a seat while he shined his shoes.

Crazy said, "Here's the thing about Wimpy: he could always draw, and a gang can always use an artist for reputational purposes. See, a gang's just muscle with some talk and a walk and names written on the wall. We didn't have a lot of muscle, so the other stuff had to be righter and tighter, so some other gang wouldn't be thinking that we were just a bunch of chumps. What we had was a proper mark: this fist in a circle with a snake around the wrist and our names written up real big. Gilligan, China, Pudly, and the Hook and me were there to make sure all the taxes got paid on time.

"What happened is I seen a new mark over by the Alcott public school. A skull and bones and the name on it said the Wrightwood Warriors. We was worried for a while until we found out instead of it being the mark of a gang, it was three little shits in the seventh grade. Nat was the shit that knew how to draw, so I told the other two to go get lost and made him part of our crew. We had him climbing up on fire escapes and spraying us on these advertising signs, and we even broke into the bus barn so as Nat could do his thing on top of fifty buses. That meant we had people chilling in skyscrapers, looking down and seeing our mark. This was some serious pub.

"Only then what happened is his mother seen one of them buses, and so she comes over to the school yard to start up yelling at me. She says her little boy's not no bum, and she don't want him going to jail and being a punk like me. I says, 'Fine. That's okay. So give me a reason I should listen to you.'

"So she takes out this ten-dollar green and says I get one for every week that her little boy don't neither get arrested by the police or drop out of school, so I says, 'Okay, fine. That's cool.' Nat do not like it much, so I say 'Okay, fine. Shut up.'

"Ten dollars. That was a lot of green back then. We could buy us some reefer and beer and food. I tell Nat to watch his step, and I tell all the rest that if he ever gets arrested or misses any school or screws up any old how, I'll have to kick out the jams. Wimpy never got in any trouble after that because these gangsters were on his case. That's where the Little Wimpy comes in since he never broke any law that I ever heard till he started doing hang time with you."

Allan covered his mouth so that Crazy Horse wouldn't get sprayed by the involuntary eruption of spittle and surprise that was rising from his gorge. They shared a silent moment, just two guys with bad teeth and a mutual friend who had left them both behind. They could have started a friendship then, but they'd grown up in different nations and the moment could not be sustained.

Crazy Horse picked up his shoeshine rag, and Allan walked away with the glass key to a city on the brink. Then the escalator lifted him from the artificial light of the Greyhound Station to the uneasy darkness of another city night.

About the Author

SEAN HANLON, a native of Chicago, is the author of *The Cold Front, The Big Dark, The Frozen Franklin,* and *Deep Freeze,* which feature sleuth Prester John Riordan. He now lives in Washington State with his wife and daughter.